Praise for Ross Mont...

'A beautifully crafted and heartwarming ...
Abi Elphinstone on *I Ar...*

'It cannot help but cheer you up'
The Times on *I Am Rebel*

'Spectacular. A story of real and rare power'
Kiran Millwood Hargrave on *The Midnight Guardians*

'Glorious. A joy of a joy of a thing'
Katherine Rundell on *The Midnight Guardians*

'A whirlwind adventure'
Daily Telegraph on *The Chime Seekers*

'A real triumph of the imagination'
The Bookseller on *The Chime Seekers*

'Marvellously funny and original'
Financial Times on *Max and the Millions*

'Cracking adventure from the wildly imaginative Montgomery'
Daily Mail on *Max and the Millions*

'Marvellously funny and original . . .
it's the tiny details that make the story work'
Financial Times on *Max and the Millions*

'A supremely readable writer [and] natural comic'
Telegraph on *Christmas Dinner of Souls*

ADVANCE UNCORRECTED PROOF COPY
NOT FOR RESALE OR QUOTATION

VIKING | 30 OCTOBER 2025
9780241766163 | HARDBACK | £16.99

For publicity enquiries, please contact:
Rosie, RSafaty@penguinrandomhouse.co.uk

@PenguinUKBooks @VikingBooksUK

#TheMurderAtWorldsEndBook

THE MURDER AT WORLD'S END

The Murder at World's End

ROSS MONTGOMERY

VIKING

UK | USA | Canada | Ireland | Australia
India | New Zealand | South Africa

Viking is part of the Penguin Random House group of companies
whose addresses can be found at global.penguinrandomhouse.com

Penguin Random House UK,
One Embassy Gardens, 8 Viaduct Gardens, London SW11 7BW

penguin.co.uk

First published 2025
001

Copyright © Ross Montgomery, 2025

The moral right of the author has been asserted

Penguin Random House values and supports copyright.
Copyright fuels creativity, encourages diverse voices, promotes freedom
of expression and supports a vibrant culture. Thank you for purchasing
an authorized edition of this book and for respecting intellectual property
laws by not reproducing, scanning or distributing any part of it by any
means without permission. You are supporting authors and enabling
Penguin Random House to continue to publish books for everyone.
No part of this book may be used or reproduced in any manner for the
purpose of training artificial intelligence technologies or systems. In accordance
with Article 4(3) of the DSM Directive 2019/790, Penguin Random House
expressly reserves this work from the text and data mining exception

Set in 13.5/16pt Garamond MT Std
Typeset by Six Red Marbles UK, Thetford, Norfolk
Printed and bound in Great Britain by Clays Ltd, Elcograf S.p.A.

The authorized representative in the EEA is Penguin Random House Ireland,
Morrison Chambers, 32 Nassau Street, Dublin D02 YH68

A CIP catalogue record for this book is available from the British Library

HARDBACK ISBN: 978–0–241–76616–3
TRADE PAPERBACK ISBN: 978–0–241–76617–0

Penguin Random House is committed to a sustainable future
for our business, our readers and our planet. This book is made from
Forest Stewardship Council® certified paper.

For Helen

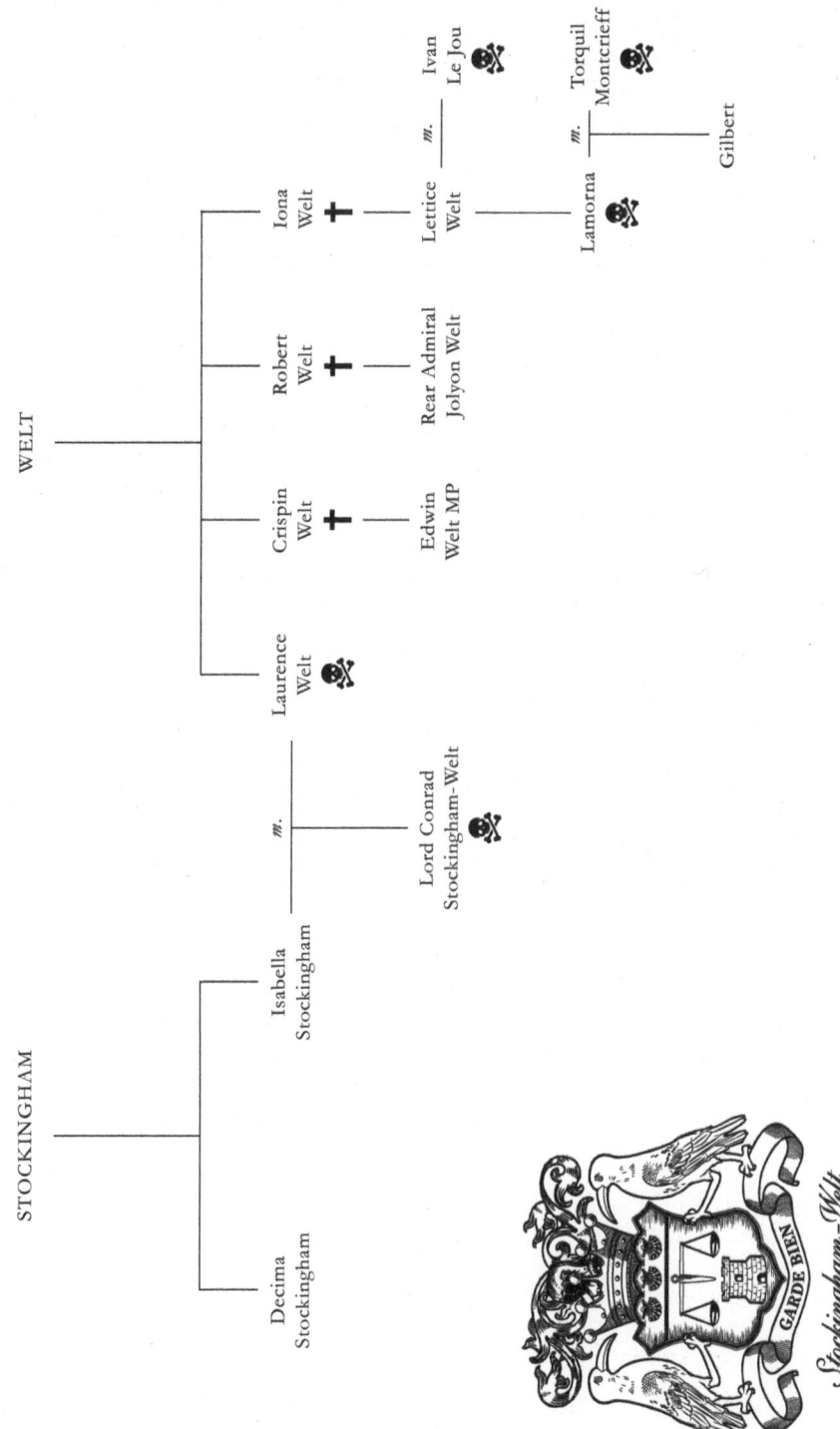

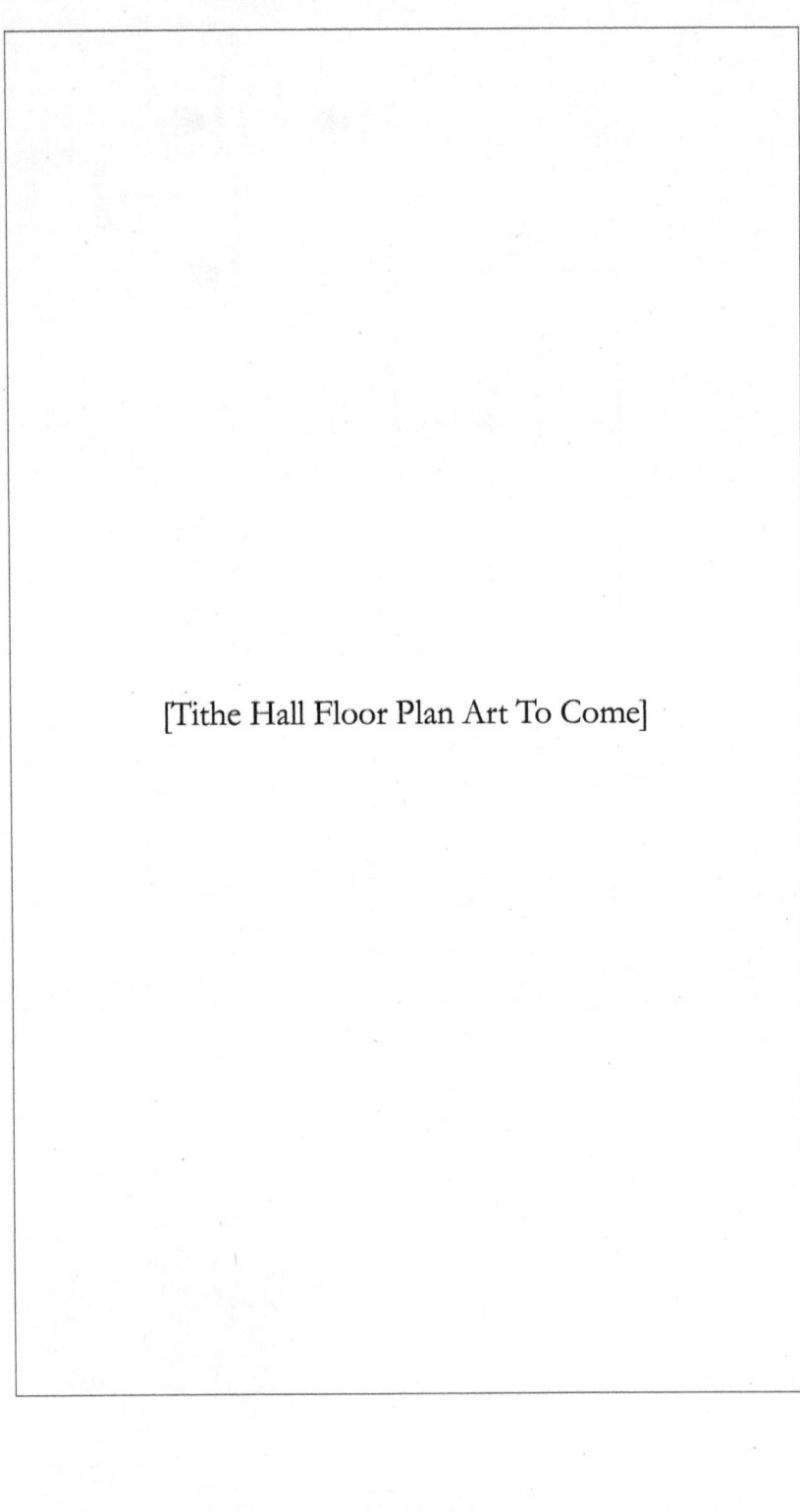
[Tithe Hall Floor Plan Art To Come]

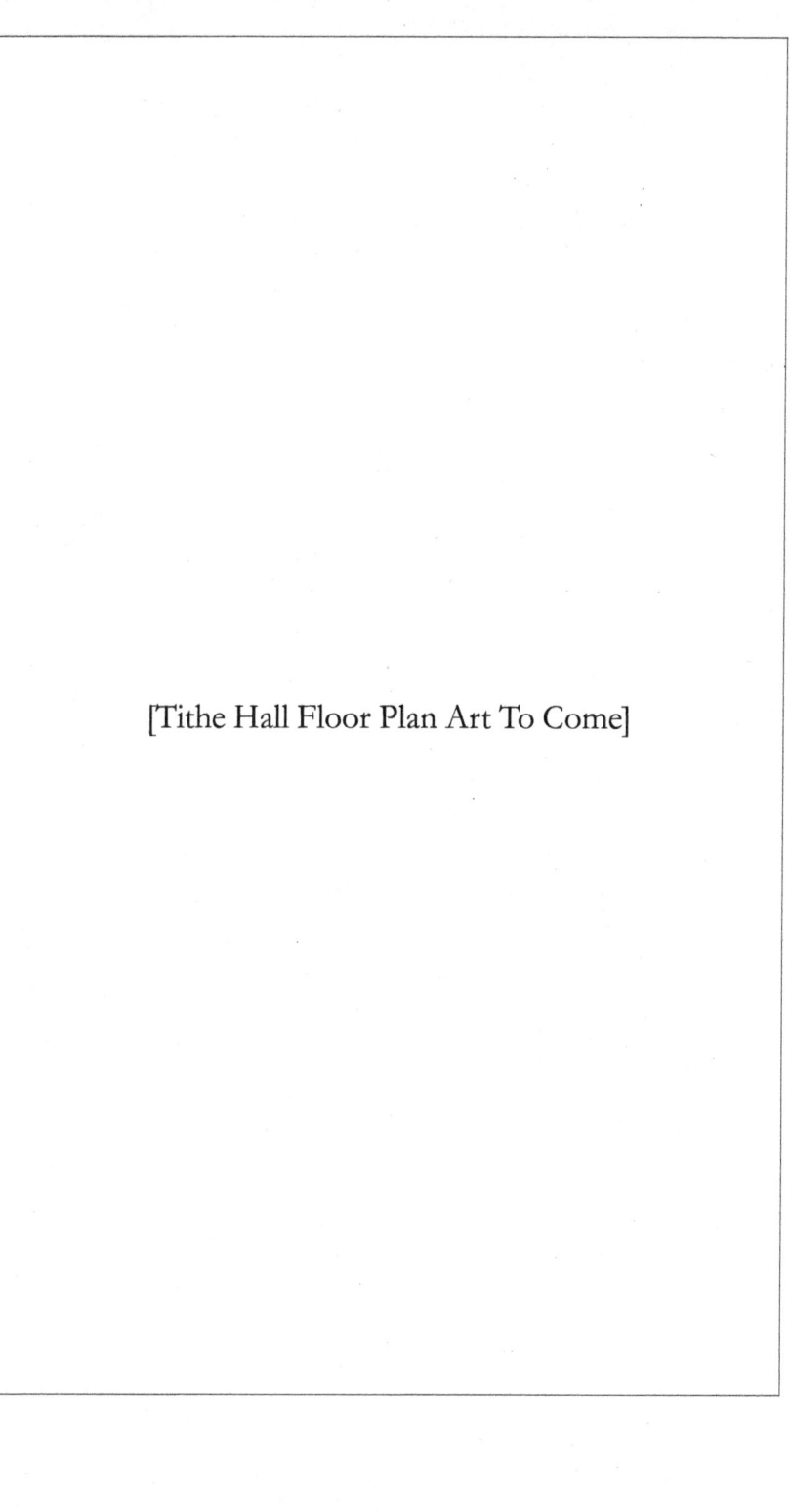
[Tithe Hall Floor Plan Art To Come]

Introduction

Comet Halley reached perihelion – the far side of the sun – on 10 April 1910. It swung in a great arc and began hurtling towards Earth at 120,000 miles per hour, just as Stephen Pike was unpacking his case at the halfway house. He had the third worst bed in the bunk room for a price of two shillings a week, paid in advance, more if you had a dog.

By 6 May, the comet was just 55 million miles away and visible during daylight hours. The global panic, which had been simmering for several months now, was about to erupt, owing to the sudden death of King Edward VII. Stephen had been sitting on his bunk when he heard the news, reading the 'Situations Vacant' section in yesterday's paper and trying to work out how many teeth he'd need to sell to make two shillings.

By 12 May, the comet was growing brighter and clearer in the sky each night, and worldwide panic had properly begun: a rush to make wills in Milwaukee, a sudden boom in the comet insurance market (not covering death by fright) and a global shortage of gas masks. Stephen, meanwhile, had just received an unexpected letter, and was wondering why it smelt so good.

By 16 May, as Stephen was stepping on to the train at Paddington to start his two-day journey to Cornwall, the comet was a mere 12 million miles away and things were beginning to get out of hand. The world was split between those who thought the comet would simply pass the Earth, as it always did, and those who thought it would bring about the End of Days. There were comet-watching parties serving comet-themed cocktails, while others dug shelters, buried love letters and prepared for certain death.

By the time Stephen started the ten-mile walk to World's End on the morning of 18 May, the comet was just twelve hours away. The last two weeks had seen it incite riots, stampedes, fits of madness and priests proclaiming the second coming of Christ. That night, the rooftops of Paris and Istanbul would be packed with spectators excitedly watching the comet reach the Earth, then either continue past it or kill every living thing on the planet.

But, before then, Stephen would arrive at the causeway that separated World's End from the mainland, wade ankle-deep through the steadily rising tides, climb the hill that led to the grand entrance of Tithe Hall, make his way to the far smaller servants' entrance tucked around the back and knock on the door to the Butler's office with a hand that wouldn't stop shaking.

He was almost an hour late, and his feet were soaking wet. Quite frankly, the end of the world was the last thing on his mind.

Wednesday, 18 May 1910

The Scranton Truth

I

Wednesday, 18 May, 9.21 a.m.

'Come in.'

It was a great voice, real proper. I could hear Mr Stokes perfectly through the wooden door, every word, which was a miracle considering the noise out here. He sounded calm, composed – *authoritative*, even. Like the judge had been at my sentencing, though for obvious reasons I hadn't been able to appreciate that much at the time. Anyhow, it was a great voice.

I opened the door. The room was serene compared with what was going on outside, everything neat and ordered, like a little tool-kit: a chair, a desk, his butler books and ledgers all filed away. Mr Stokes was like a tool-kit, too – trim and tidy, taking up the exact amount of space that he needed and nothing more. His hair was combed, his shirt was crisp, and his fingernails were spotless.

'Mr Stokes?' I squashed my accent flat, because you get only the one first impression, don't you?

He nodded, but he didn't look like he was expecting me. I'm good at noticing stuff like that – people's faces, the way they talk, the way they hold themselves . . . you had to be, in the house I grew up in. 'I'm Stephen Pike, sir.'

He just kept staring at me. I held up my suitcase. It was second-hand but it still had some shine on it. People don't muck around with suitcases like that. 'I'm supposed to be starting here today. I'm your new second footman. From London.'

Mr Stokes didn't say anything for a while. Then he blinked. He didn't look like he blinked much, but this was a big one.

'I'm afraid,' he said, 'that there's been some mistake.'

I could hear it in his voice right away, see it in his eyes, too. He was trying to get rid of me. I quickly closed the door.

'The maid who let me in said that, too,' I laughed nervously. 'But it's the truth, I swear –'

Mr Stokes was already standing up. 'I'm *afraid* that the house is closed. Tithe Hall is not receiving visitors at present. We've no call for –'

'I've got a letter here,' I said. 'See?'

I pulled it from my breast pocket – I'd put it there so it wouldn't get creased.

'From Lettice Welt,' I said. 'She's one of the Viscount's relatives. His cousin, I think.'

I stood there like a – beg your pardon – like a lemon, holding out the letter and hoping that Mr Stokes couldn't see that my hand was still shaking. I was trying not to think about the two days it had taken to get here. The train to Penzance, the early-morning bus to Tregarrick, the walk to World's End. If they kicked me out now, I couldn't even get home. The letter had only enough money for a one-way ticket. I didn't even have change for the bus. I thought about the bench in Penzance where I'd slept last night. It'd taken me ten minutes just to wipe off the bird droppings.

'If you could just read it,' I urged.

Mr Stokes glanced at the letter, taking in the delicate script, the expensive paper, the postmark. The letter was proper stuff. It even *smelt* noble. Then he sighed and took it from me. 'Sit down, Mr . . .?'

My heart pounded. 'Pike, sir. Stephen Pike.'

I sat down, giddy with relief. But I knew I wasn't safe yet. Mr Stokes could still send me packing if he wanted to, no matter what the letter said. The Viscount might be the master of Tithe Hall, but, below stairs, what Mr Stokes said was law.

I watched him read the letter, and then read it again. The room was so quiet you could hear the bedlam outside: maids charging, Cook screaming, plates being dropped, feet thundering up and down stairs. I tried to think of some nice long words to keep me calm. *Cacophonous*, I thought. *Tumultuous. Horrisonant.* It didn't work.

'It says that you have previous domestic experience,' said Mr Stokes. 'At Airforth, in Kent.'

I nodded. 'I was apprenticed as a page-boy there for a time, Mr Stokes.'

He glanced back at the letter. 'Let go at quite a young age, I see.'

There it was. I tried to think of a smart answer, but there wasn't one, so we just sat in silence. I could feel sweat starting to settle under my clothes. Ten miles, the walk had been, with that great big hill at the end. My cheap paper collar would do nothing for it.

Mr Stokes put down the letter. I could tell by the set of his shoulders that the nice bit was over.

'I'm going to be perfectly frank with you, Stephen. I've been Head Butler at Tithe Hall for twenty years. I've served the Viscount, and the Viscount's father before him, and I've hired a great number of people in my time. I have never encountered circumstances quite like these.'

I could feel the blush creeping up the back of my neck.

'Allow me to explain,' he continued, picking up the letter again. 'The Viscount's cousin – Lettice Welt, as you said – has requested that I find a place for you here, as part of her many charitable endeavours. That in itself is not unusual. But she has asked that I do so with . . . *absolute discretion*. By which she means that I do not reveal to the Viscount the nature of your hiring. In short, that I keep it a secret from him.'

Discretion. I liked that. Maybe I could put it in my notebook, just before I threw myself under the train back to London.

'I'm not in the habit of keeping secrets from my employer, Stephen,' said Mr Stokes coldly. 'Especially regarding the hiring of new servants. *Especially* when said servant last served in a house nearly ten years ago.'

The blush had reached my ears now; they'd be bright red. Nan used to call them my beacons. 'I remember the particulars of the job well, Mr Stokes.'

'I'm sure that you do, Stephen. And I'm sure you'll *also* agree that the responsibilities of a page-boy and those of a footman are remarkably different. Have you ever served at table, for example?'

He had me there. I sat up straight to stop my leg from shaking. 'I know that I have a lot to learn, Mr Stokes. That's why I'm taking a beginner's wage. And why the Society has provided me with my own livery, so I there's no unnecessary expense for the Viscount.'

A little muscle twitched in his jaw. And, right then, I knew the question he was going to ask.

'Indeed. The' – he glanced at the letter – '*Borstal Society*. Do tell me, Stephen, if you wouldn't mind – *how* exactly did you come to find yourself detained in a Borstal Institution?'

Two days. *Two days* I'd spent, working out how I was going to answer that question. And, now it was here, there was no getting away from it. The only thing standing between me and my last chance was whatever came out of my mouth next.

2

Wednesday, 18 March, 9.38 a.m.

I had to get this perfect. *Beyond reproach.* Those were the words the Governor had used in my last meeting: *beyond reproach.* I'd put it in my notebook. Now, in Mr Stokes's office, I sat up straighter, flattened my accent till there was nothing left of it and thought of the most genteel, elegant words I knew.

'I would rather not go into the details of that, sir. I made an unpardonable error of judgement, and I paid for it, as rightly I should have done. I accepted my sentence and subsequently devoted the sum of my incarceration to the complete reformation of my character. Suffice to say, I am now entirely rehabilitated.'

Mr Stokes was staring at me like I'd just talked Spanish. I kept going, sweat trickling down my back.

'I made much use of the chapel while I was there, studying the testaments and aiding the Chaplain. Indeed, the Governor said that I was the most promising young man he had come across.' I jabbed a finger at the letter. 'Which is why they cut my time to two years, instead of three. And why I was recommended to the Borstal Society for re-employment, on account of my household experience. The lady of the house said that she wanted –'

'Lettice Welt is *not* the lady of the house,' Mr Stokes cut in sharply. 'She is the Viscount's cousin. Her charitable connection to the Borstal Society may be one of *her* passions, but the same cannot be said for Lord Stockingham-Welt. He is an exacting man, with high standards. What is more, you have arrived at the house a moment of *critical* import. His Lordship has given me strict instructions not to permit any new people to enter the house, under any circumstances.'

The fancy words crumbled like pastry in my mouth. The hardness was back in his voice. I knew what that meant – I'd heard it before, at the sentencing. Mr Stokes folded his hands on the desk, making a gate.

'You see the position that I am in, Stephen. Even if I *did* choose to follow Lettice Welt's instructions, and lied to the Viscount about hiring you, I cannot possibly see how he would agree to it.'

I saw it all before me – the ten-mile walk, the bench at Penzance. Maybe if I was lucky, I could pawn the livery the Society had given me and use it to buy a ticket back to London. But then what? I had nothing. I didn't even have money for my old bunk back at the halfway house.

It's odd, seeing the end. You spend so long dreading it, and when it finally comes at you it's almost a relief. It was over: I'd done all I could. The only thing that could make it worse would be to try to fight it.

Then Mr Stokes let out a sigh and separated his hands.

'However, your timing is also in your favour. I believe that the Viscount has *greatly* underestimated the number of staff he is going to need over the next few days. We're in dire need of a young man like yourself. Someone strong and healthy and . . . *resilient*.' He folded the letter and tucked it into his pocket. 'As a result, I don't think we can turn down your offer of employment.'

I couldn't believe my ears. I wasn't going home. I had no idea what *resilient* meant, but I'd look it up later. 'Thank you, Mr Stokes. Thank you!'

'Don't thank me yet,' he muttered, standing up. 'I have to

persuade His Lordship to agree to it first. He may need some convincing.' He fixed me with an appraising look. 'I trust you understand the risk that I am taking, Stephen. Should the truth come out about the nature of your hiring, we will *both* bear the responsibility for it.'

I nodded so hard it near broke my neck. 'I won't let you down, sir.'

'I'm sure you won't,' said Mr Stokes politely. 'Come – His Lordship is in his study. I will explain the situation and impress upon him the importance of engaging you. With any luck, he will be so distracted by the current work that he'll agree to whatever I say.'

He opened the door and the sound of carnage flooded inside. I'd been so petrified for the last few minutes that I'd completely forgotten what I'd seen going on in the corridors. The maids, the shoving, the panic. It was like a train station at rush hour, not the servants' quarters of some isolated manor house. 'If you don't mind me asking, sir . . . what *is* the current work?'

There was that stare again.

I fumbled.

'Well . . . it's *odd*, is all. I thought I must have got the wrong place when I arrived. The windows being boarded up and that. The sandbags along the drive; the grounds being dug up. If there hadn't been cars parked out front, I'd have thought the house was closed. And everyone's running around like something bad's about to happen.'

Mr Stokes paused for a moment longer. Then he closed the door and turned to face me.

'Stephen, I take it that you have no other opportunities of employment, beyond this one? In other words, this is your last chance.'

I didn't have much to say to that.

'Then allow me to give you a piece of advice. Something that I have learnt from a lifetime of service.' He folded his arms behind his back. 'The success of a servant depends upon his or her ability to be *invisible*. To be as integral, and yet as indiscernible, as the furniture. To appear only when required, speak only when addressed, and otherwise draw no attention to their presence whatsoever. Would you agree?'

I nodded.

'Splendid,' said Mr Stokes, reopening the door. 'Then I suggest, if you wish to remain employed at Tithe Hall, that you never ask a question like that ever again.'

3

Wednesday, 18 March, 9.46 a.m.

The servants' corridors were packed. There were parlour maids and chamber maids and kitchen maids and laundry maids and scullery maids racing every which way, jamming doors and losing their tempers while clutching fresh sheets, hot water, scuttles of coal. I'd never seen anything like it. It was as if someone had just said that the house was on fire, and no one could go home until they'd finished work.

'As you can see, this is going to be a challenging few days, Stephen,' said Mr Stokes, gliding down the corridor like a steam liner. 'You have been dropped somewhat in the deep end. There will be a lot for you to learn, and not much time to learn it.'

We passed a larder filled with more food than I'd ever seen. 'Yes, Mr Stokes.'

'We'll restrict your duties to boot cleaning and silverware at first. Once you're more confident, you can serve at table with myself and Lowen. He's the first footman – as second footman you'll be working beneath him, of course. You must follow our lead at all times.'

We stopped to let two maids pass with a big sheet of plywood. 'Yes, Mr Stokes.'

'Naturally, with the house in its current state, you will have to think on your feet as well.'

A train of maids trooped past carrying oxygen tanks. 'Yes, Mr Stokes.'

He stopped at a corner. I couldn't see his face, but I could tell from the back of his head that he was trying to work out how best to word something.

'There may also be some . . . additional duties required of you. At times, you will assist with Miss Decima. She's the Viscount's elderly aunt, and is kept in the old Nursery, separate to the rest of the house. You will need to make yourself available to her as and when required.'

I blanched. 'I don't have much experience in that line, Mr Stokes.'

'You'll have to learn quickly,' he muttered. 'She's worked her way through all the female staff.'

We turned the corner and I saw someone slumped against the wall ahead of us. It was a maid, standing alone, weeping into her hands. No one stopped to help or ask if she was all right. Mr Stokes handed her a handkerchief as he strode past without even looking at her. I glanced over my shoulder and saw a pair of miserable eyes blinking back at me through strands of damp blonde hair.

'Tell me, Stephen – how much do you know about World's End?' asked Mr Stokes. 'Tithe Hall? Lord Stockingham-Welt?'

'A little,' I said.

Mr Stokes gave a small nod that told me he knew I was lying but didn't mind.

'World's End is the largest tidal island in the country. Over eight hundred acres, in fact. It has belonged to the Stockingham family for generations and was once considered an important military outpost. The cliffs and the hill naturally protect it from the worst of the elements, while the tides turn it into a bastion against incursion from the mainland. No doubt you noticed the causeway on your way in.'

I'd noticed it, all right. I'd waded through it while holding my shoes.

'The causeway means that the house is frequently cut off from the mainland for several hours at a time,' Mr Stokes continued. 'When that happens, we are at the mercy of the sea. The rocky coastline makes it impossible for boats to land, so the only way off World's End is to swim for the shore.'

'I can't swim,' I said.

'Probably just as well,' said Mr Stokes. 'You will get used to the isolation, in time. Just one of the many quirks of the house.'

I was about to ask what the other quirks were when Mr Stokes opened a cupboard door and stepped inside. I nearly dropped my suitcase. There was a tiny spiral staircase hidden in the cupboard, twisting up like a child's helter-skelter. I followed him inside, bent double to stop my head scraping the ceiling.

'Tithe Hall was built by the Viscount's father, Lawrence Welt, as a gift for his wife when he married into the Stockingham family,' Mr Stokes explained. 'He was a firm believer that servants and masters should be kept apart – as a result, the house contains a number of servants' staircases like these, which allow servants to access any floor, day or night, without being seen.'

I could barely believe my eyes. We passed doors labelled GROUND FLOOR – DRAWING ROOM AND NORTH CORRIDOR and JUST A CUPBOARD and WARNING! DO NOT USE before Mr Stokes stepped through one labelled FIRST FLOOR – EAST WING. I followed and found myself standing in a grand hallway hung with thick plush rugs and gleaming chandeliers. The change almost gave me whiplash.

'The servants' staircases will become a fundamental part of your life at Tithe Hall,' Mr Stokes explained. 'If you happen to see the Viscount or any of his guests, you must find the nearest one and make yourself scarce. To that end, you should ensure that you make use of the butler's mirrors, too.'

I didn't know what he meant at first. Then I saw them: round porthole mirrors in golden frames, hanging at the ends of the corridors. The glass in each one was curved like an eyeball.

'*Butler's mirrors*,' Mr Stokes repeated. 'Something of an antiquated item nowadays. They were once used to help illuminate gloomy spaces, but now they allow staff to check around corners, so they don't run into Lord Stockingham-Welt unexpectedly.'

It certainly wasn't gloomy. The light was dazzling, if anything. 'I've never seen so many electric lights, sir,' I said.

Mr Stokes nodded, pleased that I'd noticed. 'Every room is lit by them. The floors are connected by electric lifts, too, though naturally staff are forbidden from using them. All fed by a generator that runs from the waterfalls in the grounds. Lord Stockingham-Welt is considered one of the finest scientific minds in the country; he has transformed Tithe Hall into perhaps the most technologically advanced house in Europe.' He marched off, his feet barely making a whisper on the rugs. 'Come – his study is this way.'

I followed, taking in the corridor in amazement. I knew that the Viscount was rich, but I still wasn't prepared for how grand Tithe Hall was. I'd never been in a house that was protected by the sea before. The outside had been built to look like a castle, too, all turrets and battlements, like something out of a fairytale. Frankly, it made Airforth look like a toilet.

But it was strange as well. The windows had all been boarded over, making everything muffled and close, like something bottled up. I felt like I could hear my own breath. If it hadn't been for the dazzling chandeliers, the corridor would have been pitch-black.

I froze, mid-step. There was a dark figure reflected in the butler's mirror ahead of us, standing in the next corridor along, but Mr Stokes just carried on walking. When we turned the corner, I understood why – it was just a suit of armour on a plinth, with chain mail and a big, feathered helmet. It held a huge crossbow in its metal gloves, loaded with a heavy four-pronged bolt.

'His Lordship's study,' said Mr Stokes, coming to a stop at a door opposite. 'He will be busy, no doubt, with the final preparations of the day.' He glanced at me. 'Are you ready, Stephen?'

I wasn't ready at all. Standing on the other side of that door was Lord Stockingham-Welt – the Viscount of World's End. The richest and most powerful man that I'd probably ever meet. The man who was about to decide whether I had a job, or whether I was going to have to swim back home.

But there was nothing I could do about it. Mr Stokes had already raised a hand and was knocking on the thick polished oak.

4

Wednesday, 18 March, 9.52 a.m.

The sound of the knock rang out. There was a long wait before the answer came, all distant and withering.

'*Yes?*'

Mr Stokes stepped inside as I ran a hand through my hair, smoothed my shirt, held up my suitcase so the Viscount could see it and followed.

The study took my breath away. The rug alone was bigger than the bunk room in the halfway house. There was a giant set of windows on one side, stretching right up to the ceiling, that had been boarded up with sheets of plywood. On the other side was great set of shelves filled with more books than I'd ever seen in my life. There was a big stone fireplace on the far wall, so tall that I could have stood up inside it, and another one of those butler's mirrors above the mantelpiece. I could see myself reflected in it like a tiny ant, far away and insignificant.

He's done that on purpose, I thought. *Everything in this room is made to make you feel small.*

The Viscount was standing behind his desk, gazing into the biggest fishbowl I'd ever seen. He was in his forties, with greying hair and a velvet waistcoat. He didn't look up – all his attention was focused on the fish fighting for the crumbs that he scattered on the surface.

'Stokes,' he said, his voice cold, 'I said that I was not to be disturbed.'

Mr Stokes gave a deep bow. 'Apologies, sir. I have a matter of importance that I wish to –'

'The guests are all here?' said the Viscount, cutting him off. 'Maids getting their rooms ready?'

Mr Stokes nodded. 'The last car arrived just under an hour ago, sir.'

'Good,' said the Viscount, dusting off his hands. His eyes were still fixed on the fishbowl. 'I want the whole house in the drawing room at ten o'clock, then we'll bar the doors. The last thing we want is some jumpy servant trying to leave before –'

He finally looked up from the fishbowl and saw me. All the air seemed to leave the room at once.

'Who the *hell* is this?' he snapped.

I felt myself wither under his glare, and suddenly I got the feeling that my suitcase wasn't going to make much of a difference. The Viscount looked like he was about to drag me down to the causeway and drown me in it himself.

'This is Stephen, Your Lordship,' said Mr Stokes, cheerful as you like. 'A promising young man who has just arrived with *excellent* references for –'

The Viscount was aghast. 'Are you out of your mind? I said no one was to enter the grounds, Stokes! *No one!* And you're engaging *staff*?'

He was furious now, properly shouting. But Mr Stokes didn't even flinch. He just stood, letting the rage pass over him like fog.

'Hmm. I apologize, sir. I was under the impression we had discussed this matter some time ago.'

'We hadn't! The house can hold only a certain number of people! Get him the hell out of here, right now!'

Mr Stokes folded his hands. 'If you don't mind me saying, sir, I believe that Stephen's presence will be essential over the next few days.'

'I *said* –'

'We may need him to deal with Miss Decima.'

It was like watching a firework splutter out. The Viscount's rage vanished; his eyes grew massive. 'Great-Aunt Decima? Why? What's she done now?'

Mr Stokes coughed. 'She is being somewhat more ... *challenging* than usual, sir.'

The Viscount didn't know what to do with himself. He kept lifting his hands to his forehead and then changing his mind and putting them on his hips. 'But ... I thought Temperance was looking after her. The blonde one. She likes her. Well, not *like*, but –'

'She appears to have changed her mind. That's why I arranged to hire Stephen. We may be in need of brute strength.'

They turned to face me, looking me up and down like a goat for slaughter. I was beginning to understand what *resilient* meant.

'Fine,' the Viscount muttered, waving a hand. 'Find him a room and get him out of here.'

And that was it: as easy as that, I had a job. Mr Stokes took my arm and made to lead me outside, but before he could do it I gave the Viscount a deep bow.

'Thank you, Your Lordship. My gratitude knows no bounds. I hope that in time, I can evidence my devotion from London to you and –'

I felt Mr Stokes freeze beside me, and I knew right away that I'd messed up. I'd spoken out of turn. I raised my eyes and saw the Viscount staring at me with hard eyes.

'That voice,' he muttered. 'Where are you from?'

My mouth went dry. I'd tried to hide my accent, but it must have slipped out. 'Bow, sir.'

The Viscount smirked. 'Christ. No wonder you're grateful.'

I felt my fist curl up. I wanted to tell him exactly what he could do with his job, but I couldn't – I couldn't do anything. I just had to stand there and take it.

'Well, Bow, you've certainly gone up in the world,' said the Viscount breezily. 'The Stockingham-Welts are one of the oldest and most prestigious families in the country. See that armour?'

He pointed to the corridor, where the suit of armour stood framed in the doorway. The heavy four-pronged bolt in the crossbow was aimed right at me.

'My ancestor wore that at Hastings,' said the Viscount. 'That's the *very* arrow that killed Harold Godwinson. You know what happened to him, don't you?'

I nodded. 'He was shot in the eye, Your Lordship.'

'That's right,' said the Viscount. 'There aren't many people who get to work for a family like ours. So you should consider yourself extremely lucky.' He smiled. 'In fact, tomorrow morning, you're going to discover that you're one of the luckiest men on the planet.'

Somewhere in the house, a clock struck ten. The Viscount stood and listened, waiting until the last chime had rung out. It was strange – like I was watching some big ceremony. Like the Viscount was hearing it for the very last time.

'Stokes, gather everyone in the drawing room,' he said. 'The whole household, right down to the scullery maids. It's time they all found out what's going on.'

5

Wednesday, 18 March, 10.04 a.m.

My new bedroom wasn't much bigger than my cell in Borstal. A bed, a wardrobe, a basin on a washstand. It was better than the halfway house, at least. There were twenty of us to a room there, and the other men were dock wallopers who drank themselves to sleep. They snored like it was a contest.

I didn't have much time – Mr Stokes had told me to get dressed and then get back downstairs as soon as possible. I flung open the case and pulled out my livery, checking it over for creases. I was in such a hurry that I forgot about the package wrapped inside it.

It hit the floor and I thought I heard it smash. I gasped and fell to my knees, untying the string and praying *Please don't be broken, please don't be broken*. I could have cried when I opened the newspaper and saw that the frame was still intact, with only the one crack in the glass, and the picture safe inside.

There she was. Nan.

She'd only ever had one photo taken. It was at the Romney Fair, where there was a stall saying A SHADOWGRAPH FOR POSTERITY; she was wearing her good hat that day and she'd said, *Well, why not?*

That was Nan all over – she was tough, but she had a fun streak in her a mile wide. She loved having that photo taken. You can tell from her eyes that she's trying not to laugh.

Nan hadn't left much behind – what there was, Mum sold when she died. The photo was all I had of her now. I'd kept it with me through Borstal, pressed between the pages of a Bible so it wouldn't get creased. When they let me out, I'd searched through every junk shop until I found a frame I could afford, with just the one small crack in it.

I put the photo on the windowsill so she could look outside; there wasn't much of a view here, what with the boards on the windows, but when they took them off you could probably even see the sea. Nan loved having a look about. Towards the end I'd prop her up in bed so she could spend the day watching the Bow Road, saying, *Blimey, the state of her* or *That cat's back again* or *You know, I think the sun might come out.*

I kissed my fingers and held them to the glass for a few seconds. Then I got dressed and ran downstairs like I had greased shoes on.

It took ages to find the drawing room. The servants' staircases were a mess – none of them linked up properly, all blind corners with doors that led nowhere. I hit three dead ends before I finally found one that opened into the entrance hall and followed the noise to the drawing room. There was barely space to stand: the staff were crammed in like sardines, pressed to the walls, trying not to knock the furniture as they craned their necks to the front of the room.

There were five people sat there I hadn't seen before. The first was a lady in her sixties, dressed all glamorous in black from head to toe, wearing the biggest hat I'd ever seen. Beside her was a little boy, maybe seven years old, wearing a sailor suit and pulling the stitches out of the cushions. On the next chair was a huge walrussy red-faced man, who could have been anywhere between thirty and sixty, wearing a tweed suit and helping himself to a decanter of sherry. Then there was a prim-looking busybody with a thin moustache and steel glasses, clutching an attaché case. Sitting opposite them – as far away as he could, to be honest – was a man in his forties with a slick suit and a scowl. I'd never seen anyone so cold and dark and grim. He looked like an undertaker but less cheerful.

The Viscount was standing on a footstool, gazing around like an actor at the start of a big play.

'Well,' he began, 'here we are.'

The room fell quiet. The Viscount folded his arms behind him and gave himself a dramatic pause.

'I'm sure you've all noticed the changes over the last few days,' he said. 'The boarding of the doors and windows. The sandbags and sea-trenches being dug around the house, followed by the dismissal of the grounds staff.' He gazed around airily. 'I imagine you've been wondering what's going on.'

I hadn't known about the grounds staff being sacked. Judging from the dark glances and shifting feet around me, I could see it had not gone down well. In big houses like this, almost all the staff would be from the nearest village – the people who'd lost their jobs were probably brothers, cousins, neighbours.

The Viscount stood tall. 'We find ourselves on the crest of history. Even as I speak, events are unfolding across the world that will alter the course of human civilization.'

I felt a prickle up my back. The room was dead silent now, everyone holding the same breath. I looked around for any sign of what the Viscount was talking about, but they all seemed as clueless as I did.

'We've seen the warning signs,' the Viscount continued. 'Natural disasters across Europe. Floodings in Paris. Tensions in the Near East. The worsening situation in Germany. The death of our King. Though seemingly random, these events all point to a single, greater truth. One that finds its nexus this very evening.' He took another pause. 'I speak, of course, of Comet Halley.'

I blinked. I hadn't been expecting *that*. Neither, it seemed, had anyone else. At the very front of the room, I saw the man in the slick suit grip the arms of his chair like he'd just been electrocuted.

'Tonight,' the Viscount continued, 'at five o'clock Greenwich Mean Time, the comet will once more pass the Earth. Its arrival has *always* signified great change: it foretold Hannibal would fail at Carthage; appeared above Jerusalem before its fall; heralded the triumph of William the Conqueror. But, this time, its coming is more dire than ever.' He allowed another pause. 'This time, it will be the end of the world.'

A gasp of horror spread through the room. I'd heard people talk about the comet, of course – there were stories in the papers about it crashing into Earth and all kinds of daft things, but I hadn't taken any of it seriously. Nan always said that if you believed everything people claimed, you'd think the world would end every other Tuesday.

'Your government has hidden the truth from you!' the Viscount continued, shouting over the noise. 'They have insisted that the comet poses no danger. All lies! Here is the truth: tonight, the comet's path will bring it closer to Earth than ever before. So close that our planet's orbit will carry us straight through the comet's tail. A tail which spectroscope readings have revealed is full of poisonous cyanogen gases. When our planet comes into contact with that tail, our atmosphere will be flooded with them. Nothing that breathes will survive.'

Someone cried out at the side of the room – a maid had just fainted. I couldn't believe what I was hearing. It sounded impossible, like some made-up nightmare. But the Viscount wasn't just anyone: he was a nobleman. Mr Stokes had said that he was one of the greatest scientific minds of his generation. He had to be right, hadn't he?

'Only a select handful of scientists have been brave enough to speak out,' the Viscount continued. 'That is why I, and other concerned men, founded the *Cometary Cataclysm Society*: an organization committed to warning the world about the dangers of the comet. I am proud to have one of the founding members with me tonight: Professor Wolf Muller, of the Klatsch Institute in Hamburg.'

The Viscount stepped down so that the man with the thin moustache and wire glasses could take his place on the footstool. He cleared his throat. 'Greetings, ladies *und* gentlemen. Allow me, please, to explain now my own areas of research regarding the dangers of this comet.'

The man in the slick suit nearly choked. Professor Muller was German. You didn't see many Germans around nowadays – not with all the worries about invasion. People were even calling for them to be arrested, in case they were spying for the Kaiser.

'The poisonous gases are not all we must fear,' said Professor Muller. 'We must also consider the effects it will have on our oceans. Never before has something of such size, travelling at such speed, come so close to our planet! To my thinking, the consequences are clear: the Pacific and Atlantic oceans will change basins with one another, resulting in tidal waves that will sweep across America. Here, in your own country of Great Britain, you may expect the tides to cover all lands as far north as Godalming.'

This stopped the room again but not for the same reasons. People looked confused. Professor Muller stepped down, and the Viscount leapt back on to the footstool.

'You heard correctly!' he cried. 'This time tomorrow,

twenty per cent of the country will be underwater. And it gets worse! Hailstones as large as boulders will rain down across cities! Crops will wither! Wells will be poisoned! Electrical storms will blind all who set eyes on them!'

The more he talked, the more . . . well, stupid it sounded. People were beginning to look at each other. Nan had always said that no amount of money can stop a stupid person being stupid, and I was beginning to see what she meant. The Viscount was talking absolute – pardon my French – *codswallop*. The man in the slick suit was gripping the edge of his armchair so tightly that his nails had broken the fabric.

'The Cometary Cataclysm Society has done all it can,' the Viscount said sadly, shaking his head. 'We beseeched all the leading scientific institutes to take our concerns seriously. We contacted newspapers; we pleaded with governments. All in vain.' He shot the man in the slick suit a filthy look. 'Our warnings were ignored. We were mocked and ridiculed. And, now, time has run out. The End of Days has come.'

The Viscount raised his hands.

'But not for us. We few – we lucky few! – stand in the only place on Earth prepared for the cataclysm. The cliffs and sea defences of World's End can naturally withstand the worst of the rising tides. Today, we will completely seal the house, making it impermeable to the poisonous gases. Tomorrow, we will rise to a changed world. We shall rebuild from the ashes and start anew!' He kept going, his voice growing louder and louder. 'No more wars! No more hung Parliament! No more petty distractions of socialism, female suffrage or Irish independence! A new dawn of scientific enlightenment, led by men of superior brains and bloodline, returned to their rightful positions of power!'

His voice rang out across the stunned, silent room. No one could quite believe what they were hearing. The man in the slick suit looked like he was about to have a heart attack. The Viscount gazed around like a general, pulled out his pocket watch and snapped it shut.

'Right! Stokes, get the staff downstairs. They have a lot to be getting on with. The world's ending in seven hours.'

6

Wednesday, 18 May, 10.47 a.m.

Twenty minutes later I was standing around the table in the servants' hall with the rest of the staff, waiting for Mr Stokes to come back from his meeting with the Viscount. I think I was the only one who wasn't shouting.

'Hailstones? Bleeding *hailstones*?'

'He can't be serious!'

'Where's Godalming?'

Mr Stokes appeared, and everyone fell silent. He looked absolutely exhausted. He moved slowly and regally to the head of the table, like an old war hero leading his men into a massacre.

'Well?' snapped a woman at the other end of the table. 'Did *you* know about all this?'

It was the housekeeper. I could tell because she had a ring of keys on her belt and a glare that could crack an egg.

Mr Stokes sighed. 'No, Mrs Pearce. I did not. The Viscount never told me the full extent of his plans. Under the circumstances, I think that was ... probably for the best.'

He leant forwards, resting his knuckles on the worn wooden table. Then he began explaining.

'We have until five o'clock to make the East Wing entirely airtight. Block every gap, fill every crack in the floorboards, board every doorway. Then the whole house – staff and guests – will be shut inside their rooms for the night, with enough food and water to last until morning. And ... an emergency oxygen tank.'

Everyone started shouting again. A man shoved his way to the front. 'We can't do all that in six hours! It's impossible!'

It had to be Lowen, the first footman. He was in livery, too, and about my age, but barely five feet tall, with slick oiled hair pressed tight against his head that made him look like an angry pencil stub.

'And what about the grounds staff?' Lowen continued, waving his arms. 'He had them digging trenches and boarding windows for two weeks straight, then sacked them the moment they finished! No notice, no reference! Going to do the same to us, is he?'

The servants started in agreement. 'That's right! My brother ...'

'And dad!'

'They won't drown down in the village, will they?'

'*No one's* going to drown, you stupid –'

Mr Stokes raised his hands for silence. '*The Viscount has given his instructions, and we will carry them out.* That is our job: we are a mirror of the house. That matters now more than ever.' He took a moment to pick his wording. 'It is clear that Lord Stockingham-Welt is making some unusual decisions at present. Should it transpire that he is no longer ... *fit* for his role, the title will become extinct and the management of the estate will pass to the Viscount's cousin, Mr Edwin Welt – who is, one can safely assume, the person who will inherit under the Viscount's will. You all saw him upstairs just now, saw how concerned he was.'

That had to be the man in the slick suit. *Concerned* was one word for it: he looked flipping livid.

'Mr Welt has made his feelings about Tithe Hall very clear over the years,' Mr Stokes continued. 'He considers the house a frivolous luxury. He has repeatedly petitioned the Viscount to close it and move back to London. When control of the estate passes to him, every single one of our jobs will be at stake. Including mine.'

A dark wave passed over the room. If that happened, it wouldn't be just me that was stuffed – everyone here would be.

'So we do what we were placed here to do,' said Mr Stokes. 'We show Mr Welt our worth. We show him that Tithe Hall cannot possibly run without us. We will meet the Viscount's expectations, no matter how challenging, and we shall do so *impeccably*.'

The room was hanging on his every word. When times are rough, you want someone who has the guts to take charge, and Mr Stokes was that person. He was poised, composed – *magisterial*, even. He closed his eyes and started moving his hand in the air, like he was conducting music that only he could hear.

'Cook: prepare dinner as usual. A cold collation will suffice under the circumstances. Kitchen maids and scullery maids, ensure that a tea tray is left in every bedroom in the East Wing. House maids and parlour maids, a large amount of cotton wadding has been left in the dining room. You will take what you need and use it to seal every gap you can find in the East Wing. We must make that entire section of the house airtight before five o'clock: the doors, the windows, the floorboards, the fireplaces.'

I whistled under my breath. Lowen was right: it *was* an enormous amount of work. I'd no idea how many rooms were in the East Wing, but I'd seen the chimneys on the roof – there were dozens of them.

'Once the East Wing is secure,' said Mr Stokes, 'we will begin sealing people in their bedrooms. I, along with the male members of staff, will see to the Viscount's guests. Mrs Pearce, you will oversee the female members of staff. Once every single person in the house is secure, the Viscount will seal himself in his study. A telephone has been installed in my bedroom; tomorrow morning, once the Viscount is confident that the dangers of the comet have passed, he will instruct me to ring the staff bells. That will be your signal to unseal yourself from your rooms and start preparing the house as normal. Then we can begin the process of . . . welcoming in a brand-new dawn.'

Mrs Pearce folded her arms. 'You're forgetting something, Mr Stokes. *Her upstairs*. You won't get her in the East Wing – she won't be moved from that Nursery! You remember the last time we tried?'

A shudder of horror passed through the room.

'Never heard language like it . . .'

'Still got the bruises . . .'

'Big Jago never *was* the same afterwards.'

Mr Stokes nodded. 'I fully agree, Mrs Pearce. That is why Miss Decima will stay in her own rooms this evening, along with a servant.'

Mrs Pearce gasped. 'Oh, no, you don't! I'm not having you put Temperance in there all night! She's already spent the day in tears –'

'I couldn't agree *more*, Mrs Pearce,' said Mr Stokes patiently. 'That is why this evening *Stephen* will be attending to Miss Decima.'

Lowen's head snapped up. 'Stephen? Who's Stephen?'

'Our new second footman,' said Mr Stokes.

There was a moment of stunned silence – and then a hundred eyes swivelled to face me. I felt how a cow must feel when it hears a gavel come down at a meat auction.

'Stephen, you will be spending the night with Miss

Decima,' said Mr Stokes. 'You will need to seal her rooms by yourself and . . . make sure that she is comfortable.'

The room cheered up instantly. No one seemed to mind the day ahead of them now — at least they weren't *me*. The only person who wasn't sniggering and nudging their neighbour was Lowen. He was glaring at me like I was a stray dog he'd just found sitting in his favourite chair, eating his birthday cake.

'Six hours!' said Mr Stokes, clapping his hands. 'Footmen to the second floor, maids to the first. Good luck, everyone.'

The room emptied around me. I stood there like a — beg pardon — like a flipping plum, trying to work out how I'd got here.

I thought that coming to Tithe Hall would fix all my problems. Instead, I had to prepare the house for an apocalypse that wasn't going to happen, then spend the night with a woman who people spoke about the way they described dragons in old fairytales. And then, after all that, I'd probably lose my job anyway because my new master was completely stark raving mad.

Of course, back then, I didn't know how bad things were actually going to get.

7

Wednesday, 18 May, 11.08 a.m.

It took ages to find the second floor because I still had no idea how the servants' staircases worked. I finally stepped out of the right door and found Lowen skulking in a corridor with a hammer and a caulking iron.

'Sorry, I got lost,' I said, holding out my hand. 'Nice to meet you – I'm Stephen. I guess we're –'

Lowen didn't take my hand. Instead, he grabbed me by the lapels of my brand-new jacket and slammed me against the wall.

'I see you, mate,' he spat, leaning into my face. 'I see *everything*.'

'Huh?' I said.

'Think you can take my job, just because you're taller than me?' he sneered. 'Try it, tuss. I'll make a mess of you and do it with a smile on my face, too.'

I finally twigged – taller footmen got paid more than short ones. I considered saying I was only taking an entry-level wage, but I didn't want to get into the small print with someone trying to beat me up. 'Get off me, Lowen.'

But he was stronger than he looked. 'I mean it. Watch your back. One wrong move and you're dogmeat.'

He flung me hard against the wall and stormed down the corridor. I noticed, as he marched off, that his shoes had little heels on them.

I watched him go, fists twitching. I wanted to march after

him and give him a thump, I really did. But I couldn't get in trouble now – the last time I'd fought back . . .

There were voices behind me, getting closer. I spun around and saw people marching towards me in the butler's mirror at the end of the corridor. It was the Viscount's guests – the glamorous lady, the boy in the sailor suit and the walrussy man, being led by a furious Edwin Welt.

I panicked. I didn't have time to get to the servants' staircase before they spotted me – I couldn't even remember which door it was. There wasn't anywhere to hide.

Invisible. Indiscernible.

I flung myself against the wall and stood bolt upright, gazing ahead, as the guests turned the corner. It worked. They walked right past me like I wasn't even there.

'He's done it this time!' Edwin was snarling. '*A German in the house!* How in God's name am I going to explain that in the Commons?' He groaned, rubbing his face. 'I thought this was going to be some meeting about the inheritance – all that stuff in the telegram about coming here "being to our advantage". I assumed he meant the will. I'd never have set foot on this godforsaken island if I'd known he meant *this*! Poisonous gases, tidal waves up to Godalming –'

'There's a damn fine pub in Godalming,' said the walrussy man sadly. 'Say, he's not serious about shutting us in our rooms at *half past three* in the afternoon, is he? Dashed boring, that. I was hoping to get some fishing done while I was here.'

Edwin ground his teeth in exasperation. 'That should be the least of your worries, Jolyon. The Navy won't look too kindly on you if news gets out about Conrad's Bavarian guest. They'll knock you down from Rear Admiral before you can blink.'

'Poor Cousin Conrad,' sighed the lady in black, dragging the little boy behind her. 'This comet business really has got to him. Maybe Gilbert and I should leave, before it gets any worse –'

'No,' Edwin snapped. 'No one leaves. We're *all* staying until tomorrow. Including you, Lettice.'

I froze. The woman was Lettice Welt, the one who'd written to the Society and given me my final chance.

'Why?' she said innocently. 'What's happening tomorrow?'

'Nothing, that's what!' Edwin snapped. 'You heard him – he thinks he's going to become leader of the free world! What the *hell* is he going to do when he wakes up and finds out nothing has happened!' He shook his head. 'If any of this gets out, it'll make the whole family a laughing stock. I've spent *years* fixing the scandals he's caused us. That hunting accident, those girls, Great-Aunt Decima –'

'Great-Aunt Decima!' Lettice gasped, turning pale. 'She's not still . . . *alive*, is she?'

'Vigorously,' growled Edwin. 'And getting worse by the year. Conrad seems to be the only one capable of controlling her. But now we're going to control *him*.' He lowered his voice. 'So we stay here and we stop it getting any worse. Agreed?'

'Capital idea!' said Jolyon as they disappeared around the corner. 'But, er . . . you don't think we'll have to stay in our rooms *all night*, do you?'

I glanced after them. Lettice was still in the corridor, standing at a mirror and fixing her hat, while Gilbert kicked at the skirting board.

I knew I shouldn't talk to her – I'd already made that mistake once, with the Viscount. But this might be my only chance to thank her.

I sidled up and coughed. 'Miss Lettice?'

She stared at me in surprise. 'Yes?'

I did a little bow. 'It's me, ma'am. Stephen Pike.'

She gazed at me blankly. Her hands were still frozen at her hat, mid-tweak.

'From the Society,' I explained. 'I just wanted to thank you for all you've done for me. I won't let you down.'

I tried to look solemn, but it was hard because little Gilbert was kicking me in the shins. Lettice, meanwhile, was still staring at me, letting her eyes snap back to the mirror impatiently every few seconds.

'Sorry – *who* are you?' she said after a while.

'Ah, Stephen.'

I leapt a foot into the air. Mr Stokes was standing right behind me – I hadn't even heard him coming. He handed me a hammer and caulking iron.

'Lowen needs your help sealing the fireplaces. Let's leave Lettice to her busy day, shall we?' He gripped my arm and dragged me down the corridor. '*Invisibility*, Stephen. How many times do I have to tell you?'

I took a final glance at Lettice as he steered me around the corner. She hadn't even noticed I was gone. She was gazing back at the mirror, still adjusting her hat and humming under her breath.

Nan always said I was good at reading people. She said that I noticed everything around me – that I could spot a liar before a word even left their lips. *You can't hide your thoughts from Stephen*, she'd tell people. *You might as well have a glass head.*

I wasn't so sure about that. But, right now, I felt certain that that Lettice wasn't lying to me – which meant either that she was the best actress in the entire world or that she had absolutely no idea who I was.

8

Wednesday, 18 May, 4.01 p.m.

The rest of the day was bedlam.

Lowen and I dressed in overalls and went from room to room, sealing up every fireplace. That meant cutting sheets of plywood to fit inside the chimneys, before lying on our backs and hammering them in place with cotton wadding to make them airtight. It was exhausting, filthy work; before long I was covered in soot, with sore red eyes from staring up chimneys all day long. Lowen made sure my job was as miserable as possible, refusing to hand me tools and barging me whenever we had to step through a door.

The guests made our job a misery, too. Professor Muller had brought a camera so he could document the day for posterity: he took a photo of the Viscount standing grandly behind his desk in his study, and then insisted on capturing the maids sealing up the doors and windows afterwards, which meant he kept blocking the corridors with his tripod and blinding everyone with his flash bulbs. Jolyon had decided that Lowen was going to be his valet and kept sending him on personal errands, which meant that I ended up doing most of the work myself, while Lettice appeared every ten seconds demanding endless cups of tea or cakes for Gilbert.

But, thanks to Mr Stokes, it all came together. Minute by minute, hour by hour, the job got done, and by half past three we were ready to start shutting people in their rooms. Mrs

Pearce took the maids upstairs, while Mr Stokes, Lowen and I started sealing the guests inside their rooms for the night. First Lettice and little Gilbert, then Jolyon, then Edwin, and finally Professor Muller. Once Lowen and I had packed the edges of their doorframes tightly with cotton wadding, Mr Stokes would kneel down and plug the keyhole with hot candlewax to seal it completely from gas. The Viscount watched over our shoulders the entire time.

'Good,' he said, when the last guest was finally shut in their room. 'Stokes, get these two sorted upstairs, then shut yourself away. I'll go and finish preparing my study.' He glanced at his watch. 'On second thought, you can make me a tea first.'

He strolled off, leaving the three of us covered in soot and trembling with exhaustion.

'Right,' said Mr Stokes wearily. 'Lowen, start sealing yourself in your bedroom. Stephen, go upstairs and check that the maids' rooms are all airtight. I'll come presently to take you to Miss Decima.'

My mouth turned dry. It had been a long, dismal day, and it was about to get even worse. I had to seal the entire Nursery by myself and then spend the evening with Miss Decima, who frankly sounded worse than a cataclysm. No wonder Lowen was smirking over his shoulder at me as we trudged up to the top floor.

The servants' bedrooms were all at the top of the East Wing – male servants at one end, the rest for the maids. The corridor was pitch-dark when I got there, with the windows boarded and all the lights off. Even so, I could see that Mrs Pearce had done a good job. Every bedroom door was sealed tightly from the inside, with little lines of wadding sticking out of the bottom, like rows of piped icing.

Except for one. I could still see light spilling out into the corridor from under the doorway, and, when I got close, I could hear someone crying inside, too.

I shifted from foot to foot. I couldn't leave the room if it wasn't prepared – besides, something could be wrong. I knocked on the door. 'Hello?'

The crying stopped, but there was no answer. I poked my head inside. The room was just like mine: a bed, a boarded window, a blocked fireplace. The only difference was the row of books lined up all neat on the windowsill. There was a little stack on the floor beside the bed, too.

One of the maids was sitting on the edge of her bed, wiping her nose with some cotton wadding. It was the one I'd seen crying in the servants' corridor that morning. Her face was red raw. She was all on her own. Most of the other maids were two to a room, but Mr Stokes told me that ladies' maids and such like got their own quarters here.

'Everything all right?' I asked.

'Fine,' she said, utterly miserable.

'Ah, grand.'

I could tell she wanted me to go, but I couldn't. It would feel *mean*, just closing the door on someone crying like that. 'Is that a London accent I hear?'

She stared at me. 'Huh?'

'Your accent,' I said. 'You're from London.'

'Oh.' She wiped her eyes. 'Er . . . yeah, Canning Town.'

'Bow,' I said, pointing at myself.

That was it. It was awkward, truth be told. I had no idea what to say to women, let alone crying ones. I'd spent the last two years in Borstal and then a month in a halfway house. Luckily for me, she talked first.

'You're Stephen, aren't you?' she said. 'The one looking after that . . . that old *witch* tonight.'

I nodded. 'Miss Decima? She sounds like a bit of a character. Nothing I can't manage.'

It was all bluster; I was absolutely bricking myself. Luckily, it seemed to work.

'Be careful,' said the maid. 'She's bad at the best of times, but ever since the windows got boarded up she's just been . . . *awful.*'

I finally put two and two together. 'You're Temperance – the one who normally looks after her. Nice name, that.'

'My mother drank herself to death.'

'Oh.' I was in dire straits. 'Need a hand with the door?'

Temperance shook her head. 'I'm all right.'

'It's no bother, I've been doing them for hours.'

She smiled at me. 'I'm fine, really. Thank you, Stephen.'

I felt something light up inside me – like a candle, the moment the wick finally catches. The silence wasn't bad this time: it was a thing we were sharing. Suddenly I was aware of how small the space was between us, me at the door, her on the bed.

Then she stopped smiling.

'Are you all right? Your ears have gone bright red.'

Oh, God, the beacons. 'Have they?'

'They're getting worse.'

'Must be the light in here –'

'They're *really* red.'

'Well, best be off!'

I ran out, slamming the door behind me. I suppose it could have been worse. I could have been sick down myself or called her *Mum* or something. I heard a scrunching at my feet and saw a line of cotton wadding appear under the door-frame as Temperance sealed herself inside and shut away the light we'd shared together, inch by inch.

'Stephen.'

I jumped. Mr Stokes had sneaked up on me again with his silent footsteps. He was standing behind me with a flickering gas lamp in his hand.

There was a book I'd read once in the library at Borstal. It was about the Greek myths, all done with crosshatch drawings to show you the different characters. One of them had chilled my blood: it was Charon, the man who rowed you over the River Styx when you died, taking you from the land of the living to your final resting place. That's how Mr Stokes looked right then – a guide, leading me to a world of darkness.

'Come,' he said. 'Miss Decima is waiting for you.'

9

Wednesday, 18 May, 4.29 p.m.

I followed Mr Stokes downstairs and out of the East Wing. We were the only people walking the corridors now. The house was empty and muffled and silent around us. It would still have been daylight outside, but it was pitch-black inside Tithe Hall.

'The Nursery is the only section of the house without electricity,' said Mr Stokes, raising the lamp, 'so you'll need this. It means there's no staff bell either, so I'll come and collect you in the morning.'

'What time, sir?'

'Who knows. With any luck, the poisonous gases will have passed World's End and consumed the rest of Cornwall by eight o'clock.'

We came to a set of double doors, alone at the end of a corridor. They had clearly been grand once; now the brass handles had tarnished and the paint was flaking along the edges.

'I've left you enough wadding to seal the Nursery by yourself,' Mr Stokes explained, nodding me inside. 'Along with a caulking iron and hammer. You'll need to plug the keyhole to the side exit with wax, after attending to Miss Decima.' He picked up a tea tray from the floor. 'If she *does* eat, please ensure that she chews properly; the woman has absolutely no patience whatsoever. She may throw it at you, but they're wooden plates so they shouldn't hurt too much if she does.'

He pointed at the cutlery. 'This knife's for the butter; this one's for the fish.'

There were three knives. 'What's that one for?'

'That's for you,' he said darkly, putting it in my pocket. 'Miss Decima's bedroom is on the right-hand side; your room is just opposite. Take care, Stephen.'

'Goodnight, Mr Stokes.'

With that, he handed me the gas lamp; I stepped inside the Nursery and shut the doors. I was finally alone with the legendary Miss Decima.

I stood in the gloom, clutching the tray and lamp. The Nursery was tiny: a hallway leading to a side entrance, two rooms on either side. But it was in a dreadful state – chewed carpet, chipped paint, long yellow stains from a leak in the ceiling. It stank of rot and mildew. I was shocked. I wouldn't let a dog sleep here, let alone a lady of standing.

A pool of light spilt from the doorway on the right-hand side. A meal had been flung across the floor and opposite wall, probably at Temperance earlier that day, along with a number of books, a paperweight and what looked like some kind of rhino horn. I summoned up all my courage and knocked on the door.

'Miss Decima?'

No answer. I could hear sounds coming from inside, though: pen on paper, a squeaking chair. I knocked again. 'It's Stephen, Miss Decima. I have your dinner.'

Silence. I shifted from foot to foot, trying to work out what to do. Miss Decima could be stone deaf. What was I supposed to do – wait until she replied? Go in before her food got cold? I tried to work out which one was least likely to get my head caved in with a tea tray.

It was no use. I couldn't stand here all night. I took a final breath, pushed open the door and stepped into Miss Decima's bedroom.

It wasn't much bigger than my room upstairs. There was an unmade bed in the corner, a desk and a little stove. That was more or less all that I could see. The rest of it was taken up with paper: sheets and sheets and sheets of it, and any surface was made to do. Pieces were piled on the windowsills, spilling from the shelves, scattered on the floor. All four walls were pinned with hundreds more layered on top of each other from floor to ceiling, covered in spidery handwriting and so spattered with ink that the whole room looked like a great night sky with the colours flipped around.

There in the middle of it was Miss Decima.

She was sat scribbling at her desk with her back to me, surrounded by guttered candles. She was old, that much was clear. Her hair was grey, and her hands were wrinkled. But they were nimble, too, with quick sharp movements that reminded me of a blackbird. She didn't seem to know that I was there.

'Miss Decima,' I repeated.

She turned around in shock, upending an inkwell.

'Jesus! I suppose people don't announce themselves any more.'

My stomach turned to stone. Miss Decima was in a state of undress. She was wearing a long white nightgown, and her hair was loose and falling over her shoulders. I wasn't supposed to see her like this. What's more, her teeth were on the desk beside her. She followed my gaze and laughed.

'Ha! Always take them out when I'm working, helps me think.' She crammed them back into her mouth and worked the gums. '*Agony*. I've got another set for eating somewhere, but I lost them ages ago. They'll be under all that, I suppose.'

She waved her hands vaguely at the floor. I stood, clutching the tray in silence. I was in way over my head. This was a job for a ladies' maid – an experienced one at that. What on earth was I supposed to do?

'Right!' said Miss Decima. 'Step forward. Let's have a look at you.'

I did as I was told. Miss Decima peered at me, her eyes gleaming like polished silver knives.

'Hmm. I'd have thought you'd be a little stronger, all things considered. Still, beggars can't be choosers. Put down the tray and hand me my hat, please.'

She pointed to a flowery bonnet on the bed. 'Your ... your hat, Miss Decima?'

'Yes, and the coat, too. Chop-chop! We haven't got all day.'

I put down the tray and handed her the coat and hat, then watched as she put them on. I was beginning to understand the problem: Miss Decima wasn't the full shilling. At least she wasn't throwing things at me.

'I'll leave you to it, Miss Decima,' I said, backing towards the door. 'I need to seal up the Nursery.'

'You will do no such thing,' she said calmly. 'We're going outside.'

I froze. 'Outside?'

'For the comet!' she insisted. 'I have a number of observations and recordings I wish to make. I've waited seventy-five years to see it, and I very much doubt I'll be around for the next one.' She started piling paper and pens into her lap. 'Gather my things, please.'

She was being perfectly serious. 'We – we can't do that, Miss Decima. There's going to be a cataclysm at five o'clock. The Viscount's given me strict instructions to –'

'I don't give a flying fuck what Conrad says,' said Miss

Decima. 'I read some of the letters he sent from his ridiculous Society – I knew he'd end up pulling an absurd stunt like this. *Cyanogen gases!* The mind boggles. Honest to God, the man was born with shit for brains. Why do you think I called you here in the first place?'

She had me reeling. I'd never heard language like it, least of all from a refined lady. Miss Decima was clearly insane. 'You *didn't* call me here, Miss Decima. Mr Stokes told me to take over from Temperance because –'

'Good lord!' she gasped, with a groan with exasperation. 'You're even slower than I feared. Use your *brain*, Stephen. I'm talking about calling you to Tithe Hall in the first place. Getting you here has taken me *weeks* to organize.'

I frowned. 'How do you know my –'

The hammer finally fell. I stared at Miss Decima in horror.

'Lettice didn't write to the Borstal Society,' I said. 'You did.'

'*Bravo*, Stephen,' she said, with a withering look. 'I knew Conrad would never allow me outside to study the comet, so I had to ensure I had a suitable servant on hand. Someone young and strong and willing to break the rules if need be. I decided a reformed criminal would be the ideal candidate: morally flexible, a natural disregard for law, useful in a tight spot should it come to violence. Better than some wet, weepy maid who can't even defend herself from a flung lunch.' She grabbed a telescope. 'So! I faked Lettice's handwriting, wrote to the Borstal Society pretending it was one of her charity schemes, then made sure that it all went via Stokes. Good old Stokes – he always knows when discretion is best. And here you are, right on time!' She handed me the telescope. 'Quick, please. We are already in the path of the comet's tail, but the comet itself won't be visible for a few hours. It's going to take us at least an hour to get in place, and then we have to set everything up.'

I stood rooted to spot, flooding with panic. 'If anyone sees us –'

'They won't,' said Miss Decima. 'Thanks to my idiot nephew, every single person in Tithe Hall is now sealed on the other side of the house. They couldn't see you even if they wanted to, and, quite frankly, Stephen, I can't see why anyone would want to. Now stop being impertinent and help me to my bath chair. We are not getting any younger.'

She grabbed a stick and started struggling to her feet. I watched in alarm. The stick shook in her grip, her legs trembling with the effort. 'Stop it, Miss Decima – you'll fall!'

'Then you'd better start fucking helping me, hadn't you?'

It was no use. If I helped Miss Decima, I'd lose my job. If I *didn't* help her, she'd end up breaking her hip, and then I'd be in even more trouble than I already was. I took her arm and led her into the corridor, feeling like a ship about to be smashed between two rocks.

Sure enough, there was an old wicker bath chair tucked into an alcove. It hadn't been used in years – the back wheels were both rusted. A cloud of dust burst out of the cushion when Miss Decima sat down.

'There!' she wheezed. 'See to the door, Stephen, and gather my things.'

She sat up like Cleopatra on the Nile and pointed ahead. I glanced up. 'The door?'

'The door, yes.'

I didn't move. Miss Decima looked like she was about to start shouting at me again, but then, all of a sudden, her eyes filled with pity. 'Oh, Stephen. *Please* don't tell me you believe any of that nonsense about poisonous gases.'

I blushed. 'It's not just the Viscount who thinks it, Miss Decima. It saw it in a newspaper, too. I know it *sounds* unlikely and all, but, well . . .'

I trailed off. Miss Decima gave a deep sigh and folded her hands in her lap.

'*Yes*, there are cyanogen gases in the comet's tail. *No*, they will not kill us. They're so rarefied that our atmosphere will pass through them like an elephant stomping through a cobweb. The entire scientific community has been saying so for months, and the only people that have said otherwise have been given the front page of every single newspaper in this country and beyond, precisely *because* what they have to say is outlandish. Sadly, my nephew is one of those men who thinks that disagreeing with established thought is a prerequisite of genius. People listen to him because he is rich and has the great fortune to having been born a man. Tomorrow morning, when the world is still very much here, he will somehow turn his failures into further confirmation of his theories. He will say that solar rays displaced the poisonous gases, or that the scientific community lied about the comet's distance, or blah blah blah . . .' She windmilled her hands. 'And on it will continue. The only tragedy is that people will *still* continue to listen to him.'

I glanced at the door. 'You're certain, Miss Decima?'

'Open the door and see for yourself.'

I believed her. If Miss Decima had told me that dogs were cats and my name was Nancy, I'd probably have believed *that*, too. She just had that way about her: she dragged you along whether you liked or not.

I stepped towards the door and opened it. It was a gorgeous summer's evening; the light was still out. A breath of cool, clear air flooded inside, rich with the smell of the sea. After a whole day trapped in that dark house, it was like a tonic, to tell you the truth. *Ambrosial*, even.

'*S-S-Stephen!*'

I turned in horror. Miss Decima was shuddering in her

bath chair, the rusted wheels squeaking as she choked for breath, her eyes bulging out of their sockets.

Then she laughed.

'Too easy,' she said. 'Now, for the last time, gather my fucking things.'

10

Wednesday, 18 May, 5.14 p.m.

I heaved the bath chair outside and closed the door. I hadn't seen this side of the grounds yet; we were in some ornamental gardens, all cobbled paths and tinkling stone fountains. The lawns led up to a hedge maze, and some cedars in the distance. I could hear crashing waves that I couldn't see.

'We'll head to the south-west prospect,' Miss Decima announced, checking her pocket watch. 'That should give us the most uninterrupted view of the comet. It should be visible to the eye within the next couple of hours. To the arboretum, please.'

I froze. 'Er . . .'

'The *trees*, Stephen.'

That was easier said than done: the rusted wheels of the bath chair screamed blue murder as I pushed it over the gravel. *Surely* someone was going to hear us? It didn't help that Miss Decima kept shouting at me.

'Left, Stephen. Past the agapanthus. *Your other left!* Good grief. A little faster, if you please, I should like to see the comet before the world really *does* end.'

Things calmed down once we were further from the house. The ground suddenly sloped down, forming a steep path, lined with twisted trees, that led towards the sound of the sea. This could almost be a normal day out: a manservant taking the lady of the house for an evening turn. *Nan would have liked this*, I thought. And then I stopped thinking that because it was like a knife in the ribs. 'How much further, Miss Decima?'

'Just keep going. You'll know when we get there.'

On we went. Any sign of a path began to disappear, and the woods became more overgrown around us: jagged rocks, strange plants, windswept grass that got caught in the spokes of the wheels. The sound of the sea grew louder and louder, but I still couldn't see anything. *Eight hundred acres*, I thought to myself. *Where on earth is she taking me?*

Finally, just as I thought the forest would never end, it did. A flat heath stretched out before us, stopping as suddenly as it started and plummeting down to the sea. Beyond that was nothing but ocean. It fair took my breath away. There were no boats, no lights from distant towns, just sea and wind and sky for miles and miles and miles.

'Hmm,' said Miss Decima, inspecting the horizon. 'Some light cloud cover, but it should be gone within the hour. Set us up over there, please.'

I did my best, but it took several tries. Miss Decima would pick a spot and get the whole thing set up, then would take one look down the eyepiece and decide we had to go to the other side of the heath instead. By the time she finally had it the way she wanted, the sun was sinking and the sky was ripening up in peach and auburn. 'What now, Miss Decima?'

'We wait.'

'But it's going to get dark soon.'

'Good. Some things only reveal themselves in darkness.'

And so we waited. We stood side by side in silence as night fell around us. At first, all I could think about was how much longer we were going to be out here, how cold it would get, how soon until we were back safely inside the house, but slowly, bit by bit, I felt myself relax. I'd spent all day feeling like a box being flung from person to person; now there was nothing to do but gaze out at the ocean and listen to the sound of waves beating the rocks far below. I felt an iron band break from around my chest.

Ah!' said Miss Decima. 'There she is. *Mademoiselle Halley.*'

I looked up. Night had fallen: the sea was one great mirror to the sky. The clouds had parted like curtains, just as Miss Decima had predicted, and there behind them was the comet.

It wasn't the first time I'd seen it. Its picture had been in the papers for months now, and over the last few weeks you had only to look up on a clear night to see it with your own eyes. But I'd never seen it like *this* before. It was bright as the point of a needle, the tail streaking behind it like long strands of soft hair, surrounded by stars and clear as anything. Out here, in the middle of nowhere, you could see every star that God had ever made.

'Quite something, isn't it?' said Miss Decima. 'Formed four and a half billion years ago, from the same primordial matter that birthed our solar system, and it's been trapped here ever since. Nero saw that, and St Paul, and the Prophet Muhammad, and William the Conqueror, and Genghis Khan and Shakespeare, and now us.'

I frowned. 'Wait a second: the tail's on the wrong side. It's flipped around.'

'It's passed the sun,' Miss Decima explained. 'The tail is made up of gases streaming away from the nucleus, which is made of ice. So the head leads the tail on the approach to the sun, then the tail leads the head on the way back.' She pointed. '*Two* tails, you see? The white one is vaporized dust, reflecting sunlight; the blue one is incandescent gas particles. *There* are your cyanogens, Stephen. Each one of those tails is twenty-four million miles long.' She folded her hands in her lap. 'I was four years old the last time I saw it. My father said that I'd be in my seventies if I saw it again. I never forgot that. I never quite believed him either.'

I could have stood there all night, listening to Miss Decima describe the heavens. 'It's beautiful, Miss Decima. *Diaphanous*, even.'

She glanced at me. 'Goodness me. *Diaphanous*. Time to put that vocabulary to good use.' She thrust a notebook into my hand. 'I'm going to dictate and you're going to write down everything I say. Light measurements, time readings, that sort of thing.'

I panicked. 'Perhaps it would be better if you did it, Miss Decima.'

'Stephen, I did not spend seventy-five years waiting for the comet to return so I could spend all night gazing at a sheet of fucking paper. Do as I say, please.'

There was no point arguing with her – you might as well argue with an iceberg. She adjusted the telescope and peered down the sight. 'Begin, please: *Right ascension of nucleus three hours, twenty-five minutes, thirty-nine point two seconds . . .*'

I scribbled like a man possessed. 'How do you spell *ascension*?'

'However you like. *Declination nineteen degrees, twenty-three arcminutes, twenty-seven point eight arcseconds . . .*'

I kept going as fast as I could, and found, to my surprise, that Miss Decima was right. I *could* do it. I was good at it even. There I was – Stephen Pike, not even twenty years old, three days out of a halfway house and already taking notes on learned matters for a lady of standing. I couldn't keep the smile off my face.

For a brief moment, we were perfectly in balance out there on that heath: Miss Decima with her eye to the heavens, and mine to her notebook, keeping the comet company like we were the only people left in the world.

11

Wednesday, 18 May, 11.21 p.m.

Pushing the chair back *up* the hill was a whole lot harder than getting it down, let me tell you.

By the time we got back to the house, there wasn't a hair of light to be seen at the windows. Everything was dead silent. I didn't dare breathe until I'd heaved the squeaking chair along the last stretch of garden and locked the door behind us.

I could have danced a jig: we were back in the house, and we hadn't been caught. Miss Decima was exhausted, though. She was leaning hard on my arm as I led her back to her room and settled her into her desk chair.

'Will that be all, Miss Decima?' I asked.

She shook her head. 'I need to translate your notes for my readings. Make me some tea, please. The jar of leaves is on that shelf, next to the Bible.'

I glanced at the bookshelf above her head. 'I'm surprised you have a Bible, Miss Decima. You don't seem like the religious type.'

'I like to have things nearby to throw that I don't mind breaking . . .' She smacked my hand away. 'No! Not that jar. Use the other one.'

I rubbed my hand. She had a slap like a dog-whip. 'Why?'

'Because I *say* so, Stephen. Stop being so fucking impertinent.'

With that, she took out her teeth, kicked off her shoes and began writing. I took the other pot of tea leaves and searched for the kettle – it was already on the little iron stove beside the desk, half full and still warm. It wouldn't take too long to boil. I knelt down and started stoking the coal.

I glanced to the side as I did, and nearly dropped the poker. It was the first chance I had to see Miss Decima's feet. They were in a terrible state: the soles were cracked, the skin so red they were almost purple. They were even worse than Nan's had been, right at the end.

'You must be wondering what I'm writing,' she said, all casual.

I nodded quickly. 'That's correct, Miss Decima.'

'I'm preparing an essay on the comet for the Royal Society,' she said grandly. 'I have a number of different theories that I've been working on for some time. I do believe they're going to make quite an impact.'

The kettle was already ticking away. I spooned some leaves into the teapot. 'Sounds like a passion for science runs in the family.'

She frowned. 'What do you mean?'

'Well, your nephew. The Viscount. Mr Stokes said that he was considered one of the finest scientific minds of his –'

It was the wrong thing to say. Miss Decima spun in her chair.

'*Conrad?* A scientific fucking mind! You could fill a warehouse with what that man doesn't know, and what he *does* know, he stole from me! I swear to God, if that horse-fucking little bastard ever . . .'

There followed a string of invective that I don't wish to record, repeat or remember. It near took the skin off my teeth. *Causticizing*, it was. I'd never heard language like it, not from a lady or otherwise, and I'd just spent the last month sharing a bunk with a man called Filthy Mick.

'. . . in his own mouth, and I bet he'd like it, too,' Miss

Decima concluded. 'Even his title is invented – did you know that? "Lord Stockingham-Welt" – ha! The only reason he has a peerage is because he saved the King's dog from drowning in the fucking causeway eight years ago, and he acts like he's stamped with the caste of Vere de Vere! I know what *I'd* like to stamp him with! He might call himself "Stockingham-Welt", Stephen, but, trust me, the man is pure Welt down to the marrow. Edwin, Jolyon, Lettice, that revolting little Gilbert . . . Welts, the lot of them! Nothing but drunks, parasites, hypocrites and whoremasters, without two brain cells to rub together between them!'

'Yes, Miss Decima,' I burbled, pouring the tea through the strainer as fast as I could.

But there was no stopping her now. 'The Stockinghams were one of the noblest families in England, Stephen. Did you know that? Then my useless, weaselling father squandered our fortune. He had to marry my sister Isabella to Lawrence Welt for his money, then kept *me* unmarried so I could look after him; then, when Isabella died, everything I should have inherited passed to the Welts. Can you credit it?' The anger was steaming out of her. '*I* was one of the finest scientific minds of my generation, Stephen! Sir John Herschel himself stood up after my presentation to the Royal Society and said that I would achieve great things. *Great things!* And look at me now!' She held out her hands in despair. 'My work, ignored! My talents, squandered! My ambitions, sacrificed at the altar of mediocre men! Confined to rotten rooms with nothing but criminals for company –'

'Your tea, Miss Decima.'

I handed over the rattling cup and saucer, trying to hide that my hands were shaking and I'd just given her a weapon. 'I-I should go. I have to get on with sealing the doorways.'

She looked surprised. 'Why?'

'Mr Stokes asked me to.'

She blinked. 'But there's no gas. It's pointless.'

'I don't want to let him down, Miss Decima.'

She gave a long, deep sigh. 'No. No, I suppose you wouldn't. Goodnight, Stephen.'

'Goodnight, Miss Decima.'

I fled, closing the door and almost fainting with relief. I was beginning to understand why people were so scared of Miss Decima. Being around her was like getting caught in a rip tide, then spat out the other end into a furnace. No wonder she'd been hidden away on the other side of the house by herself.

But it wasn't *right*, keeping a woman of her age in conditions like that. Her rooms were filthy and damp and badly kept. It wasn't right that she should swear like Filthy Mick either, but at least her rooms could be fixed. I decided I'd talk to Mr Stokes about it first thing in the morning, right after the cataclysm.

It didn't take long to seal the Nursery, now that I didn't need to worry about doing it well. Within an hour the doors were packed shut and I was feeling my way back along the hallway with the gas lamp. To my relief, Miss Decima's light had finally gone out. I felt my way to the room opposite, where I was going to sleep that evening. It was pitch-black and stank of damp bedding, but I didn't care. I'd been awake for eighteen hours and hadn't had so much as a bite to eat all day. All I wanted was to collapse into bed and close my eyes.

But there was something important thing I had to do first.

I knelt down by the bed and clasped my hands together. The very last time I saw Nan – that morning when the police kicked in the door and dragged me away – she told me to keep God in my thoughts, and I had. Every night in Borstal,

I'd taken her photo from out of the Bible, put both in front of me and finished the day with a prayer. I didn't care if the other lads laughed at me. I was talking to God and Nan was with him, and that was all that mattered.

First, I thanked the Lord for gifting me the job. I prayed for Mr Stokes, and then I prayed for Mrs Pearce and Temperance and all the other servants. I even prayed for Lowen and asked God to help him find the strength not to thump me in the mouth. I prayed that God would keep and protect *everyone* in the house, both staff and guests, and bring them to no harm.

Because that was the problem. I had known, from the very first moment that I laid eyes on Tithe Hall, that there was something wrong with it. Something bad. I could feel it, like a splinter under my thumbnail, and there was nothing I could do to stop it. So I prayed for the souls of everyone in the house. Edwin, Lettice, the Rear Admiral, Gilbert, the German . . .

I never got around to praying for the Viscount's soul. I'd started leaning forwards while I was praying and then my head met damp sheets, and before I knew it I was out like a snuffed candle.

12

The comet sailed past the Earth, continuing its great arc towards the Milky Way, onwards through the stars.

Not a single thing stirred in the corridors of Tithe Hall. It was the deepest, darkest part of night. The house was asleep. All was still, and all was silent.

But there were three people who did not sleep.

One was Miss Decima, who sat alone in the darkness, watching her bedroom door with eyes like polished silver knives.

One was the Viscount, who was dead.

And the other was the man who had watched him slowly die.

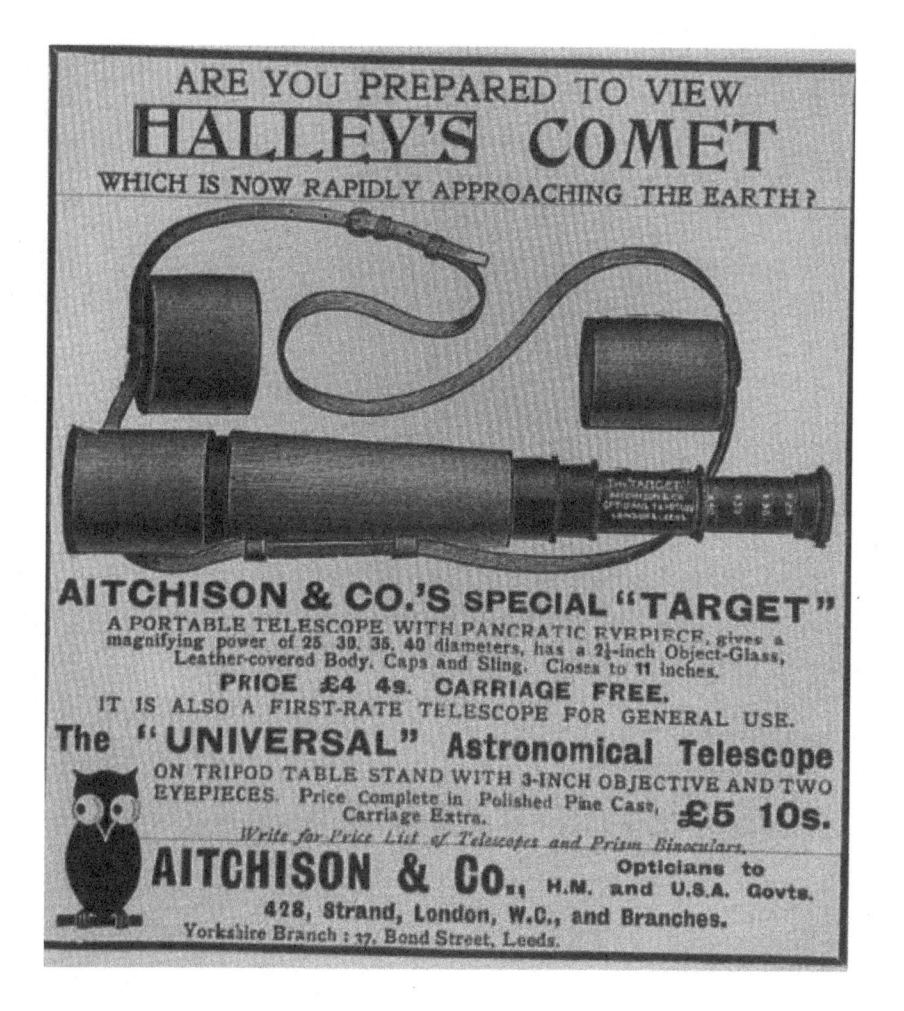

Thursday, 19 May 1910

13

Thursday, 19 May, 7.49 a.m.

I was having the usual dream when the knocking woke me.

I sat bolt up. The room was pitch-black and I was twisted up in the sheets, still wearing all my clothes. I must have climbed into bed during the night.

'Stephen!'

It was Mr Stokes. I didn't have time to find the gas lamp, so I had to feel my way along the peeling wallpaper until I found the door. 'Sir?'

'There you are,' came his voice, all muffled through the wood and wadding. 'I have just received the call from His Lordship. We need everyone up and out and preparing the house immediately. Go upstairs and fetch Temperance, please – she'll take over from you.'

I glanced over my shoulder. 'Should I check on Miss Decima first, or –'

Too late – I could already hear him striding away down the corridor. I swore. There was no time to check on Miss Decima – Temperance could deal with that. I found the gas lamp and unsealed the door as fast as I could, retracing my footsteps from the night before and racing to the top of the house. All the lights were still off, and the staircase was pitch-black – if I hadn't had the gas lamp with me, I wouldn't have been able to see a thing.

The maids' corridor was empty when I got there. Everyone was still trapped in their rooms, struggling to prise the wadding from under their doorframes so they could let themselves out. I headed straight for Temperance's door – sure enough, she hadn't even started unsealing it.

'Stand back!' I shouted.

I counted to five, then ran at the door as hard as I could, slamming it open. Temperance was inside, sitting on her bed and blinking at me.

'That sounded really painful,' she said.

'It wasn't, actually,' I just about managed to choke out.

'Stephen!'

I turned around. Mrs Pearce was marching down the corridor towards me. 'What are you doing up here? You're supposed to be letting the guests out!'

I frowned. 'Temperance is supposed to relieve me in seeing to Miss Decima.'

'She looks pretty relieved to me!' she snapped. 'What are you standing around for? Lowen's already started! You're supposed to be helping him!'

I could make out a muffled hammering coming from below us. I groaned. If I was late, Lowen would absolutely make me suffer for it. I grabbed the lamp and raced down to the second floor as fast as I could. The lights were all off there, too, and the hallway was pitch-black. I fumbled my hand along the wall to find the switch, trying to work out why it was still so dark. Why hadn't Lowen turned the lights on?

I nearly leapt out of my skin. There was a light flickering at the far end of corridor. I swung up my lamp in panic – sure enough, the distant light swung too. It was just my own lamp, reflected in one of the butler's mirrors.

'Idiot,' I muttered.

The hammering was coming from down the corridor. I didn't have time to find the light switch; I marched towards the sound as fast as I could, keen to get there before Lowen started shouting at me. But then I turned the first corner and stumbled to a halt. The suit of armour was standing in front of me.

My heart sank. The hammering was coming through the ceiling. I wasn't on the second floor: I'd got lost on the servants' staircases and skipped a whole floor. I was outside the Viscount's study. Lowen was going to skin me alive.

At least there was no chance of bumping into the Viscount now — I could see that the study door was still sealed shut. That meant I could nip past and use the next servants' staircase along to save time. I scurried past, glancing at the suit of armour as I did.

I stopped dead. The bolt was missing. The crossbow string had been loosed, too; it must have been fired.

I turned around, expecting to see the bolt jutting from the study door, but there was nothing. The wood was completely undamaged. A bolt like that was made to punch through metal armour — it should have left a mark. I lowered the lamp to see if it had fallen out of the crossbow and was lying on the floor.

I froze. There was a large, red stain in the centre of the white wadding under the door.

I stared at the stain. I knew what it was. 'Y-Your Lordship?'

Absolute silence. I peered through the keyhole, but it was sealed with candlewax from the inside. I raised a trembling hand and knocked.

'Everything all right in there, Your Lordship?'

Nothing. I felt a rising panic. Why wasn't the Viscount replying?

Because he isn't in there. But he had to be. The door was sealed.

Because he's asleep. But he'd already phoned Mr Stokes.

Because he's ignoring you. But the bloodstain . . .

'*What are you doing?*'

Lowen was striding down the corridor towards me, a hammer in one hand and a crowbar in the other. He was absolutely fuming.

'Where the hell have you been? I've been looking for you everywhere. You're supposed to be helping me get the guests out!'

He tried to grab my arm, but I snatched it back. 'Look.'

I pointed at the bloodstain. Lowen's eyes widened. 'What's that?'

'It's blood.'

'I *know* it's blood, you stupid . . . What's it doing there?'

'I don't know, do I?'

Lowen stared at me for a moment. Then he glanced at the door. 'Knock, then.'

I knocked, louder this time. Lowen and I looked at each other. The seconds ticked down, one by one. The silence was so loud it buzzed.

'Get Stokes,' said Lowen, his voice suddenly very small. 'Now.'

'But where –'

'*Now!*'

I tore through the corridor, back to the staircase I'd come from, and scrambled down to the servants' quarters. I was going so fast that I crashed into someone coming upstairs – it was Temperance, carrying a breakfast tray that she almost dropped.

'*Hey!*' she snapped. 'For God's sake, look where you're –'

'Stokes,' I burbled. 'Where is he?'

Her eyes widened. 'He's in the kitchen. Sorting the Viscount's breakfast.'

'Tell him to come the study. Now.'

'But —'

'*Just get him!*'

I raced upstairs, hurtling back to the study. Lowen was already flinging himself at the door, trying to break through with his shoulder. 'Help me!' he shouted.

We threw ourselves at the door together, but the wood barely shifted: it was solid oak, packed with wadding. We tried over and over, until my bones were throbbing and my shoulder screamed. Sure enough, bit by bit, the frame around the door began to crack and loosen. Suddenly I could hear raised voices from the end of the corridor and glanced up to see Temperance flying around the corner, waving her hands. 'Mr Stokes! They're here! They're —'

Lowen and I hit the door together, and the frame finally gave in. I lost my footing and stumbled inside, landing in the middle of the rug. I looked around, head spinning, but the study was pitch-black — the lights were all off. 'Your Lordship? Is everything —'

The lights slammed on, stinging my eyes like salt water. For a few seconds, all I could do was blink away spots until the room finally came into view.

It had changed since I last saw it. The fireplace had been boarded up, and all the papers and books had been cleared off the desk. Only the fishbowl was left. The fish inside it were dead, floating belly-up on top of the water, their bodies shifting and swaying from when I'd disturbed the rug.

The Viscount was sitting behind his desk, between two oxygen tanks. He was wearing the same clothes as the day before, and his hair was still neatly combed. His arms were on the armrests, and his head was flopped to one side, his cheek and neck and chest covered in blood.

The crossbow bolt was buried deep in his eye.

He was dead. And the look on his face told me he hadn't died easy either.

There was another crosshatch drawing I'd seen in that book of Greek myths – men who'd been turned to stone by Gorgons. That was how the Viscount looked in that chair: screaming, petrified, frozen at the exact moment he laid eyes on the monster that killed him.

There was a sudden smash behind me. Lowen was standing at the light switch, his face a mask of fear. Temperance was in the study doorway, her hands clutching the broken doorframe, holding in a scream.

Standing behind her, a tea tray hanging limply from his hand, was Mr Stokes. He looked pale as death. The remains of the Viscount's breakfast lay shattered across the floorboards at his feet. The teapot had smashed to pieces, spreading a dark stain between his leather shoes, and I heard a single teacup roll over and over, until that, too, fell silent.

14

Thursday, 19 May, 10.14 a.m.

It took two hours for the tides to go down and the causeway to open up, so that Chief Constable Penrose could reach the house.

He arrived with a police surgeon and two more officers. They took a sketch of the Viscount's body, and then they took sketches of the rest of the room. The whole study was searched from top to bottom. Every cupboard was opened, every shelf examined. The chimney was unboarded, the plywood taken off the windows, and the last of the broken doorframe pulled apart.

Nothing was found.

Chief Constable Penrose questioned everyone. He sat down Lowen, Temperance, Mr Stokes and me, and had us all explain how it happened – what we'd seen, how we'd seen it, who did what when. Then he ordered a full search of Tithe Hall. The boards on the windows were removed, and every single room was inspected under his close eye. The driveway around the house, the gardens, the forest and the maze were all searched, too.

Nothing was found.

It was mid-afternoon by the time Chief Constable Penrose called Edwin to the drawing room for a private meeting. The rest of the staff had all been told to wait in the servants' quarters, but Mr Stokes had made Lowen and me stay with him, so that we were on hand to help the police. The three of us stood in the entrance hall in silence. We couldn't even look at each other. I kept my eyes fixed ahead, trying not to think about the image of the Viscount's body in the study.

But I was thinking about it, even then. I remember that. I remember standing there and thinking, over and over, that there was something wrong with that room.

The drawing-room doors opened, and Edwin and Chief Constable Penrose stepped out.

'Thank you again for your cooperation, Mr Welt,' the Chief Constable was saying. 'I appreciate that this must come as a terrible shock to you.'

'That's one way to put it,' muttered Edwin.

Right on cue, two officers appeared at the top of the staircase with the Viscount's body under a covered gurney.

'We'll have the post-mortem results for you on Monday,' said the Chief Constable. 'For, er . . . all of them.'

He held up a greaseproof paper bag, which was filled with a dozen dead fish.

'The Inspector from Scotland Yard should be here tomorrow afternoon,' he added. '*Jarvis*, he's called. I believe he knew the Viscount personally. Sounds like the right man for the job. He should have all this unpleasantness cleared up within a few days.'

Edwin clenched his jaw as the corpse was carried past. 'Quite. As you can imagine, Chief Constable, this is going to cause some . . . *considerable* family embarrassment. I trust that I can count on your discretion in this matter?'

The policeman nodded. 'Of course, Mr Welt. You needn't worry.' He gave me and Lowen a sideways glance. 'But you might want to have a word with your staff. Gossip travels fast in houses like these. You don't want them telling their families or there'll be reporters everywhere before long. Maybe you should nip it in the bud, while you can?'

They shook hands, and a police van drove off with the Viscount's body. Edwin stood watching the van disappear down the winding driveway until it had crossed the causeway and left World's End for good.

'Stokes,' he said, without turning around, 'summon the household. Immediately.'

Within minutes, everyone was back in the drawing room. It was exactly like it had been the day before: standing room only, shoulder to shoulder, family and guests at the front. The only difference was that it was Edwin standing on the footstool now, rather than the Viscount. He waited until everyone was silent before talking.

'I'm sure you've all heard the news,' he said coldly. 'That Lord Stockingham-Welt was found dead in his study this morning.'

Everyone gasped. People *knew*, of course, but hearing it said out loud made all the difference. I glanced at the Viscount's family. Jolyon looked a state – he was red-faced and bleary-eyed, clearly the worse for drink. Lettice was tearily fussing at Gilbert's hair while he tried to struggle away. But Professor Muller looked the worst by far. He was a shaken man, smoking like a chimney and stubbing out the butts with a trembling hand.

'The study is now a crime scene,' Edwin continued. 'No one is to set foot on the first-floor corridor before the Inspector from Scotland Yard arrives tomorrow. Until he has concluded his investigations, Tithe Hall is in *complete lockdown*. No one leaves the island under any circumstances, and no one from the mainland is to set foot here. Excursions to the village are cancelled. You are not to write to any relatives or discuss matters with any tradesmen who might appear at the causeway. Anyone found breaking these rules will have their position terminated, immediately, without reference.'

He glanced at his family. 'The same applies to guests. No one leaves World's End before the will reading next Friday.'

'But, Edwin, I have plans!' Lettice begged.

'Me, too!' said Jolyon, choking on the glass of raw egg he was drinking. 'I have an important meeting with my turf commissioner!'

'I must be back in Hamburg on Monday!' said Professor Muller, wringing his hands frantically.

'I don't give a toss,' snapped Edwin. 'I'm not letting *a word* of this leak to the press. Thanks to Conrad's plans, the house has more than enough provisions to last until the will reading. We stay until the matter is concluded. Until then, I will be assuming the role of master of the estate.' He glanced to one side. 'Anything to add, Stokes?'

Mr Stokes cleared his throat. 'Only to request that all staff assemble downstairs, please. There are a number of further details that I wish to make clear.'

Edwin nodded. 'Very well. This meeting is over.'

Lettice leapt out of her chair to plead with him; Jolyon switched from his glass of egg to a nearby decanter; Professor Muller fled from the room, shoving people aside as he did so. The staff filed out in dark silence. I could tell from the looks around me that they were going to have a few choice words to say about this once they were out of earshot.

But I didn't follow them. I hung around at the back, holding open the door of the servants' staircase until I was completely alone. Then I crept upstairs to the first floor.

The hallway was different in daylight, with the boards off the windows. The walls almost seemed a different colour. I made my way down the corridor in silence, my eyes fixed to the butler's mirrors ahead to make sure that no one was coming.

The study doorframe was still broken, hanging off its

hinges. I took a final glance behind me, then slid inside without so much as a sound.

It was a mad thing to do. *Uncountenanceable*, really. If I was caught sneaking in here now, after everything I'd just heard, Edwin would have me thrown me out in a heartbeat.

But I couldn't help it. There was something about that room that had been nagging at me ever since I fell into the study that morning. Something that was screaming at me to go back to find out what it was, before it was too late.

The study looked different in daylight, too. The Viscount's body was gone; the dead fish had been scooped from the fishbowl, leaving only a glass bowl of water. The bloodstained wadding was gone, too, and the crossbow bolt. Everything else had been left untouched, ready for the Inspector to begin his investigations.

But I knew that something was wrong with it.

You notice things, when you're a servant. You have to. You have to spot when a plate's been nudged or a fork's got a smudge of silver polish on it before anyone else does. It's all part of the job. And, right now, I knew that something in this room had changed. Something had been tampered with since I first stepped into the study on Wednesday morning and when I broke down the door the next day. I knew it, as sure as I knew myself.

But what?

'*Ach!*'

I nearly had a heart attack. Someone had just crept into the room behind me – someone who had sneaked down the hallway so they wouldn't be heard. Someone who wasn't expecting to see me either.

Professor Muller stumbled back to the broken doorway, tripping over his own feet. His eyes were bulging with terror, like a trapped animal.

I quickly bowed. 'B-beg your pardon, sir.'

I raced past him and fled down the corridor, my back breaking out in sweat. It was all over – I was surely done for now. When Professor Muller told Edwin that he'd just found me snooping around the crime scene . . .

But then I realized Professor Muller wouldn't tell Edwin a thing. Because *he* wasn't supposed to be in there either. I glanced up at the butler's mirror as I turned the corner, and, sure enough, Professor Muller was leaning out of the study door and watching me as I left. You'd never seen a guiltier face in all your life.

15

Thursday, 19 May, 4.33 p.m.

No one noticed me slipping in at the back of the servants' hall. Cook had had a funny turn while I was upstairs, and was now collapsed in a chair, maids flapping her bright red face with their aprons.

'*Murder!*' she kept saying, in between gasps. 'In this house. I can't believe it. Never in all my life would I have dreamt it!'

'*Hush*, Jenni,' Mrs Pearce muttered, shoving a mug of water in her hand. 'We don't *know* it's murder, do we?'

Lowen was smoking against the wall, scowling. 'Course it's murder. Police wouldn't do this for suicide, would they?'

Mrs Pearce tutted. 'It could've been an accident –'

'An *accident?* Ha!' Lowen laughed. 'Just like his father, eh?'

A weird quiet seemed to pass over the room. Suddenly everyone was shifting their feet. I looked around at them. They all knew something, something important, but no one wanted to say it out loud.

'What happened to the Viscount's father?' I asked.

Mrs Pearce tutted. 'Never you mind! Shame on you, Lowen, bringing that up. There's a man dead in this house – we've got no time to go dredging up old gossip!' She paused. 'But, if you must know, it was a hunting accident. He got shot with a crossbow.'

I jumped. 'Where?'

'On the grounds. Down by the waterfall.'

'I meant where in his *body*.'

She glared at me. 'Why would *anyone* want to know morbid details like that? Honest to goodness! What's done is done!' Another pause. 'But, seeing as you asked, it was in his eye. Not many people know that.'

Lowen and Temperance and I shared a stunned look. We were the only people in the room who had seen the Viscount's body: the only ones who understood the significance. He'd died in the exact same way as his father.

'Christ,' said Lowen, with a shudder. 'That's weird, that is.'

Mrs Pearce frowned. 'What's weird?'

Lowen shifted. We'd been told by the police not to breathe a word about what we'd seen. If Edwin found out Lowen had been talking about the crime scene, he'd be sacked in seconds.

'Nothing,' said Lowen, stubbing out his cigarette. 'But, let's face it – no one thought his father's death was an *accident* either, did they? The Viscount and his dad go hunting on the grounds, only the Viscount comes back alive. Everyone figured he murdered his own father for the fortune. Big scandal, and that.' He paused. 'But maybe the Viscount *didn't* kill him. Maybe someone else did. And maybe that same person killed the Viscount last night.'

Everyone was muttering now. 'He had plenty of enemies . . .'

'A lot of money involved . . .'

'Even his own family seem to hate him . . .'

Mrs Pearce glared around her. 'Listen to yourselves! Have you no respect for the dead? Why on earth would anyone –'

'Maybe it weren't anyone on Earth.'

Everyone turned at the same time. A maid was sat at the end of the table, her palms pressed to the wood. She was young, her cheeks thick with spots.

'I always said it would happen, didn't I?' she said, her voice getting higher. 'I *said* the ghost was going to get revenge.'

Lowen rolled his eyes. 'Oh, for *pity's sake*, Merryn –'

'What's she talking about?' I asked.

'She thinks she's got the bleeding second sight,' muttered Lowen.

Merryn looked around, her eyes wide and frightened. 'The Viscount's father. His soul's been wandering Tithe Hall for years. I've seen him. He was angry about being murdered, he was, so angry –'

'Enough, you stupid girl!' snapped Mrs Pearce.

But Merryn had already worked herself into a frenzy. 'Don't you see? The ghost killed the Viscount! And now we're all stuck here with it!'

She collapsed on the table in floods of tears. At that moment, Mr Stokes entered the room. He gazed at Merryn and sighed wearily. 'Mrs Pearce, if you wouldn't mind.'

Mrs Pearce bundled Merryn from her chair and marched her outside, where she could be heard giving her a sound drubbing two rooms away. Mr Stokes took us all in with a piercing, steady glare.

'I want to make this absolutely clear,' he said. 'No more gossip, no more speculation. When the Inspector arrives tomorrow afternoon, you will all make yourselves available to him for questioning.'

Lowen scowled. 'Course. They won't question gentry, though, will they? It'll be the staff in the firing line for this, mark my words.'

'I'll remind you to keep remarks like that to yourself, Lowen,' said Mr Stokes darkly.

But Lowen wasn't stopping now. 'Doesn't matter that we were *all* in the East Wing together, does it? They're not going to arrest his family over this. They'll pin it on one of us!' He paused. 'Course . . . not *everyone* was in the East Wing, were they?'

The room fell silent. Then, one by one, everyone turned to look at me.

I couldn't let the panic show on my face. That only makes you look guilty, which is exactly what had happened in the dock. 'What do you mean by that?' I said, as calmly as I could manage.

Lowen shrugged. 'It's just funny, isn't it, all this happening right after you turn up –'

'*That is enough, Lowen!*' Mr Stokes bellowed, slamming his hand on the table.

It was the first time I'd heard him shout. Judging from the reaction around me, it was the first time *anyone* had heard it. He glared around the room.

'That is the last accusation I will hear in this house. Anyone who breaks that rule – *anyone* – will have me to answer to. Do I make myself clear?'

Everyone muttered quickly. Lowen nodded, his cheeks turning an ugly red.

'Kitchen staff to the kitchen,' Mr Stokes barked. 'Parlour maids to the fires. Lowen and Stephen, get upstairs now. We have dinner to prepare.'

The room emptied at lightning speed. No one spoke, but I knew that the moment I was out of sight they'd all be talking about me. Chief Constable Penrose was right: houses like this ran on gossip. I'd just seen that with my own eyes. And, right now, thanks to Lowen, everyone was going to be trying to remember when they'd last seen me on the night of the murder.

At least I had Mr Stokes on my side. I gave him a look of heartfelt gratitude as I stepped past him . . . but the second his eyes met mine, he looked away.

It stopped me dead. I'd just seen something in his eyes that hadn't been there before. Something that I recognized. A flicker of doubt. *Fear*, even. And I knew why it was there.

Mr Stokes was the only person in the house who knew about my past. The only person who knew that I had a criminal record. And he had just pieced together that the very same day I'd arrived at World's End, the Viscount had been murdered.

16

Thursday, 19 May, 5.33 p.m.

The dining room was a dim and gloomy space. The table was a dark mahogany and the silk walls were the colour of blooming blood, lined with more of those butler's mirrors.

'Stephen, you will observe for tonight,' said Mr Stokes. 'Stand behind the screens and don't draw any attention to yourself, please.'

There was a coldness in his voice that hadn't been there before. I understood why he'd brought me up here – he wanted to keep an eye on me. I stood at the side of the room, feeling my stomach turn to stone as Lowen and Mr Stokes prepared the table, flapping out the tablecloth and screwing the electric candles into their sockets. Before long, a line of maids trooped upstairs with crockery and cutlery. Mr Stokes went around the table with a rule measure, giving instructions.

'Oyster forks don't go there, Alice. No, Betty, not those glasses, this is a family occasion. Third chest in the kitchen. Make sure they're washed, and make sure Mary doesn't do it.'

The maids all shot me glances as they scampered out of the room, whispering to each other. I knew what they were saying. I knew what they were all thinking, too.

The clock struck seven just as the table was finally set. The family arrived dressed in mourning: Edwin in a black suit,

Jolyon with a black armband tied around his sleeve, Lettice in a long sparkling black dress and veil. She'd even dressed up Gilbert in a little black sailor outfit. She had a real flair for mourning wear.

Edwin took the chair at the head of the table. 'Well,' he said solemnly, 'I think a prayer would be suitable under the circumstances, don't you?'

Lettice frowned. 'Conrad *loathed* religion.'

'Yes, well, lots of things are going to start changing around here,' said Edwin icily. He bowed his head. 'Dear Lord, we beg that you display some leniency in your consideration of Cousin Conrad's soul.' He paused, and decided not to add any more. 'Amen.'

Lowen and Mr Stokes moved around the table with a tureen of soup, ladling it into bowls. I stood against the wall, watching the butler's mirrors. I could see it all from where I stood: every setting, every plate, every face lit from beneath by a candle.

'*Scotland Yard!*' Lettice was saying, shaking her head miserably. 'I don't see why you couldn't do something about it, Edwin. Connie would be so humiliated.'

'I imagine he wouldn't be too thrilled about being dead either,' Edwin muttered. 'It's out of my hands, Lettice. An investigation like this is well beyond the capabilities of a rural police force.'

'Well, I don't see why they had to go through my room!' Jolyon muttered, catching Mr Stokes's eye and jabbing a finger at his already empty wine glass. 'That was most unnecessary. Not that one has anything to hide, or any cause for embarrassment, or, er . . . so on.'

I saw Edwin thin his eyelids, just a fraction.

'There'll be much more prying than that when the Inspector arrives, Cousin,' he said carefully. 'We shall all have to get used to it. Before long they'll be on their way, the matter will be concluded, and this whole tragic episode will be –'

'Who murdered Cousin Conrad?' said Gilbert.

On every side, I saw faces snap towards him in the butler's mirrors.

'*Gilbert!*' Lettice laughed nervously. 'What do you mean? Cousin Conrad wasn't *murdered* –'

'Yes, he was,' said Gilbert. 'I heard Uncle Edwin talking to the fat policeman about it. Someone shot him in the head with a crossbow and all his brains came out of his eye.'

'That wouldn't have taken long,' Jolyon muttered.

'Gilbert! What a *terrible* thing to say!' Lettice gave Edwin a beseeching look. 'Honestly, Edwin, he shouldn't be eating so late. It stirs his blood.'

'He shouldn't be eating with us *at all*,' muttered Edwin. 'He should be upstairs on his own, with a soft posset and a shut door.'

Lettice gasped. 'Leave him alone, on a night like this? Have a heart, Edwin! I'm all the poor boy has left!'

Edwin glanced at them distastefully. 'Yes, I was sorry to hear about his parents. It must have been a terrible shock to you, losing them both like that. Especially after you'd only just lost your husband.' He took a sip of his soup. 'Gastric flu must run in the family.'

Lettice's mouth twitched. She hadn't liked that.

'So kind of you to say, Edwin,' she replied sweetly, an edge to her voice. 'I must say it's terribly hard, providing for a grandchild at my age. I'm doing all I can for him.' She took a dainty spoonful of soup. 'On that subject, I've been trying to organize a place for him at Eton but I'm having some trouble securing the funds. Conrad must have somehow missed my letters about it –'

Edwin snorted. 'The family money won't stretch to Eton, Lettice. It'll be Lancing or Gresham's.'

'I'm not sure *Lancing* is quite right.' She made it sound like medieval torture. 'Gilbert is a sweet, sensitive boy.'

'Will Cousin Conrad's ghost come back?' Gilbert was saying. 'I hope he does. Maybe he'll come back and haunt the murderer until they go mad and die.'

Lettice was turning pale. 'Gilbert, stop it! There is no *murderer* in this house!'

'Hmm,' said Jolyon, slurping at his soup. 'That's not necessarily true, is it?'

Everyone stared at him. Jolyon waved Mr Stokes over to refill his wine glass for the third time.

'Well, there *has* to be,' he said. 'Stands to reason! Causeway was closed. Tide was up all night. No one left World's End before, and no one's left since. So whoever did it is still here. Including, ahem . . .'

He gave a nod to the empty chair beside him. Professor Muller was the only guest who hadn't come down for dinner; I hadn't seen him since running into him in the study.

Lettice's eyes took on a sudden gleam. 'Indeed. Such a pity Herr Muller couldn't bring himself to join us. How . . . *Continental* of him.'

'A little *too* Continental, if you ask me,' muttered Jolyon. 'Murdering a chap in his own home strikes me as a decidedly un-British thing to do.'

'I'd rather we didn't go around accusing our unwanted German of *murder*,' said Edwin through gritted teeth. 'It's bad enough that he's here in the first place. I want him gone as soon as possible, along with this whole scandal.'

There was a sudden change in the room. I could feel it, see it, hear it all around me.

'Of *course* you do, Edwin,' said Lettice. 'You've got everything you ever wanted, haven't you? The estate, the fortune –'

'Hold on a minute,' muttered Jolyon, suddenly annoyed. 'Just because he's *managing* the estate, it doesn't mean he'll inherit it. Same with the money. They're separate.'

Edwin fixed Lettice with a glare. 'Indeed they are, Cousin. Conrad had no children, no heir. The estate and fortune were free to distribute as he saw fit.'

'But you're the eldest male relative,' she said sweetly, like rot beneath honey. 'It stands to reason that you'll inherit the estate. And you can't run a house like *this* without money. The two are bound to go hand in hand.'

'I imagine we'll find out at the will reading,' said Edwin, dabbing his mouth with a napkin. 'You know an awful lot about wills, don't you, Lettice?'

The atmosphere had turned ice cold. Every word had a weight to it. I glanced between the butler's mirrors, seeing every side glance, every clenched jaw, every twitch of the lip. *They're hiding something*, I thought. *They all know something and they're hiding it.*

The silence lasted only a touch longer. Then Jolyon burst out laughing.

'Say! I've just had a rum thought.' He waggled his glass. 'There's someone else in the house who could have done it. Someone who hated Conrad more than anyone.'

He looked around, waiting for them to guess.

'Don't you see?' he said. '*Great-Aunt Decima!* Maybe she finally did away with him, once and for all!'

He guffawed loudly at his own joke and drained his glass. Edwin glared at him with disgust . . . but then, all of a sudden, his face softened.

'Hmm. An interesting point, Cousin. She has threatened

to kill him a number of times, hasn't she? We all remember that shooting weekend. My footman didn't walk properly for months afterwards.'

'She certainly has a violent side,' agreed Lettice. 'And that *temper* —'

'Don't remind me,' said Jolyon, with a shudder. '*Getting Decimated*, we used to call it. What I never understood is why Conrad called her *Great*-Aunt Decima. Wasn't she just his mother's sister?'

'She added the *Great* part herself,' Edwin muttered, running a finger around the rim of his glass. I could tell, with one look, that he'd made his mind up about something. 'Hmm. Great-Aunt Decima, the shame of the family, arrested for murder.' He took a sip of wine. 'It'd be a terrible pity, wouldn't it, if she got taken away because of all this?'

Lettice rolled her eyes. 'Don't be ridiculous, Edwin. She *can't* have killed Conrad. She can hardly walk!'

'But she wouldn't have been alone last night, would she?' said Edwin. 'She'd have had someone with her — a servant, or something.' He glanced over his shoulder. 'Stokes, who was with Great-Aunt Decima last night?'

I didn't look up. I didn't dare move. I felt like my skin was on fire. I knew — just knew — that Lowen's eyes were boring into me from the other side of the room.

Mr Stokes cleared his throat. 'Sir, that would be —'

He was cut off by a knock on the door. Temperance stepped inside, curtsied to the table and then ran over to whisper something to Mr Stokes. Mr Stokes managed to hide his shock but only just. He bowed to Edwin.

'Forgive me, sir,' he said. 'I have a message for one of the servants.'

He stepped across the room and stood in front of me. Everyone was watching now: Temperance, Lowen, Edwin,

Jolyon, Lettice, Gilbert, a wall of eyes surrounding me from every angle in every mirror.

'It's for *you*, Stephen,' said Mr Stokes in a quiet voice. 'Miss Decima has requested that you come to her quarters immediately.'

17

Thursday, 19 May, 7.37 p.m.

I walked to the Nursery like a man making his way to the firing squad. I was done for: tomorrow afternoon, the Inspector would arrive and he would talk to Mr Stokes, and then it would be over. It didn't matter that I was innocent. I had no alibi. I had a criminal record. Edwin wanted the mess to disappear quickly, and he'd use his powers to make it happen. I would be taken away and, this time, it would be for the rest of my life. It felt like the corridors of Tithe Hall were swallowing me up, one gulp at a time.

Miss Decima was in her bedroom, gazing out of her newly opened windows with a telescope.

'You wanted to speak to me, Miss Decima,' I said miserably.

'Yes, Stephen,' she said, without turning around. 'My tail's disappeared.'

It took me a moment to realize she was talking about the comet. I looked up – sure enough, the blue-white streak of the tail was gone.

'Most unusual,' she muttered. 'We'll have to make some further recordings when we have the time.'

I nodded, numb. There wouldn't be any more recordings. She'd just sealed my fate, and she didn't even know it. 'Will that be all, Miss Decima?'

She glanced at me haughtily. 'No, Stephen, it will *not* be all.'

She reinserted her teeth and turned to face me.

'You are going to tell me what has happened today. Every

last detail. I will *not* have secrets kept from me in my own house. The policemen who took the boards off my windows were *most* uncooperative, and Temperance hid from me the moment I started asking polite questions.'

I doubted any of her questions had been polite, but I didn't see the point in saying that. I didn't see much point in lying either. 'The Viscount's dead, Miss Decima.'

'I see. How did he die?'

'Crossbow bolt to the eye.'

'Goodness. Any sign of a perpetrator?'

'The police searched every inch of his study and found nothing.'

'I see. And the room itself?'

'Locked, empty, sealed from the inside.'

'Hmm. The Inspector from Scotland Yard is –'

'Arriving tomorrow afternoon.'

'Splendid. Anything else?'

'Edwin's put the house in lockdown.'

'Of course. And the servants?'

'They think it's ghosts.'

'Naturally.'

I swallowed. I had reached the sharpest point yet, the worst one of all. 'And . . . they think *I* did it, Miss Decima. The servants, the family, everyone. Because I was here last night, and because I turned up only yesterday. When they find out about Borstal, and about you bringing me here, it's . . . well, it's *ineluctable*, is what it is. By which I mean they're going to stitch me up.'

Miss Decima sat back, mulling this over.

'Hmm. I see what you mean. A reformed criminal arrives at Tithe Hall under a veil of secrecy, and that very same evening his master is brutally murdered. His only alibi is the mad old lady who lives on the other side of the house, who got him here under false pretences. And I suppose the crime that you were arrested for was –'

'Attempted murder, Miss Decima.'

She nodded thoughtfully. 'Ah, yes. That does tie up rather neatly, doesn't it?'

I wrung my hands. 'But I didn't *do* it, Miss Decima! You have to believe me!'

'*Hush*, Stephen,' she snapped. 'I wouldn't be talking to you now if I thought you did it. I happen to know for a fact that you're innocent.'

I blinked. 'You do?'

'I stayed up all night, watching your bedroom door,' she explained. 'I'd just locked myself in with a convicted criminal, I'm not a complete idiot. You didn't leave your room. The fact of the matter is that I've known plenty of murderous little twats in my time, and frankly I don't think you have it in you.'

I was relieved, if a little offended.

'So!' said Miss Decima. 'Herein lies the problem. If *you* didn't do it, who did?'

It took me a while to find the right words.

'I don't know, Miss Decima. But I know one thing for certain. A great wickedness has happened here. Something *worse* than murder.'

'Meaning?'

'Well, they could have killed the Viscount a thousand different ways if they wanted to – shot him or stabbed him or clubbed him or poisoned him. Why did they go about shooting him in a locked room with a crossbow?'

'Because a crossbow is silent, for one,' said Miss Decima. 'And can be fired across a great distance. But I suspect that the real reasons are far more complicated than that.'

'What do you mean?'

She turned back to gaze out of the window, to the empty space where the comet's tail should have been. It was a long time before she spoke again.

'Take a look at that comet, Stephen. It has held an unwavering course in our solar system for thousands of years; you can calculate exactly when and where it will appear, almost down to the time of day. It is saturated with law and order: regular orbits, regular intervals. Yet, despite that, over the last few weeks, we have seen it reduce the world to outright panic. It has been blamed for earthquakes, volcanoes, plagues, floods – even the death of the King. It does not seem to matter that Edward VII had been ill for many months, or that freak weather incidents occur regularly without once being reported. Give people the choice between a fact and a passing fancy, and they'll pick the fancy nine times out of ten.'

She drummed her nails across the top of her walking stick.

'The same goes for what happened at Tithe Hall last night. This was no accident, no act of ghostly revenge. Conrad was *murdered*, pure and simple, by someone inside this house. Someone whose aim was not simply to kill him but *to make it seem like it was impossible*. Because that would produce suspicion, hearsay, prejudice and all the worst excesses of human nature. Because that would elicit so much chaos and confusion that the truth would become occluded. And, as a lady of science, I cannot in good conscience allow gossip and speculation to be given as much weight as fact.'

She clapped her hands.

'So! We shall fight chaos with clarity. We shall use reason and rationality to come to the only logical conclusion that can exist and solve this murder *scientifically*.'

It took me a moment to realize what she'd just said. '*We*,' I repeated.

'Yes, we!' said Miss Decima. 'I'm the only person in the house clever enough to solve the mystery, and you shall push my bath chair. I'll also need you to investigate my relatives, eavesdrop on conversations, threaten suspects, lie to the police and maybe break a few fingers. And you're going to have to be rather efficient about it, too, Stephen, because, if we don't work out who did it, fast, I think it's safe to say that you're completely fucked.'

I didn't have anything to say to that. I just stood opening and closing my mouth like a fish pulled out of the ocean and slapped on the deck. Miss Decima gazed through her window and gave a long, satisfied sigh.

'Goodness me! A murder at World's End. My own nephew, slaughtered under the grisliest of circumstances. A ticking clock. A house filled with suspects. An unsolvable case that would confound even the most brilliant of minds. Dearie, dearie me!'

I didn't know much about Miss Decima. What I did know, I didn't really understand. But I was fairly certain that, at that moment, she'd never been happier.

18

High above World's End the comet soared on, cutting a line through Aquila and on towards Taurus, tracing its solitary way between the stars.

Stephen and Miss Decima talked for hours, making their plans. By the time they were finished, it was so late that Stephen went straight to his room without checking in with Mr Stokes. He lay on his bed for some time and stared at the ceiling, trying to work out how his life had ended up like this and what Nan would have said about it all.

Far below him, the man who'd watched the Viscount take his final choking breaths was standing in the study, gazing out of the window at the darkening lake.

Friday, 20 May 1910

POPULAR FALLACY.

MISFORTUNES ASCRIBED TO THE COMET.

The fact that Halley's comet was first seen with the naked eye in England on the eve of King Edward's death has lent a new force to the old belief that the coming of comets is in some inscrutable manner connected with the fortunes of the great and of the kingdoms over which they reign. It is this belief which is embodied in Shakespeare's famous lines:

When beggars die, there are no comets seen;
The heavens themselves blaze forth the death of
  princes

Daily Mail

19

Friday, 20 May, 6.00 a.m.

The staff bell rang on my bedroom wall, screaming away.

I lay like a plank of wood. I'd been awake all night, thinking about what might be in store for me today. I was about to become the chief suspect in a murder case. In the next few hours I had to avoid a police inspector, clear my name and help Miss Decima to catch a murderer, all while not getting sacked.

I didn't have time to worry about it. I could already hear the other servants through the thin walls, opening their wardrobes and washing their faces. Miss Decima's words from last night rang loud and clear in my head.

Stephen, stop fretting like a fucking nursemaid and listen to me. Here's what we're going to do.

I flung on my clothes and peeked out of my bedroom door. The hallway was empty.

The moment you wake up tomorrow, come straight back here. Make sure no one sees you. If anyone asks why you haven't gone to serve at breakfast, say that I insisted that you wait on me and not Temperance.

I crept to the staircase and scurried downstairs, my ears pricked for any sound. The rest of the house was still quiet around me; this early, only the downstairs staff would be working.

We need to work out your alibi for the night of Conrad's murder. And we'll need to be quick about it, too, because we'll have only a few hours before –

A scream ran through the house.

It was a real scream this time. A woman's scream, coming from somewhere below me. I froze. No one screamed like that for anything good.

The scream came again, louder this time. It was coming from the ground floor. I flew down the stairs two at a time, following the sound to the entrance hall.

It was turmoil when I arrived. Five maids were already there, clustered around someone collapsed on the floor. It was Merryn, her face wet with tears.

'It was him,' she was saying, over and over again. 'It was him!'

'Who?'

'*The Viscount!*' Merryn screamed.

It chilled my blood. Merryn kept babbling, gasping for breath and shaking as she did.

'I was in the servants' staircase. I heard this sound coming through the door that goes to the first floor. This . . . *horrible* sound.' She wiped her face with a trembling hand. 'It was the Viscount. Moaning and crying and saying he was going to get the person who killed him!'

It stopped the room – no one knew what to do. Suddenly Mrs Pearce barrelled through the door behind me, shoving me aside and snapping her fingers at the maids. 'For heaven's sake. Get her out before anyone sees!'

The maids practically carried Merryn out of the hall. I took a good look at her face. She wasn't acting. She meant every word. I'd never seen anyone look so frightened.

'Ah, Stephen.'

I gave a yelp of fear when I realized Mr Stokes was standing right behind me. He was good at that.

'You didn't return to me last night,' he said sternly. 'I'm sure you realize that you are *not* to end the day without being dismissed.'

I went clammy all over. 'S-sorry, sir. Miss Decima insisted I stay with her for some time. I *did* look for you, but . . .'

I trailed off. Mr Stokes didn't exactly seem convinced.

'Come with me, please,' he said coldly. 'There's a matter of great importance I need to speak to you about.'

I felt my legs go weak. 'M-Miss Decima asked me to see her first thing, sir –'

'That can wait. Follow me, please.'

He turned and marched downstairs. There was nothing else for it – I followed like a condemned man, my heart pounding in my chest. The plan was already in tatters. I racked my brains, trying to think what I could do or say to Mr Stokes to persuade him that I was innocent, but it was too late now. We stepped into his office and he closed the door softly behind him. 'Sit down, Stephen.'

I did as I was told. Mr Stokes made his way to the other side of the desk. The room felt like a cage. Sweat was sticking my shirt to my back. 'What seems to be the matter, sir?'

'I need to give you these.'

He opened a desk drawer and handed over a set of black gloves.

'Orders from the new master. The house is in mourning, and he has asked us to dress accordingly. These will replace your white gloves for the time being. I'll be replacing all the writing paper with black-lined mourning stationery, too.'

I took the gloves. 'I thought we couldn't write any letters.'

'We can't,' he sighed. 'But those are the instructions, regardless. Furthermore, I have given it some thought and decided that you shall replace Temperance and attend to Miss Decima for the time being. It's imperative that we keep her under control while the Inspector is here, and sadly Temperance doesn't have the strength for it.' He sat down opposite me. 'I trust you understand.'

I couldn't believe it. I wasn't in trouble. What's more, I'd just been handed a reason to spend all day with Miss Decima. *Fortuitous* didn't even cover it. 'Of course, Mr Stokes. I'll go to see to her now.'

I made to stand but he stopped me with a single hand. 'Not quite yet, Stephen. There's . . . another matter I wish to speak to you about.'

My guts twisted. His voice had changed. I sat back down, feeling the room getting smaller and smaller. Mr Stokes folded his hands in front of him, fixing me with a look.

'I've worked for the Welt family for almost forty years, Stephen. Did you know that?'

I shook my head. I had no idea where this was going.

'My father was their Head Butler before me,' he said. 'I started as a page-boy at the age of ten and worked my way up to the top. I've attributed my success to three types of loyalty: loyalty to my master, loyalty to my staff and loyalty to God.'

He nodded to the wall behind him. There was a little crucifix hanging above his chair that hadn't been there before.

'I haven't had much opportunity to practise my faith these last twenty years,' he explained. 'The Viscount had rather strong feelings about religion. He banned staff prayers, refused to recognize holidays. As Head Butler, I had no choice but to follow his orders. But at heart, Stephen, I am a God-fearing man. I always have been. I believe in His judgement. I gather that you are a God-fearing man yourself?'

I nodded. 'Yes, sir. Very much so.'

Mr Stokes smiled. 'It's one of the reasons that I agreed to hire you, Stephen. You can always trust a man who believes in heaven and hell. Do you believe in hell, Stephen? That when we die, there is a place tailor-made for those who have sinned?'

I was baffled but nodded anyway. 'Of course, sir.'

'Splendid.' He reached into the desk drawer and brought out a leather Bible. 'In that case, I would like you to place your hand on this Bible and swear to God that you did not murder the Viscount.'

I might as well have been bolted to my chair. 'I . . . what?'

'I am not a stupid man, Stephen,' said Mr Stokes amiably. 'I know that Lettice did not write that letter. I gave you a chance because I do not believe that a man who has repented for his sins should be made to suffer for the rest of his life. And I believed, Stephen, that you were deserving of a second chance. For my own sake, I need to know that I did not make a dreadful mistake. I need to know right now, upon your soul, that you did not murder the Viscount. That you had nothing to do with his death.'

He really meant it. I put my hand on the Bible and held the other to my heart. 'I didn't kill him, sir.'

'The Lord is watching you. He sees into the hearts of men. He knows if you are lying.'

'I swear it, sir. By the Almighty God and all his angels. I didn't kill him.'

Mr Stokes watched me for a long, long time. Then, finally, he nodded.

'Good.' He took back the Bible. 'I believe you. For that reason, I will *not* be mentioning anything to the Inspector about the unusual nature of your hiring.'

I near fell out my chair. 'You won't?'

He shook his head. 'I told you, Stephen – I am loyal to my master, my God and my staff. I have seen the wrong man unduly punished many times, simply due to his circumstances, and I will not sit back and watch it happen to you.' He returned the Bible back to the desk drawer. 'I will burn your letter of recommendation and tell the Inspector that I applied for you via a regular agency at the Viscount's request. Do *not* make me regret that, Stephen.'

I could have told him the whole truth, then and there – how Miss Decima had hired me, how we'd been out all night to look at the comet, how she could vouch for me until morning. But I didn't want to risk fumbling the good fortune that had just fallen into my lap.

Mr Stokes let out a long, weary sigh. 'Now, if you don't mind, I have rather an enormous amount to organize. The Inspector will be here this afternoon, and I have a number of staff adjustments to make. Merryn isn't good for anything at the moment so I'll have to place Temperance with Cook until we can find someone more suitable. You may return to Miss Decima.'

I could have cried for joy. Mr Stokes was on my side. I had hours to work out my alibi with Miss Decima. 'Thank you, si—'

There was a knock at the door. Before Mr Stokes could reply, it swung open and there was Mrs Pearce, her eyes wide with panic.

'What is it?' asked Mr Stokes.

She swallowed. 'It's . . . the Inspector, Mr Stokes. From Scotland Yard. He's just arrived.'

20

Friday, 20 May, 7.11 a.m.

By the time the family arrived downstairs, it was gone seven. They appeared in the drawing room in various states of undress, absolutely fuming. I stood waiting to one side with Lowen and Temperance, my stomach in knots. I still had no alibi; I still had no defence. It was too late for me to work anything out with Miss Decima. What was I going to say when the Inspector started asking questions?

Mr Stokes appeared at the door and cleared his throat. 'Everyone, may I present Inspector Jarvis of Scotland Yard?'

I took in the man who was about to ruin my life. Inspector Jarvis certainly looked the part. He was wearing a three-piece suit with silver chains crossed between the pockets, and held a clay pipe in one hand. It took me a moment to realize that he hadn't actually lit it.

'Welcome to Tithe Hall, Inspector,' said Edwin, in the least welcoming voice he could manage. 'How good of you to arrive eight hours before anyone was expecting you.'

Jarvis nodded magnanimously, not seeming to realize that Edwin hadn't meant it. 'The pleasure's all mine, sir! The Viscount was a close personal friend, as you know. I leapt on the milk train the moment I heard the news. It's an honour to be here to solve his fascinating murder; indeed, one that seems beyond the understanding of man. A lord of the manor, slain with his own beloved crossbow!'

I frowned. Jarvis didn't really seem that bothered about his friend's having been murdered. If anything, he seemed glad of the work.

Edwin glowered. 'We were hoping you might keep the more scandalous elements under wraps, Inspector. Just do it by the book – that sort of thing.'

Jarvis waved him quiet. 'You have nothing to fear, my good man! I'll have the killer in chains before the weekend is out. I believe that the slaying at Tithe Hall will be my greatest achievement yet.'

'Please stop calling it a slaying,' Edwin repeated.

I was doing everything I could not to tremble where I stood. Jarvis didn't sound like he was interested in the truth – just a quick arrest. I could feel my last minutes of freedom slip between my fingers.

Mr Stokes stepped in. 'Allow me to take your bags, Inspector. Perhaps you will have some tea?'

He nodded at Temperance, who instantly reached for the teapot beside her. Jarvis shot out a hand. 'No! I shall pour my own tea, thank you.'

Temperance blinked. 'It's no bother, sir, I can –'

'I will not be waited on while I am here!' said Jarvis, grabbing the teapot. 'I am my own man, and I am *more* than capable of pouring my own tea, thank you very –'

Within seconds, Temperance was on her hands and knees mopping up the puddle of tea while another maid swept up the pieces of broken china. Their scowls said it all. No one liked a rude master, but what servants *really* hated was a man like Jarvis, who didn't understand the order of things and wouldn't let staff do their jobs.

But I wasn't looking at them. I was watching Temperance mop the steaming tea from the floor and trying to understand what in my head was screaming to be noticed.

'Perhaps we should just get on with it, Inspector?' suggested Edwin wearily.

Jarvis nodded. 'Right you are, sir! I shall begin by observing the crime scene, along with the people who were present when the body was found. I imagine these rural police forces have made a number of elementary errors.'

Mr Stokes led him to the first floor, and we followed in silence – Lowen, Temperance and me. This was it – any moment now, the whole sorry thing would come out. What would I do when the Inspector's eyes turned to me? I tried to think what Miss Decima would say.

You're fucked.

That sounded about right.

We came to the study. The Inspector stepped inside and stood in the centre of the room, gazing around. 'This is all exactly as it was yesterday morning?'

'The police officers took the boards off the windows and the fireplace,' said Mr Stokes. 'Apart from that, nothing's been touched.'

Mr Stokes was right – the room was exactly the same. Yet there it was again – the sense that something was wrong. That something was missing. Something *had* been changed.

'And you were the ones present, when the body was found?' asked Jarvis, turning to us.

Mr Stokes nodded. 'Lowen and Stephen broke the door down. Temperance came to find me once it was discovered that the Viscount was not responding.'

Jarvis pulled a notebook from his pocket, flicking through the pages. 'You were the last person to see the Viscount alive on Wednesday evening, Mr Stokes, correct?'

Mr Stokes nodded gravely. 'I believe so, sir.'

'Perhaps you can describe, in your own words, your last interactions with him.'

Mr Stokes cleared his throat. 'It was shortly before five o'clock. I came here to inform the Viscount that the East Wing was fully sealed, and asked permission to shut myself in my own room. He was boarding up the fireplace when I found him.'

Jarvis frowned. 'I thought the manservants had boarded the fireplaces.'

'The Viscount insisted on doing his own, sir. He had been studying several books on carpentry.'

Jarvis flicked through the notepad. 'You spoke to him the following morning as well, correct?'

Mr Stokes paused, and then nodded. 'I did, sir.'

Jarvis glanced up. 'Is there something else you'd like to add, Mr Stokes?'

He shifted uncomfortably. 'I would rather explain in private, sir.'

'*I* would rather you explained now,' said Jarvis.

Mr Stokes gave a sigh of resignation. He folded his arms behind his back.

'The Viscount telephoned me at half past seven on Thursday morning. He repeated his instructions from the day before, telling me to wake the staff and prepare him breakfast. But just before he ended the telephone call, he . . .' Mr Stokes paused again. 'He said that he could hear a sound outside his study door. A scratching, like someone trying to get inside. Then he hung up.'

I felt a chill up my spine. No one spoke for a moment. Jarvis stroked his chin thoughtfully, then clicked his fingers at me and Lowen. 'These two were first to enter the study, correct?'

'Stephen got here first,' said Lowen quickly. 'He never

showed up to work so I went looking for him. I found him standing outside the study door, on his own.'

I nearly choked. Lowen was trying to dob me in, make me look guilty.

'Is that true?' said Jarvis, glancing at me.

I nodded. 'I – I got lost trying to find the guest bedrooms, sir. I was walking past the study door when I noticed that the bolt was missing from the crossbow.'

'This one?' said Jarvis, marching to the suit of armour. 'This held the bolt that killed the Viscount?'

Mr Stokes nodded. 'The very same, sir.'

Jarvis inspected the crossbow from different angles. 'And there were no telltale signs that it had been fired? No bloody fingerprints on the trigger, perhaps?'

Mr Stokes blinked. 'None that I recall, sir.'

Jarvis stepped on to the plinth and crouched behind the suit of armour, gazing down the length of the crossbow. He clicked his fingers at me. 'You! Where was the Viscount's body, when you found it?'

I gulped. 'In his chair, sir.'

Jarvis waved a hand towards it. 'If you wouldn't mind.'

I felt a lurch in my chest. 'You . . . want me to sit in the chair?'

'Exactly as you found it, yes.'

I walked over to the desk, stomach churning, and sat down while everyone watched in silence. I put my arms on the armrests, and then let my head loll to one side. *This is exactly what he would have seen*, I thought, *just before he died.*

Jarvis gazed down the length of the crossbow at me.

'Interesting. Very interesting,' he muttered. He stepped off the plinth and strode back into the study. 'Very well! I will need private access to this study for the rest of today, while I make my preliminary inspections. I'll visit the police station at Tregarrick this evening and collect their notes and sketches. First thing tomorrow, I shall begin my questioning of the household. From the Cook right down to the lowliest, least-educated maid.'

Lowen was right – he didn't so much as mention the guests. But, even so, I felt a wave of relief. I had another day to prepare – enough time to find Miss Decima and work out my alibi.

'Very good, sir,' said Mr Stokes, with a bow. 'Let us know if there is anything else you require.'

'Nothing, my good man, nothing at all!' said Jarvis. 'Except . . .'

He turned around at lightning speed, his eyes fixed on me.

'*You* can stay here, Mr Pike. I have further questions I would like to ask you.'

21

Friday, 20 May, 7.44 a.m.

I felt my soul leave my body. This was it – the beginning of the end. There was nothing I could do to stop it now. I watched in stony dread as the others left the study, leaving me and the Inspector alone. Lowen shot me a knowing smirk as he went, the insufferable – beg pardon – *twerp*.

Jarvis strolled casually around the room, which suddenly felt enormous with just the two of us. 'Quite an unusual set of circumstances, eh, Stephen? A man brutally murdered in a locked room. No signs that anyone left or entered.'

I swallowed. 'It's certainly a conundrum, sir.'

'Is it!' Jarvis barked, whipping around to face me again. 'Perhaps it is, to those unfamiliar with the devilish world of crime. But, to a man like me, the answer is deceptively simple!'

He spun the Viscount's chair around and sat down dramatically. There was an audible *crunch*, followed by the faint gasp of a man who's just accidentally sat on himself.

'Are you all right, sir?' I asked.

'Quite fine, thank you,' he replied delicately, standing up again and walking towards me with a slight limp. 'Tell me, Stephen, where were you on the night of the murder?'

There it was. I tried to keep my breath steady, clenched my fists to stop them shaking. 'I – I was taking care of Miss Decima, sir.'

He glanced at his notebook, frowning. 'Miss Decima?'

'The Viscount's aunt, sir. She lives in the old Nursery.'

Jarvis frowned. 'So you were not in the East Wing on the night of the murder?'

My throat was like ash. 'No, sir.'

He was staring at me now. 'Quite unusual, is it not, for a footman to attend a lady?'

I swallowed. 'I was asked to step in at the last minute, sir.'

'How long have you been employed at Tithe Hall, Stephen?'

I closed my eyes. 'Since . . . Wednesday, sir.'

Jarvis froze.

'*Wednesday*,' he repeated, his voice soft and low. 'You began your employment the day before your master dies. Does that not strike you as unusual, Stephen?'

The room was starting to spin. 'It's perplexing, sir.'

'*Is it?*' Jarvis cried, striding towards me. 'Perhaps there's nothing perplexing about it at all!' He leant in close. 'I've met your type before, Mr Pike: a man who'll stop at nothing to get what he wants. A man prepared to use a weak, defenceless old lady as an alibi. She must have been easy prey for you!'

He threw me with that. 'Huh?'

Jarvis shook his head hatefully. 'Don't play innocent with me, Stephen! How did you break her spirit? Foul language? Violence? Perhaps it was even more sickening than that – perhaps you seduced her, until her resolve finally caved in! You wore her down with ravishment upon ravishment, until she succumbed to your every whim!'

I wanted to defend myself, but I was too busy choking on my own spit.

'Admit it!' Jarvis barked, jabbing me in the chest. 'You wore down poor, defenceless Miss Decima – almost certainly with ravishments – until she agreed to provide you with an alibi!

Then you sneaked through Tithe Hall under cover of darkness and murdered Lord Stockingham-Welt!'

It was like a bell was ringing in my ears, drowning out everything else. 'No, sir! I've done nothing wrong! Ask her yourself, ask Miss Decima. She'll vouch for me!'

'Ha! I'm sure she will!' Jarvis sneered. 'You've done more than enough damage to the poor old lady, Stephen.' He picked up the telephone on the desk. 'Come! You shall accompany me to the police station at Tregarrick for further questioning!'

And that was it. The end had come. I was going to jail. Not even Mr Stokes could save me now. I had to accept my fate and –

'Ahem.'

There, framed by the doorway in her bath chair, was Miss Decima.

'I believe, Inspector, that Stephen was asking for me.'

I could have wept. Miss Decima – my hope, my salvation – was here. She'd even dressed for the occasion, in a big purple gown and pearls. Her chair was being pushed by a young maid who was shaking like a leaf.

Jarvis frowned. 'Are you Miss Decima?'

'The very same,' she replied haughtily. 'I apologize for my lateness, Inspector, I came as fast as I could.' She glanced at the maid. 'Go away.'

The maid fled so fast the air whistled.

'Now! Indulge me, Inspector. I believe you were about to take Stephen away for questioning. On what grounds?'

Jarvis hadn't been expecting that. He put down the receiver of the telephone. 'Standard police procedure, Miss Decima. I have questions regarding his whereabouts on the night of the murder.'

'Well! Ask away,' said Miss Decima, all cheerful. 'Stephen was with me all night.'

Jarvis glanced between us, shifting on his feet. 'With respect, Miss Decima, I have a number of rather *sensitive* theories which –'

'Yes, I heard your rather sensitive theories from the end of the corridor,' said Miss Decima. 'As did the rest of the household. What a lovely loud voice you have. Tell me, Inspector, do I strike you as a lady who is easily ravished?'

Jarvis didn't know how to answer that question. I don't think anyone would.

'I'm . . . simply trying to clear up some peculiarities, Miss Decima. It strikes me as strange that Stephen – a young, *male* servant – was attending to a lady of your standing on the night in question.'

Miss Decima gave him a look that could have melted bricks.

'Inspector, this may have escaped your notice, but I am unable to walk without assistance. I had just learnt from my nephew that the world was about to end. I was trapped on the ground floor of the house, with the sea levels threatening to rise by several hundred feet. Of *course* I had a manservant! I hardly think a housemaid would be capable of helping me to safety, do you?'

Jarvis was stumped. 'Be that as it may, Miss Decima, there isn't even any evidence that Stephen was actually *with* you . . .'

'On the contrary.' She reached into her bath chair and held up her notebook. 'Stephen stayed up with me all night, taking recordings of the comet for me. I'm afraid to admit that we broke my nephew's rules and used an old back window which the grounds staff had neglected to board up, in order to observe the comet's movements.' She handed him the notebook. 'Stephen's recordings correspond to its exact locations, at the exact times they occurred, and are made in his own handwriting. They cannot be faked. I suggest that you contact the Royal Observatory and ask them to confirm his readings; you will find them to be scientifically accurate to within a mere handful of miles.'

I could have kissed her. Checking those readings would take Jarvis the best part of a day, at least. Miss Decima had turned the conversation on its head. Jarvis was speechless but only for a moment.

'My word,' he said, with an edge of menace to his voice. 'I was wrong about you, Miss Decima. You are no frail, defenceless old lady.'

'I find it sharpens one's mind to stay interested in things,' she replied coolly.

Jarvis folded his arms. '*Sharp*'s certainly one word for it. I always said that this crime was beyond the bounds of man's understanding. Perhaps I was more correct than I realized. Perhaps this crime is so warped, so sinister, that *no man* would be capable of committing it! Perhaps, this is the sort of unnatural murder that only a *woman* could conceive!'

Miss Decima lifted one eyebrow. 'Fascinating. Do carry on.'

Jarvis stroked his chin. 'Yes, it's all falling into place now. A woman who applies herself to a task almost invariably overdoes it; this murder *reeks* of feminine overcomplication. But an uneducated maid? No, it stretches credibility. This crime would need to be committed by a woman of standing. A woman of influence. A kind of "social hermaphrodite", if you will, elevated to an indulged position by circumstance, and desperate to wreak her revenge on the stronger sex! A woman with access to a young male servant, whom she could force to do her bidding.' He fixed her with a glare. 'Am I getting close, Miss Decima?'

I was terrified. But Miss Decima wasn't. She was giving Jarvis the biggest, widest smile you've ever seen.

'What remarkable theories. You certainly have a lot of them. I'm sure you have eyewitnesses, too?'

Jarvis frowned. 'I beg your pardon?'

She folded her hands in her lap. '*Eyewitnesses*, Inspector. I believe it's the 1903 Wanstead Ruling that says suspects cannot be taken for questioning without substantive evidence, and then only if vouched for by an eyewitness. I don't believe that there's a scrap of evidence for the crime you're suggesting – nor, indeed, a single eyewitness – which would make it illegal for you to take either Stephen or myself in for questioning. Is that not right? Do correct me if I'm wrong, Inspector, I would so hate to be wrong.'

Jarvis stared at her in dumb disbelief.

'The onus is on you to provide evidence to back up one of your claims,' said Miss Decima. 'Until then, we shan't impose on you for a minute more.' She rapped her stick on the ground. 'On we go, Stephen!'

I was so stunned that it took me a moment to realize that she was talking to me. I grabbed her chair and squeaked her out of the room while Jarvis stood fixed to the spot, opening and closing his mouth with nothing to say. We made it halfway down the corridor before I heard him bellow with rage and kick the desk.

'Well!' said Miss Decima. 'I've been called plenty of things in my time, but a *social hermaphrodite* – that's a new one.'

I shook my head. 'How did you do that, Miss Decima?'

She shrugged. 'It's nothing. You have to stand your ground with men like Jarvis. He's not used to having people disagree with him, least of all women. There's no such thing as the 1903 Wanstead Ruling, but he's not going to realize that for some time. Those comet readings won't provide you with much of an alibi either, truth be told, but they should buy us a day or two until he works it out.'

'No. I mean . . . how did you know I was in the study?'

Miss Decima frowned at me. 'How do you think? I saw the Inspector's car pull up outside and knew that I'd have to find you as soon as possible, so I screamed that the house was on fire until someone came to find me. Stop here, please.'

We came to a stop at a set of doors to a lift. Miss Decima reached over with her walking stick and jabbed at a button on the wall beside them. The lift doors opened.

'Marvellous thing,' she muttered. 'I could do with something like this in the Nursery, you know.'

I wheeled her into the lift. 'Thank you, Miss Decima.'

'For what?'

'For coming to get me. If you hadn't, I'd be on my way to the police station now.'

Miss Decima snorted. 'Ha! I didn't do it for *you*, Stephen. I wanted to get a measure of Inspector Jarvis. He's going to help us solve this case more quickly than anyone else.'

I frowned. 'He is?'

'Of course!' she said, pushing the button for the ground floor. 'Didn't you hear him? He just accused the two people who, we know for a fact, did not commit the murder. Which means that whatever Inspector Jarvis thinks, we can safely assume the opposite to be true. The man's a fucking idiot.'

22

Friday, 20 May, 8.23 a.m.

The lift shunted to a stop by the entrance hall. I made to push Miss Decima back to the Nursery, but, before I could, she ground her stick into the floor.

'No, Stephen. Turn left here, please.'

'That's the breakfast room, Miss Decima.' I never could get over that at Airforth – a whole room, just for breakfast.

'I'm aware of that,' said Miss Decima. 'Take me inside, please. It's for our investigation.'

'But your family are in there.'

'Stephen, you don't have to describe everything that is happening; we are not a Greek chorus.'

I turned left and wheeled her into the breakfast room, where the family were helping themselves to kedgeree from a set of brass burners on the sideboard.

I might as well have walked in carrying a lit bomb. Lettice was trying to feed Gilbert when she caught sight of Miss Decima; she made the same sound a mouse makes when it's stepped on and jumped out of her seat. Jolyon choked on his kedgeree. Edwin took one look at her and emptied a cup of coffee on to his shoes.

'She – she's out of her room,' said Edwin. 'What's going on? Why the hell is she out of her room?'

Lettice had turned as pale as a ghost. 'This can't be happening.'

'It's her, all right,' said Jolyon in dread. 'Look, she's even got the same stick. What was it called again?'

'Brat's Bane,' said Edwin weakly.

On cue, Mr Stokes strode into the room. The maid who'd pushed Miss Decima must have run downstairs to tell him what was happening; I could hear the rest of the staff clambering through up the entrance hall behind him, peering through the doors. Mr Stokes saw me, glanced at the family and gave Miss Decima a deep bow. 'Miss Decima. How nice to see you out and about again.'

She nodded. 'Thank you, Stokes. I felt compelled to finally leave my rooms, having heard the tragic news about my poor nephew. I must say, I'm rather enjoying the experience.' She grinned at the trembling Welts. 'So you can all expect to see a lot more of me from now on.' She rapped her stick on the ground. 'Stephen! Back to my rooms, please! We've delighted my family long enough.'

We left the breakfast room in absolute stony silence, the squeaky wheel of the bath chair echoing behind us like the shriek of a gleeful banshee. The staff scattered the moment we came into the entrance hall. I had to admit, the power felt good.

'Well!' said Miss Decima, when we were out of earshot. 'What did you make of that reception, Stephen?'

I considered the politest way to say it. 'They seemed a little surprised to see you.'

'*Surprised* is one word for it,' she muttered. 'It was like Conrad's corpse had just strolled in, asking for a Scotch. All rather suspicious, if you ask me.' She rubbed her hands. 'We shall have to keep shaking that jar of hornets and see what happens.'

I frowned. 'You're not really meant to shake jars of

hornets, Miss Decima. Perhaps we should be keeping our heads down. We're trying to find a murderer.'

'Nonsense,' she said. 'Keep your head down and you won't see anything. Besides, half the fun is in the fighting.'

I wheeled her into the Nursery and back to her bedroom, where she flopped into her chair with a groan of relief. Her dinner from last night was still on her desk, completely untouched. 'You haven't eaten.'

'Of course I haven't!' she snapped. 'I had to figure out your alibi, and then I was up for the rest of the night working on my comet essay.' She shoved over the plate. 'Help yourself. You look like you need it.'

I frowned. It wasn't *right*, a lady her age not eating. But frankly I was so hungry I could've eaten the plate. I shovelled it down gratefully while Miss Decima clapped her hands.

'Now! We must stop wasting time and begin our investigation proper. From now on, Inspector Jarvis is going to be searching for any evidence he can get against you. We must stay one step ahead of him at all times.'

I miserably gulped down the food. 'How?'

'We shall begin with the obvious,' said Miss Decima. 'What has happened since we last spoke? I need to know every detail, please.'

I started with the biggest bombshell. 'Mr Stokes isn't going to tell Jarvis anything about me and Borstal.'

'Why?'

'He made me swear on the Bible that I didn't kill the Viscount.'

'Ha! I should have thought of that. Anything else?'

'He said something funny while we were upstairs, Miss Decima. He said that the Viscount told him he could hear scratching outside the study door yesterday morning. Like something was trying to get inside.'

She frowned. 'Interesting. Did *you* hear anything when you walked past the door on Thursday morning?'

I shook my head. 'Nothing. But something's up with that room, Miss Decima. I sensed it the moment I broke down the door. Something in there had changed since when I first went in on Wednesday morning.'

She tutted. 'Of course it had. Conrad had closed up the fireplace –'

'Not just that. There was something else, too. I'm certain of it. And when I went back in yesterday afternoon –'

'You went back into the study?'

I nodded. 'To see if I could work out what had changed. But I didn't have time because Professor Muller came in and I had to run. I guess he must have been . . .'

I trailed off. Miss Decima had her head in her hands.

'Let me get this right,' she said. 'You found one of our suspects sneaking back to the crime scene yesterday . . . and you didn't think to tell me!'

I blinked. 'I didn't know he was a suspect.'

'Of course he's a fucking suspect, Stephen! *Everyone* is a suspect!'

She swept the desk clean, leaving only a star chart, which she flipped over so she could use the underside as a blank sheet. She weighed it down with a book at each corner, using her false teeth for the final corner.

'Thanks to Edwin's lockdown, the murderer has no choice but to remain here until all suspicion has passed,' she said. 'The guests arrived on Wednesday morning, the entire household was locked in their rooms by five o'clock, and the causeway was completely impassable until Thursday morning. The Viscount was killed sometime between making that telephone call to Stokes and your breaking down the door – no one has left World's End since. Which means that we can say, with absolutely certainty, that the murder was committed by someone who is still inside the house.'

She started writing down a list of names. She began with us, then the guests, moving quickly on to the servants. I was impressed – she knew the names of every single member of staff. She had lovely handwriting, too.

'Our job,' she said, 'is to whittle down this list, suspect by suspect, until only a single name remains. We shall do so *scientifically* – applying theories one at a time with methodical rigour, until we can prove beyond doubt that one of them is correct.' She glared at me. 'Which means, Stephen, that from now on you must tell me *everything*. Everything you see, everything you hear, everything you notice. No detail is too small. Do you understand?'

I nodded sheepishly. 'Yes, Miss Decima.'

'Good.' She moved to the top of the list. 'Let us begin by removing the two people whom we know, for a fact, did not commit the crime.'

She started crossing our names off the list. I opened my mouth to say something, then quickly shut it. Miss Decima's pen froze over the paper. 'Something on your mind?'

'No, Miss Decima.'

'Stephen, this unusual arrangement will work only if we are honest with one another. Right now, I know that you are lying. Your ears are putting the Lighthouse of Alexandria to shame.'

Flipping beacons. 'It's just that ... if we're being scientific and all, Miss Decima, I don't know *for certain* that you didn't do it. You could have done *anything* while I was asleep.'

Miss Decima nodded. 'A fair point. You did not see me, so you cannot prove that I was here.' She put down her pen. 'Are you familiar with the great Edmund Halley?'

I nodded. 'He discovered the comet. That's why they named it after him.'

'He didn't *discover* it, Stephen. It had been recorded by astronomers for centuries, and orbiting our solar system for millennia. But Halley was the first person to realize that multiple observations of supposedly different comets were, in fact, one and the same comet. So certain was he of his hypothesis that he correctly predicted the date that the comet would next reappear, fifteen years after his death, and so it did. He was a brilliant man. If he hadn't been alive at the same time as Newton, he would have been the greatest mind of his generation.'

She pressed her hands together.

'Halley did not need to *see* the comet to know that he was correct: his logic was irrefutable. And so must ours be. We cannot discredit something because we do not see it – we have to *prove* that it was not so. Let me put it to you this way: in order for me to murder Conrad, I would have had to unseal the Nursery by myself, find a way upstairs to his study, kill him without leaving a shred of evidence, come back here afterwards and reseal the doors from the inside, all without waking you. Do you think I would be capable of doing that?'

I shook my head. 'No, Miss Decima.'

'Well, there we have it. As *thrilled* as I would have been to murder Conrad, it would have been impossible for me to do so.' She crossed our names off the list. 'Next, we shall remove those who had no opportunity to commit the murder. When you left the East Wing on Wednesday night, the rest of the household was in their rooms, correct?'

'Correct, Miss Decima. Everyone except the Viscount, Lowen and Mr Stokes.'

'When did you last see them?'

I thought about it. 'Lowen was on the second floor,

and Mr Stokes led me here. He left to make the Viscount some tea.'

'Hmm. Interesting,' said Miss Decima, underlining his name twice.

I balked. 'Wait, it *can't* have been Mr Stokes. Now the Viscount's gone, he could lose his job.'

'Everyone is a suspect, Stephen,' she repeated gravely. 'We're not concerning ourselves with *motive*. We are simply looking at who had the *opportunity* to commit the murder. And Mr Stokes had more opportunity than anyone. As Head Butler, he has access to every part of this house. He was the last person to speak to the Viscount, and the last to see him alive.'

I looked at his name on the list. I hated to admit it, but she was right.

'Now, let us consider who was in their rooms,' said Miss Decima. 'Whose rooms did you seal yourself?'

I thought it over. 'All the guests: Edwin, Jolyon, Lettice, Gilbert, the Professor. I unsealed them all the next morning, too.'

She frowned, crossing their names off the list. 'Hmm. And the maids? Cook? Mrs Pearce?'

'They were already sealed in their rooms when I went upstairs.'

'Did you see them get shut inside?'

I shook my head. 'Except for Temperance – I saw her seal herself in. I let her out the next morning, too.'

'I'm amazed she had the strength to lift her own wadding,' Miss Decima muttered, crossing her name off the list. 'Very well. Temperance is accounted for; the rest are unconfirmed. Their rooms might well have been sealed, but, for all we know, they weren't inside them.'

I frowned. 'But they were sealed from the inside. They *had* to be in their rooms.'

'And you checked all of them, did you?'

I opened and closed my mouth. I hadn't, truth be told. What's more, I had no idea who was supposed to be in which room.

'Which brings us to the conundrum of Professor Muller,' said Miss Decima, circling his name. 'He was sealed inside his room before the murder and unsealed afterwards. Logically, there's no way he could have done it. And yet, for some reason, he returned to the study the next day. There must be a reason for it, and I suspect that someone else in this house will know what the reason is.' She shifted in her chair. 'I've had some further thoughts about that, in fact.'

There was something in her voice that I didn't like. 'What kind of thoughts?'

She steepled her fingers.

'I have been considering our position, Stephen. There are only so many places in this house that the two of us are able to be at once. In order to understand how this murder was achieved, we need a *confidante*: someone who knows what was going on in this house *before* you arrived. Someone who can fill us in on all the missing details. A maid, for example.'

I brightened up. 'We can ask Temperance, Miss Decima. She's the only one we know we can trust.'

'My thoughts exactly,' said Miss Decima. 'Your job is to get information out of Temperance.'

'How?'

'Use your imagination.'

I frowned. 'I can't *threaten* her, Miss Decima. That's not right.'

'I wasn't suggesting you threaten her.'

I gazed at her blankly. She let out a big, long sigh. 'Good lord! I've got my work cut out for me here. I am suggesting, Stephen, that you seduce her. Beguile her with your charms. What is it you youngsters call it nowadays? "Spooning".'

I felt the blood drain from my face. I actually felt it. 'I don't think you know what that word means, Miss Decima.'

'I know exactly what it means. I spent a weekend on the Côte d'Azur with the Duke of Edinburgh – believe you me, I know what spooning is. And, right now, spooning with a maid may be our only option. With a number of seduced maids in our arsenal – say, four to six – we would be able to create a clearer picture of what was happening in Tithe Hall in the weeks leading up to the murder, and if you had any energy left we could . . . Stephen, are you all right? You're looking rather pale.'

'I just need some air, Miss Decima.'

I fumbled with the window latch and leant outside, gasping for breath. Miss Decima shook her head pitiably. 'Bless my soul! All this fuss over a little spooning?'

'Please stop talking about spooning.'

'Honestly, I thought spooning would have come as some light relief, after two years in Borstal.'

I turned around. 'That's the problem. I'm not *used* to . . . entertaining the company of ladies. I've never . . . I don't know how . . . by which I mean . . . I wouldn't even know what to say!'

Miss Decima sighed. 'Have you considered *not talking*, Stephen?'

I stared at her in disbelief.

'There's nothing to it!' she insisted. 'Maids are already bored out of their wits, trust me. New lad in the house, touch of a cockney accent, "How's it going, darlin'" . . . you're more or less halfway there.'

I closed my eyes. I had to stand my ground. I knew that once Miss Decima got an idea in her head, there was no stopping her. 'No. I won't do it.'

She frowned. 'Stephen –'

'*No*,' I repeated. 'I appreciate all you've done for me, Miss Decima, I really do, but there has to be another way.'

'*Stephen –*'

'No! You can threaten me all you want, but I won't be made to do it. No, no, no!'

23

Friday, 20 May, 10.48 a.m.

Temperance closed the door to the larder and jumped. I was standing behind her, leaning on the doorframe.

'How's it goin', darlin'?' I said.

Temperance looked baffled. 'Do you need something?'

She had me there. I hadn't thought this far ahead. I searched for something else to talk about. 'Ham, eh?'

Temperance glanced down at the ham in her hands. 'Cook asked for a ham.'

'And what's a nice girl like you doing with a ham like that, eh?'

She blinked at me. 'Cook asked for a ham,' she repeated.

This wasn't working. She was looking at me like I had a brain injury. Time to think on my feet. I tried to remember what the lads in Borstal used to say when they talked about spooning.

'Work, work, work!' I said, swaggering towards her. 'Always work with you, isn't it? How about we forget work for a little while, and –'

I lay on the floor and blinked away the spots. I'd been hit plenty of times in my life, but I'd never been hit in the face with a salted ham. It did the job just fine, let me tell you.

Meanwhile Temperance was standing over me, screaming. 'That's right! And you can stay down, too, you filthy pervert!' She stepped over me. 'I'm telling Mrs Pearce.'

I panicked. 'No! You can't – I'll get sacked!'

'Good!' Temperance shouted over her shoulder.

I scrambled to my feet. If Temperance told Mrs Pearce, I'd be in even more trouble than I already was. I tried to stand up but was so dizzy that I fell to my knees, which was fine, because right now begging was the only option I had left.

'Temperance, *please* don't tell Mrs Pearce. It was a stupid thing to do. I'm sorry.'

That stopped her at least. She stood at the door, her eyes getting redder and redder.

'I thought you were nice, you know,' she said quietly. 'I thought we might be friends. But you're just another *horrid* man who . . . who . . .'

Her voice crumpled and she started crying, burying her face into her apron. I could have died of shame. 'Please don't cry,' I begged.

'*Oh, don't you start!*' she snapped. 'Why shouldn't I cry? I can cry if I want to. I hate it here. *I hate it!*'

I stared at her, clueless, while she sobbed. The seduction plan was a washout. Temperance was in tears, my head throbbed, and my face smelt like ham. What was I supposed to do now?

Stop dawdling like a twat and help her, Stephen.

I took Temperance by the arm and gently led her to the table. She let me pull out a chair for her and then wept over the table.

'You don't know what it's like,' she whimpered softly. '*Everyone* here hates me. Even the lowest maids treat me like dirt. They all think I'm some Londoner trying to steal a job off their cousin. I'm supposed to be a ladies' maid, but they make me do all the downstairs jobs I shouldn't be doing, and, when I complain, they say I'm stuck up!' She wiped her face.

'I've no one to talk to. I've no one even to *write* to. All my people back home are gone.'

I felt a pang of guilt. I knew how it felt to be alone in a house full of people. Ever since I arrived here, I'd felt like a button in the wrong buttonhole. 'I'm sorry, Temperance. I feel terrible, I really do. I never should have agreed to do it in the first place.'

Her head snapped up. 'What do you mean, agreed to it?'

I froze. 'Er . . .'

'Someone put you up to it? Like a *bet*?'

'Ah . . .'

I was beginning to understand why Miss Decima had told me not to talk. All of Temperance's rage was back in an instance. 'Who was it – Lowen?! Or was it . . .' She suddenly gasped. 'Oh, my God, it's *Miss Decima*, isn't it? I don't believe it! She's trying to get rid of me, just like she gets rid of *all* her ladies' maids! And you just went along with it, did you? *Stephen, you must dispose of her at once! Yes, Miss Decima, right away, Miss Decima!*'

I hated to say it, but it was a spot-on impression. I'd have clapped, if I hadn't been busy going blind with panic. 'No, that's not –'

It was no use – Temperance was back on her feet, marching towards the door. This time, I knew that she wouldn't come back. My future hung by a single thread.

'It's because of the murder!' I cried out.

She stopped at the door. I kept going – I had no other choice.

'Miss Decima thinks she can solve it,' I explained. 'She wanted me to get close to you – find out what you know, that sort of thing.'

Temperance snorted. 'By touching me up in the larder?'

I blushed bright red. 'That was . . . more or less the plan, yeah.'

Temperance still didn't look convinced. I leant forwards, pleading.

'I'm in trouble, Temperance. Deep trouble. Everyone in the house thinks I did it. If I don't work out who the real murderer is fast, I'm doomed.'

Temperance was confused. 'Why?'

I swallowed. I'd already told her far more than I should have done. But I was a servant: if I had to make my bed, I was going make it with hospital corners. 'Because I've been in prison.'

She stared at me in shock. 'You're not serious.'

I nodded. 'Right now, the only people who know about it are Mr Stokes and Miss Decima. But if Jarvis finds out . . . well, he'll arrest me. So my one hope is that Miss Decima find the murderer first. I know you're angry with me. You probably don't even believe me. But I need your help. Please.'

I looked up, and my heart clenched. Temperance had alarm written all over her face. She leant back in her chair, arms folded tightly on her chest.

'I'm sorry. I just . . . I need a minute.' She shook her head. 'I don't believe it. Miss Decima, a real-life *lady detective!*'

I paused. Temperance wasn't horrified – she was thrilled. Her eyes were sparkling like Christmas trees.

'I can see it, you know,' she said. 'She's got a right mouth on her, but a mind like a whip, too. Like Miss Cayley, or Lady Molly of Scotland Yard.'

I suddenly remembered all the books I'd seen stacked up beside her bed. 'You like detective stories?'

'Love them,' she said breathlessly. 'I get them from the library in Tregarrick on my days off. Miss G, Mrs Paschal . . . anything with lady detectives. I can work out the endings before I finish them sometimes.'

She looked different all of a sudden – sitting a little taller in her chair, almost. *Revivified.* I glanced over my shoulder and then leant in closer. 'Miss Decima thinks it might be Professor Muller. You've seen how he looks now – guilty as anything.'

She snorted. 'Trying to leave the house as soon as he could, too. Funny that, isn't it? Booking a ticket to Hamburg for Monday when you think the world's going to end on Wednesday.'

I hadn't even thought about that. Temperance was smart. 'Have you noticed anything else odd? Something that could explain what's going on here?'

She looked at me for a moment. Then the corners of her mouth went up, like stage curtains being lifted.

'As a matter of fact, Stephen,' she said, 'I have.'

24

Friday, 20 May, 11.52 a.m.

Ten minutes later, I was knocking on Miss Decima's bedroom door.

'Back so soon!' she exclaimed, turning in her chair. 'Either the spooning went better than I planned, or even worse than I...'

She trailed off. I wasn't alone – Temperance was standing beside me. Miss Decima's eyes flicked between us. 'What's going on?'

I cleared my throat. 'Temperance and I have been talking, Miss Decima...'

Miss Decima froze. '*Talking*,' she repeated.

I gulped. This didn't feel like a good start. 'I – I told her what we're doing. And it turns out she knows something that could help us.'

I waited for Miss Decima to ask what it was, but she didn't say anything. She just stared. Her gaze went through me like a hot knife through cream cheese.

'Temperance,' she said calmly, 'please excuse us for a moment. I would like to have a private word with Stephen.'

My stomach dropped. I gave Temperance the kind of look that drowning sailors give to lifeboats, but she was already scurrying out of the door. I turned to Miss Decima, braced for the rhino horn that would come at my head, but to my surprise she was leaning back in her chair and fanning herself.

'Are you all right, Miss Decima?' I asked, concerned.

'I'm feeling a little out of sorts, Stephen,' she said breathlessly. 'Would you mind feeling my head, please?'

I frowned. 'Your head?'

'Yes, my head. Feel it and see if you notice whether anything has changed.'

I was baffled but did what she asked. 'I can't feel anything, Miss Decima.'

'Are you sure? The shape hasn't changed? It hasn't become tall and conical perhaps, with a big letter *D* painted on the front?'

The penny dropped. I stopped checking her head. 'No, Miss Decima.'

'Oh! What a relief! Then it is safe to say that there is no dunce's cap on my head? I assumed I must be wearing one, since you thought it fit to suggest such an unbelievably fucking stupid idea in the first place.'

'There's no need to swear, Miss Decima.'

'I beg to differ: swearing is an absolute fucking imperative at this point. What on earth were you thinking? You have just ruined our entire plan! I have been waited on by that useless little tart for months on end –'

I was starting to bristle. 'She's not useless, Miss Decima. She can help us.'

'Do *not* contradict me, Stephen! She can barely string a fucking sentence together, let alone –'

'You're wrong.'

It just came out. Miss Decima was stunned into silence.

'You're *wrong*, Miss Decima,' I repeated. 'She's smart. You'd know that, if you listened to her.'

'How dare you?' said Miss Decima, her voice deep and low. 'The sheer impertinence. I should have you sent back to fucking Borstal.'

I had to keep going before I lost my nerve. *Half the fun is in the fighting.*

'Solving this mystery might be a game for you, Miss Decima, but it's not for me. If we don't find the murderer quickly, I'm going to jail whether you send me there or not. We need all the help we can get. And, if you won't let Temperance help us . . . well, then, I won't help you.'

I closed my eyes, counting down the seconds before the horn hit me square in the face. But nothing happened. When I opened my eyes, Miss Decima was gazing at me calmly.

'Very well,' she said. 'Bring her back in. Let's see what she has to say for herself.'

I thought it might be another trick at first, but Miss Decima just waited. I opened the door and Temperance shuffled inside, looking petrified. She'd clearly heard every word. The glow that I'd seen downstairs had been totally snuffed out.

'Temperance, you said you'd noticed Lettice doing something unusual,' I said. 'Is that right?'

Temperance nodded. 'She . . . she's hiding something,' she said in barely a whisper. 'I walked into her bedroom yesterday and she closed one of the drawers really quickly and then shouted at me for not knocking. I thought it seemed . . . odd.'

Miss Decima said nothing. The silence was ear-splitting.

'Temperance reads detective stories, too,' I said, trying to sound cheerful. 'I thought she might be good at, you know . . . detecting.'

Miss Decima raised her eyebrows. 'Detective stories! Well, that's certainly put me in my place. I wasn't aware that I was in the presence of a budding young sleuth!' She folded her arms imperiously. 'Go on, then, my dear. How did they do it?'

Temperance blinked. 'Do what?'

'The murder! How did someone kill the Viscount in a

locked and sealed room and then escape without being seen? Please, do tell, we're all ears.'

I clenched my jaw. 'You don't need to be rude, Miss Decima.'

'I'm not being rude, Stephen! You're the one who said an old biddy like me couldn't solve this mystery by herself, or perhaps my ear trumpet didn't pick up the –'

'It's a machine.'

Miss Decima was cut off, mid-rant. We both turned to Temperance. She was standing on the spot, fussing her hands.

'A machine murder,' she repeated. 'Someone set up a machine in the study that would kill the Viscount after he'd locked himself inside. That's why the room was still sealed and empty when we found him.'

Miss Decima snorted. 'Impossible. The crossbow was outside an undamaged door –'

'That's *why* it was done with a crossbow,' said Temperance. 'So everyone would think it came from the suit of armour *outside* the door. But that's just a red herring, to stop people searching *inside* the study for the real murder weapon. A crossbow doesn't need someone to fire it either – just something to pull the trigger when it's loaded. That . . . that could have been what made that scratching sound that the Viscount heard, right before he died.'

Miss Decima shifted in her chair. 'Ludicrous. The police would have spotted such a contraption by now –'

'Not if the murderer removed it before the police came,' said Temperance quickly. 'It was hours before the causeway opened up. And a machine like that would need to be carefully camouflaged anyway, so that the Viscount wouldn't spot it. It could still be in there now.'

I brightened. 'I *said* something in that room had been

changed, didn't I? Maybe someone put a machine in the study after I first went in on Wednesday morning. They could have done it while the house was being sealed up!'

Miss Decima was speechless for a moment. She looked like someone who'd just had their pocket picked.

'The exact conclusion I was about to arrive at!' she announced. 'Indeed, I do believe it was my very next line of enquiry!'

She turned back to her list of suspects, flustered. I shot Temperance a look. We had just achieved the impossible: we'd made Miss Decima feel out of her depth.

'A machine murder opens up our list of suspects *dramatically*,' said Miss Decima. 'If the Viscount was killed by a machine in his study, the crime could have been committed by someone who was locked in their room all night – it gives them ample opportunity.' She removed her teeth. 'We have a theory. Let's put it into practice. Stephen, Temperance, talk me through everything that happened on Thursday morning. From the moment you woke up to the moment you stepped inside the study and saw the Viscount's body.'

I did the best I could. I told her about being woken up by Mr Stokes, going upstairs to get Temperance, looking for Lowen, seeing the missing bolt, finding the bloodstained wadding, breaking down the study door. Temperance explained running into me with the breakfast tray, racing down to the kitchen to find Mr Stokes, bringing him back up just as the door was smashed open.

'Now, tell me *exactly* what you saw when you entered the study.' She pushed a sheet of paper across the desk to me. 'Draw it, Stephen.'

I'd never used a pen before – just pencils. I did the best I could, scratching and splodging ink across the paper.

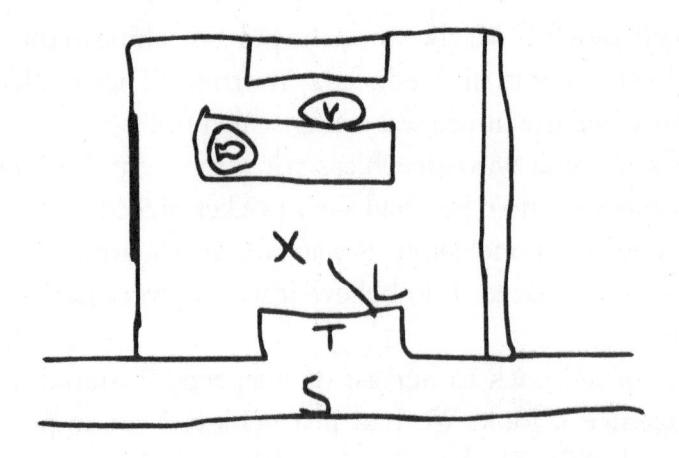

'There,' I said. 'I was the *X*, in the middle of the room. The Viscount was behind the desk, between two oxygen tanks. Lowen was by the light switch, Temperance was at the door. Mr Stokes was in the corridor behind her.' I glanced at Temperance. 'Right?'

She pointed at the drawing. 'The fish were dead – don't forget that.'

I thought about it. 'That could have something to do with the murder machine, too. Maybe *that's* why Professor Muller came back to the study on Thursday, after Edwin announced the lockdown. To get rid of the evidence.'

'And he was in the study on Wednesday afternoon as well, wasn't he?' said Temperance excitedly. 'Taking the Viscount's photograph. He could have set up the machine then!'

Miss Decima nodded thoughtfully. 'And as a man of science – even a terrible one – Herr Muller would have sufficient means to build, or acquire, a murder machine. Very well! Herr Muller has just become our chief suspect.'

She double underlined the Professor's name. I beamed. This was going even better than I'd hoped.

'We have a theory,' said Miss Decima. 'Now, we must prove

it beyond all doubt, with scientific rigour. We shall inspect the crime scene and find evidence of this murder machine. I doubt that Jarvis will leave the study before the end of the day, so we shall have to wait until our next opportunity, then act fast. For now, over here, please, both of you! I have a number of additional jobs for you to complete, and we've already lost enough time as it is.'

I looked at Temperance, beaming from ear to ear. Maybe I was wrong, but I had the feeling we'd just become a team.

'Stephen, for heaven's sake!' Miss Decima snapped. 'Stop being such a clod and make some room for Temperance!'

Temperance giggled. 'He is clumsy, isn't he?'

'I'm amazed he can walk through a door without assistance.'

'He's all elbows.'

'I've met cows with more grace!'

Maybe *team* wasn't the right word for it.

25

Friday, 20 May, 3.42 p.m.

Temperance and I left the Nursery hours later, reeling. Neither of us had expected it to go so well. Neither of us had expected to be given so much to do either.

'Well done,' I said. 'You were brilliant in there – just brilliant.'

Temperance perked up. 'Was I?'

'Of course!' I nodded. 'All that stuff about a machine murder. I think you really impressed her.'

There was that sparkle again. 'I mean – it's obvious, isn't it? The house was complete chaos on Wednesday afternoon. Muller could have set up the machine, using the servants' staircases to move around the house without being spotted.'

'Yes!' I said. 'And after the murder happened, he must have –'

A pair of maids suddenly appeared around the corner. They took one look at us, standing together in an empty corridor flushed with excitement, and scurried off down the hall, bursting into giggles the moment they were out of earshot.

Temperance bit her lip. 'We should be more careful.'

I nodded. 'You're right. No more talking about the murder outside the Nursery.'

'No,' said Temperance quickly. 'I mean . . . about being seen together.'

It took me a while to twig what she meant. Then my ears burned. Romance between servants was forbidden in houses like these. If Mrs Pearce or Mr Stokes thought anything was going on, they'd come down on us like a ton of bricks. 'Yes. Let's avoid each other for the rest of the day, then.'

'Good idea,' she said quickly. 'I'm supposed to have been with Cook all day; she'll *kill* me when I get back. And Miss Decima gave us plenty of other things to do, didn't she?'

'She did,' I said. 'Well, ta-ra.'

Temperance sped off. I headed in the other direction, cursing myself all the way.

'*Ta-ra*,' I muttered. 'You could have said anything you wanted, and you said –'

Just as I was opening the door to the nearest servants' staircase, someone crashed right into me. I gasped with pain and looked straight into the eyes of . . .

Lowen. He was out of breath. He hadn't been expecting to see anyone. He shoved me aside, barging straight past. 'Watch where you're going!'

I watched him race up the stairs two at a time, until I heard a door slam far above me.

I stood in the dark, watching the spot where I'd last seen him. I had no idea where Lowen had been, but I'd seen the look on his face just before he ran into me. He was frightened. He'd been looking over his shoulder like he was running away from something.

Dinner was much the same as the night before. Miss Decima had told me to keep my eyes peeled and my ears open for anything unusual, *anything* that could be useful, but there was nothing. Jolyon drank too much, Gilbert had a tantrum about his soup, Edwin and Lettice shot barbed comments at each other over venison, and Professor Muller didn't show his face. Jarvis had left World's End the moment the causeway opened, heading straight to Tregarrick. I kept one eye on Lowen the whole time, waiting to see if I could work out what he'd been running from, but he didn't so much as look at me.

I was polishing the silver hours later when Mr Stokes called me to his office. He was sat behind his desk, scowling down at a ledger.

'Ah, Stephen,' he said. 'Just the man I was looking for. Do you remember how many bottles of Château Margaux we had at dinner tonight?'

I thought back. 'Two, sir. Three if you include the one the Rear Admiral took upstairs afterwards.'

Mr Stokes tutted. 'Hmm. Something's not adding up here. I shall have to check the cellar when I have a moment.'

I thought back to Lowen, running up the stairs. 'Anything wrong, sir?'

Mr Stokes sighed. 'A number of things around the house have become unaccounted for. Some of the laundry has . . .' He stopped himself. 'On second thought, never mind. I'm sure there's a perfectly reasonable explanation for it all.'

Laundry. I made a note for later. 'Will that be all, sir?'

He paused for a moment, and then closed the ledger. 'No, Stephen. Shut the door, please.'

I sat down, my stomach in knots. This had to be about the maids, seeing me and Temperance. How was I going to find an explanation that covered up what we were *actually* doing? Mr Stokes gazed at me, all calm and collected.

'You caused quite a scene today in the breakfast room,' he said.

I hadn't been expecting that. 'Sorry, sir. Miss Decima insisted on it. There wasn't much I could say to dissuade her.'

Mr Stokes nodded. 'Indeed. I know that refusing her is quite impossible – she is a forceful woman. But I would appreciate it, Stephen, if you did everything you could to keep her contained while the Inspector is here. Is she planning on making any more excursions around the house?'

I winced. 'Not *today*, sir.'

His jaw went tight. There was a long silence before he spoke again. 'Do you remember what my first piece of advice to you was, Stephen? *A servant should be invisible.* And, right now, you are drawing far too much attention to yourself. I saw Mr Edwin's face when you left the breakfast room today: he was furious. He has noticed you, and he is far from happy about it. You seem to forget how much effort I have made to keep you away from scrutiny.' He drummed his fingers on the desk. 'Perhaps it might be best to change your duties, for the time being.'

I panicked. If I got moved from Miss Decima now, solving the mystery would be impossible. 'I think I should stay with her, sir. I'm getting good at looking after her. We get on, truth be told.'

Mr Stokes fixed me with a look.

'Indeed. I have noticed that there is something of the ... growing relationship between the two of you. You must remember that you are not intended to mix. She is of this house, and you are below it. I trust you remember the words of the hymn? *The rich man in his castle, the poor man at his gate: God made them high or lowly, he ordered their estate.*' He paused to let the words settle. 'Miss Decima has very little to lose by angering Edwin: her misdeeds are easily covered. But it is not the same for you. I have seen people of gentry fall into close relations with their servants many times before, without a care for the consequences. You would not be the first servant that Miss Decima has cast off, once you have ceased to be of use to her.'

I remembered what Temperance had said earlier: *She's trying to get rid of me, just like she gets rid of all her ladies' maids.* 'I know, sir. I'll be much more careful from now on. But I think I should stick with her. She'll only kick up more of a fuss if I don't.'

Mr Stokes let out a weary groan. 'I suspect you're right. Frankly, I'm loathe to make any more changes to the household. I've already had to make Temperance stand in as Lettice's ladies' maid; she's running everyone ragged, making them change her mourning outfits five times a day.'

I tried to hide the excitement on my face. Temperance was Lettice's ladies' maid; now she had an even better chance of working out what she'd been hiding in her bedroom. 'Is that all, sir? Only I'm halfway through polishing the silver, and it's getting late.'

Mr Stokes nodded quickly. 'Yes. The silver. Of course. Please return to it, Stephen.' He sighed. 'I confess that I have somewhat allowed things to . . . fall apart in recent days.'

I frowned. 'What do you mean, sir?'

He didn't reply for a while. He just sat there, staring over my shoulder.

'It's my job, Stephen, to keep this house running smoothly. That affords me a certain degree of influence. You saw, for example, how I was able to persuade Lord Stockingham-Welt to hire you. I wonder if I could have said or done anything that would have stopped him from going through with his plans, in the weeks leading up to his death. If I had, perhaps . . . well.'

He trailed off, gazing grimly ahead. I felt for him then. 'You can't blame yourself, sir. It's not your fault someone went and murdered him.'

He glanced up sharply. 'Perhaps not. But, then, someone must be held to account, mustn't they?'

I had no idea what to say. He just sat in his chair, looking like the saddest man in the world. There was another drawing in that book of myths that I read: Damocles, the King, sat beneath a sword that always hung above his head. That was how Mr Stokes looked then, with the crucifix hanging on the wall behind him. 'Anything I can do to help, sir?'

Mr Stokes sighed. 'No. Just finish the silver. If you could check that the lights are all off on the ground floor when you head upstairs, that would be most useful.'

'Yes, sir. Goodnight.'

'Goodnight, Stephen.'

I finished the silver and made my way to the ground floor, turning out the lights in the drawing room. I was thinking about Mr Stokes's name on Miss Decima's list. Professor Muller might be our main suspect, but she was still right about Mr Stokes having the opportunity to kill him. *In the weeks leading up to his death.* No one could have set up a murder machine, I realized, more easily than Mr Stokes. He had the whole run of the house. I couldn't get that out of my head, no matter how hard I tried.

But I was thinking about what he said about Miss Decima, too. He was right: gentry always got second chances but not us. I thought about how easily I'd lost my job at Airforth – how one mistake had got me sacked. That one mistake had put me on a path to the gang and then Borstal, almost to oblivion. It would never be the same for someone like Miss Decima. There might be one roof over Tithe Hall, but there were two very different worlds beneath it.

'You there!'

I froze. Edwin was marching towards me, clicking his fingers. 'Get out. I need to use this room.'

I frowned. It was near eleven o'clock – what on earth did he need the drawing room for? I wasn't going to argue with him, though. I bowed my head and sped out of the room, closing the doors behind me, when Miss Decima's voice suddenly popped into my head.

Keep your head down, Stephen, and you won't see anything.

I paused. Edwin was behaving suspiciously, and I was supposed to be keeping an eye out for anything suspicious. The hall was empty. I leant forwards and placed my ear against the crack of the drawing-room doorway. Sure enough I could hear his voice inside, just over a whisper. 'Streatham 2109, please. Right away.'

The telephone. That's why he needed the room – he was calling someone. I stood frozen on the other side of the door, not even breathing. It took ages before Edwin spoke again.

'Finally. What took you so long?'

Pause.

'Yes, I *know* what time it is, that's why I'm calling your house. I can't wait until Monday to . . .'

Pause.

'You *know* who it is. Don't make me say it over the phone, you cretin, I can't . . .'

Pause. He groaned.

'*Edwin Welt.* There, are you happy? Now stop wasting my time and tell me what the hell's going on!'

This time, the silence was much longer. A whole minute passed while I stood there, listening. When Edwin next spoke, his voice was like something crawling out of a cave.

'Tell me you're joking.'

Pause.

'Last Thursday? That's impossible.'

Pause.

'And you didn't think to tell me!'

Pause.

'No, Wilkins, as a matter of fact it is *highly* important, because the man in question is now dead, and the will reading is being held in a week's time. What do you think I've been paying you for!'

The wires in my brain all switched on at once. I pressed my ear even closer to the crack in the door.

'And I suppose you don't have a clue what changes he made, do you? . . . Well, can you find someone who does? Yes, *now*! And it had better be damn fast, because I'll be phoning you the moment I . . .'

There was another pause. This time, I knew the silence wasn't because Edwin had been interrupted. It was because he'd just thought of something so startling that it had stopped him in his tracks.

'Wilkins, has anyone else spoken to you?'

Pause.

'I'm not a hundred per cent sure I believe that.'

Pause.

'For a start, because you're already accepting bribes from *me*, you idiot. Let me put it to you this way: if I *do* find out that you've gone over my head on this, I'll come to your poxy little office and I'll stuff that will right up your – hello? *Hello? GAH!*'

The phone slammed down and footsteps came striding towards the door. I leapt to the side just before Edwin flung open the door and marched across the entrance hall, leaving me pressed to the wall.

I caught sight of his face as he stormed upstairs. He was pale and his teeth were clenched, his eyes so full of rage and fear that I couldn't tell which one he felt the most.

26

High above, the comet soared further from the Earth, tracing past Epsilon and Zeta, the Tauri stars.

Stephen made his way upstairs and lay in bed, thinking about everything he had just overheard; it was a long time before he finally fell asleep. He was not the only one. There were two worlds under the roof of Tithe Hall, but, that night, servants and guests slept just as uneasily as each other.

The scullery maid who had worked in the house since she was twelve years old tossed and turned, thinking about what she'd heard the ghost whisper through the door.

The daughter of a viscount who had once dined at the same table as the Prince Regent sat alone by the light of a single candle, reading and rereading her own notes, until she fell asleep with her head on her chest.

The man who had served at Tithe Hall since he was a boy sat alone in his room with his head in his hands, thinking about the mistakes he had made.

And, all the while, the murderer stood in the dark and gazed out at the lake.

Saturday, 21 May, 1910

"Have we struck into the [comet's] tail?" and "What will be the upshot of it?" were the questions that came to most minds. So to-day we have all been busy with conjectures about the affair. Meteorologists, who are, generally speaking, wise after the event, say [the reported storms across Europe were] simply due to the atmospheric conditions, and had nothing whatever to do with the comet. But you can't persuade the man who was awakened by the war of the elements that this was the case. And who can dogmatise as to cause and effect in the present instance?

Leeds Mercury

27

Saturday, 21 May 6.00 a.m.

In the dream, Nan was further away than ever before.

It was always the same, the dream. I'd had it all through Borstal and every night since. I was in a river up to my chest. Nan was upstream, floating on her bed with her nightgown and duvet, calling out for me to help her. I was fighting with everything I had, but the water was like a landslide against me and no matter how hard I tried I only ever got further away. Soon I couldn't even hear what Nan was saying any more. Not that it mattered, because she was always saying the same thing.

You can't fight a river.

Then I'd wake up, drenched in sweat.

You can't fight a river. That's what she always said, when nothing went our way. When I got the sack, when we had to move back to Bow, when we got bumped from squalid flat to squalid bedsit because I couldn't get a job, when her cough got worse and she couldn't leave her bed, when I got arrested and dragged away, never to see her ever again. *You can't fight a river.* You can't change what can't be changed, and, if you don't accept that, you'll only go mad or drown.

She was right, in a way. Everything in my life had been fine, until I'd fought back.

The staff bell was ringing. I got dressed as fast as I could and made my way downstairs. I had to find Miss Decima and tell her what I'd overheard last night; I knew she'd want to know straight away. I was going down the stairs so fast that I ran into someone on their way up.

It was Lowen again. This time, he didn't look so surprised to see me. 'Where are you going?'

'Miss Decima,' I said, trying to sidestep him.

He blocked me. 'No, you're not. Go and do the breakfast room.'

I bristled. 'That's your job. I'm supposed to be with Miss Decima.'

'And I'm first footman,' Lowen bit back. 'You answer to me. And I *said*, go and do the breakfast room.'

'Why aren't *you* doing it?'

'That's none of your business, mate.'

We stood, facing each other in the dim stairwell. I thought about how easy it would be to tell him to stuff off. But I couldn't do that, could I? 'Fine.'

I pushed past, feeling his eyes burn into the back of my head. I had no idea why Lowen was making me do breakfast and no idea what he was going to do instead. Maybe he was up to something. Or maybe he was just being a – beg pardon – *pillock*.

It didn't matter. Breakfast wouldn't take long: at dinner and lunch you had to serve the guests in the dining room, but at breakfast they helped themselves. All I had to do was to set up the food burners on the sideboard and then clear up afterwards. I'd soon be free to find Miss Decima.

I helped the maids load the trays and set up the burners, watching as the family arrived one by one. Edwin came first, helping himself to bacon before scowling in a corner. Next came Jolyon, slumping into the room with bloodshot eyes, clearly hungover for the third day in a row. I watched him pile his plate with four huge servings of bacon and hunch over his food. I didn't know what to make of him. Back when I lived in Romney, there was a prize boar which weighed nearly 2,000 pounds and which had to be retired because it was so big it kept breaking the sows' spines. Jolyon looked like that, with trousers.

There was no sign of Lettice or Gilbert – Temperance was probably with them right now. No sign of Professor Muller either. He hadn't left his room for days. I hadn't so much as heard a peep from him since . . .

I froze. Mr Stokes had just strolled in with Inspector Jarvis close behind. I quickly turned away and fussed at one of the trays before he could notice me.

'Ah, *Inspector*,' said Edwin, pronouncing it distastefully, as if it were a disease. 'I trust you had a comfortable night in Tregarrick?'

'Indeed I did, sir! I spent the evening reviewing the crime-scene notes from Chief Constable Penrose.' He waggled a folder stuffed with paper. 'I also spent a rather *illuminating* few hours discoursing with the locals at the tavern. Quite incredible, the memories of these simple country folk.'

Edwin winced. 'We were hoping for a little more discretion, Inspector. There's no need to discuss matters with the locals. I'll ensure all servants are available for questioning today, as you requested –'

'That can wait, sir! I now have a number of new lines of enquiry to follow.' He glanced around the room enigmatically. 'I trust you'll allow me full access to the house today, including the cellars?'

Jolyon choked on his bacon – no one else noticed, but I did. Edwin was too busy grinding his teeth. '*Naturally*. Do ask if you need anything.'

Jarvis strolled out of the room. Edwin glared after him with loathing. '*Discoursing with the locals*. God, this is getting worse by the second. What the *hell* is that idiot saying to people?'

'Oof – keep it down will you, old boy?' Jolyon groaned. 'Not feeling myself this morning. Er . . . you don't think he meant that about going in the cellars, do you?'

I had no idea what Jolyon was so worried about, but I was thinking about the cellars, too. If Jarvis was downstairs, that meant he wouldn't be in the study. And, if the study was empty, that meant Miss Decima, Temperance and I could search it for the murder machine. I sidled out of the room, heading towards the Nursery as fast as I could. If I could get to her before the rest of the family came down for breakfast . . .

'*Nein*, it is impossible!'

I skidded to a halt. It was the Professor – he was coming this way. And he was arguing with someone. I flung myself behind an old cabinet just as they turned the corner ahead.

'I'm afraid that you are going to have to *make* it possible, Herr Muller. Or would you rather I told everyone about what I saw?'

It was Lettice. She was marching coolly ahead while Professor Muller followed close behind, wringing his hands. It was the first time I'd seen him out of his room in days, and he looked dreadful. He was wild-eyed, desperate, unshaven.

'Ach – you saw nothing!' he cried. 'It is all, how do you say, a terrible misunderstanding –'

'I think the photograph says otherwise,' said Lettice curtly. 'I've made my situation *quite clear*. You have until tomorrow, or the deal is off.'

With that, she clipped shut her purse and flounced away towards the breakfast room. Professor Muller grabbed his hair and let out a wail of misery, tearing back down the corridor and out of sight.

I stood pressed to the wall, my heart racing. I couldn't decide which barnstorming piece of news I was going to tell Miss Decima first: that the Viscount had changed his will a week before he died, that Jarvis was checking the cellars, or that Lettice was blackmailing Professor Muller.

'It's like buses,' I said. 'You spend ages waiting for one clue, and then three come along at once!'

It was the first joke I'd managed to make since I'd arrived, and no one was around to hear it. I can't tell you how annoyed I was about that.

28

Saturday, 21 May, 8.27 a.m.

Miss Decima and Temperance were both waiting for me when I finally made it to the Nursery.

'About fucking time,' Miss Decima barked. 'Perhaps you can start by explaining why you're so late. You clearly have something important to tell us. Might as well say it before you wet yourself.'

I hardly knew where to start. I told them all about Edwin's telephone call from the night before, Jarvis checking the cellars, and what I'd just overheard between Lettice and Herr Muller. Temperance's mouth fell open; Miss Decima glowed with pride.

'Well!' said Miss Decima. 'You have outdone yourself. A new line of enquiry, blackmail *and* a recently changed will!'

Time to give it another shot. 'They're like buses, aren't they? You spend *ages* waiting for one clue, and then –'

'You have just provided us with an element that has been sorely missing from our investigation,' said Miss Decima, cutting me off completely. '*A motive.* So far, we've only focused on who had the *opportunity* to kill Conrad. But now we have discovered something just as important: a reason *why* someone might have decided to do it in the first place.'

Temperance nodded. 'He changes his will; a week later, he dies. It *is* pretty convenient, isn't it?'

Miss Decima nodded. 'Indeed. Conrad was unmarried,

childless. Without an heir, it's all up for grabs: the island, the estate, the house, the fortune.'

She found the list of suspects and spread it on the desk before her, weighing down the nearest corner with her false teeth.

'We will apply a new theory: whoever believed that they might benefit from Conrad's will could have committed the murder. Let us begin with the candidates.'

She drew a circle on one side of the paper and labelled it VISCOUNT. Then she traced a spidery line from the circle and wrote another name at the end.

'Suspect number one: Edwin Welt, MP,' she began. 'The grasping little toerag's been after the Welt family fortune for as long as I can remember. There's a motive, right there.'

I frowned. 'I'm not sure, Miss Decima. He didn't sound too happy about the will being changed.'

'He wouldn't be, if he'd been under the impression that he was going to benefit from it,' Miss Decima muttered. 'Did Edwin murder Conrad for the fortune, only to discover that the will had been changed at the final second? As for means – well, I once saw him strangle a swan to death with his bare hands. He's as vicious as they come, and he and Conrad *loathed* each other.'

'I heard him talk about the will on Wednesday,' I said, suddenly remembering. 'He said he only came here because he thought the Viscount was going to discuss it!' I frowned. 'But . . . *murder* him? With a crossbow? It doesn't seem right. Edwin's been bending over backwards to hide the scandal.'

'*And* he had no idea about the Viscount's plans,' Temperance added.

'Making it the perfect alibi,' said Miss Decima. 'Perhaps Edwin knew more about Conrad's plans than he lets on. Perhaps his fear of a family scandal is just an act. Fooling everyone into believing that you're someone you're not comes with certain benefits. Which brings us neatly to . . .'

She drew another line from the circle and wrote a new name at the end.

'Suspect number two: Rear Admiral Jolyon Welt,' she muttered. 'The shame of the British Navy. A drunkard, a gambler, and up to his eyeballs in debt. He's always had his sights set on World's End – sees it as his own personal fishing lodge. And Conrad was a petty man: I can well imagine him passing the estate on to Jolyon in his will, just to spite Edwin. If Jolyon somehow knew about that . . . well, there's his motive. And, as a military man, he certainly had the means to commit murder. Remember, he took part in the official *and* unofficial massacre of Derdepoort.'

Temperance and I glanced at each other. We were both thinking the same thing.

'Er . . . I'm not sure, Miss Decima,' I said.

'I don't think he's been sober since he arrived,' said Temperance.

'Precisely the point I'm trying to make, if you'd let me!' Miss Decima snapped. 'You're a lad from Bow, Stephen. I'm sure you and your "muckers" enjoy a "punt" at the "dogs" on a Friday night?'

'I've been in prison for two years, Miss Decima.'

She frowned. 'Well, you're more or less familiar with the concept.'

'More or less, yeah.'

She shifted irritably. 'Racing greyhounds are graded according to their speed to keep the races competitive. Say you have a greyhound who can finish a 550-yard sprint in 20 seconds. That might place them in the top grade. If you wanted to *fix* a race, all you'd need to do is to make your super-fast dog run slowly for a few races by, say, lightly sedating them. Your sedated dog now finishes the 550 in 23 seconds and gets grouped with other slower dogs. Wait a few days for the sedative to wear off, place your super-fast greyhound against a handful of duds, and boom! You'll win any race you care to name.'

I tried to get my head around this. 'You're . . . you're saying that Jolyon drugs greyhounds?'

Miss Decima rolled her eyes. 'I'm *saying* that he might not be the man we think he is. Perhaps the drunken buffoonery is all an act. *Perhaps*, in truth, Jolyon Welt is far more cunning, and far more dangerous, than we give him credit for. And speaking of cunning . . .'

She added a third name to the list.

'Suspect number three: Lettice Welt. A viper in a tea gown. As a distant female relative, she's unlikely to inherit anything from the will, but she could get something far more valuable. *Influence*. With another relative in charge of the fortune – say, Edwin or Jolyon – she'd have a much better chance of twisting their arm to get whatever she wants. Gilbert's school fees for Eton, for example. There's our motive. As for *means* – let's face it, people around Lettice have an unfortunate habit of dying. Her husband, her daughter, her son-in-law . . .'

I choked. 'Edwin said they died of gastric flu.'

'Ha! A common smokescreen for a far more pressing ailment,' said Miss Decima. '*Arsenic poisoning*. Don't let the twenty-five-inch waist fool you, Stephen: the woman is capable of anything. Which brings us, rather nicely, to this secondary matter of blackmail . . .'

She drew a fourth line from the Viscount, leading to another name.

'Professor Wolff Muller. Our current chief suspect. Conrad might well have left a legacy to that ridiculous Society and appointed Herr Muller as its head in the event of his death. Perhaps *that* was the recent change to the will, which would then place Herr Muller in control of a large sum of money and give him a more than credible motive for murder.' She tapped Lettice's name. 'If Lettice found out about that, she could blackmail Muller to get her hands on some of it. Which would explain the conversation that you just overheard.'

Temperance gasped. 'Wait a minute – she said something about a photograph, didn't she? Maybe it's the photograph Muller took on Wednesday afternoon: the Viscount standing in his study. Maybe there's something in it that proves he committed the murder.'

'The murder machine!' I said.

Temperance nodded. '*That's* what she could be hiding in her bedroom drawer – one of those glass camera plates he was using. Lettice has the telltale photo, and she's blackmailing Professor Muller with it!'

'As a theory, it certainly holds water,' said Miss Decima. 'Motive, means *and* opportunity. Of course, none of it's worth a bent penny without proof.'

I frowned. 'How do we do that?

Miss Decima shoved in her teeth with a flourish and grabbed her walking stick.

'How do you think?! Fetch me my best hat and bath chair, Stephen. We have a crime scene to investigate.'

29

Saturday, 21 May, 10.07 a.m.

The lift shunted to a stop at the first floor. The corridor was still and empty. The rusty wheel of the bath chair shrieked as I pushed Miss Decima towards the study. I could have kicked myself for not having oiled it.

'You're sure Jarvis is in the cellars?' Temperance whispered.

I nodded. 'He said he had a number of new lines of enquiry. I don't know what for, though.'

'Even if there *is* something, I doubt he'll find it,' Miss Decima muttered. 'The man couldn't find his own arse with both hands.'

We turned the corner and there was the suit of armour, tall and silent in the gloom. I hated that thing, got the shudders just from looking at it. Miss Decima put on a pair of glasses and began closely inspecting it. 'The bolt in the Viscount's eye was the one taken from this very crossbow, correct?'

I nodded. 'Amazing, considering how old it is.'

Miss Decima frowned. 'What do you mean?'

'The Viscount said it was from the Battle of Hastings.'

She barked with laughter. 'Pah! Good lord. That man was so full of shit it's a miracle he didn't sprout flowers.'

I blinked. 'He said it was the one that killed Harold Godwinson.'

'About fifty other families claim the same thing,' muttered Miss Decima. 'If all of them were to be believed,

Harold Godwinson would have left the battlefield looking like a hedgehog. It's *fake*, Stephen – another Welt trick to appear noble. Why do you think Lawrence Welt built this house to look like a castle? It's barely fifty years old.' She kept studying the crossbow. 'But it's still important. A tale travels further than a fact: whoever killed Conrad *wanted* people to think about how Harold Godwinson and, more importantly, Lawrence Welt, had died, in order to make it seem like grisly fate and ghostly revenge. It's all a distraction from the truth.' She turned around. 'And the bloodstained wadding? Where was that?'

I pointed to a spot on the floor. Miss Decima leant low to search the floorboards.

'Hmm. Nowhere near the keyhole – not even in the path of the crossbow.' She clapped her hands. 'Very well. In we go.'

Temperance held the shattered door aside, and I pushed Miss Decima into the study. There it was again – the sense that something had changed, that something was missing. Like an itch at the small of my back that I couldn't quite reach.

'Now, think carefully,' said Miss Decima. 'Is this all as it was on Thursday morning?'

I gazed around. 'They've taken the boards off the windows and fireplace. The dead fish are gone. That's it.'

'And the oxygen tanks?'

The two cylinders still stood behind the desk, either side of the Viscount's chair. 'They were here, Miss Decima.'

'Take me closer, please.'

I did as she said. Miss Decima twisted the nozzle on the cylinder, until the sound of hissing gas filled the room. A rubber hose led from the top to a canvas nosebag. She lifted it up and sniffed it. 'Hmm. Looks like it's just oxygen after all.'

I frowned. 'What else would it be?'

'Just making sure it wasn't cyanide gas,' she said, twisting the nozzle back. 'After all, one of our key suspects is a prolific poisoner. But there's no smell of bitter almonds, and I very much doubt the murderer would kill Conrad with something the police could so easily spot. Especially when they'd already fired a crossbow bolt into his brain. Still! Worth a try.'

'You . . . you were going to breathe in cyanide gas?' said Temperance, stunned.

'Science rides on the backbone of risk, my dear,' said Miss Decima. 'If we wish to understand this murder, then we must –'

She froze. Her gaze was fixed to something on the table.

'These papers,' she murmured. 'Have they been moved at all?'

I glanced at the desk. There was a handful of books and documents lying in front of the Viscount's chair. Miss Decima picked up the nearest sheet of paper, and I saw right away what she'd noticed.

A little sketch, doodled in the margin. Some kind of symbol or hieroglyph. 'What is it, Miss Decima?'

She didn't reply. In fact, she'd gone deathly pale. When she put down the sheet of paper, and I saw her hand was trembling slightly.

'It's nothing,' she said. 'Nothing at all. I – I just thought I saw something.'

I glanced at Temperance. She looked as baffled as I did. It was the first time that we'd seen Miss Decima look shaken.

'Well, what are you both waiting for?' Miss Decima snapped, suddenly waking up. 'We're supposed to be looking for a murder machine! Stephen, start with the door and work your way around; Temperance, you can focus on the furniture. We're looking for *any* indication that the room has been tampered with. Chop, chop!'

We did. We checked every wall panel, the windows and the fireplace; we checked the desk and the chair; we checked every book on the shelf. We must have searched that room for an hour at least, top to bottom. But it was no use. There was *nothing* – no sign of tampering, no secret compartments, no damage except the doorframe that I'd broken. When we met up in the centre of the room at the end, our faces said it all.

'They might have moved it already,' said Temperance, scuffing her feet. She was clearly embarrassed that her idea hadn't paid off.

Miss Decima sighed. 'We cannot allow ourselves to ignore the facts. If there is no evidence of a murder machine, the most likely reason is because there *wasn't* one. Which means, sadly, that our first theory cannot work. There must be *another* explanation for how the murderer was able to kill the Viscount and then leave this room without using the study door.'

I shook my head. 'There isn't one. The windows were boarded. The fireplace and chimney, too. Even the keyhole was plugged up.' I pointed to the blob of wax that was still below the door handle. 'See?'

'I didn't mean *that*,' said Miss Decima, 'I have another idea. Over there, please, Stephen.'

She pointed at a small cabinet in the corner. I wheeled her over and she opened up one of the drawers, revealing rows of tiny cards inside.

'A card catalogue!' said Temperance brightly. 'They've got one of these at the library in Tregarrick.'

'Indeed,' said Miss Decima, skimming through the cards. 'It's for Conrad's book collection – not that he read them.

Fossils, continental drift, eugenics . . . he'd skim-read a few chapters, then call himself an expert. Shifted his interests in women just as quickly, from what I hear.' She moved on to the next drawer. 'Most of them aren't even his. They're *mine*. He confiscated them from me, along with all my chemicals and equipment, when one of my experiments went wrong.'

'Experiments?' asked Temperance.

'Bombs, mainly,' she said breezily. 'Any excuse – Conrad always was a thieving little toad. How do you think he wrote all those famous scientific papers? *They* were mine, too. He intercepted the ones that I tried to submit to the Royal Society, rewrote a few lines, then claimed them as his.'

I was astounded. 'Didn't you tell anyone?'

'Of course I did!' said Miss Decima, moving on to the next drawer. 'I wrote to the Society and complained. Never did me any good. Conrad always knew the right people to talk to. It wasn't as if I had any friends of influence, stuck on an island at the far end of the country looking after my father. It was always my word against his. Conrad stole my inheritance, my sister, my career . . . everything. For a long time, all I had was a ladies' maid, and he took *her* away from me, too.'

I gazed at her back as she hunched over, sorting through the cards. 'That's terrible, Miss Decima.'

'It was,' she replied. 'I was absolutely furious about it for about ten years, and then miserable for another five, and then furious again up until a few days ago. Still! We move on.' She pulled out a card. '*Voilà!* Find this for me, please, Stephen.'

I peered at the card. There was a title on it and then a load of tiny numbers. 'Er –'

Temperance sighed and plucked it out of my hands, then looked along the shelf of books until she found the right one. It was huge, so thick and heavy she could barely carry it.

'What ... *is* ... this?' she gasped, heaving it down on the desk.

Miss Decima opened the book with a flourish. '*These* are the original floorplans for Tithe Hall. A map of the entire house, from top to bottom.'

It was beautiful. The paper showed every floor of the house from all four sides, covered in endless notes and measurements. *Meticulous*, they were. 'It looks complicated, Miss Decima.'

'It is,' she grumbled. 'This house is constructed like an ants' nest. The servants' staircases alone offer a murderer a million different routes around this house without being spotted, and, as such, I do believe that they might hold the answer to how this murder was committed.' She peered a little closer. 'For example, I can *now* see that the guest bedrooms are located directly above us. Which offers a rather interesting development, doesn't it?'

I glanced up. She was right: the ceiling would meet the floors of the guest bedrooms. 'What do you think it means, Miss Decima?'

'That is for *me* to find out,' she said primly. 'I am going to check every inch of these plans for secret passageways. If there's a concealed entrance somewhere in this study, I intend to find it. Meanwhile, you two are going to go upstairs.'

'We are?' said Temperance.

'Of course!' said Miss Decima. 'Lunch is about to be served. Which means that you have just over half an hour to sneak into Lettice's bedroom and find the glass plate that she's using to blackmail Herr Muller. Quick now!'

30

Saturday, 21 May, 12.02 p.m.

The second floor was empty, just as Miss Decima had predicted. The family were all downstairs at lunch, and there was no sign of Jarvis. Temperance and I sneaked down the corridor until we came to a closed door. Temperance knocked softly, waited for a moment and then stepped inside.

It was the first time I'd seen Lettice's bedroom properly. Like everything else in Tithe Hall, it looked ten times bigger in daylight. There was a beautiful, big mahogany wardrobe on one side, and a huge four-poster bed with velvet curtains.

Temperance pointed to a dresser covered in gloves and jewellery. 'There – *that's* where I saw her hiding something. She shoved it in the top drawer when I walked in.'

We searched the top drawer, but it was empty. So were all the other drawers. We moved on to the rest of the room: the wardrobes, the curtains, the rugs, everywhere. Temperance even went through Lettice's – pardon me – *particulars* while I searched under the bed. There was nothing. No sign of any glass plate.

'She must still have it with her,' Temperance groaned. 'In her handbag or something. She probably doesn't want to let it out of her sight.'

'We should keep going. We've still got time before they finish lunch.' I pointed to the other door on the opposite wall. 'What's in there?'

Temperance shuddered. 'That's Gilbert's room.'

I frowned. 'What's wrong with it?'

She sighed. 'Let's . . . let's just get it over with.'

When we walked through the door, I understood. Gilbert's bedroom was a chamber of horrors. The floor was covered in old clothes, broken toys, glasses of spilt milk. He'd stamped mud into the carpet and spit ink on the bedding. There were bedsheets everywhere.

'Blimey,' I said. 'No wonder Mr Stokes said laundry's gone missing.'

'It's not *bedding* that's gone missing, it's . . . never mind,' Temperance sighed. 'Honestly, the state of this place. I've never known a messier child.'

I picked my way over the wreckage. 'You'd think Lettice would make him keep it tidier.'

'Why?' she muttered. 'That's what *we're* here for. Honestly, the way that woman treats servants is disgusting. Yesterday, she dropped one of her earrings, and, when I knelt down to get it, you know what she did? She *kicked* me! Not even out of anger – just to show me where it was. Like you would a dog, or something.'

I shook my head. 'They're all as bad as each other. The Viscount, Edwin . . . even Miss Decima, sometimes.'

Temperance shrugged. 'She's different. She's rude to *everyone*. Besides, she's a hundred times better than she normally is.'

I found that hard to believe. 'Really?'

'It's this murder – it's given her something to do,' said Temperance. 'I can't tell you how awful she was before you got here. The maids she's had sacked over the years, simply because she was bored . . . and that's just for starters.'

I suddenly remembered something. 'That thing she saw downstairs – the drawing in the Viscount's papers. What was that about? I thought she was going to faint.'

Temperance shrugged. 'I didn't see. What did it look like?'

'It was a symbol,' I said, struggling to remember. 'I couldn't make it out properly. Like a hieroglyph, or something.'

'Who knows?' said Temperance. 'Maybe it reminded her of something from her past. Have you heard about some of the stuff she got up to when she was younger? *Apparently*, there were these two handsome Bulgarian counts, both twins, and one night she –'

'Wait a minute,' I muttered. 'What's that?'

There was a desk in the corner covered with paper. I picked up a sheet and my blood turned cold.

It was a drawing of Gilbert cutting off someone's head with a broadsword. The sheet underneath showed him burning someone alive in a bonfire. *All* the pictures were of him killing people. One of them showed him shoving Jolyon into a big mincing machine; another showed him using a large circular saw to slice Edwin in half; one showed him closing the door of an Iron Maiden, and through the barred window you could just make out the face of –

I started. 'That's me!'

Temperance looked over my shoulder. 'Oh! That's quite good, you know. He's definitely got the knack.'

I fumed. 'The little creep. What's he killing me for?' I looked closer. 'And what's all that green stuff coming out of the door?'

'I think he ran out of red crayon.'

I suddenly felt a chill, like damp bedding, settling all around me. 'You . . . you don't think *he* did it, do you?'

Temperance grimaced. 'Kill the Viscount? No. He's seven. I mean, he's a nasty piece of work but . . . *murder?*'

I shuddered. I didn't want to think about it. 'We should go. Lunch'll be over soon.'

We left the room and walked miserably back to the

servants' staircase. It didn't need spelling out – the investigation was a shambles. We'd managed to hit two dead ends in the space of an hour. 'So, what now?' I asked.

Temperance sighed. 'I'll have to attend to Lettice for the rest of the day. She always gets changed after lunch. And before dinner. And again after dinner. Maybe I can look for this glass plate then.'

I perked up. 'Good idea. I'll help Miss Decima look for these secret passages and –'

I stopped dead. Temperance froze beside me. 'What? What is it?'

I pointed. There was a butler's mirror hanging on the wall beside us. 'That's new. That wasn't there on Wednesday.'

Temperance frowned. 'You're sure?'

'Positive.' I walked up to it, studying it all over. 'Why would someone put a mirror here?'

'There's mirrors *everywhere*,' Temperance pointed out.

'But the others are in the corners,' I said. 'This one's right in the middle of a wall. It's not like there's anything around here to . . .'

I trailed off. I was right up close to the mirror, and I'd just seen the flicker of a shadow appear in the curve at the edge of the glass.

A figure, peering around the far end of the corridor behind us.

I clamped my hands around Temperance's wrist and marched off. 'Hey!' she said. 'What are you –'

'We're being followed,' I muttered. 'There's someone else up here.'

Temperance tried to turn around, but I jolted her back.

'*Don't!* Just keep walking. We can't let them know we've spotted them.'

We kept the pace steady, our eyes fixed on the butler's

mirror at the end of the corridor. Sure enough, the moment we got close to it, a dark figure leant around the corner behind us.

'Is it Muller?' Temperance whispered.

'I don't know,' I said. 'They're too far away to see.'

'What do we do?'

'We keep walking.'

'And after that?!'

I began to sweat. She was right – as we turned the next corner I saw that the person in the mirror was getting closer, catching up behind us. Sooner or later, they were going to realize that we had nowhere to go. 'After the next corner, we run. We hide in the first room we find.'

'They'll see us!'

'Not if we're fast.'

'But what if –'

'*Now!*' I hissed.

We turned the corner and bolted, scrambling through the first door we came to. I closed the door, and the stench hit me more or less immediately. I clamped a hand over my mouth and nose.

'*Fu*— oh, my goodness,' I gagged. 'Who . . . whose room *is* this?'

'The Rear Admiral's,' Temperance gasped, choking into her apron.

The stink was unbelievable. Tobacco and stale beer and meat sweat, all mixed together. The windows were closed and the curtains drawn, making it even worse. The bed was an abomination. It looked like you'd find a chicken drumstick under the pillow, if you had the stomach to go looking. 'Why hasn't anyone cleaned it?'

'He won't let the maids in,' said Temperance. 'Whenever they try, he –'

I could suddenly hear footsteps, marching down the corridor towards us. There was no time to think: I grabbed Temperance by the wrist again. 'Under here! Quick!'

I dragged her under the bed just as the handle clicked. We lay frozen in place, holding our breaths in the fetid air. There was silence for a moment, then the door cracked open and a bar of light slid across the carpet.

We'd been caught. Whoever was following us knew that we were in here. They moved slowly and silently. They didn't need to be fast. They had us trapped.

A single foot stepped into the room. My stomach dropped. There was only one person who had feet that small, and heels that big.

It was Lowen. He had followed us.

31

Saturday, 21 May, 12.44 p.m.

I lay like a corpse, flattened to the floorboards. I was beginning to realize how stupid we'd been. If we'd run to a servants' staircase, we could have gone anywhere we wanted. Now we were trapped. It was only a matter of time before Lowen looked under the bed and found us.

But Lowen didn't move. He was standing at the door, as if he knew he wasn't supposed to be in here either. Then the smell hit him: he gagged and took a surprised step back. He tried to take another step forward, gagged again, and then quickly closed the door behind him in disgust and marched off. I listened as his footsteps carried on down the corridor, until they faded into silence

Temperance and I lay for a moment, trying to steady our breaths.

'He must have been waiting for us outside Gilbert's room,' I muttered. 'He's trying to get me in trouble. He thinks I'm trying to steal his job.'

'Why?'

'Because I'm taller than him.'

'*Everyone's* taller than him.' She glanced at me. 'You don't think *he's* the murderer, do you?'

I swallowed. 'He *could* be. I never saw him go to his room on Wednesday night. But . . . why?'

A silence settled between us. At least the smell was better under the bed.

'We should go,' I said. 'Jolyon could be back soon.'

'Let's wait a bit longer,' said Temperance. 'Until we know that Lowen's gone.'

I nudged her. 'Anything to get out of work, eh?'

She grinned. 'Can't get the staff nowadays.'

We giggled. The room was utterly disgusting and we were more or less trapped, but I felt content, lying there in the dark with Temperance.

'Stephen?'

'Yes?'

'Why did you go to prison?'

I was glad she couldn't see me blushing. 'It's a long story.'

'We've got time.'

I considered lying to her. But, for some reason, I didn't want to lie to Temperance. I'd started my time at Tithe Hall with a lie, and where had that got me?

'I was in a gang, back in Bow. There was a fight one night. The police thought it had been planned because it was in another gang's pub, so I got charged with attempted murder. In the end they couldn't prove anything, so it got reduced to GBH instead.'

Temperance stared at me. 'Grievous Bodily Harm? *You?*'

'I didn't mean to hurt him. It was self-defence. I'd just been stabbed.'

'Where?!'

'In the billiards room.'

'I mean in your body.'

'Oh, the arm.'

Temperance shuffled. 'I'm surprised.'

'Why?'

'You don't really seem like the gang type.'

'I didn't do it for me. It was for my Nan.'

'Your Nan wanted you to join a gang?'

I shook my head. 'No. She'd never have wanted me to do it. It broke her heart that I did.'

I gazed at the underside of the bed. I thought that if I kept all my attention focused on that, it'd be easier to keep talking.

'She was the one who raised me. I lived with my parents when I was a kid, but it was horrible. Dad had turned to drink and Mum could barely look after herself. All they did was fight. The late nights, the funny turns . . .'

'The hunger,' said Temperance quietly.

I didn't even need to see her face to know she understood. It was right there, in her voice. She had lived it, too.

'Nan took me away from all that,' I said. 'Just turned up one day and brought me back to Romney with her, wouldn't take no for an answer. She was a tough woman – *very* tough – but she was fair. Like Miss Decima, in a way – you couldn't get anything past her. She saw the good in things, too. She saw good in me when no one else did.'

I took another breath in the dark. *Why are we still here?* I thought. *Why aren't we leaving?*

'She got me a job at the big house in the village, called Airforth,' I said. 'I was a page-boy. It was great; I'd work there all week, then I'd come back to Nan's on Sundays and look after her. She was getting old by then and needed the help, but I liked looking after her. I was *good* at it.'

I fussed my hands, pulling at the knuckles.

'Then I got into a fight with one of the servant boys at the house. He said something about where I came from and I thumped him and they threw us both out, there and then. There was no work for me after that. Nan was getting sicker and we had no choice but to move back to Bow. Dad was long gone by then and so we had to stay with Mum in her bedsits. *Pits*, they were. Damp and horrible. It was killing

Nan to stay in them, and I knew it. I'd try to take her out for walks and read to her, but she just kept getting worse.'

I knew I wouldn't be able to stop, once I'd started. I had to keep going.

'I wanted us to get our own place. Somewhere warm, just the two of us, where I could take care of her properly. But if I took a job to pay for it, there'd be no one to look after Nan. I didn't trust leaving Mum with her.' I sighed. 'Then one day, a boy on my street asked if I wanted to earn some extra money. He was in the local gang and said they needed help that night. I couldn't believe my luck. I'd sneak out when Nan and Mum were asleep, earn a little money, and no one needed to know about it. What was the harm?'

I stared at the wooden slats, the lumpen mattress, the dark.

'Course, it didn't turn out that way. We went to smash up another gang's pub, but they were already in there waiting for us. The fight went wrong and the police found me at home and I got arrested. Nan died while I was inside. I never saw her again.' I dug my nails into my palms. 'That's why I'm doing all this now, you see. It *killed* Nan, me going to prison. I have to fight it. I can't let her down like that again.'

'You're too hard on yourself.'

'I'm not hard *enough*.'

I felt Temperance's hand take mine. 'That's not true.'

I turned to face her. It had been a long time, so long, since anyone had held my hand. Since anyone had said something gentle and kind to me. And here we were, close again – that golden light was between us, even here in this dark, horrible place. How easy it would be, how perfectly natural and obvious, to lean a little bit further forwards and close the last few inches of space.

I turned to her, and felt something clink against my leg. 'Oh, God. There's something under here.'

Temperance clutched my arm. 'It's not moving, is it?'

I shook my head. 'No. It's . . .'

I reached out and pulled it towards me. It was an empty bottle of wine. I reached again and found another one, and another, and another.

'Blimey. There's a whole stash here. No wonder he's so hungover all the time.'

I glanced at Temperance, but she didn't look very interested. In fact, I'd say she looked pretty hacked off. She'd folded her arms and was glaring at the underside of the mattress. I understood why. I'd cocked it up completely. Our moment had come and gone, like the comet streaming to the edge of the universe.

'Maybe we should get going,' I said. 'Miss Decima will be wondering where we are.'

'*Yes, Miss Decima,*' Temperance muttered, scrambling from under the bed. '*Right away, Miss Decima.*'

I hated to say it, but she had me perfect. 'You're good at that, you know.'

'Don't try to butter me up.'

'I mean it,' I said, clambering out from under the bed. 'You could be on the stage.'

She snarled at me. '*I said* that's enough, *you snivelling little worm.*'

She had Edwin nailed: the cut-glass voice, the clenched jaw, the spat words. She sounded just like him. Temperance must have seen the look on my face, because she stopped dead, too. 'What? Is someone coming?'

'No,' I said, taking her wrist for a third time. 'I've just had an idea.'

32

Saturday, 21 May, 12.58 p.m.

Miss Decima sat in the centre of the study, staring at us.

'*Impressions,*' she repeated.

I nudged Temperance. 'Go on – just like you showed me.'

Temperance turned bright red and shuffled her feet. 'Er . . . *Stephen, stop dawdling like a twat and bring me my tea this instance!*'

Miss Decima's nostrils flared. I winced.

'I meant Edwin,' I whispered.

'Oh! Umm . . .' She tried again. '*What's wrong with you? Am I the only one in this miserable house with an ounce of intelligence?*'

Her voice wasn't as deep as Edwin's, but it was still good. Good enough for what I had planned, anyway.

'Forgive me if I'm wrong,' said Miss Decima, with a glare, 'but I was under the impression that you two were looking for some fucking evidence.'

I pointed to the telephone on the desk. 'Don't you see? Temperance, call up that clerk Wilkins, pretending to be Edwin. We can find out what was in the will. He's expecting a call from him, isn't he? He won't be able to tell the difference over the telephone.'

Miss Decima's eyes kindled with interest. 'Are you up to it, my dear?'

Temperance was getting smaller before my very eyes. 'Er . . .'

'Splendid,' said Miss Decima, lifting the receiver. 'We'll

do it now. The family are still at lunch ... Hello, operator? Streatham 2319, please. Thank you.'

She thrust the receiver at Temperance. Temperance held it in horror. 'I don't know what to do!' she squeaked.

'I'll tell you what to say,' said Miss Decima, grabbing a sheet of paper. 'If in doubt, be rude. You'll be amazed how often that works.'

'But...'

Temperance froze. I could hear that someone had already picked up at the other end of the line. She stared at us helplessly while Miss Decima scribbled something and held it up. A single word: WILKINS.

'H-hello? I mean ... *Hello?*' said Temperance, dropping into her Edwin voice. 'I'm looking for, er, Mr Wilkins ...'

Miss Decima scribbled something on the paper. RUDER.

Temperance floundered. 'Now, please.'

Miss Decima scribbled some more. RUDER!!

Temperance gritted her teeth. 'Stop blathering on at me and get him, you stupid woman. I'm in a hurry!'

She waited, breath held, then gave us a relieved thumbs-up. I glanced at the door. We were still alone, but I could hear voices coming from below. Lunch was over, and we were running out of time. Miss Decima began frantically writing on another sheet of paper while Temperance paced on her feet, then snapped to attention. I could hear a voice on the other end of the line.

'Wilkins? Is that you?' said Temperance. 'It's Edwin Welt. I ...'

There was a pause. Then she glanced up, eyes widening in terror.

'Er ... never you mind what's wrong with my voice! I have a cold, that's all. Yes, I *know* I said that, but er ... umm ...'

Miss Decima held up the sheet of paper just in time. Temperance stared in disbelief at what she'd written down, but Miss Decima just gave her a curt nod. Temperance took a deep breath, and began.

'No, you listen to *me*, you cretinous little mole. You know how miserable I could make your life if I chose to, so why don't you tell me what was written in that new will before I march over to your scummy little office and have you strung up by your' she frowned – '.genoas?'

Miss Decima moaned with exasperation and furiously scribbled something, jabbing at it with her pen.

'Gonads!' Temperance corrected. 'Sorry, I meant gonads.'

There was a long pause while Wilkins replied. Temperance's eyes flickered between us.

'Very well! I'll get back to you on Monday. But you'd better have something good for me, Wilkins, or I'm going to use all my powers to make sure you spend the rest of your pitiful career in the smallest, dampest office I can find.'

I was blown away – Temperance was brilliant, even better than I'd hoped. I could tell Miss Decima was impressed, too.

'Umm . . . No, that is most certainly *not* all!' Temperance gawped at us, wide-eyed, wheeling her hand. 'I also want to know . . . I also want to know . . .'

Miss Decima held up the paper again, her hands now spattered with ink spots.

'I want to know how this disaster happened in the first place,' said Temperance with relief. 'When did Conrad change the will?'

I winced.

'Er . . . yes, I know you told me that yesterday,' Temperance said, blushing. 'I mean . . . when in the day? And . . . and you can tell me *what* he said, too. I want details, man!'

As saves went, it wasn't terrible. This time, the pause was

much longer. I could hear Wilkins talking at the end of the line, but the words were all muddled and tinny in the telephone. The only clue to what he was saying was there, on Temperance's face. Confused, then shocked, then amazed. She tried mouthing something at us, but I couldn't make it out. Miss Decima handed her the pen, and Temperance scribbled something down as fast as she could before holding it up. VISCOUNT NOT ALONE.

'Well, who was he with?' Temperance snapped.

Pause.

'What did they look like, then? No, I won't wait until . . . Hello? Hello? Gah!' Temperance rattled the receiver. 'He hung up on me!'

Miss Decima was glowing. 'Temperance, my dear, you are a born actress. That was splendid work.'

'Call him back,' I said, heading for the telephone.

But Miss Decima stopped me with an outstretched hand. 'There's no time. Just tell us what he said, Temperance.'

She stared at us, breathless and flushed bright red.

'He . . . he said that when the Viscount went in to change his will, he arrived with someone else. *A man*, he said. No one in the office recognized him; they didn't get a name or anything like that, and Wilkins was out having lunch. He didn't even know it had happened until a few days later, when someone else mentioned it. Then he said he'd been trying to get hold of Edwin *for days* to tell him after it happened, but he couldn't find him anywhere. Because he came here, I guess.'

Miss Decima and I stared at each other in amazement. It felt like we'd just stumbled upon a hidden treasure trove, buried beneath the desert.

'My, my,' said Miss Decima grandly. 'Congratulations, my dear. Thanks to you, I do believe that we may have just –'

She never finished the sentence. There was a sudden shout from the floor below us. Then there was another, and another, and another, until it felt as if the whole house was shouting.

Something had just happened in the dining room.

33

Saturday, 21 May, 1.11 p.m.

By the time we got downstairs, the dining-room door was already blocked by servants. People were shouting hell for leather inside. Temperance found Merryn jostling for space at the back. 'What's going on? What's happening?'

'It's Mr Stokes,' Merryn whispered. 'The Inspector's trying to arrest him!'

Miss Decima swung her stick at the servants' legs like a scythe. 'Let me through! Out of my way!'

I pushed while she battered her way to the front. It was a right scene when we got there: the family staring on, aghast, as Inspector Jarvis tried to drag away an ashen Mr Stokes.

'What the hell's going on?' Edwin was bellowing. 'For the last time, explain yourself!'

Jarvis bowed. 'Mr Welt, I am simply trying to clear up some irregularities . . .'

Mr Stokes was trying to lead him out by the elbow. 'Inspector, I really do feel that we should continue this conversation in private –'

Jarvis whipped his arm away. 'We shall discuss it now, sir! After all, this is no regular crime we are investigating – this is *murder*!' He caught sight of me standing in the doorway and his face lit up. 'Aha! And, right on time, we have our second culprit. You tried to pull the wool over my eyes, didn't you, young man? But you cannot escape the law! *You* shall be accompanying me to the police station, too!'

I gripped the handles of the bath chair in terror, but Miss Decima just sighed wearily. 'Inspector, we have already been through this. Stephen has an alibi for the night in question —'

'But he doesn't have one for *Thursday morning*, does he?' Jarvis bit back.

He reached into his pocket and brought out Miss Decima's notebook.

'Six long hours, I spent, poring over these comet observations. And, lo and behold, they only go up to eleven o'clock! After that, Stephen's whereabouts are entirely unaccounted for. That provides him with more than enough opportunity to commit the crime on Thursday morning!'

I was shaking on my feet. It was all nonsense, but what difference would that make? Every set of eyes in the room was on me now.

'I knew, from the moment I met Stephen Pike, that he was guilty!' said Jarvis, pacing the room. 'All I had to do was to connect the dots: why was he hired the day before his employer was killed? How could he have organized this fiendish murder in such a short space of time? And *why* would he kill the Viscount in the first place? The answer to all three questions lies right . . . here!'

Quick as a flash, he whipped something from his pocket and leapt at Mr Stokes. Everyone gasped, but Jarvis wasn't trying to attack him. He'd put a set of metal compasses over Mr Stokes's head.

'Aha! There is the answer, ladies and gentlemen, as clear as day! The calipers do not lie!' He started measuring Mr Stokes's head from all angles. 'Observe, if you will, the bulge of self-destructiveness above the ear . . . See, too, the cavernous pit of self-esteem beneath the crown . . . And when that is paired with . . . Aha! Yes! The exceptional thickness of the skull at the base, indicating a lack of morality –the truth is laid bare for all to see!'

Jarvis closed the calipers with a triumphant *clip*.

'Phrenology. A fascinating subject. All entirely self-taught. I also practise a number of Eastern mesmeric techniques.'

The room was baffled. Edwin had started to lose patience. 'What the *hell* does that have to do with anything?'

'It has everything to do with it, sir!' He thrust a finger at Mr Stokes. '*Here* is the mastermind behind the murder of Lord Stockingham-Welt. It was your plan all along, wasn't it, sir? Your act of vengeance! Stephen Pike may have committed the deed, but he was merely your hired thug, your paid assassin!'

The room was in uproar. The only person who wasn't shocked was Miss Decima, who was leaning on the arm of her chair and looking bored stiff. Jarvis, meanwhile, was on fire.

'I always knew that there was more to the slaying at Tithe Hall that met the eye!' he said, waggling a finger. 'I knew that in order to solve the Viscount's death, I would have to search for answers that lay deep in the past . . . And last night, in the tavern at Tregarrick, I found them! I spoke with the locals: simple, uneducated folk who nonetheless retain memories as deeply carved as their native Cornish stone. What they told me was enough to chill my blood. And just now, in the cellars, I have found all the evidence I need to confirm it!' He pulled out his pipe and strode around the room. 'Your father was the Head Butler at Tithe Hall before you, was he not?'

Mr Stokes nodded. 'He – he was, sir.'

'And is it *true*, sir, that he was sacked from his position for the crime of peculation – that of stealing wine from his master's cellar?'

Mr Stokes flinched, like he'd taken a punch in the gut.

'That is not *quite* correct, Inspector. My father suffered from an addiction to drink. As a result, his work began to suffer towards the end of his career. It was deemed appropriate that he retire earlier than initially planned, so that –'

'That's not what I heard last night, sir,' said Jarvis darkly. 'The locals told me that your father was caught red-handed with bottles of Lord Stockingham-Welt's wine hidden in his room. Rather than press charges, the Viscount chose to terminate your father's contract and gave his job to *you*. The locals said that in later life he was a sorry sight indeed: propping up the bar at all hours, debilitated by drink and railing against the treacherous son who had stolen his job!'

The servants were horrified. I could tell that none of this was news to them – houses like this ran on gossip – but no one could bear seeing Mr Stokes humiliated like this, in front of his staff and masters.

But there was no stopping Jarvis now. He jabbed the air with his pipe. 'Admit it, sir! On Wednesday, 18 May – on the *exact date* of the twentieth anniversary of your father's dismissal –'

'My father was dismissed in August,' said Mr Stokes, confused.

'Within a six-month period of the twentieth anniversary of your father's dismissal,' corrected Jarvis, 'you set the wheels in motion for the Viscount's grisly death. First, you hired Stephen – a cold-blooded thug, I am certain – to carry out your fiendish plot. Then, you ensured he had an alibi for the night of the murder by placing him in the Nursery, under the pretence of caring for Miss Decima. Then, on Thursday morning, you ordered him to unseal the Viscount's study . . . but of course the Viscount never left his study alive. For the moment that Stephen opened the door, he plucked the Viscount's beloved family crossbow from the suit of armour, aimed it at the Viscount's head and slew him with it!'

I was soaked with sweat. It was all made up, all of it. But what did that matter, when no one in the house trusted me? When Edwin wanted someone arrested? Miss Decima was right: give people a juicy story, and they'll always listen. Jarvis whipped a drawing from his folder and waved it above his head.

'Behold! The truth is right here, in this sketch of the crime scene. The angle of the bolt in the Viscount's eye corresponds *perfectly* to a killer standing at the doorway! A swift, silent death that allowed Stephen to reseal the study door behind him, replace the crossbow in the armour and wait for Lowen to find him in the corridor . . .'

'And the keyhole?' said Miss Decima cheerfully.

Jarvis paused. 'I – sorry, keyhole?'

'The keyhole in the study door,' said Miss Decima. 'The one that was sealed with candlewax. *From the inside.* It's in the crime scene drawing, too.' She pointed at the picture. 'I hardly see how Stephen could have managed to do that. The door was still locked when Stephen and Lowen broke it down – you can see *that*, too, in the damage to the doorframe. A doorframe which was also sealed from the inside.'

Jarvis stared at the sketch and went slowly pale. She folded her hands in her lap.

'Conviction should *follow* facts, Inspector, not precede them. Your theory is impossible. You have yet to provide us with a single piece of evidence that backs up any one of the scurrilous claims you just made.'

There was a muttering of agreement around the room. I could have picked Miss Decima up and kissed her. She had just *exonerated* me in front of the whole house. Jarvis didn't have a leg left to stand on.

'Scurrilous, madam? Then explain this! Explain how I have just found six – six! – bottles of wine missing from the cellar, entirely unaccounted for in Mr Stokes's house records!' He thrust a finger at Mr Stokes. 'That's right! Explain that, sir! The wine has gone missing, just as it did with your father! Is *that* why you killed your master? Did he discover the truth, and threaten to terminate your position, too?'

Mr Stokes's face fell. 'Inspector, if there is any wine missing –'

'There is, sir! I know the exact ones! I have written them down here, somewhere, in my notepad . . .' He started fumbling at his pockets. 'Drat, where is it – I had it just a moment ago . . .'

'Two bottles of Château Margaux 1869,' I said. 'Three bottles of Romanée-Conti 1858. And a bottle of fine Madeira.'

Everyone turned to face me. Jarvis looked at the list in his notebook, and then gazed at me in surprise. 'How did you know –'

'They're under the Rear Admiral's bed,' I said. 'I just found them while I was . . . helping to clean his room.'

There was a moment of stunned silence. Then the whole dining room turned to face Jolyon, who took a while to notice because he was busy pouring himself a large sherry. His face turned even redder than usual.

'Er. Yes. Well. I might have helped myself to a few bottles. Nothing wrong with having a drink or two to see you through the night, is there? No crime in that.' He shuffled in the chair. 'I doubt Conrad would have minded. Especially as we were about to be locked in our rooms all night without warning, and so on.'

The room stank of embarrassment. Jarvis looked like

a slowly deflating football. Probably because everyone – Miss Decima, the staff, the guests – were staring daggers at him.

'Right!' he said, putting his notebook back in his pocket. 'If anyone needs me, I'll be in the study.'

With that, he strode out of the dining room as if nothing had happened.

34

Saturday, 21 May, 2.06 p.m.

'Poor Mr Stokes.'

The three of us were back in the Nursery, helping Miss Decima to her desk. The house had only just returned to normal after Jarvis's accusation.

'Imagine having that brought out in front of the whole house,' muttered Temperance. 'All that stuff about his father.'

Miss Decima sighed. 'Yes, Stokes senior served the Welts for many years. He did try to hide his addiction, but towards the end he could barely carry a tray without his hands shaking. All rather sad.' She clapped her hands. 'So! Let's see what this does for our investigation, shall we?'

She unrolled the list of suspects without a care in the world. I frowned. It was easy to forget how thoughtless Miss Decima could be sometimes. She had been wronged in so many ways – by her family, by Conrad – that it had hardened her, made her selfish. She had no time to think about anyone else.

'Our murder-machine theory is dead,' she said, crossing out the words at the top of the sheet. 'I think, at this point, we can also remove Jolyon from our list of suspects. The man can't even steal a few bottles of wine without being caught. So much for him being a secret Machiavellian genius.'

I made a note to look up *Machiavellian* later. 'We should get rid of Mr Stokes's name, too.'

Miss Decima frowned. 'Why?'

'Because of what just happened. He's innocent.'

Miss Decima shook her head. 'Jarvis's *reasoning* may be wrong, Stephen, but his *answer* could still be correct. Mr Stokes's movements on Wednesday night are still unaccounted for. He had a better opportunity to commit this murder than anyone else.'

I was beginning to lose patience. 'But it doesn't make any sense. He's still covering for me. He could have thrown me under the bus ten times over, and he hasn't. Surely that stands for something!' I looked at Temperance pleadingly. 'Right?'

She bit her lip. 'I don't know. I mean . . . I don't *think* Mr Stokes could have done it either. But it would make sense, wouldn't it? Everything that happened after we were locked away – we have only his word for it.'

Miss Decima nodded. 'Correct. You are setting conviction before facts, Stephen. Until we have indefatigable proof that Mr Stokes did not do it, he must remain a suspect.'

I gazed miserably at his name on the sheet of paper. I hated to admit it, but they were both right.

'Meanwhile, we must work faster than ever to stay ahead of Jarvis,' said Miss Decima. 'After that scene in the dining room, he'll be keen to find a culprit and keep his complexion egg-free. And, let's face it, Stephen, you're still first in the firing line.'

She brought out the enormous book of floorplans from beneath her skirts.

'So! We shall separate our tasks accordingly. I'm going to spend the rest of the day continuing to study these rather complex plans for any sign of a secret passage.'

I gawped. 'How long have those been there, Miss Decima?'

'Long enough,' she wheezed. 'Meanwhile, we still need to find the glass plate that Lettice is using to blackmail Herr Muller.'

'Oh, God – *Lettice*!' Temperance cried, leaping to her feet. 'I'm supposed to be looking after her! She always changes after lunch. At least this means I can stay close to her. I'll be back the moment I find anything!'

With that, she flew out of the room and disappeared. Miss Decima watched her go, nodding with approval.

'Well, I must say that you were right, Stephen. Temperance is not the insipid little milksop that I thought she was. It's the first time I've been served by someone with a backbone since Elsie.'

I tried not to smart at that. 'Elsie?'

'My old ladies' maid,' she sighed. 'Temperance has her spirit. It just goes to show, people can still surprise you.' She paused. 'You two seem to be getting along rather nicely.'

I blushed. 'I don't know what you're talking about, Miss Decima.'

'Ha! Your lips say one thing, Stephen, but your ears say another.'

Flipping beacons. 'What about me, Miss Decima? What shall I do?'

'*You*, Stephen, shall keep your eyes and ears about you. There are several unanswered questions still at play, which can be only solved by careful listening and close watching. Have you noticed anything suspicious about our remaining suspects?'

I glanced at the list. 'Lowen was following us earlier, Miss Decima. I spotted him in one of the butler's mirrors on the second floor.' I shuddered. 'I hate those things.'

'Ah, yes, the butler's mirrors,' said Miss Decima absent-mindedly. 'The French call them *œil de sorcière*, you know – witch's eye. Very well! In that case, I suggest you follow Master Lowen. Find out where he fits into all this.'

I stood up. 'I'll be back later with your dinner, Miss Decima.'

'No Stephen, I do not wish to be disturbed for the rest of the evening.'

No lunch, no dinner. I thought of Nan, coughing in her bed. 'Some fruit, then.'

'No.'

'Perhaps some beef tea.'

'I said no.'

I stole another glance at her feet – they were worse than ever. 'You should eat something, Miss Decima.'

'You should mind your own business, Stephen. Stop fussing me and get out.'

I fumed. 'As you wish.'

I turned from the room, bristling all over. It was bad enough being spoken down to, being ordered about, being insulted, but this was too much. I couldn't watch as she starved herself to death. If she wasn't going to look after herself properly, what could I do?

As a matter of fact, I had a few thoughts about that.

'And Stephen?'

I stopped. 'Yes, Miss Decima?'

She didn't turn around. She kept her eyes on the floor-plans and her head bowed over the desk.

'Watch how you go,' she muttered. 'There's a murderer in this house.'

35

Saturday, 21 May 5.52 p.m.

I spent the rest of the day searching for Lowen, but there was no sign of him. He wasn't in the servants' hall; he wasn't in any of the corridors, and he wasn't on the stairs. I still hadn't found him when I knocked on Mr Stokes's office door.

'Come in,' came the weary reply.

I poked my head inside. Mr Stokes sat hunched over his desk, the Bible open in front of him. It was clear that he'd been reading it for some time.

'Cook asked me to pass on a message, sir,' I said quietly. 'We need to start laying the table for dinner.'

Mr Stokes glanced at the clock in surprise. 'Goodness. Dinner. I quite forgot.' He sighed. 'You'll be serving with me this evening, Stephen. Lowen is no longer allowed upstairs.'

I frowned. 'He's not?'

Mr Stokes shook his head grimly. 'He's been demoted. It transpires he was stealing bottles from the cellar for the Rear Admiral. Lowen will be relegated to downstairs work from now on.'

Suddenly, it all made sense: Jolyon sending Lowen on all those errands on Wednesday, the panic in Lowen's eyes when he ran into me on the staircase. He'd been sneaking bottles up from the cellar. 'But that's not fair, sir. The Rear Admiral made him do it.'

Mr Stokes grimaced. 'You are correct. But, sadly, that is not how these things go.'

I had nothing to say to that. It was just as Mr Stokes had said – servants were always made to suffer for their masters. They stood to lose nothing, while we stood to lose everything.

'I'm sorry for what happened earlier, sir,' I said. 'It was wrong of the Inspector to speak to you like that in front of everyone. He didn't need to bring up that stuff about your father.'

Mr Stokes looked so worn down then, so heavy. Like a statue in a graveyard. 'Thank you, Stephen. It was a rather unfortunate matter. I spent many years trying to live down my father's misdeeds. But I suppose that the past cannot always stay in the past, no matter how much we might wish it would.'

I gazed at him. I was thinking about his name on the list of suspects, and how he was the last person to see the Viscount alive.

'I understand, of course, why the Inspector accused me,' said Mr Stokes. 'Being Head Butler gave me a greater intimacy with Lord Stockingham-Welt than most. I served him for twenty years. I washed his clothes, combed his hair, knew about his most personal matters. But such service has a reverse side. I made a great many sacrifices to serve him, and I was often made to suffer for it.'

I felt like I was seeing a hidden part of him: a closed room, glimpsed through a crack in a doorway. 'What do you mean, sir?'

Mr Stokes took a moment to decide on his wording.

'Lord Stockingham-Welt was not a good master. I do not believe that he was even a worthy one. He treated his staff with the utmost contempt. But I served him anyway. Because that is what I am: a servant to my master, a servant to my staff and a servant to my God.'

I picked up the Bible. The cover was worn smooth: Mr Stokes had clearly reread it many times. 'You must have hated him, sir.'

'Yes, Stephen. At times, I rather think I did.'

I handed him the Bible. But the moment Mr Stokes's fingers touched the leather, I kept hold of it.

'Did you kill him, sir?'

Mr Stokes sat frozen in shock. He lowered his eyes to the Bible, to his fingers on the cover. Then his gaze met mine. I'd never seen sadder eyes in all my life.

'No, Stephen,' he said quietly. 'I hated him. I often wished him dead. But I did not kill him.'

'You'll swear it, sir?'

'On anything you care to name.'

At that moment, I knew a handful of things to be true. I knew that I was innocent; I knew that the killer was still inside the house; and I knew, as sure as I knew anything, that Mr Stokes was telling the truth. 'I'll go to set up the dining room, sir.'

Mr Stokes nodded, shaken. 'Thank you, Stephen. I – I shall join you presently.'

I let myself out of the office, heart thundering. I couldn't believe I'd done it. A week ago, I would never have *dreamt* of speaking to Mr Stokes like that. Maybe being with Miss Decima was rubbing off on me.

I stopped. Lowen was staring at me from the end of the corridor. It was the first time I'd seen him out of livery. He was in work clothes, the kind you wore if you were a coal boy. He had the sullen eyes of a struck dog. His lips twisted when he saw me, and he turned away.

'Lowen,' I called after him. 'I'm sorry. It's wrong, what they've done to you.'

Lowen paused. For a moment, I thought he was going to

shout at me again. But instead he walked up to me and leant in close, so I could just about hear him whisper.

'I know it was you,' he said. 'I *know* you did it. And I'm going to make it my business to prove it.'

And with that, he marched down the corridor and out of sight.

36

Stephen served at dinner for the first time that night, alongside Mr Stokes. There was nothing to overhear: the family ate in strained silence. Herr Muller was nowhere to be seen.

Stephen wasn't really taking any of it in anyway. He was thinking about what Lowen had just said to him and wondering how much time he had left.

He was still thinking about it when the family went to bed; when he polished the silver; when he moved through the house at the end of the night, pulling the curtains closed and locking the doors and windows, turning out the lights and dressing the house in darkness.

He never noticed the murderer, watching him from the shadows.

Sunday, 22 May 1910

COMET CAUSES PANIC.

The inhabitants of a small Hungarian village have prepared for the end of the world, which they have been expecting for some weeks, believing that on the appearance of Halley's comet the whole globe will be smashed to atoms. When a large fire broke out towards midnight in a neighbouring village, the watchman seeing the skies lighted up, walked through the streets blowing his horn to rouse the inhabitants, and shouting "The last day has come!" The people rushed half-clothed from their abodes to die in the open. What followed was curious. The simple people considered first that all the provisions in the village should be consumed. A large fire was lighted in the square in front of the church, and there food and drink of all kinds was brought out of the houses. Everyone joined in a hurried orgy, while hasty prayers were made between bites for the salvation of their souls.

Jarrow Express

37

Sunday, 22 May, 5.52 a.m.

The scream woke me before the bell did.

I almost fell out of bed. The scream was coming from this floor, loud enough to wake the dead. I threw on my clothes and ran out into the corridor.

There, lying crumpled in a heap, was Merryn. Her face was red and wet, and her breath came in sobs. A few maids were already out of their rooms and trying to help.

'*He was here! He was in my room!*'

I caught Temperance's eye down the corridor. Merryn wasn't mucking about. She was beside herself. I tried to help her up, but I was shoved aside by Mrs Pearce, who dragged Merryn to her feet and started slapping ten bells out of her. 'For heaven's sake, girl! What's wrong with you?'

Merryn finally caught a breath between slaps. '*The – the ghost!*'

By now, the corridor was lined with maids looking out of their doors in fear. Merryn kept going. 'It took my cross. My special silver cross. I take it off every night and put it under my pillow. But last night, I . . . I *felt* it go. Like someone reached under and grabbed it. And, when I woke up, it was gone!'

Mrs Pearce looked like she was about to wring her neck. 'You *stupid* girl! *That's* what you've woken up half the house for? You probably dropped it between the floorboards!'

Merryn shook her head wildly! '*No!* The ghost took it! He got the Viscount, and now he's trying to get me, too!'

Mrs Pearce dragged Merryn down the corridor. 'All of you – stop gawping! *No one* is to talk about this! You hear me? No one! And, for God's sake, Stephen, do your flies up.'

I looked down at my open flies. A whole corridor of maids snorted into their hands, slammed their bedroom doors and burst out laughing behind them.

As mornings went, I'd had better.

I got dressed and trudged downstairs. I figured I might as well start early; I'd be sorting the breakfast room every day by myself now Lowen wasn't allowed upstairs. It took me nearly an hour to lay out all the burners, plates and cutlery by myself, and then carry up all the food. I left for Miss Decima in a foul mood. I was supposed to be solving a murder and clearing my name, but I still had my duties to attend to *and* Lowen's as well. I bet Miss G never had to search for clues between sharpening knives.

'You there!'

I stopped. Edwin had just staggered through the breakfast-room door, clutching a large marble bust of his own head. 'Take this,' he barked.

I dutifully held it while Edwin lifted the bust of Conrad from a nearby plinth and replaced it with his own. He stood admiring it just as Lettice flounced into the room with Gilbert.

'Oh!' she said with a grimace. 'That's, er –'

'Good, isn't it?' said Edwin proudly. 'Got it express-made in Tregarrick. And to think they said it'd be impossible to achieve a tasteful likeness from an old newspaper photograph, and at such short notice!'

'You certainly proved a point,' Lettice muttered. 'Er – any reason *why* you're removing Connie's bust, dear Cousin?'

Edwin adjusted the statue by a hair. 'I want everyone to

see that Tithe Hall is changing for the better. Out with the old, in with the new. That's why we're all going to Matins this morning.'

Lettice winced. '*Matins?*'

'I don't want to go to church!' wailed Gilbert.

'Hard cheese,' said Edwin. 'Thanks to that idiot Jarvis, the whole village is going to be talking about us now. As a result, I'm loosening the lockdown so that we can attend the church service in Tregarrick. Conrad and Great-Aunt Decima have spent *years* damaging our name. We're putting on a show of unity to make sure that everyone knows that the Welts are a collection of perfectly respectable –'

At that moment, Jolyon bustled in wearing a deerstalker and rubber galoshes, and carrying a set of fishing rods. Edwin stared at the ceiling and slowly counted to ten under his breath. '*What* are you doing?'

'What does it look like?' Jolyon muttered. 'I'm going fishing.'

'No, you're not,' Edwin snapped. 'You're coming to church with us. And we're inviting the Reverend Wellbeloved back to World's End this evening, too. He'll be our guest of honour at dinner.'

Jolyon groaned. 'Oh, Christ, not *him*.'

'He is awfully dull, Edwin,' Lettice begged.

'Tough,' snapped Edwin. 'The Reverend's going to see that anything he might have heard about *murder* is nothing but gossip. Conrad suffered a tragic accident – that's all.' He pointed at Lettice, Gilbert and Jolyon in turn. 'And *you're* going to be normal; *that's* going to be on its best behaviour; and *you're* going to be sober throughout the whole thing. Understood?'

Jolyon sulked. 'Well, I don't see why I have to come to church. I could stay here and catch us something for dinner.'

His eyes darkened. 'Besides, I don't much like the thought of leaving *Fritz* alone in the house. Turn your back on a Kraut and he'll have us all for bratwurst, mark my words.'

Edwin set his jaw. Clearly, the prospect of Jolyon staying at home and not showing him up in public was an appealing offer. '*Fine*. Go fishing. But you'd better be on your best behaviour tonight, Jolyon. No drinking – understand?'

Jolyon turned bright red. 'A big misunderstanding. A load of fuss over nothing.'

'It'd better be,' Edwin spat. He glanced at his watch. 'Come! Let's all get out of here, before that idiot Inspector turns up.'

My mind was already whirring. The family were out all morning, which would leave us free to go investigating. I had no idea if Miss Decima had found any secret passages yet, no idea what she'd discovered hidden inside Tithe Hall. I was desperate to find out what she knew.

But, first, I had to find Temperance. There was something very important we needed to do.

38

Sunday, 22 May, 9.04 a.m.

We found Miss Decima hunched in her desk chair, surrounded by guttered candles. The floorplans of the house were still open in front of her. She'd clearly been working all night.

'Ah, there you are,' she said weakly. 'I'm afraid I'm going to need something a little stronger than tea this morning . . .'

She turned to face us, and trailed off.

'What is *that*?'

I held up the jar. 'It's a herbal liniment, Miss Decima. For your feet.'

'My feet,' she repeated. 'And the, er, basin and towels?'

'Also for your feet,' said Temperance, putting them on the floor.

I put the kettle on to the stove to warm up. 'This liniment's good,' I explained. 'I used it on my Nan, and it did wonders for the swelling. Cleaned up the skin, too. Two foot rubs a day should make a world of difference to you. Mrs Pearce said we can keep the whole jar.'

Miss Decima stared at us in outrage. '*Neither* of you will be touching my feet! Now stop wasting my time and –'

Temperance and I folded our arms, facing her like a pair of bailiffs.

'*No*, Miss Decima,' I said. 'Your brain's all well and good, but it won't mean anything if you're ill. Keep this up, you're going to hurt yourself. Either you let us sort those feet out, or we're not helping you.'

Miss Decima puffed out her chest. 'You are quite certain of this?'

''Fraid so,' I said.

She glared at us for a heart-stopping moment longer. No one moved. Then – like a lion with a thorn in its paw – she raised her feet. 'Very well. Get on with it, then, Judas. And make me a sodding cup of tea while you're at it.'

I let out the breath I'd been holding. Temperance got to work, pouring warm water into the basin while I took Miss Decima's feet and lowered them into the bowl. She winced at first but relaxed as soon as I started rubbing in the liniment.

'I will begin with some bad news,' she said. 'I have spent *all night* searching these godforsaken floorplans from top to bottom, and there is nothing. No secret passages into the study, no hollow wall spaces, no unexpected voids . . . nothing. That whole theory is a dead end.'

I hadn't been expecting that. 'We're back where we started?'

'Sadly, yes,' she sighed, holding out her hands to the floorplans. 'And yet I feel as if the answer is right here, on the edge of my vision, waiting to appear.'

I glanced at Temperance. This was worse than I thought. 'But if there's no murder machine, no secret entrance, no way anyone got in or out . . . how did the murderer do it?'

Miss Decima didn't reply.

'Miss Decima?'

There was a long pause before she finally spoke.

'Please return you attention to that particular area of my heel just there, Stephen.'

I smiled. 'Yes, Miss Decima.'

'Might I recommend a gentler swirling motion this time?'

'Yes, Miss Decima.'

'And then do the other one, so they match.'

She lay back, basking like a cat in the sun as I rubbed her feet.

'Our only hope,' Miss Decima continued, 'is to return to what we know. You are still certain, Stephen, that something changed in that study between Wednesday morning and Thursday morning. Correct?'

I nodded. 'I'd swear my life on it.'

'Very well,' said Miss Decima. 'Then we shall make that the focus of our investigation. If we can pinpoint what changed in the study, we might be able to work out *how* the murderer did it and, from there, *who* did it. We just need to find some way of comparing the room at those two points in time.'

I sighed. 'I don't see how we can do that.'

'I do,' said Temperance excitedly.

She reached into her apron and brought out a small sheet of glass in a wooden frame, no bigger than a letter.

'It's the photographic plate!' she said, almost in a whisper. 'The one that Muller took of the Viscount's study on Wednesday! See?'

She held it up. The whites and blacks were all reversed, but it was just as she said: the Viscount standing behind his desk, framed in the great wide fireplace.

'You found it!' I said. 'Where was it? Lettice's bag?'

Temperance shook her head. 'No, I still haven't had a chance to go through that. She keeps it with her the whole time. This isn't what she's using to blackmail Muller. I stole *this* from his bedroom.'

I nearly dropped Miss Decima's feet into the basin. 'You did *what*?'

'He turned up at Lettice's bedroom this morning, just after I helped her get dressed,' Temperance explained excitedly. 'Begging her to listen, saying he needed more time. Lettice chucked me out before I could hear any more. But then I realized, if he was with Lettice, his room would be empty, wouldn't it? So I sneaked inside to see what I could find. And there were all these glass plates, stacked up to one side!'

I was fuming, truth be told. 'What were you thinking? For all we know, he's the killer!'

But Miss Decima beamed. 'Outstanding work, my dear. You have once again excelled yourself. Now we have an image of the study exactly as it was on Wednesday afternoon!'

I grumbled. 'It's still not enough. We need another photograph of the study *after* the Viscount died, so that we can compare the two.'

'But we have one, don't we?' said Temperance impatiently. '*The crime-scene sketch!* The one Jarvis was waving about yesterday. It was made just a few hours after you broke down the door . . . It's perfect!'

My heartbeat quickened. She was right. 'Well, I'll be.'

'A splendid plan,' said Miss Decima. 'Though it presents us with a series of further tasks. First, we need to get our hands on Jarvis's crime-scene sketch. Then we need to develop and enlarge this glass-plate negative so that we can compare the two images properly.' She steepled her fingers. 'In the absence of a darkroom or any developing equipment, I propose we make a cyanotype print using natural sunlight and a simple mixture of chemicals. I've made plenty in my time. All the equipment we need will be in Conrad's study, seeing as the thieving little prick took them off me. Though we shall have to be rather quick about doing it, as I suspect it's only a matter of time before Jarvis finds a new way to implicate you, Stephen.'

I grimaced. 'He's not the only one.'

I told them both about what Lowen had said to me last night. Miss Decima raised her eyebrows. 'Good grief. Is there anyone in this house who *doesn't* hate you?'

'It's not my fault,' I muttered.

Miss Decima sighed. 'Then we have even less time to lose. Temperance, find Jarvis and stick close to him. It's imperative you get your hands on this crime-scene sketch. Stephen, finish this foot rub and then head straight to the study. I'll make you a list of chemicals to collect, so that I can prepare the development fluid.'

I blinked. 'You want me to finish the foot rub first?'

'Yes! And jolly well put your back into it this time,' she muttered, leaning back in her chair. 'I am feeling especially tense.'

39

Sunday, 22 May, 10.43 a.m.

I peered down the first-floor corridor.

It was empty: the family were still at church, Jolyon was out on the lake and Jarvis had announced he was going to spend the day searching the grounds. Even so, I still felt like I was being watched as I walked towards the study, my eyes fixed to the butler's mirrors for any sign of Lowen.

I stepped silently through the shattered doorframe. The room was still, dead, like it had been jarred in aspic. I looked around, hoping I might finally spot what had changed since the first time I came in here, but it was no use. I still couldn't work it out. For some reason, all I could think about was the crash of the teapot on the floor.

I didn't have time to worry about it; I needed to find Miss Decima's chemicals, and fast. There was the cabinet she'd told me about, tucked into the corner. I knelt down and opened it; sure enough, it was filled with glass jars and vials, all labelled with the Viscount's careful handwriting. I pulled the list from my pocket and carefully read through the chemicals that Miss Decima had given me.

Potassium ferricyanide, citric acid, ferric chloride, hydrogen . . . Are you listening, Stephen? Jesus, it's like I'm talking to myself sometimes . . . Hydrogen peroxide, ammonia, and get a few beakers, too – decent-sized ones, please, no need to go scrimping . . .

It was a long list, but Temperance had lent me her big tapestry handbag to carry them all. I searched through the bottles one by one, checking the labels before placing them in the bag. The potassium ferricyanide took the longest to find: a jar of sticky orange-red, tucked at the very back with a peeling label.

Soon enough, the bag was fat and clinking. I breathed a sigh of relief. I'd been worried that at least one chemical would be missing, but we had everything we needed. Time to get back. I was grateful to leave the room, to be honest – being here by myself gave me the willies. Especially with all the talk that morning about Merryn and ghosts. I sped out of the room, taking a final glance behind me . . .

I was wrong. Something in the room *had* changed.

The fishbowl was gone.

I walked over to the desk in disbelief. It was there yesterday, when we were with Miss Decima; now it was gone. There was a ring on the wood where the water had stained it. Someone had moved the bowl, but why? And who?

'What are you doing?'

I spun around so fast, I nearly dropped the bag.

'M-Master Gilbert! Why aren't you at church?'

Gilbert was standing in the doorway, wearing his little sailor suit and with a sinister smile on his lips. 'I didn't want to go to stupid church,' he said. 'I cried until Grandma let me stay. She thinks I'm napping!'

He started skipping around the room, pulling faces at me. My heart pounded. I had to get rid of him before he noticed my bag. 'You're not supposed to be here, Master Gilbert. This room is out of bounds.'

'Then why are *you* here?'

I thought fast. 'I'm . . . doing jobs.'

'So am I,' said Gilbert, in a sing-song voice. 'I come down here all the time. I'm allowed to. It's *my* house.'

He started skipping in circles around me, blond ringlets

bobbing. I frowned. 'That's not true, Master Gilbert. It's your cousin Conrad's house. I don't think your grandmother would be happy to know you're in his study.'

'Cousin Conrad's dead,' said Gilbert, still skipping. 'And if you tell Grandma that you saw me here, I'll say you struck me.'

I froze. 'Pardon?'

'Grandma listens to everything I say,' sang Gilbert. 'I'll say you struck me with the back of your hand and laughed!'

I glowered. Striking Gilbert was beginning to sound pretty tempting. 'Very well, Master Gilbert. I'll leave you to it.'

I made to leave, but he stepped in my way. 'Not so fast! *You're* going to take me to the waterfall!'

I frowned. 'What waterfall?'

'The one by the lake!' said Gilbert. 'Lowen said he'd take me, but now I can't find him. So *you're* going to take me instead!'

He made a lunge for my arm, but I stepped back. 'Why do you want to see the waterfall?'

'I'll never tell. Tralalalala.'

The poisonous little – excuse my French – *cherub* started skipping around me again. I had to get him talking. I thought of all the gruesome drawings I'd seen in his room.

'If you tell me why, I'll tell you what Cousin Conrad's dead body looked like.'

It was like offering a dog a hot sausage. Gilbert stopped skipping and blinked up through his ringlets. 'You *will*? Including all the viscera?'

'Yep. Horrible, it was.'

Gilbert was finally ready to cooperate. He took my hand, led me to the window and pointed outside. You could see almost all the grounds from up here. There was the hedge maze, and the lawns, and the forest.

'See that lake?' said Gilbert, pointing between the trees. 'There's a waterfall on one side, a big one that becomes a river that goes all the way to the sea. Lowen said *that's* where Cousin Conrad murdered his father!'

It chilled my blood. 'Why is Lowen telling you things like that?'

'Never you mind why!' snapped Gilbert, twisting my wrist. 'I want to see it, and *you're* going to take me! Otherwise, I'll tell Grandma that you and Lowen *both* struck me! I'll say you took it in turns! With belts!'

I'm sure he'd have carried on describing it for the rest of the day, but I wasn't listening to him. I'd just spotted someone through the window.

It was Professor Muller. He wasn't in his room any more – he was inside the maze. I could just make out his face over the hedges, his wire-frame glasses catching the sun as he glanced over his shoulder.

'*Hey!*' cried Gilbert. 'Where are you going? Come back here!'

I was already out of the room, tearing down the corridor so fast my shoes practically made scorch marks on the carpet. I had no idea what Professor Muller was doing in the maze, or what I was going to do when I caught up with him. But I could already hear Miss Decima's voice in my head, loud and clear.

Get after him, Stephen. And do it fast, before you miss your chance for good.

40

Sunday, 22 May, 11.44 a.m.

I stuffed the tapestry bag behind a piano in the servants' quarters and flew out through the back entrance. The grounds were completely empty – no sign of Muller and no sign of Jarvis, just a small bonfire, smouldering away at the edge of the trees. I frowned. Something about that seemed odd, but I didn't have time to think why. I had a chief suspect to follow.

I marched across the lawns towards the maze. It was the first time I'd seen it up close. The hedges were tall and carefully clipped, stretching just over my head. The entrance split into two paths – one left, one right. A wooden sign hung inside:

DON'T GO THE WRONG WAY

I frowned. What did that mean? What happened if you went the wrong way?

You get lost, came Miss Decima's voice in my head. *That's the whole point of mazes, Stephen.*

I groaned. It was a puzzle. I hated puzzles. I closed my eyes and tried to think like Miss Decima. 'Don't go the wrong way,' I recited. 'Don't go the *wrong way* . . .'

And the opposite of wrong, Stephen?

'Is right,' I said. 'But that could be left or –'

I stopped. *The wrong way* was *not right* – *not right* was *left*. I took the path on the right, feeling extraordinarily pleased with myself.

Bravo came a weary voice in my head.

I made my way through the maze, blood pounding in my ears. I had no idea how to get to the middle, or if I was going to turn a corner and suddenly run into Professor Muller. The hedges were too tall to peer over, too thick to see through. I could hear the faint sound of tinkling water coming from somewhere in the centre. Apart from that, it was silent.

I glanced down. The path was made of gravel; I should have been able to hear Professor Muller's footsteps. He must have been walking along the sides, where it was still tufted with grass. If he was silent, I'd need to be silent, too. I stepped to the edge and crept my way towards the sound of water.

It took me longer than I'd hoped. The further I got into the maze, the more overgrown it became – clearly no one used it any more. The Viscount must have become bored by the maze, like he became bored by everything else. The grounds staff had given up trying to tidy it, so the hedges bagged and spread from the edges. I made my way patiently to the centre, pushing through the twisted yew and checking every corner for the first sign of Professor Muller.

Finally, I turned the last corner and there it was: the centre of the maze. Like all mazes, the middle was a let-down: a small grass square with a few benches and a tinkling fountain. There was no sign of Professor Muller, no sign of anyone. It was empty. I groaned with frustration. There was another exit on the other side of the square. No wonder I hadn't been able to hear the Professor: he must have already been and gone. I'd missed him.

But, then, why had he come here in the first place?

I looked around. It might have been a pretty spot once, but it had been left to decay for a long time. Now it was all neglected turf and quiet stone. *Ethereal*, I thought. There was a little sign dug into the ground, written in the Viscount's handwriting, saying that the hedges were made of a rare poisonous yew. I walked over to a tinkling fountain, which was in the middle of a fishpond. Next to it was another sign, also written by the Viscount, explaining that it contained a number of freshwater carp that he was attempting to crossbreed with koi. I couldn't see any inside, but the water was too green and murky to make out anything.

There was a statue in the middle of the fountain, green with algae. It was a woman with her face in her hands; the water tinkling from between her fingers and running down to her feet made you think of tears.

THE HONOURABLE ISABELLA WELT
Dearly departed wife and mother
1830–1865

Isabella. Miss Decima's sister and Conrad's mother. I quickly did some calculations: the year 1865 suggested she must have died around the time that Conrad was born. I glanced at the statue. It was weird, I thought, covering up her face like that. It made me think of Nan, how she'd looked on the day the police took me away. Hunched in bed, head in her hands, sobbing. Why would you want people to think about stuff like that?

I stopped. Something had just caught my eye at the bottom of the pond: a glimmer, hidden in the murk. I rolled up my sleeve and dipped my hand inside. The water felt thick and warm, the bottom covered in slime. My fingers closed around what I was looking for, and I held it up to the sunlight.

It was a curved shard of glass, as long as a dagger.

Crunch.

My body clenched like a fist. I knew what I'd just heard.

A footstep on the gravel.

There was someone else in the maze.

I stood up, heart pounding. I didn't dare breathe; my senses were wide open now, hunting for the next footstep, trying to work out how close it was.

It came, then another, and again. They were heading to the centre of the maze. They were getting faster.

Perhaps now is the time to run, Stephen.

I threw the glass back into the pond and skidded out of the exit on the opposite side to where I'd come in. I didn't bother trying to hide my footsteps now; I had to get out, before whoever was in this maze caught up with me. I scrambled around corners, searching for a way out, my ears trained for the sound of footsteps behind me.

Suddenly they weren't behind me; they were louder than ever, right on the other side of the hedge beside me. I stopped dead. The person on the other side stopped dead, too. I couldn't see who it was, but I could hear their voice.

A man. Panting, muttering under his breath. Trying to work out where I was. Then the footsteps raced off.

I understood what was happening. It was Professor Muller; he'd seen me sneaking into the maze and now he was chasing me. If I didn't find a way out, I'd never leave here alive. I spun on my heels and raced off, near blind with fright, scrambling around corners and stumbling into dead ends, certain with each turn that I would suddenly find myself face to face with Muller, the shard of gleaming glass clutched in his hand like a knife . . .

Then I turned a corner and saw, with a cry of relief I couldn't help but make, the wooden sign at the entrance. I'd made it; I was free. I flew out of the maze and ran across the lawn, not even daring to check if Professor Muller was behind me. I had to get back inside the house – that was all that mattered now. Once I was inside the servants' quarters, there was no way that Muller would dare to . . .

I flew so fast around the corner of the house that I crashed straight into someone walking in the opposite direction. It blew all the wind out of me. I choked out a breath, turned around . . . and found myself eye to eye with Professor Muller.

He looked worse than ever. His skin was pale; his eyes were red. His face was hungry and haunted. He looked as shocked to see me as I was to see him.

'*Aus'm Weg!*' he spat, shoving me aside and lurching into the ornamental garden.

I watched him go, my head reeling. The realization was dawning on me, slow and dismal. If Professor Muller hadn't been chasing me in the maze . . . who had?

I pricked up my ears. Someone was shouting around the corner behind me.

'*Calm down*, you stupid man.'

'*Nein*, Frau Lettice! There is no calm!'

Lettice was back from church, earlier than I'd expected. I peeked around the corner and saw them both, arguing. Professor Muller was pulling at his hair and raving like a madman.

'I have done all you asked of me, Frau Lettice! I cannot do more – I must leave!'

'Out of the question,' she said icily. 'Half the village already know that there's a German in the house. Edwin needs to make a good impression on the Reverend, and he's said he'll allow Gilbert to dine with us if I convince you to come. So tonight you're going to shave, dress properly, join us for dinner and *behave perfectly*. Or else you know what I'll do.'

I gasped. She was talking about blackmailing the Professor again. I fell to the ground and commando-crawled behind a topiary dog, until I was close enough to hear them properly. When I peered around the side, Lettice was leaning into Muller's trembling face.

'Tell me, Herr Muller – what would Hamburg society say if I were to tell them what I caught the *esteemed Professor* doing? What would happen to your career – your reputation – if I explained that, on the day of the Viscount's murder, I walked into your room and discovered . . .'

I listened as Lettice recounted Professor Muller's sins, one by one. I listened as Herr Muller tried to defend himself, and, bit by bit, I was able to piece together the truth.

Then, very slowly, my mouth fell open.

41

Sunday, 22 May, 2.33 p.m.

I stepped through the side exit with the carpet bag of chemicals and made my way to Miss Decima's bedroom. She and Temperance were both already there.

'Stephen!' Miss Decima snapped. 'Where the hell have you been? We've been waiting for you! You'll be pleased to know that Temperance has outdone herself, yet again.'

Temperance held up a sheet of paper excitedly. 'The crime-scene sketch! I managed to sneak it out of Jarvis's folder while he was wringing out his clothes. He fell in the lake while exploring the grounds.'

'An *exceptional* piece of detective work,' said Miss Decima, her eyes glowing with pride. 'You are coming into your stride, my dear. Ah, and I see you found my chemicals, Stephen. Very good. Anything else to report?'

'I've just found out how Lettice is blackmailing Professor Muller,' I said quietly.

Temperance gasped. 'You *have*?'

I nodded. 'We've been wrong this whole time. Lettice isn't blackmailing Muller for the murder. It's . . . something else.'

There was a long silence. Miss Decima and Temperance glanced at one another.

'*Well?*' said Miss Decima. 'What is it?'

I opened and closed my mouth several times, trying to work out how to explain what I'd just heard. The options were all pretty poor, to be honest. I'd started blushing some time ago. 'If you don't mind, I'd rather not say.'

'Of course I fucking mind!' Miss Decima snapped. 'Whatever Herr Muller said or did, we need to know!'

'She's right, Stephen,' said Temperance. 'You have to tell us.'

I groaned. I decided to give myself three more seconds of not saying anything, as a treat. Then I closed my eyes, took a deep breath and thought of all the most elegant words that I knew.

'On Wednesday afternoon, Herr Muller was tasked with taking photographs of the sealing of the house, so that the Viscount could document the process for posterity.'

'Why are you talking like that?' muttered Temperance.

'Get to the point!' snapped Miss Decima.

'It seems that,' I said, my voice cracking, 'on that very same afternoon, Lettice got lost and accidentally mistook Herr Muller's bedroom door for her own. As a result, she walked in on Herr Muller while he was engaged in a . . . private position. An *extremely* private position. Doing something' – I windmilled my hands – 'untoward.'

Miss Decima grinned. 'I see! Something untoward with one of the maids, perhaps? Has our German guest been doing a little *spooning* of his own?'

'I'll bet it was Maud,' muttered Temperance. 'She'll be as untoward as you like for tuppence and a ham sandwich.'

'No,' I said desperately. 'Herr Muller was . . . alone. *Entirely* alone. By himself. With the glass negative plates he had taken. He had assumed that he would be undisturbed, and so he had made himself comfortable. Really very comfortable, in fact. Is it hot in here, Miss Decima? It's really hot.'

Hot was an understatement. You could have fried an egg on my ears at this point. But Miss Decima and Temperance just kept staring at me, waiting for me to go on.

'The photographs were . . . *of the maids*,' I said miserably. 'Sealing the floors and doors. The *bottoms* of the doors, in particular. Bending over.' I cleared my throat. 'Professor Muller had also taken a number of . . . personal items from the laundry room. Belonging to the maids. Their . . . their particulars, in fact. He'd taken some of Lettice's particulars, too.'

Temperance gasped. 'So *that's* where all the underwear's been going!'

Miss Decima frowned. 'I don't understand. What did he want with their underwear?'

I closed my eyes and silently wished for death. I didn't know how much more of my blood supply could fit inside my head.

'Stephen, this is intolerable. I cannot solve a mystery through suggestion and innuendo. I insist that you tell me at once what he was doing!'

I let out a small, feeble sigh.

'He . . . he had arranged them all into a small pile, Miss Decima. In front of him. Along with the glass negatives. Of the maids. And he was, er . . . he was . . .'

I windmilled my hands some more. The penny finally dropped. Miss Decima's face fell. 'Ah. I see. So when Lettice walked in, he was –'

'He was spooning with himself, Miss Decima,' I said, 'into her particulars.'

The silence that followed could have filled the Royal Albert Hall.

'That's why he's been acting so guiltily,' I mumbled. 'Lettice got hold of one of the glass negatives that he took of the maids. She said that if he doesn't give her the money for Gilbert's Eton fees, she'll contact all her friends in Hamburg and tell them what he was doing.'

Miss Decima made a sound like an over-pumped tyre releasing air. '*My!* This is quite the development. No pun intended.'

Temperance and I stared at her.

'Photography joke – never mind,' she sighed. 'Excellent work, both of you. Thanks to your dutiful service, we can now clear *two* chief suspects from our list.'

She unrolled her chart of suspects and crossed out Lettice's and Professor Muller's names.

'If Herr Muller is so tormented over a little *self-spoonage*, I think we can safely assume he would have confessed to a brutal murder by now. As for Lettice – if she *did* plan this murder, I highly doubt she'd have any need to blackmail the Professor for money as well. Two *utterly revolting* characters, all in all, but neither guilty of murder.'

'Just wait a minute,' said Temperance, turning to me. 'What were you doing outside anyway? I thought you were going to the study!'

I told them what had happened that morning: the missing fishbowl, being caught by Gilbert, following Professor Muller into the maze, finding the shard of glass in the pond, being chased out by a mystery assailant.

'I've no idea why Muller was going into the maze,' I said. 'And I've no idea who was chasing me either. It was a man, I know that much.'

'The plot certainly thickens,' said Miss Decima, holding up the glass negative and crime-scene sketch to the light. 'For now, we have work to do. Somewhere within these two images lies the answer to how the murder was committed. In order to compare them properly, we'll need to develop and enlarge this glass negative to the same size as the sketch. Sadly, we've missed our chance to do it today; we need strong sunlight, and it will take me some time to mix the chemical solution that's needed. You can assist me, Stephen.'

'I won't have long,' I sighed. 'Mr Stokes will need me to help with dinner in a few hours.'

Temperance shook her head. 'He doesn't! He told me earlier that he wants me to serve at dinner instead. You're to stay with Miss Decima tonight and keep her under control. Edwin doesn't want to risk her causing a scene with the Reverend.'

'*The Reverend Wellbeloved?* Here?' Miss Decima winced. 'Still, I suppose these things are sent to try us.'

Temperance leapt to her feet. 'I'd better get back –Lettice will be wanting to change out of her Sunday mourning dress and into her afternoon grief-wear. I'll come back later and see how you're getting on. Good luck!'

With that she raced off, face flushed.

'Well, Stephen, let us begin,' said Miss Decima. 'We have no time to lose. Pass me the bag of chemicals and the telescope.'

'Telescope?'

'Yes, for later. It's by the window.'

I glanced at the sky where it was pointed. There was the head of the comet, faint in the midday sun.

'Still no sign of our missing tail,' she sighed, arranging the jars on her desk. 'Almost four days it's been gone now. Wonders never cease.' She paused for a moment. 'Remind me, what was it you found in the pond today?'

'A shard of glass, Miss Decima.'

'Anything else?'

'No, it was empty.' I paused. 'I saw your sister's statue, though. She died younger than I thought.'

She huffed. 'Yes. Isabella was desperate for babies – it's why she agreed to marry Lawrence Welt in the first place. I told her she was too old for that sort of thing, but she didn't listen to me – Isabella never did. Went ahead with it regardless and died at the first. All rather sad.' She sighed. 'Still, if we wept for every woman who suffered, we'd never stop weeping, would we?'

I thought about Nan, covering her face as the police dragged me out of the door.

'Right!' said Miss Decima. 'Enough talk. We have two fluid ounces of ferric ammonium citrate solution to make before dinner. First, you shall carefully take apart that telescope and lay out the pieces on my bed. Then you must oil the squeaky wheel on my bath chair and get my best gown out of mothballs.'

I paused. 'Your gown?'

'Yes! We must both look our best for tonight. We're joining the family for dinner.'

I gawped at her. 'We are?'

'Of course!' she said. 'A dinner with the Reverend? A table surrounded by suspects in a house full of secrets? I wouldn't miss it for the world. Time to give that jar of hornets a good old shake.'

42

Sunday, 22 May, 7.09 p.m.

I spent only one night in the gang. The plan had been to smash up the other gang's pub after closing time, but we hadn't known they were all waiting inside for us with sticks and clubs. I'll never forget how it felt to storm through the doors and hear twenty chairs being scraped back at the same time.

That was nothing compared with walking into the dining room with Miss Decima. At first, no one noticed we were there – they were all making polite conversation. Then they looked up, and fell silent one by one. Edwin was sat at the head of the table talking to the Reverend, when he finally saw us.

'. . . a terrible accident, Reverend. The police have insisted on staying to clear up a few irregularities, hence the local gossip, but I'm sure you can see for yourself that –' He saw Miss Decima in the bath chair and turned pale. 'Oh, fuck.'

I gazed around, palms sweating. Mr Stokes stepped from the shadows with a look of genuine panic. 'Miss Decima. I was unaware that you would be dining with us tonight.'

'She can't,' said Edwin quickly. 'No place has been laid.' He glared at me with murderous eyes. 'I'm sure she'd be much more comfortable *in her own rooms*.'

'With my nephew slaughtered, and the murderer on the loose?' Miss Decima exclaimed. 'Heavens, no! I feel much safer down here, with my beloved family.'

The Reverend looked startled. In fairness, he seemed like the sort of person who'd be startled by a stiff breeze. 'Goodness – *murder?*'

'She doesn't mean that,' Edwin snapped.

'On the contrary, Reverend!' said Miss Decima darkly. 'Murder of the most diabolical kind! And unsolved! It chills my blood to think that the killer could still be here, in this house, walking among us.'

The Reverend was turning the colour of a raw oyster. Miss Decima rapped her stick on the ground. 'Come, Stephen! Take me to the table.'

I gulped. Mr Stokes was rapidly shaking his head. Edwin looked like he was trying to strangle me by using just his eyes. Even Temperance was gawping open-mouthed from the side of the room – Miss Decima had insisted that we keep our appearance tonight a complete secret, even from her. I took a deep breath, and remembered the last words that Miss Decima had said to me.

Just follow my lead, Stephen. It's all part of the plan.

I wheeled her to the end of the table, planting her next to Herr Muller. The Professor finally looked halfway normal, now that he had shaved and dressed. He was clearly following Lettice's orders to be on his best behaviour, but I noticed that his hand was trembling as he sipped a glass of water.

'Honestly, Edwin, your manners!' Miss Decima chided. 'Sitting a guest without a partner? We can't have Herr Muller left alone in the dark, revelling in his solitary pleasures.'

Herr Muller choked on his water. I got to work drying him off with a napkin while Miss Decima turned her attention to the rest of the table. 'How nice to have us all together like this, even if it must be under the most gruesome of circumstances. Dear Nephew Jolyon! You look utterly dreadful, even for you.'

She was right. The Rear Admiral had now been sober for almost twelve hours, and was suffering for it. He looked like an old cushion found in a ditch. 'Never better, Aunt Decima,' he wheezed.

'Are you sure you wouldn't like a glass of wine?' she said. 'Have mine.'

Edwin jolted to attention. 'No, Jolyon can't drink tonight. Because of . . . his stomach ulcer. Isn't that right, Cousin?'

'Yes,' muttered Jolyon, his eyes fixed on the glass like a circling vulture. 'That's right. Terrible, dreadful, thirsty ulcer.'

'Really?' said Miss Decima, scandalized. 'After you spent all afternoon gallantly fishing for our dinner? That hardly sounds fair.'

Jolyon growled. 'No, it doesn't. Now that I think about it, it doesn't sound fair at all.'

'I don't think your ulcer would be *very happy* if you did, Cousin,' Edwin insisted through clamped teeth. 'In fact, I think your ulcer would be *absolutely furious with you.*'

'I've read that moderate wine consumption prevents ulcers,' said Miss Decima.

'Is that so?' said Jolyon quickly. 'Well, can't argue with science.'

He grabbed the glass and drained it before Edwin could stop him, then let out a gasp like water flung on to a steam engine. '*Christ*, that's better! Good old science, eh?'

The maids arrived with the fish course. There was a moment of stunned alarm as each of them spotted Miss Decima, before I stepped forward to take the plates from them. Mr Stokes joined me, grabbing the plates and leaning close to hiss into my ear, '*What on earth are you doing!*'

I did my best to act naturally. 'Miss Decima insisted I bring her to dinner, sir.'

He groaned. 'This is a disaster. Good lord, the Rear Admiral's already finished the rest of that bottle.'

I glanced in the butler's mirror opposite. Sure enough, the Rear Admiral had managed to polish off two more glasses and was well on the way to being drunk, waving his arms like a conductor. 'Look at these goddamn beauties, Reverend!' he bellowed. 'Fresh carp, all from the Viscount's own lake. They put up a fight, by Christ, but God knows I got them in the end!'

The Reverend didn't reply, probably because he was reeling from the Lord's name being taken in vain three times in as many seconds.

'Damn fine lake that is, damn fine,' murmured Jolyon, necking another glass. 'Mark my words, tomorrow I'll come back with the biggest whopper you've ever seen!'

'Perhaps Herr Muller can photograph it,' said Miss Decima. 'If he has any plates left.'

'*Mein Gott*,' cried Herr Muller, spilling his second glass of water.

I set down the plates as fast as I could. By now, the table was chaos – no one knew where to put the remaining plates, now that there was an extra guest disrupting the place settings. The maids crashed and bumped into each other, while Mr Stokes tried frantically to direct them.

'Hey!' Gilbert demanded as a plate was carried past him. 'Why aren't I getting fish?'

Lettice shook her head. '*No*, Gilbert, no fish for you. You might choke on the bones.'

'I want fish!' Gilbert screamed.

'Have mine – I don't want it,' said Miss Decima, pushing over her plate. 'I'm not in the least bit hungry.'

Before Lettice could stop him, Gilbert had already grabbed the plate and started shovelling forkfuls into his mouth. Lettice squeaked and started frantically pulling out the bones while Miss Decima turned, like a swooping raptor, to her next victim.

'Ah, Reverend Wellbeloved. It's been too long. How is that sturdy young daughter of yours? Still stomping around the village?'

The Reverend blinked at her nervously. He looked like the kind of man who'd apologise to a door for walking into it. 'Er ... Clemency is doing well, Miss Decima. She has hopes of a scholarship to Oxford.' He blushed. 'In fact . . . I hear you're quite a learned woman yourself. I wonder if you wouldn't mind casting an eye over her application essay, and advise her how best to –'

'I would rather kill myself,' said Miss Decima calmly. 'Here, Jolyon, you might as well finish this second bottle. Lettice, leave the boy alone for five blessed seconds; frankly he's safer without you. Maybe use your left hand to eat, Herr Muller, your right one must be rather tired . . . Oops! That's another glass gone!'

I gazed in awe as Miss Decima laid waste to the entire dining table. In fewer than ten minutes, she had turned Edwin's dinner into a complete disaster. He was glaring at her with absolute loathing from the other end of the table.

'You'll have to forgive Great-Aunt Decima's behaviour, Reverend,' he said, bristling with menace. 'She's been the victim of a rather sad decline these last few years. Conrad did his best to contain her, but, as you can see, she is beyond anyone's help.'

'Yes!' Miss Decima exclaimed. 'Conrad tried to contain an awful lot of things, didn't he, Edwin? But ghosts have a habit of returning, no matter how much you strive to hide them. We can't forget the old family scandal, can we?'

There was the faintest flicker in the corner of Edwin's

eyes, the slightest clench of his jaw. '*Please.* Everyone knows that story about Conrad murdering his father is absolute –'

'Oh, I'm not talking about *that*!' said Miss Decima cheerfully. 'I'm talking about the *other* scandal. The real one. The one that you think no one else knows about.'

Edwin froze.

'You know the one I mean,' she said calmly. 'And you and I *both* know that it's the key to this whole murder.'

'Stokes,' said Edwin. 'I think it might be time to take Miss Decima back to her rooms.'

Mr Stokes instantly marched over and grabbed the bath chair, but, before he could move her, Miss Decima ground down the handbrake.

'You *must* know the truth, Reverend,' said Miss Decima desperately. 'There is a darkness at World's End. An ancient, secret darkness that must finally show its face!'

The room was silent now; the whole family were gazing on in shock. Even Gilbert was growing paler and paler.

'A guilty person sits at this table!' Miss Decima cried. 'A person whose soul is in torment! And until their crime is confessed –'

'*All right! I confess!*'

Herr Muller flung himself from the table and threw himself at the Reverend's chair.

'I know it is wrong, Reverend, terribly wrong!' he sobbed. 'Always I am trying to stop! But the corsets and fine silks, they call to me like demons!'

Edwin finally exploded. He slammed his fist on the table and leapt to his feet. 'That's it! You are OUT of here, you mad old witch! You hear me? OUT!'

'Perhaps I should be going . . .' the Reverend squeaked while Herr Muller clawed at his trouser leg.

'*Sit down!*' Edwin roared. He stood at the head of the table, glaring around the room with biblical rage. '*No one* is leaving until *I* say so. *I am the master here!* You hear me? The MASTER! And, until the will reading, I will not hear another –'

Gilbert vomited down the length of the table.

In the madness that followed, Miss Decima's outburst was more or less forgotten. Jolyon leapt back from the table in shock and tripped over the Professor, who was still clinging to the Reverend's ankles; Lettice screamed and grabbed Gilbert; the Reverend bolted, dragging the Professor with him along the carpet; Edwin tried to race after him, only to fall foul of Gilbert's second outpouring of vomit, which tripped him up and turned him on his back, flailing like a spider crab.

Mr Stokes, Temperance and I stood locked to the spot, watching it all unfold in speechless silence. Miss Decima nodded, satisfied, and released the handbrake.

'There, Stephen. *Now* you may take me out.'

43

Sunday, 22 May, 8.01 p.m.

I managed to get Miss Decima back to her rooms without anyone stopping us. Frankly, they had enough to be getting on with. I could still hear the shouting from the other end of the house.

'Well!' said Miss Decima as she settled back at her desk. 'That went rather well, I thought.'

I said nothing. Just stared at her in furious, trembling silence.

'What going on?' Miss Decima snapped. 'What's wrong with you?'

'Do you understand what you've just done?'

She looked at me bullishly. I took a deep breath and slowly counted to ten. All I could see was Mr Stokes's face as he stared at me across the room with a look so cold it almost burned.

'Miss Decima. That might have been great fun for you, but it wasn't for me. You've just put me in the firing line *again*. The only thing that's stopped me being arrested so far is that I've managed to lie low, and you've wrecked my chances. You've lost me any support I had from Mr Stokes, *any* ability to hide from Edwin –'

'Good grief,' she muttered. 'Were you a schoolmistress in another life, Stephen? Stop being so priggish. I wasn't doing any of that for *fun*. There was a purpose to it.'

I laughed bitterly. 'Like what?'

She began unpinning her hat.

'I *told* you at the start of all this, Stephen: we must approach this mystery scientifically. Science rides on the backbone of adventure; one must take risks, if one wishes to proceed. I knew that tonight, the family would be desperate to appear perfect in front of the Reverend, so I wanted to see what would happen when I placed pressure on them. To turn the rack a little and gauge their reactions. And I found a number of fascinating insights.'

I frowned. 'Is that why you were rude to the Reverend?'

'Ha! No, that *was* just for fun,' said Miss Decima. 'That daughter of his, Clemency? Absolute dud. *Scholarship to Oxford!* I've got a better chance of representing Britain at the next Olympic Games.'

She handed me her hat.

'But take, for example, my mention of the *old family scandal*. Jolyon couldn't have cared less – he was far too interested in his wine. Lettice seemed a complete blank, too – unusual, I would say, for a piece of gossip to have escaped her. But did you see Edwin's face? He almost died in his chair. *That*, Stephen, tells us all we need to know.'

'What *is* the old family scandal?' I asked.

'There isn't one,' she said. 'At least, not that I know of. I just made it up, to see what would happen when I said it. And after Edwin's reaction . . . well, I think we may have stumbled upon a path that leads to the solution.'

I was confused. 'What do you mean?'

She began removing her gloves.

'Think about our comet, Stephen. It was only when Halley studied the past that he was able to predict the future and calculate when the comet would next appear. So it is with this murder. There's something hidden in this family's history – something buried deep in the past – that explains how, and *why*, Conrad was killed. In order to solve this murder, we must discover what that secret is.' She gave a deep sigh. 'Tomorrow, we must redouble our efforts. Our work has just become significantly more dangerous. If we don't solve the mystery soon, I rather fear for the worst.'

I gulped. 'What do you mean?'

I waited for her to explain, but she was too busy unpinning her brooches and placing them on the desk before her.

'I already told you,' she said. 'I took a number of risks tonight. One of them was choosing to attend the dinner in the first place. You just saw what happened to Gilbert. Don't make me spell it out for you.'

I blinked at her. She groaned.

'Good grief! You really are dense sometimes, Stephen. The fish was poisoned. The killer is trying to kill again.'

44

Far above World's End the comet carried on, deeper into dark and endless space.

And, down below, the murderer was planning the next step.

Monday, 23 May 1910

The local population is convinced that the earthquake and the abnormal weather of the present spring stand in some mysterious relationship to Halley's Comet. After weeks of almost constant rain and cold winds the thermometer rose yesterday to summer level. The earthquake was immediately preceded by a violent tempest.

Evening Mail

45

Monday, 23 May, 6.00 a.m.

The nightmare was still stuck on my eyes when the bell woke me.

Nan had been further away than ever before. The force of the river was like machinery against me, driving me down and down and down. Nan's face was in her hands, her voice growing fainter as the water swept over my head.

You can't fight a river.

I gazed up at the ceiling with dread. I was trapped on an island with a killer who was trying to kill again. The chances of Inspector Jarvis catching them before they did was zero. In the meantime, Edwin wanted to pull my arms and legs off. If we didn't solve the murder soon, I was either going to get sacked, arrested or murdered myself.

Miss Decima's orders from last night were still running through my head.

Listen carefully, Stephen. This is important. Tomorrow morning, find Temperance and bring her to my rooms as quickly as you can.

I got dressed and made my way to Temperance's bedroom. It was empty: she must have already started work. I crept downstairs and poked my head inside the breakfast room, but there was no sign of her there either.

Of course – she'd be attending to Lettice. After everything that happened last night, she probably hadn't even gone to bed.

'Stephen.'

I leapt a foot in the air. Mr Stokes was standing behind me with a glare as cold as stone.

'How marvellous of you to finally reappear,' he said. 'I never saw you after last night's events. I was hoping you might help me to clear up the mess in the dining room. And in the entrance hall. And down the length of the central staircase.'

I swallowed. 'Is Gilbert all right, sir?'

Mr Stokes sighed. 'Improving. I'm afraid the same cannot be said for the master's mood. He's utterly furious, and I can hardly blame him. If I were you, I would stay well out of his way.' He glared at me. 'What on *earth* possessed you? You assured me that you would keep Miss Decima contained.'

I swallowed. 'I'm sorry, sir. She was . . . in high spirits.'

'I'm sure she was,' Mr Stokes snapped. 'I have rarely seen her spirits higher. If you could ensure they do not ascend further, Stephen, I would appreciate it. I have enough to be dealing with already.'

With that, he marched off. I felt awful, truth be told. I'd lost his trust; the hurt in his eyes was terrible. I was desperate to tell him everything and explain myself . . . but how could I?

'*Aha! There he is!*'

My heart sank when I saw who was marching towards me. It was Inspector Jarvis, and he was in a proper state. The strain of failing to solve the mystery was beginning to show; he seemingly hadn't slept in days. I couldn't help but notice that he had his shirt buttoned up the wrong way.

'Stephen Pike – the man himself!' Jarvis cried. 'Thought you could wriggle past me, did you? Well, you thought wrong, sir!'

Jarvis's shouting was bringing everyone from all over the house. Mr Stokes came back, trying in vain to settle him, but it was no use. Edwin stormed in behind them, looking like he was ready to shred the rugs with his teeth. 'Oh, not this *again*!'

The rest of the family appeared: Jolyon limped into the room, holding his head and wincing like a dog that's had an operation, while Lettice, pale and fraught, scrambled in after him. 'Can you *please* keep the racket down? My beloved grandson is on the verge of death!'

Jarvis nodded savagely. 'You are right, madam; we have talked long enough. Perhaps *now* is the time that the slaying at Tithe Hall was finally brought to the most shocking of conclusions!'

I stood, sweating on the spot. I had no Temperance, no Miss Decima, not even Mr Stokes in my corner. I was trapped. The entire house was trickling into the room, peering through doorways and whispering. Was this the moment that I finally got arrested?

Jarvis reached inside his jacket and pulled out an envelope. 'Behold! Last night, I retrieved these from the police station at Tregarrick: the post-mortem results. And their findings are most ... *unexpected*. For they reveal that Lord Stockingham-Welt's death was not caused by a crossbow wound to the brain, but by ... *asphyxiation*.'

There was a gasp throughout the room. Even I was surprised at that.

'That is correct,' Jarvis continued. 'And allow me to shock you even further. The post-mortem toxicology results conclude that the cause of asphyxiation was the administration of a *lethal poison*!'

Poison. I glanced at Lettice, but she barely even blinked. Of course she didn't – she could surely see, as well as I could, that Jarvis was going to somehow pin this on me. I stood, sweat prickling over my forehead. How on earth was I going to get out of this?

'Most unusual, do you not think?' said Jarvis. 'Stranger still, the poison in question is no common-or-garden one – it is a poison called *rotenone*. Late last night, I demanded that the library at Tregarrick was reopened for me. And there, in the small hours of the morning, I discovered that rotenone is derived from the tropical plant *Pachyrhizus erosus* – otherwise known as jicama vine, or the "Mexican turnip". The roots of this plant are perfectly harmless, but the leaves, skin and seeds? Quite the opposite. Indeed, were a person to ingest even *five grains* of the rotenone found in their cells, death would occur within the hour!'

He fell silent for a moment.

'But *how*? *How* could such a quantity of poison be administered to the Viscount? As always, the answer was staring me in the face. *The crossbow bolt!*' He gazed at the room in triumph. 'Lord Stockingham-Welt did not *ingest* poison – the poison was fired directly into his brain! The bolt that killed him was laced with rotenone!'

There was a murmur of confusion around the room.

'Through a locked door?' said Mrs Pearce.

'Aha!' cried Jarvis, slapping the mantelpiece. 'You have it on the nose, my good woman! Your feminine mind cannot conceive of the true barbarity of this crime – a crime that upends all our expectations. The crossbow was not fired through a locked door. It was fired through an open door . . . *which was then locked*!'

Jarvis kept going, his voice low.

'On Wednesday evening, Lord Stockingham-Welt walked to his study to seal himself inside, but, just as he reached the study door, he was distracted by a noise behind him. *What is this?* he must have wondered; whereupon, turning to the suit of armour, he was met with the shock of a lifetime . . . or, indeed, of a *death-time*!' He raised a finger. 'For the suit of armour was no longer empty. On the contrary – concealed inside it was Stephen Pike, cradling a crossbow into which he had loaded a bolt laced with lethal rotenone, which he fired directly into the Viscount's eye!'

The room was silent. It was safe to say that no one was convinced.

'I've never *heard* of anything so absolutely ridiculous!' Edwin spat. '*That's* what you've been doing, all this time?'

'Of course!' said Jarvis, undeterred. 'I can see from the looks on your faces that you are unconvinced! *But how, then, was Conrad's body found inside a locked and sealed room?* you must be thinking! Exactly what Stephen Pike was relying on. The answer is obvious! Shocked from his attack and fearing that the suit of armour was in fact the vengeful ghost of his murdered father, Conrad reacted as *any* man would: by striving to preserve himself. Perhaps, even then, the rotenone was befuddling his powers of rationality and logic. Thus, with his last ounces of strength, he fled into his study, locked the door behind him and sealed himself inside, before sitting down on his chair and expiring!'

Mr Stokes coughed into his hand. 'And, er . . . the telephone call that he made in the morning?'

'All Stephen Pike!' Jarvis announced triumphantly. 'It was *he* who called you, sir, from one of the many other telephones in the house. This was a murder that was meticulously planned, right down to every last devious detail!'

He shoved the post-mortem results into my hands.

'Read them and weep, Mr Pike! This time, you have no Miss Decima to protect you. The post-mortem results are emphatic: death by rotenone poisoning. And here is the evidence!' He reached into his pocket and held up a jar of powder. 'Rotenone, which I found just now in Conrad Stockingham-Welt's study. It was Stephen Pike's final, ingenious flourish – hiding the very poison he had used to commit the murder in among the victim's own chemicals. The

Viscount's body displayed all the signs of rotenone poisoning: hypoxemia of the blood, metabolic acidosis –'

'Necrosis of the gills?' I read aloud from the list.

'Yes, and . . .' Jarvis stumbled, mid-sentence. 'Gills? What do you mean, *gills*?'

I glanced up. The whole room was looking at me now. I held up the post-mortem results and pointed at them.

'*Necrosis of the epithelium cells of the gills*. That's what it says here.' I handed back the post-mortem. 'I think you've got confused, Inspector. These aren't the post-mortem results for Conrad. They're for the fish in the fishbowl.'

Jarvis stared at me blankly for a few seconds. Then he gazed at the jar of poison in his hand. 'But . . . but then how . . .'

'*Mein Gott!*'

Everyone turned around. Herr Muller was standing in the doorway, pointing at the rotenone in Jarvis's hand.

'You . . . you have found it,' he choked. 'My poison! I must beg you, I had nothing to do with Lord Stockingham-Welt's death. I gave him the jar but that is all, I swear of it!'

Jarvis was turning paler by the second. 'This is . . . yours?'

Professor Muller nodded feverishly. 'Conrad asked me to bring it from Germany, so that he could test it on his own fish.' He glanced around the room. 'For the sharks, no? They would be most disorientated, after the comet drove them from their native waters and infested the Cornish coastline.'

Inspector Jarvis made a small, gurgling sound at the back of his throat. I turned around. The entire room was staring at him with absolute loathing.

'Well,' I said cheerfully, handing him back the post-mortem results. 'I'd best be off. I have my duties to attend to.'

I gave a bow, then strolled out of the room like I was wearing the biggest boots you've ever seen in your life.

46

Monday, 23 May, 7.33 a.m.

By the time I made it to Miss Decima's rooms, Temperance was already there. Her face was completely white.

'I've just been updating Temperance on the events of last night,' said Miss Decima grandly.

'I can't believe it,' said Temperance in a hushed voice. 'Gilbert's been *really* ill. I thought he was a goner at one point. Why would someone try to poison him?'

'They *didn't*,' I said. 'The plates all got mixed up, remember? Gilbert wasn't even supposed to have fish. It was meant for someone else at that table. Edwin, the Reverend, Jolyon, Lettice, Muller –'

'Miss Decima?' Temperance whispered.

She shook her head. 'No one was expecting me to be there. That was why I decided to keep our arrival a complete secret – even from you, Temperance. I hope you don't mind.' She drummed her fingers on her cane. 'That's not all we learnt last night, is it? *The old family scandal*: a secret buried deep in this family's past, which leads the way to the murder.'

Temperance shrugged. 'I haven't heard anything. But, then, I've not been here for long.'

'We could try the older servants,' I suggested. 'Mrs Pearce?'

Temperance rolled her eyes. 'She's all gossip.'

Miss Decima harrumphed. 'Gossip is no good to us now. We need facts, and we need them fast. Our web is becoming more complex with each passing minute. Jarvis will no doubt attempt to accuse you again, Stephen –'

I puffed out my chest proudly. 'He just did, actually.'

I explained everything that had happened in the breakfast room: the post-mortem results, the rotenone, Jarvis making a fool of himself in front of the whole family. I thought that Miss Decima would be pleased with me, but instead she just gawped.

'The rotenone belonged to Herr Muller?' she repeated.

I nodded. 'He was worried that the police might somehow use it to make him a scapegoat for the murder. What with him giving it to the Viscount, and being a German and all.'

'Indeed,' said Miss Decima. 'It certainly explains some of his movements over the last few days. It *also* provides a complete and comprehensive explanation for what happened last night, and several other unsolved elements of this case.'

Temperance and I stared at her blankly.

'Oh, come on,' Miss Decima muttered. 'It's obvious. Please don't make me spell this out for you.'

We kept staring. Miss Decima sighed and removed her teeth.

'The fish that made Gilbert sick last night wasn't poisoned. *All* the fish served at dinner were poisoned. With rotenone, to be precise.'

Temperance frowned. 'That's impossible. Nobody else got sick.'

'Because rotenone,' said Miss Decima haughtily, 'while highly poisonous to fish, is only *slightly* poisonous to humans. The amount under discussion would have been extremely dilute, too: practically homoeopathic. A tiny amount in the flesh of a cooked fish isn't going to kill anyone, but it *might* make a seven-year-old child extremely ill, right down the length of a dining-room table.'

I tried to put two and two together, and made minus eighty-six. 'But . . . how did the fish get poisoned in the first place?'

Miss Decima steepled her fingers. 'Remind us – what did you find in the ornamental pond at the centre of the maze, Stephen?'

'A shard of glass.'

'Quite. And how do you think it got there?'

My eyes widened. 'The fishbowl! From the study!'

Miss Decima nodded. 'Follow, if you will, the trajectory of this logic. Conrad poisoned his fish on Wednesday to test the efficacy of the rotenone, as part of his final preparations for the cataclysm. Naturally, the fish were dead by Thursday morning. Herr Muller, fearing that the rotenone would be used to implicate him, entered the study on Thursday afternoon to find and remove it, which is where you ran into him, Stephen. That was enough to scare him off for a few days, long enough to realize that there was something *else* in that study that would connect him to the poison.'

I frowned. 'I'm not following.'

'I know you're not,' she snapped. '*The water in the fishbowl.* It would also be tainted with rotenone. Herr Muller, upon learning that the family were leaving for church on Sunday, sneaked into the study to take the tainted fishbowl and remove all traces of his link to the poison in the crime scene. He carried the fishbowl somewhere he thought that *no one* would see him: the maze.'

I shook my head. 'But I saw him from the window. He didn't have a fishbowl with him.'

'Of course he fucking didn't,' she snapped. 'Because he was *leaving* the maze, you dolt, not entering it. It's awfully hard to tell the difference, which is a fact that will come up again in a moment, if you'd let me fucking finish.'

She took a breath.

'Herr Muller carried the fishbowl to the centre of the maze and emptied the tainted water into the ornamental pond – sadly, the bowl slipped from his grip and smashed in the pond. Hence the reason why you found a curved shard of glass inside it.' She smiled wryly. 'I can't for a moment wonder why his hands were so slippery. And tell me – what else did you find in the pond?'

I stared at her blankly. 'Nothing. The pond was . . .'

And suddenly, it all made sense.

'The pond was empty,' I said excitedly. 'It was supposed to be full of fish, but it wasn't. Because Jolyon had just scooped them all out!'

Temperance blinked at me. 'You what?'

'He told everyone he got them from the lake, but that was a lie. Jarvis probably scared all the fish off when he fell inside it! So, to save face, Jolyon sneaked into the maze to net the fish from the pond and serve them at dinner. *That's* who I heard chasing me in the maze!'

Miss Decima smiled. '*Bravo*, Stephen. Jolyon wasn't actually *chasing* you – he was trying to sneak out of the maze before you spotted him. But, as I said, when you're stuck in a maze, running *away* from someone sounds an awful lot like running *towards* them.' She sighed contentedly. 'All in all, this has worked out rather well for us! We no longer have a killer who's trying to kill again, and we've cleared up some extraneous loose ends. Speaking of which, I trust that there were no further ghost sightings this morning?'

Temperance and I shook our heads.

'Naturally,' said Miss Decima. 'That's because our ghost is currently in bed, spewing his little guts out.'

Temperance choked. 'The ghost was . . . *Gilbert*!'

'Who else?' said Miss Decima. 'The mop-haired little

psychopath must have leapt at the chance to get up early, moan through some closed doors and terrify an impressionable maid. I imagine that Merryn's missing crucifix will be somewhere in his bedroom, alongside a number of other items taken from the house. I imagine we won't have any more ghost sightings until he's back on his feet again – leaving us ample time to focus on the task at hand!'

She held up a vial containing a small amount of bright green liquid.

'*Ferric ammonium citrate* solution,' she announced grandly. 'Not much, but enough to produce a few cyanotype prints. We shall finish constructing the enlarging equipment, then head out at midday and develop the image in natural sunlight. Then we can finally compare it to the crime-scene sketch and discover what it was that was changed about the study.'

Temperance and I were in awe.

'We shall have to be rather quick about it, though,' Miss Decima muttered. 'I do believe a rather violent storm is due to appear later this afternoon, which will cut off World's End for a number of hours, trapping us in the house with the killer and increasing the likelihood of somebody *actually* being murdered.' She rubbed her hands gleefully. 'Goodness! Nothing like a bit of drama to focus the mind, eh?'

47

Monday, 23 May, 12.04 p.m.

By the time we had Miss Decima back in her bath chair with the equipment she needed, it was midday. I led her out on to the gravel, glancing over my shoulder to make sure we were alone. 'Where to, Miss Decima?'

'The south-west prospect, Stephen. We need maximum seclusion and maximum sunlight.'

We took the exact same path that we'd taken the night we first met, past the stone fountains and flowerbeds and into the trees. So much had changed in the space of five days. When we were last here, the Viscount was alive and Temperance and I had barely spoken. Now, here we were, two servants and an Honourable Miss, working together to solve a murder. Funny how life works out.

Then there, through the trees, was that bonfire again – the one I'd seen on the lawn yesterday. It had only half burned through. I frowned. Why did it keep bothering me so much?

Miss Decima suddenly whipped out a hand. 'Stop! Take me to the *Hyacinthus orientalis*, if you please.'

I looked blank.

'The hyacinths.'

'The blue ones over there,' muttered Temperance.

I pushed her over and Miss Decima leant down to grab a handful of bright blue flowers. She pulled a short sharp knife from a pocket to cut through the stems. 'Are they for the cyanotypes, Miss Decima?' I asked.

'Mind your own business, Stephen.' She pointed ahead. 'Carry on!'

We kept going, twisting down through the trees. The path became grass, the grass became bare earth, the forest around us turned wilder and the sound of the sea grew and grew. Finally we found ourselves standing on the cliff at the edge of the estate, the whole great ocean sparkling before us and whipping our faces with salt. There was so much of everything here – so much air, so much space, so much sunlight. In that house we were like fish in a fishbowl, but now it felt like standing on the edge of the world.

'We'll need an hour of uninterrupted sunlight for a full development,' said Miss Decima. 'We must work fast: the solution will start developing the moment it is on the paper. Stephen, start flattening the grass into a square of roughly two feet by two feet, if you please.'

I stamped the grass flat while Miss Decima shoved jars and bottles and brushes into Temperance's hands. Then she took a beaker of green solution and emptied a separate paper sachet of red powder into it, stirring all the while. She pulled out a large sheet of watercolour paper from her chair and, spreading it across her lap, smeared the liquid across it in great long green streaks with a paintbrush.

'I thought you said the picture would be blue,' I said.

'It will be, once the image has developed.' She held up the damp paper. 'Now lay this on the ground, please. Careful not to touch the solution.'

I picked up the paper at the edges and laid it flat. Miss Decima reached into her bath chair and produced the contraption she'd built this morning. I'd been in awe, watching her make it. She'd taken apart her telescope and removed the two curved glass lenses from inside, then arranged them facing each other inside a wooden box, which was now resting on top of a wicker footstool that she'd gutted.

'Place this over the paper, please,' she instructed. 'Very carefully. Just as we discussed.'

I took the footstool and placed it so that the legs stood either side of the treated paper. I could see right away that sunlight was striking the lenses.

'Good.' She took the glass negative plate and handed it to me. 'Even more carefully now, Stephen. We'll only have one chance at this before the sunlight fails us completely.'

There was a little slot that Miss Decima had made for the negative, barely a fraction of an inch beneath the two lenses. She'd spent hours getting the exact distance right – if I nudged the lenses now, it'd all be over. I slid the negative into place, my breath held and my hands trembling. With a gasp of relief, it fell perfectly into position.

'Good,' said Miss Decima quietly. 'Now, open the aperture, Temperance.'

'The biscuit lid?'

'The biscuit lid, yes.'

There was an old round lid strung over a hole at the bottom of the footstool. Temperance took it off, and it was like magic. Sunlight streamed through the lenses at the top, right through the glass plate negative and through the hole in the footstool and on to the paper. The image was now projected at twice the size on to the paper. The blacks and whites were still flipped, but the lines were all crisp and sharp; Miss Decima had calculated the distances perfectly. There was the Viscount, standing in his study.

'Splendid,' said Miss Decima, her breath notably tighter. 'I must say, that's looking better than I'd hoped.'

Temperance frowned. 'The blacks and whites are the wrong way around.'

'The image will be developed exactly as we need it to be, my dear. All we have to do is wait.'

I glanced at the sun. It was bright, but there were clouds on the far horizon. 'How long will it take?'

'We should have brought a picnic,' muttered Temperance.

Miss Decima didn't reply. She was gazing out at the ocean.

'Miss Decima?' I asked.

It took a long time for her to speak again. When she did, there was a softness to her voice that I hadn't heard yet.

'Just before he died,' she began, 'Newton said that he felt like a boy playing on the seashore, while the great ocean of truth lay all undiscovered in front of him.' She nodded to the sea, stretching out to the horizon. 'Those words ring truer to me now than ever before. I've devoted my whole life to pursuing truth, and yet, the older I become, the more I begin to see how little I have understood.'

Temperance and I glanced at each other. There was no point trying to stop Miss Decima when she was like this. You might as well try to stop a landslide. She pointed to the other side of the heath. 'Wheel me over there, if you please.'

'Why?'

'It's none of your f—'

'All right, all right.'

I pushed her to the other side of the heath. It was only when we got closer that I saw what we were walking towards: a stone in the ground, hidden by long grass. Miss Decima made me stop the chair beside it and leant down to carefully cut away tufts with her knife, grunting with effort.

Temperance knelt down to help her. 'Let me, Miss Decima –'

'No, girl,' she said. 'This is my job to do.'

She spent some time clearing the grass, while Temperance and I stood to one side, baffled. Then she took the blade and scraped away the moss that had caked over the stone. It was only then that I could read the words carved into the stone, and realized what it was.

ISABELLA STOCKINGHAM
1830–1865
AD ASTRA

Miss Decima took the hyacinths from her lap and placed them carefully on the ground beside her.

'It's been a long time since I visited,' she explained. 'Her body's in the Welt family crypt and Conrad commissioned that statue for her in the maze. But neither of those ever struck me as right for Isabella. Who wants to spend an eternity trapped inside marble or hidden in walls of poisonous yew, when you could be out here, in the glory of the world?'

She held out her arms to the wide open sea, stretching on to the horizon.

'I made this memorial for her,' she said. 'My own way to remember her. I could have visited it when we were out here on Wednesday night – I *should* have visited it – but, as usual, I was . . . rather distracted. I've always been like that. I never had much time for Isabella when she was alive either.'

A wind flicked at the grass, carrying the smell of the sea. Miss Decima shifted in her chair.

'This heath was where my father took us to see the comet when it last passed, you know. Back before the Welts turned up, before Tithe Hall was built, when Isabella and I were just a few years old. We called it our Star Garden.' She smiled. 'All of my fondest memories of Isabella were spent here, looking out over the world and imagining what our lives would be like when the comet next passed. The things we would achieve, the lives we would lead. We used to say that we would marry good husbands and have dozens of children and hundreds of grandchildren. As I got older, I realized that none of those things mattered to me very much. But Isabella never stopped wanting a family. So when our father said that she had to marry Lawrence Welt, I couldn't help but feel that part of her was delighted about it.'

Her hands fussed at her cane, worrying it this way and that.

'At the time, I thought that I had the worst part of the deal – having to forgo my career to look after our parents, while she was left to satisfy some stupid man. We'd always spoken about wanting so much more for ourselves; how could she throw it away now, at the first opportunity? I begged her to reconsider. I told her that she was betraying her sex, her worth, her intelligence, our promise to one another, and I told her that, until she saw things for what they really were, I couldn't speak to her.' She smoothed the skin of her hands. 'Then, of course, she died. So she never saw things the way I did, and I never spoke to her either. I think, if I had my time all over again, I would much rather have said that I was wrong. *Pretended*, even. So that we could talk again.'

We stood in silence, listening to the waves.

'I never understood Isabella,' Miss Decima whispered. 'I never understood why she made the choices that she made. Her son grew up to be cruel and stupid, lazy and unjustly entitled. But I suspect that, despite all that, she would still have loved him. Isabella had a habit of loving people who were not necessarily deserving of it.'

She reached around her neck and pulled out a locket on a silver chain, opening it with a thumbnail. Inside was a silhouette of a young woman. Miss Decima turned to us, her eyes more serious than I'd ever seen them.

'I need you both to understand,' she said quietly. 'Solving this murder is not a game for me. It is not a matter of intellectual pride. I failed Isabella in her life, but I can make up for it now. I can find out who killed her son. I can do that for her, with the little time that I have left. Do you understand?'

I thought of Nan's photo on my windowsill, kept in the best frame that I could afford. The Bible I prayed to every night. 'Yes, Miss Decima.'

'Of course,' said Temperance quietly.

Miss Decima gave a short sharp nod, and clipped the locket shut. 'Splendid. Now if you don't mind, I would like to be alone for a moment.'

Temperance and I did as we were told. We stepped over to the other side of the heath, leaving Miss Decima with her thoughts and the headstone she'd made.

'Is she going to be all right?' I whispered, once we were out of earshot.

Temperance nodded. 'Of course she will. She's Miss Decima. She's *always* all right.'

I wasn't sure about that. Temperance was a servant; surely she had spotted those tiny details that told all. Surely she'd seen the redness in Miss Decima's eyes as she spoke; the way that her voice broke on her last instruction. Surely she'd noticed that, when Miss Decima thought we'd turned away, she reopened the locket and kissed it a final time before placing it back beneath her gown, where it stayed hidden beside her heart.

48

Monday, 23 May, 2.48 p.m.

Miss Decima's grieving ended as quickly as it'd begun.

'Right!' she barked from the other side of the heath. 'Stop shirking. Our cyanotype must almost be done!'

Sure enough, the paper had changed when we came back to it. The bright green colour had turned dull and murky, like seaweed. Miss Decima nodded, and I carefully removed the footstool. Where the picture had been projected, the paper had been scorched muddy brown.

'You said it was going to be blue,' I muttered.

'It *will* be,' she said, picking up the paper and handing it to me, 'once you wash off the ferriate. You'll have to do it quickly, too. The image is still developing.'

I panicked. 'It'll take me at least twenty minutes to get back to the house.'

'I wasn't suggesting you go to the house, Stephen.'

I stared at her blankly, until I noticed the sound filling the silence between us. Waves. My heart sank. I turned to the slope behind us. 'You want me to wash it in the sea?'

Miss Decima rolled her eyes. 'Don't be ridiculous! Of course not.'

I sighed. 'That's a relief –'

'Salt water will damage it,' she said. 'You can wash it in the river. You should be able to access it through those trees.'

I gawped at her. 'But I can't swim.'

'Stephen, I am not suggesting you perform lengths. Find

a still, shallow pool in the waterfall and wash off the ferriate. Quickly as you can, please. Chop, chop!'

'But –'

She folded her arms. 'Do you *want* to catch the person who murdered my nephew? Or perhaps you'd rather wait until I was murdered in my bed, too?'

I sighed wearily. 'No, Miss Decima.'

'How reassuring! Mind how you go now.'

I gave Temperance a pleading look, but she was far too busy laughing behind her hand to notice. I set off grumbling down the slope. 'I should have stayed in bleeding prison,' I muttered.

Getting to the river was as bad as I'd feared. There was no path, just a steep slope covered in ferns and thorns and sudden drops. I had to cling on to roots with my free hand so I could clamber down, step by step, until the noise of the waterfall grew louder and louder.

It was more like a series of waterfalls than just the one. It started at the lake at the top of the hill – I could see a little wooden bridge passing over it – and then plummeted in a series of stone pools, until it became a river at the bottom, twisting through the trees and out of sight. I was about halfway down, next to one of the smaller waterfalls. The water was fast – the only place where I could safely kneel and wash the paper without it being ripped from my hands was on the opposite bank. The only way to get there was by crossing some wet stepping stones near the edge. If I slipped, it was going to be a hard, nasty fall. I gazed over the edge, and then wished I hadn't.

You might want to get on with it, Stephen, came Miss Decima's voice.

The print in my hands was getting darker. I whispered a quick prayer and scampered over the stepping stones, losing my footing near the end and soaking one of my shoes before finally standing on the opposite bank, panting for dear life.

Bravo, Stephen.

Time to get it over with. I held the paper at the corners and lowered it into the water, making sure the current didn't whip it from my hands.

It was just as Miss Decima had said. The murky brown was magically swept away, flake by flake. Hidden beneath it was the Viscount's study in rich crystal blues. There was the fishbowl; there were his books, the window, the fireplace. There was the Viscount standing behind his desk, his haughty face lit up by Professor Muller's flashbulb. There was something secretive and mocking in his eyes – *derisory*, I thought, like he was goading me to work out who had killed him.

I lifted the dripping paper out of the water and got to my feet. I couldn't go back up the way I'd come: the slope was difficult enough to stumble down, let alone climb up again. I gazed along the river, searching for another way up . . .

There was Lowen, barely twenty feet away.

I flung myself to the ground. There was no doubt it was Lowen. He was by himself, walking upstream. What was he doing down here?

You're going to show me where Cousin Conrad murdered his father. Lowen said he'd take me, but now I can't find him.

I raised my head, peering over the edge of the waterfall. Lowen wasn't walking towards me; he was marching along a path that ran beside the river, one that led up to the other side of the lake.

No, not marching – *running*. Almost stumbling. Like he was trying to get away from something. He stopped at the top one final time, glancing down the slope he'd just come from, and his face was a picture. I'd never seen anyone look so frightened in my life. Then he disappeared, just like that.

I lay on the spot, my heart thumping on the ground. I'd just seen one of our suspects out in the middle of the grounds. In the place where Lawrence Welt had died, twenty years ago. He looked like a man who was being hunted.

And what do you propose to do about that, Stephen?

I steeled myself. I draped the wet paper over a nearby rock, climbed over the edge of the waterfall in a series of faltering, painful steps and made my way downriver.

It was not a nice place to die, that much was certain. The estate around Tithe Hall had been made to look perfect; this part of it had been neglected and left to rot. The air was cold and damp and smelt of illness; the path was mud, the trees bent low with their branches bowed like the heads of grieving women.

But I could hear something new, now that I was further away from the waterfalls: the whine of machinery, coming through the trees up ahead. I kept going until I saw a tin shed, built across the river. There wasn't much to it – a few sheets of corrugated metal hidden in the shadows, all rusting and sad and dilapidated. It looked like a dying animal, crouched beneath a bush.

I finally twigged. It was a hydroelectric turbine – the one that provided the electricity for the house. The river passed through a hole at the front, where a metal sluice gate caught any fallen branches, and anything smaller got sucked inside and under the wheel itself. I frowned. Was *this* why Lowen had come down here? An old shed?

There was a door at the side. It wasn't locked. I opened it and peered inside, blinking away the gloom. There was nothing to see. Most of the room inside was taken up by the huge wheel, as tall as a fairground ride, churning in the darkness. The water crossed the shed from one end to the other, beside some dusty floorboards strewn with dead leaves. There was a large thundering generator, and that was it. Nothing had been hidden here; nothing stored.

I closed the door, my mind ticking over. The path carried on past the shed and towards the coast. I walked down it, waiting to see if there was a boat or anything else waiting there, maybe even some people, but there was only a rocky inlet, and the sea stretching on ahead. The sky was getting darker in the distance. The waves that stuck the shoreline were angry now, smashing against the jagged stone.

I felt a nagging doubt in my chest. Apart from the shed, it didn't look like there was a single reason to come down here. So why had Lowen? What had he seen that scared him so much? I shook my head, turned to go back up to the path . . .

And stopped.

I was right. There *wasn't* any reason for someone to come down here. Which was precisely the reason it had been chosen.

There was a row of trees hidden behind the shed; I'd had no idea they were even there. Each trunk had been painted with two white marks. The marks were at head height, all of them. Like eyes.

I walked up to the nearest one and ran my hand over the bark. The wood around the marks was splintered – like something sharp had pierced it repeatedly.

I knew what I was looking at. It was a target-practice area. A place hidden away, where no one would ever think to come and look; where they could never be seen, and never be heard; where they could fire an arrow at a pair of eyes, over and over again, until they got it perfect.

49

Monday 23 May, 3.48 p.m.

It took a while to climb the waterfall and clamber back up the slope with the dripping cyanotype in my hands, even at the speed I was going. By the time I reached the heath, I was covered in dirt and sweat. Miss Decima and Temperance watched me pace towards them with curiosity.

'Good grief,' said Miss Decima. 'You look like you hit every tree on the way down.'

'Where have you *been*?' said Temperance.

'Lowen,' I gasped. 'I – I just saw him. By the waterfall. And that's not . . . all I saw.' I swallowed. 'The trees. By the turbine. They have marks on them. Arrow marks. Like eyes, painted on the tree trunks.'

Temperance turned completely white. 'You don't think –'

I nodded. 'Lowen. It's a target practice. He must have gone down to –'

'We should not jump to conclusions,' said Miss Decima quickly. 'He could have been doing *anything* down there – he might even have been searching for something to implicate *you*, Stephen. How did he look, when you saw him?'

I gulped. 'Terrified, Miss Decima. Like he was being hunted.'

'Perhaps he was,' said Miss Decima darkly. 'Perhaps he stumbled upon the very same practice area, if that's what it is. Perhaps he feared the killer was after him.' Her fingers worked at her walking stick. 'But the fact of the matter is, this discovery changes everything. We now know for certain that the Viscount was *not* murdered by a member of his family.'

Temperance stared at her. 'How?'

'Because they all arrived at World's End on Wednesday morning,' she replied. 'And, from the sound of it, the damage to the trees was done over a long period of time. Correct?'

I nodded. 'There were dozens of arrow marks, Miss Decima.'

'Precisely,' she said. 'Which means that the Viscount was killed by someone who's been here for a while. Someone in the house. Someone who was able to spend day after day down by that turbine shed, practising how to kill him.'

We stood in silence as the realization fell heavily on us. We'd been wrong, all this time. 'But . . . all that stuff about the will –' I said.

'Now is not the time to ruminate,' said Miss Decima. 'We must work faster than ever to solve this mystery, before it's too late. Stephen, the cyanotype. Temperance, the crime-scene sketch. Lay them side by side. Quickly!'

I did as I was told, and lay the dripping cyanotype print on the grass while Temperance placed the sketch of the crime-scene alongside it. There they were: two studies side by side, from almost identical angles, one with the Viscount alive, one with him dead.

'Come, Stephen,' Miss Decima said. 'This has never been more important. We *must* discover what was changed in that study!'

The blue cyanotype of the study was just as I remembered: the Viscount standing tall and proud behind his desk, the fishbowl, the oxygen tanks, the window, the fireplace. In the crime scene, it was all the same, except this time, of course, the Viscount was slumped in his chair, the fish floating dead on the surface of the bowl. But what else was different?

I stared at the pictures until my eyes burned. I studied them from top to bottom, side to side and corner to corner. I looked at the desk, the shelves, the wall, the fireplace, searching for anything that stood out, anything that was different, *anything* that could explain how the murder was done . . .

But there was nothing. I turned to Miss Decima and Temperance, and saw the same grim acceptance on both their faces.

'They're . . . identical,' said Temperance. 'They're exactly the same.'

Miss Decima sucked at her teeth. 'Oh, dear. We have hit another dead end.'

I shook my head. 'No. I know I'm right. I *know* something changed in that room!'

'But *what*, Stephen?'

I swallowed. 'I . . . I don't know. All I can think about is that stupid teapot. The one that broke on the floor.'

We stared at the pictures in miserable silence. We had placed all our hopes on their holding the answer: providing one miraculous clue that would somehow solve the whole mystery. But we were wrong. We were back where we started – in fact, we were further from the truth than ever before. We saw no motive, no means, no opportunity. In the distance, the sky had started to scab over with clouds. The storm was getting closer.

'Well,' said Miss Decima. 'I think it's safe to say that we're absolutely –'

The scream came shrill and distant, carried by the wind. It took only a second of us staring at each other to hear it again. Another scream – more than one. And they were coming from the house.

We didn't pause for a second longer. Temperance grabbed the pictures from the ground and stuffed them all into Miss

Decima's lap; I spun the chair around and pushed her bath chair up the hill, back bent and legs pumping. None of us spoke. We all knew, deep down, what we were going to find when we got back to the house.

The grounds were empty when we reached the top of the hill, but the screams that reached us from inside the house were louder and clearer now. So were the shouts of disbelief, the bellowed orders. We tore over the lawns, down the gravel path and past the Nursery, making for where the noise was loudest: the entrance to the drawing room, where the crowds had gathered in horror.

It wasn't difficult to push Miss Decima to the front of the crowd. The staff and guests let themselves be pushed aside, as if there were nothing really holding them to the ground any more. Besides, it was easy to see what was on the drawing-room floor. And no one wanted to look at it for any longer than they had to.

The marble bust of Edwin was lying beside the fireplace, chipped and smeared with blood. Slumped beside it, like a gruesome mirror image, was the body of Inspector Jarvis. A waterfall of blood had spilt from a wound on the back of his head and was pooling beneath him. His mouth was open in shock as he gazed back at us with eyes as cold and empty as the bust that had been used to club him to death.

50

Monday, 23 May, 5.47 p.m.

The next few hours were a blur, to tell the truth.

We pieced together what had happened from the rest of staff. Merryn had found the body. Mrs Pearce had asked her to do the ground-floor fireplaces, seeing as they were short of above-stairs servants, and she'd walked into the drawing room to find the Inspector dead.

Mr Stokes telephoned the police straight away. No one came. It became clear what the problem was, long before anyone called back: the coming storm had caused the tides to rise, and the causeway was flooded. There was no way for the police to access World's End, and there was no way that any of us could leave it.

We were trapped on the island with the killer.

Edwin acted fast. Every single person in the house – every family member, every guest, every servant, every maid – was ordered to shut themselves in their room, just as we had on that first, fateful night. Doors that could be locked were to be locked; doors that couldn't would have beds pushed up against them. No one would be allowed to leave their room until Chief Constable Penrose arrived.

Until then, all we could do was wait.

That was how Miss Decima and I finally came to find ourselves back in the Nursery. We had no Temperance: she was shut in her bedroom on the top floor, with the rest of the maids. Outside, the storm had finally arrived. The trees were being whipped all around us, and the rain was driving at the windowpanes. Tithe Hall felt more like a castle than ever, battening down against the besieging outside world.

I gazed at my shoes. 'I'm sorry, Miss Decima.'

She frowned at me. 'Why?'

I shifted. 'Thinking that the study had changed ... That was all my idea. And I've been wrong this whole time. If we hadn't been focusing so much on *that* ... well, maybe we'd have found the murderer by now. Maybe Inspector Jarvis would still be alive.'

It was a miserable thought. A man was dead, and it was my fault.

'Jesus!' Miss Decima groaned. 'I didn't realize I was going to be treated to a performance by the divine Miss Sarah Bernhardt. Stephen, stop complaining. This is all marvellous news.'

I blinked. 'It is?'

'Of course!' said Miss Decima. 'Jarvis is finally off your back, and we're closer to catching the murderer than ever before!'

I didn't think it was fair to describe Jarvis as *off my back* when he was dead, but I didn't see the point in arguing with her. She turned to her desk. Every single piece of evidence we'd collected was there: the list of suspects, the map of the study, the plans of Tithe Hall, the cyanotype, the crime-scene sketch.

'I admit that, at times, I have lost sight of this investigation,' she said. 'We have indulged ourselves, and allowed ourselves to forget that it was our intention to solve this murder *scientifically*. We have spent four days removing untruths from the wealth of material before us. Ghosts, blackmail, poison, photography, inheritances ... Now, at last, we can focus on the facts that remain. A locked room. A scratching at the door. Blood on the wadding. Targets in the trees. *These* are the only details that matter.'

I shook my head. 'But . . . we've tried everything we can think of, Miss Decima, and we're still no closer to working it out. We don't have a clue who did it, how they did it, or why. We're further away than *ever*!'

'On the contrary, Stephen,' she said coolly. 'It is only when the comet is at *aphelion* – the furthest extent of its orbit, the furthest point from the sun – that it can begin its return. So, too, has our investigation reached its critical turning point. With every passing moment, we come closer to the truth. Better yet, the murderer had just been forced to show their hand by killing again! And whom did they kill, Stephen?'

'Jarvis,' I said blankly.

'Precisely! A moron! A man who's proved himself to be utterly incapable of solving this mystery! So, answer me this, Stephen: *why* would the murderer go to such lengths to kill such a stupid man?'

I took a breath. 'Because – because he'd worked out who did it.'

'*Bravo*, Stephen. Like a stopped clock telling the right time twice a day, Jarvis had somehow managed to say something that was correct. The murderer had to kill him before he revealed the truth. And we must discover what that is.'

I gasped. 'Jarvis's notebook – he wrote everything in it. I saw it sticking out of his jacket pocket when we went into the drawing room!'

'Splendid!' said Miss Decima. 'Try not to disturb the body too much when you get it. And don't tread in his blood either; that'll be a dead giveaway.'

With that, she turned back to the evidence and started

arranging it before her. I blinked. 'You . . . you want me to ransack his corpse?'

'Yes, and be quick about it. We don't want the murderer to get their hands on it before we do.'

I stared at her in disbelief. Was I *really* going to walk through an empty house containing a double murderer, unarmed, and steal something from a dead body, just because she told me to?

Of course I was. I made my way to the door, trying to work out the point at which my life had stopped making sense.

'And Stephen?'

I turned around, but Miss Decima didn't meet my eye. She was gazing out of the window, to the point where the treetops were being beaten into a frenzy.

'Watch how you go,' she muttered. 'With a storm like this, I doubt anyone would hear you scream.'

51

Monday, 23 May, 6.00 p.m.

I made my way through the house as quickly as I could. The corridors were dark and gloomy now, the storm making the electric lights flicker on and off around me. A door had been left open somewhere, and wind was whipping through the corridors, rattling picture frames against the walls.

The drawing-room doors were shut. My hand was trembling as I turned the handles and slowly opened them. A part of me that was certain that I'd look inside to find the dead body gone or, worse, Jarvis sat up with his face all covered in gore, just like the Viscount had been. Or I'd open the doors to find the murderer standing inside, finally unveiled.

But, of course, the room was just as I'd last seen it. There was Jarvis's body, lying in a pool of blood beside the marble bust. My stomach flipped at the sight of it. I couldn't imagine what kind of person would pick up a big heavy bust and bring it down on another man's head like that.

Probably the same kind of person who'd pick a corpse's pocket.

I swallowed. I could see the shape of the notebook in Jarvis's jacket. I gulped and knelt beside him to pull it free; slowly, the notebook inched out . . .

Clang.

The sound made me leap out of my skin. Something had fallen out of his pocket and on to the floor: his metal calipers – the ones he'd used on Mr Stokes – had been tucked behind the notebook. I closed my eyes, let out a shaky sigh of relief and carefully placed them back in his pocket. I got to my feet, taking a final glance at his body. I had to make sure it looked right – I couldn't risk anyone noticing what I'd just done. I arranged his jacket carefully, straightening the sleeves and collar.

There it was. A tiny detail. The kind that only a servant notices. I knelt close to the body again, as close as I could stomach, trying to work out if what I was seeing was really there.

Tiny black specks, all over his hair. Soot. I glanced down at his hands. His fingertips were stained with soot, too.

Outside, the storm screamed. It was even closer now, great waves of wind swelling over World's End and battering the house. There was no time to waste – I had to get back to Miss Decima and give her the notebook, now. I closed the drawing-room doors behind me and paced down the corridor, my skin itching with fear, trying as hard as I could not to think about the look in Jarvis's dead eyes when I –

'Stephen!'

A hand clapped my shoulder. I couldn't help myself – I screamed. It was Mrs Pearce, glaring at me with a face like bad milk.

'What are you doing out here? You're supposed to be in your room!'

I gasped with relief. My heart was going like the Grand National. 'S-sorry, Mrs Pearce. I had to get something for Miss Decima.' I paused. 'What are *you* doing out here?'

Mrs Pearce shifted. 'Lettice is insisting I make her some tea. Why? What's it to you?'

We both gazed at each other uneasily, neither of us trusting the other.

'Well, I'd better get going,' I said, backing away.

Mrs Pearce grabbed my arm. 'No, you don't. I need you downstairs. There's no way I can carry a full tea set for Lettice and a whole cake for Gilbert up three flights of stairs on my own.'

Gilbert was better, then. I thought fast. 'Miss Decima won't like to be left waiting –'

'She can start learning; it'll do her the world of good. Honestly, the things that woman used to get up to! I could tell you stories that would make your hair stand on end, Stephen. This way, please.'

She marched off. I cursed under my breath and followed her downstairs. There was nothing I could do – she'd already been looking at me suspiciously. The quicker I got this done, the quicker I could get back upstairs to Miss Decima.

'What a storm!' Mrs Pearce muttered. 'Rain enough to soak the dead in their graves. That causeway will be six feet under by now. Stephen, get the kettle on and help me with these.'

I filled the kettle and heaved it on to the range. Mrs Pearce was already taking out the cups and handing them down to me.

'Honestly, the state of this service! Mr Stokes is getting slack. It wasn't like this when Stokes Senior was in charge, let me tell you. His father might've been a demon for the drink, but at least he ran a tidy ship!'

I glanced over my shoulder. How long was this going to take?

'That's right – thirty years I've been here,' said Mrs Pearce, like I'd asked her a question. 'From scullery maid right up to housekeeper. Does anyone ever ask my opinion? Believe you me, Stephen, I've seen it all. There's no one who knows more secrets about this place than me!'

I paused, one hand on the plate she'd just passed to me. 'Do you know what the old family scandal is?'

'Ha! Which one do you want? There's plenty to pick from! But I'm not one to gossip, so we'll leave it at that.'

I put down the plate, counted to ten in my head and waited. Mrs Pearce lasted seven seconds.

'There's Lawrence Welt's murder,' she said. 'He was a tough man, cold as you like, but no one deserves to die the way he did. Mr Stokes swears blind that the whole thing was an accident, but, if you ask me, that man's always been far too loyal for his own good.'

I glanced up in surprise. 'Mr Stokes was *there*? When Lawrence Welt died?'

'Of course!' she replied. 'He was the one who ran up to the house to say that he'd been shot. He was only Under-Butler back then, assisting on the hunt with his father. By the time anyone got down to the river, Lawrence Welt was dead and Conrad was sitting right by his corpse, without so much as a tear in his eyes.' She shuddered. 'Twenty years, Mr Stokes hid the truth for that odious man. It's not like me to speak ill of the dead, but, mark my words Stephen, if there's a Hell, Conrad Welt is roasting in it. *Everyone* knows the real reason he killed his father. And it wasn't for money, let me tell you!'

I took a cup from her, my heart pounding. The kettle had begun to hiss behind me. 'Why did he do it?'

'Ha! Wouldn't you like to know? My lips are sealed, Stephen. We've no time for idle gossip now!'

She made it to twelve seconds this time.

'Yes, a bachelor his whole life but always with an eye for the ladies, that Conrad,' she muttered. 'Got better as he got older, but he wasn't so careful back then.'

I had stopped breathing some time ago. 'What happened?'

Mrs Pearce harrumphed. 'He had a reputation, let me put

it that way. I used to make the maids work in pairs, so they were never alone in a room with him. He never tried it with *me*, of course, because he knew exactly what I'd say to him if he did!'

'That was surely it, Mrs Pearce.'

She sighed. 'But there's only so much you can do, isn't there? I work with what I'm given. I can't protect someone if they already have a bad character.'

The hiss of the kettle was rising now, the copper drumming as it swelled. 'Like who?'

Mrs Pearce didn't reply at first. She was too busy rooting around in the back of the cupboard.

'Miss Decima's old ladies' maid. *Elsie*, her name was. Turns out she and Conrad had been meeting for months in secret, and then she was with child and there was no doubting it was his.' She handed down a milk jug. 'Conrad had to confess everything to his father, and, bless my soul, what a falling out! You could hear it though the whole house. Miss Decima had her sacked for it, and Lawrence sent her back to London. She used to write to Conrad asking for help. I always recognized her letters when they came in. But he never replied, the bounder.'

I took the jug. If I said one wrong word now, it would all fall apart. 'What happened to her?'

'Ha! Who knows. She had the baby. I asked a housekeeper I was friends with in London to keep an eye on her, but then she disappeared and no one heard from her ever again. She probably ended up on the streets, poor thing. Let's face it, she wouldn't have got work as a ladies' maid after that!' She paused for a moment. 'It's funny – I haven't thought about her in years. It's only with all the goings-on this last week that I even remembered it at all.'

The kettle was boiling now. 'A baby,' I said.

'That's right, a baby. I often wonder what must have happened to them. They'd be about twenty by now – Lawrence sent them away just before he died. Conrad won't have left them anything. He always denied that the child was his. But, illegitimate or not, a child is still a child!'

She heaved herself out of the cupboard.

'Right! That's the last of them. You get a tray and I'll . . . Oh, Stephen, for heaven's sake, can't you see to that kettle? I can barely hear myself think –'

I never heard the rest of what she said. I was already racing up the servants' staircase three steps at a time, the kettle overflowing behind me.

52

Monday, 23 May, 6.44 p.m.

'A child,' I gasped. 'An illegitimate child.'

Miss Decima sat staring at me in disbelief. I had run all the way back to the Nursery. I pulled out a chair and sat as close to her as I could, my words tumbling over each other. The rain outside was coming harder now, filling the room with a dull white roar.

'Mrs Pearce. She just told me. Conrad had a child. In secret. With your maid. Elsie. Lawrence Welt sent her away. Just before he died.'

Miss Decima's face lit up. 'Elsie. Of course. But . . . a *child*?'

I nodded. 'Mrs Pearce said she wrote to Conrad asking for help, but he never wrote back.'

'Yes,' said Miss Decima quietly. 'She wasn't the first maid that Conrad tried his luck with, and I very much doubt she was the last. I had warned her about him; told her to steer well clear of him, in fact. But the girl had other ideas. She never much listened to me at the best of times. When I found out that they'd been caught, I was furious with her. Dismissed her on the spot and told her never to return.' She drummed her fingers on her walking stick. 'I had no idea that she was with child. She wrote to me once, asking for help, but she made no mention of it. I never wrote back. I was too busy with my work at the time, and I was *angry*, too. The last thing I wanted was to get drawn into some mess with a disgraced maid. Of course, if I'd known . . .'

She trailed off, her face flickering with doubt. I leant forwards. 'Mrs Pearce said that Conrad and Lawrence had a big argument about it. Maybe they had another one, on the day of the hunting accident. Maybe *that's* why Conrad shot his father.'

Miss Decima nodded, her mind whirring. 'And all this time, he had a child. Not an *heir*, of course –'

'Unless he changed his will,' I said. 'A week before he died.'

Her eyes shot to me. 'You think –'

I nodded. 'The second man. The one who came into the clerk's office, with the Viscount. The one that no one recognized.'

Miss Decima's eyes were widening right in front of me. She clapped her hands. 'Come. We have a new motive: an illegitimate heir to the fortune. Someone who murdered Conrad, in order to benefit from this new inheritance. We must draw all this together, Stephen, to find the one and only remaining answer!'

She turned back to her desk and began rapidly arranging the evidence in front of her: the plans of the house, the map of the study, the list of suspects, the sketch of the crime scene, the cyanotype. I stared at everything, baffled. It was like gazing up at the night sky, trying to link the stars into constellations that made sense.

She whipped out a hand. 'Jarvis's notebook – do you have it?'

I gave it over. She took it from me and started flicking through it at rapid speed, her eyes darting left to right. The look on her face changed quickly as she took it in what Jarvis had written: irritation, confusion, then bafflement, before opening up the final page . . . and the sharpness came back to her eyes.

'Well,' she said archly. 'That certainly answers *one* of our questions, if not the entire mystery.'

'What does it say, Miss Decima?'

'Never mind.' She slapped the notebook down on the desk. 'For now, we must start from the beginning. Talk me through everything that happened on Thursday morning. Leave nothing out.'

I groaned. '*Again?*'

'Yes, again!'

I closed my eyes and went back to the morning of the murder. 'There was a knock at the Nursery door. It was Mr Stokes. He said I had to help Lowen unseal the guest bedrooms.'

'And then?'

'I went upstairs and got Temperance, and Mrs Pearce shouted at me. I could hear hammering downstairs.'

'And then?'

'I ended up on the first floor. I thought I could run past the study door and find another staircase, and that's when I noticed the crossbow bolt was missing.'

'And then?'

It was like being back in the dock. 'I saw the blood on the wadding. I called for the Viscount, but he didn't reply. I tried to look through the keyhole, but it was sealed with wax.'

'Then?'

'Lowen came. He told me to get Mr Stokes, so I ran downstairs and found Temperance and told her to get him.'

'How long was Lowen on his own?'

I fumbled. 'A minute. Maybe less. Not long.'

'And then?'

'We broke down the door.'

'And then?'

'I ran into the room. Fell, really.'

'And what did you see?'

I thought it over. 'Nothing, at first. All the lights were off.'

It was like she'd been electrocuted. She sat bolt upright. 'What did you just say?'

I blinked. 'The lights were all off. It was too dark to see anything.'

She stared at me in disbelief. 'Jesus fucking Christ, Stephen! You told me that the first thing you saw was the fucking fishbowl!'

I nodded, confused. 'Well, it *was*. But Lowen had to turn the lights on first.' I pointed at my hand-drawn map of the study. 'See? That's why he was behind the door. Where the switch is.'

Miss Decima's face was turning bright red in front of me.

'Stephen, I told you to tell me everything! *Everything!* Every last detail!'

'I didn't think it mattered.'

'Of course it matters! Everything matters! And that one detail has just made all the difference in the world!' She grabbed the lapels of my jacket. 'Conrad was killed sometime between making that telephone call to Stokes and you breaking into the room. Why would he have made that phone call while sitting in darkness?' She suddenly froze. 'Unless . . . No, impossible. *Unless . . .* But then that would mean . . .'

I watched as she muttered to herself, her eyes darting left to right once more. It was like she was reading another notebook at double speed, one that existed only in her head, recounting the whole sorry story from beginning to end. 'Of course. *Of course!* How could I not see it before?'

'See *what?*'

She didn't answer. Instead, she scooped all the papers into her lap and rapped her stick on the ground. 'Hurry, Stephen. Get me to my bath chair. We have no time to lose.'

'Where are we going?'

'Where do you think? The study. I've just worked out how the murder was done.'

53

Monday, 23 May, 6.59 p.m.

The walk to the lift and the ride up to the first floor felt like they took forever. I pushed the bath chair along the corridor as fast as I could, watching as we swelled and shrank in the butler's mirrors. The storm was lashing the windowpanes now, thickening the shadows and sending the curtains rippling. The study was gloomy when we got there; I flicked the switch, snapping the room back into bright.

'Over there, Stephen,' Miss Decima ordered. 'Take me to the desk.'

I wheeled her over and she flung her papers over the top, knocking over an inkstand and sending books crashing to the floor. 'Be careful, Miss Decima,' I muttered. 'It's a crime scene.'

'A crime we are about to solve, Stephen.' She gazed around the room, nodding frantically. 'Yes, it makes sense now. The paths are converging; a picture is finally beginning to emerge.' She rifled through the papers and held up the cyanotype print, cackling with glee. 'And of course! *Of course!* No *wonder* we could not see it!'

I gazed at her, utterly baffled. 'See *what?*'

She turned to face me. 'Indulge me. Turn out the lights. Draw the curtains. I wish to see the room exactly as it was when you first burst in.'

'Are you sure that's wise, Miss Decima?'

'Yes, Stephen. Some things only reveal themselves in darkness.'

I did as I was told, pulling the curtains and then flicking the switch by the door so that the room was fully dark. The only light came from the glow of the corridor outside.

'Now, wheel me over to the light switch,' she ordered. 'And then show me exactly what happened when you came in on Thursday morning, one step at a time.'

I groaned. '*Again?*'

'Yes, again!'

I pushed her to the light switch and stepped back. 'I ran into the door with Lowen, and it broke.'

'Show me where you ended up.'

I took a few stumbling steps forward. 'About here.'

'You were standing?'

'Kneeling.'

'Then bloody well kneel, Stephen.'

I did as I was told. 'Like this.'

'That's right,' said Miss Decima. 'You knelt in a pitch-black study, dazed and unseeing, while Lowen ran in behind you and flicked the light switch. How long until the lights came on?'

I shrugged. 'A few seconds? Three, maybe?'

'*And then there was light.*'

She flicked the switch and the room lit up in dazzling brightness. I blinked away the spots from my eyes. 'Now,' said Miss Decima. 'Tell me what you saw.'

I rubbed my eyes and pointed to the desk. 'The fishbowl. It was right there.'

'And then?'

I traced a finger along the back wall. 'The oxygen tanks.'

'And then?'

'The Viscount's body.'

'Exactly,' said Miss Decima. 'But tell me, Stephen: what did you *not* see?'

I gawped at her. 'How am I supposed to answer that?'

She pointed to the desk. 'Look at the cyanotype of the murder scene, and then look at the room in front of you. Tell me what is different.'

I held up the photograph, and then looked around the room. It was no use: they were both exactly the same. There was the desk, there was the chair, there was the fireplace.

'Try above the mantelpiece,' she said.

I looked above the mantelpiece. 'There's nothing there –'

'Isn't there?'

I opened my mouth to argue with her, but my mouth stayed open. Finally, after all this time, all this confusion, I had worked out what had changed about the room.

'The butler's mirror, Miss Decima,' I said. 'It's gone.'

I pointed above the fireplace. There, like a ghost, was the faintest outline of a circle on the wall, where the wallpaper had discoloured over time. There was even a tiny hole near the top, where a nail had been removed.

'*That's* what was different!' I gasped. 'There was a butler's mirror above the mantelpiece when I came in on Wednesday, and it had gone the next morning!'

Miss Decima nodded. 'Precisely, Stephen. It *should* have been in the cyanotype of the study, too, but it wasn't. Professor Muller had removed it for the photograph. Because if it was there –'

'The flashbulb,' I said breathlessly.

'Bravo,' said Miss Decima. 'The reflected glare would have spoilt the image. So Professor Muller removed the butler's mirror before he took the picture. *That's* why we couldn't spot the difference between the cyanotype and the crime-scene sketch. The butler's mirror was missing from both of them.'

It was all making sense now. 'The one that suddenly

appeared on the second floor – the new one that I noticed on Saturday. It must have been the one that was here!' I frowned. 'But . . . why didn't it just get hung up back here? There's not even a nail in the wall any more.'

'Because the murderer removed it, Stephen.'

'*Why?*'

'You tell me.'

I turned to the empty patch on the wall. I thought about the first time I'd walked into this room and seen it: the way it made me look so small, so tiny and insignificant. The way it warped the room around it so that all the walls and windows, the ceiling and bookshelves, became twisted into shape . . .

There was a sudden snap of lightning outside. And the answer came to me, all at once.

'The mirror was removed,' I said, 'because the murderer didn't want me to see what was behind me.'

'Very good, Stephen. And the murderer didn't want that because . . .'

I saw it again, exactly as it happened: Lowen, frozen at the light switch, all the colour draining from his face; Temperance standing in the doorway, clinging to the frame, her mouth open in a silent scream; Mr Stokes in the corridor behind her, the teapot smashing on the floorboards at his feet.

The teapot.

'Oh, my God,' I whispered, as the whole truth came crashing down on top of me, *cataclysmic.*

Then all the lights in the house went out.

54

Monday, 23 May, 7.07 p.m.

The study was pitch-black; all the lights in the corridor were off, too. I could hear shouts throughout the house, footsteps pacing the ceiling above us, servants calling for each other.

'The electrics have gone, Miss Decima,' I said. 'The storm must have short-circuited them.'

'Are you *quite certain* of that, Stephen?'

Even in the darkness, I could feel the weight of her look. 'You don't think –'

'That's exactly what I think.'

My stomach dropped. The thunder bellowed. She was right. The murderer had cut the electricity to the house, and I understood why. Tithe Hall would be in chaos. No one would notice him sneaking through the darkness.

'Block the door,' Miss Decima ordered. 'We'll barricade ourselves inside.'

'The lock's broken. It won't keep him out if he comes here.' I grabbed the bath chair. 'Have you still got that knife?'

Miss Decima stared at me, alarmed. 'Yes, of course.'

'Good. Have it ready.'

She gripped her chair in alarm. 'Stephen –'

'Stop arguing with me!'

We charged out of the study and down the hall, careering around the corners as fast as I dared. The corridors were dark tunnels now; the storm was wild and bristling at the window-panes, clawing to get inside. But I couldn't think about any of that; I had to get Miss Decima downstairs and back to the Nursery – somewhere I could lock the doors and keep us safe. I turned the final corner and there was the lift door, right ahead of us. I slammed my hand on the button . . . and nothing happened.

'An electric lift,' said Miss Decima drily. 'In a power cut. *That* was your plan, Stephen.'

My guts clenched. We were stuck on the first floor. 'Wait here!'

I flew down the rest of the corridor, heading towards the shouts that I could hear coming from the main stairwell. The entrance hall below was bedlam: the front doors were open and a gale was howling inside, maids scrambling to steady the ornaments in near-total darkness while Mr Stokes handed out candles and barked instructions. There was no way I could get Miss Decima downstairs on foot without anyone –

I froze. Someone was racing up the stairs to meet me – Temperance, a candle in her hand. She caught sight of me in the darkness and nearly jumped out of her skin. '*Jesus!* What are you doing? You almost –'

I dragged her up the last of the stairs and held her close. 'Get to the Nursery, as fast as you can. Lock the side exit and get ready to barricade us inside. Get a weapon.'

Her eyes widened. 'But –'

'The murderer's going to kill again.'

She opened her mouth, but another peal of thunder burst above us. She nodded quickly and turned to leave.

'And . . . Temperance,' I said. 'Be careful.'

She nodded again, just the once. And there we were again, a final time, in that moment of whirling chaos – just the two of us, held in the golden light of her candle. And then she turned and was gone, forever. There was no time to lose. I tore back to Miss Decima, spinning her chair around and steering her down the corridor.

'Listen, Miss Decima. There's only one way for us to get downstairs. But it's not going to be easy.'

I threw open the first door I came to. There was the servant's staircase, a tight twisting coil in the darkness.

'No one will expect us to use these now. It's the safest way for us to get down. It means you'll have to walk, but . . .'

I trailed off. Miss Decima was already pinning her stick into the carpet and pushing herself to her feet. 'What are you waiting for? Come on, Stephen!'

I took her by the arm and led her downstairs, step by spiralled step. It was slow, exhausting work: at every moment, I was expecting Miss Decima to slip and fall, or for the sound of footsteps to come racing up the stairs to meet us, and there would be the murderer, a knife in his hand . . . But we reached the ground floor, and I led Miss Decima out into the corridor. I felt a clutch in my heart as I watched her lean against the wall to catch her breath. Her face was creased in pain. The walking stick in her hand didn't shake; it fluttered. She looked even worse than Nan had, right at the end.

'Wait here,' I said, turning around. 'I'll go back and get your bath chair.'

She shook her head. 'No. No time. We walk.'

'It's too far. You might fall.'

'It's preferable to dying. Now stop wasting my time and help me!'

I held her up and we staggered down the corridor, an inch at a time, as the house descended into chaos behind us. I kept all my senses trained, waiting for the moment that the darkness would suddenly shift and *he* would leap out of the shadows towards us, eyes white with rage . . .

But finally we turned the corner, and there were the

Nursery doors, already opened for us. Temperance had made it, and not a moment too soon: Miss Decima was exhausted, her face red and dripping sweat.

'We made it,' I said, leading her through the doors. 'Look – we're safe! We'll barricade the doors and –'

I froze.

The hallway was empty. The side exit was open, flapping in the wind. Through the darkness, I could just make out the forest in the distance. There were two figures, barely visible through sheets of rain.

One of them was Temperance.

And the other was a man, dragging her, screaming, into the trees.

55

Monday, 23 May, 7.29 p.m.

I watched in horror as Temperance was carried into the forest. The murderer had been here the whole time; he had been lying in wait for us. And I had sent Temperance . . .

I made the decision fast. I heaved Miss Decima into her bedroom with all my strength and more or less dropped her into her desk chair. 'Don't move.'

She held up a hand, gasping for breath. '*Stephen –*'

I raced out before she could stop me. I grabbed the caulking iron from the side exit, left there from the night I'd sealed the doors, and flew across the grounds to the point where I'd seen Temperance disappear. The rain was a downpour now, and my clothes were soaked in seconds, the lawns hissing around me like the roll of a snare drum.

I met the trees and kept on running. I knew they couldn't be much further ahead of me; the murderer couldn't drag Temperance faster than I could run. And I knew exactly where he was taking her, too.

I found the path and flew down it, until I reached the wooden bridge over the waterfall. The surface of the lake was churning under the downpour, like it was boiling over; the waterfall was raging white, louder than ever, bursting the riverbanks. Whole branches were being carried over the edge, crashing into the foam below.

Temperance was nowhere to be seen.

'I know you're out here,' I shouted. 'I know you're hiding!'

No reply. I gripped the caulking iron and turned on the spot, my eyes peeled for any signs of movement around me.

'Just let her go,' I called out, my voice lost to the storm the moment the words left my mouth. 'Let her go, and we can talk it over.'

Silence. I turned, my eyes slowly scanning every tree trunk.

And then I saw it – a shape hunched low in the ferns, barely a stone's throw away. The curve of a back.

Someone crouched, lying in wait.

I tightened my grip on the iron and stepped forwards, silently. 'It's over. We know how you did it. And we know *why* you did it, too.'

The murderer didn't move. I knew he would be lying on top of Temperance, his hand clamped over her mouth, stopping her from screaming. He thought I hadn't spotted him; he thought I was going to walk straight past and carry on further down the slope. I had to make sure he didn't hear me creep towards him.

'It was clever, we'll give you that,' I said, keeping my voice low and steady. 'And it was nothing like we thought. *That's* why it took us so long to work it out. But we got there, in the end. We know everything now.'

The murderer stayed where he was. I was only a few steps away. I kept going, waiting for the moment to strike.

'This had nothing to do with money. This was revenge, pure and simple. For the way that Conrad treated your mother, Elsie. And it worked. You've killed your father, so don't make it any worse. Just let her go, Lowen.'

Lowen stayed frozen on the ground, crouched and waiting. This was it. I was right beside him. If I kept going, he'd jump up behind me. If I leapt now, and got it wrong . . .

'We know who you really are,' I said. 'Conrad had a son that he abandoned, twenty years ago. And that son is you.'

It was now or never. I gripped the iron and leapt into the ferns, raising it above my head to strike . . .

I was wrong. Lowen wasn't lying on his front. He was lying on his back, his coat thrown over his body. His face stuck out from the top, pale and sodden. He'd been dead for hours.

'It was a daughter, actually.'

The voice came from close behind. I swung around, just as Temperance brought a hammer down on my head, and my world turned black.

56

Monday, 23 May, 7.44 p.m.

I opened my eyes.

I was lying on my back, the trees twisting above me. My head throbbed and my clothes were soaked. My mouth tasted of blood.

Something was tugging at my ankles. I raised my head to look, but dropped it straight back down. It hurt too much to move. I knew what I had seen, though: Temperance tying my legs together with cord.

'What was it she said?' she muttered, tugging at the knots. 'Something like *Your answer is right, but your reasoning is wrong.* She was spot on there. Not that she'll be saying it for much longer.'

I tried to move my hands, but I couldn't. They were bound at my chest. Temperance tightened the cord on my ankles a final time.

'He did everything he could to break my mother, you know,' she explained calmly. 'He didn't just abandon her. He made sure that no one ever believed her. He made sure she never got to work again. Her own family turned their backs on her. She died alone, penniless. The things she had to do. The things *I* had to do . . .'

She trailed off, checking the knots again, wiping the rain from her eyes. Her hands were raw and ragged, her clothes smeared in dirt.

'I spent years trying to find a way back so I could kill him.

It took me so long, Stephen. I worked so hard at it, and it all came together so perfectly. It was the only thing that had ever gone right for me in my whole life. And then you and that *bitch* . . . You ruined it. You ruined everything.' She was crying now, her voice choked with tears. 'Look at what you made me do.'

She nodded to the body of Lowen, stretched out in the ferns beside us.

'He was *nothing*. Some nasty little twat who had nothing to do with any of this. Then he went snooping around looking for you and found those targets and . . . Well, what else could we do?'

'*We?*' I tried to say. But nothing came out – a mumble drowned out by wind.

Temperance grabbed the rope that bound my ankles and began to drag me across the ground, her breath heaving with the effort. I tried to fight against her, but I had no strength. My hands were bound too tightly; my head was swimming. All I could do was watch the trees slipping past me.

'One . . . death. That was . . . all we . . . wanted,' she panted. 'I *promised* him it was – just the one. We knew we'd have to . . . separate you, if we were going to . . . fix the . . . mess you made. He's up there right now, finishing . . . finishing the job.'

Miss Decima. I felt my back slide across slick wood. She'd brought me to the bridge. I could hear the waterfall below the wooden planks, the white noise of water. Temperance was kneeling at my side, stuffing rocks into my pockets. And I understood right away what was about to happen.

'I know you can't swim,' she said, not meeting my eyes. 'They say it's quick, drowning. It'll look like a suicide. Killed the Viscount, killed Jarvis, killed Lowen, killed Miss Decima, confessed to everything in a letter, drowned yourself. Edwin's so desperate to put the whole thing to rest that they'll never even question it. Even the ropes on your hands and feet won't make a difference, if they find them.'

She wiped her hands clean on my clothes and leant back, bracing her feet against me.

'I'm sorry, Stephen. I really, *really* didn't want to have to kill you.'

I found my voice. '*Temperance!*'

With one great push, she heaved me over the edge of the bridge. For a single second, there was nothing around me but air and rain as I tumbled through space, like the comet crashing to the Earth, before the water cut through me like cold slate and the pain in my head didn't matter one bit.

57

Monday, 23 May, 7.48 p.m.

The breath was knocked out of me in one blow. I opened my mouth and water poured in, choking me. I lifted my head above the water, spluttering for breath. '*Hel—*'

Crack. The first boulder hit my side, sending a savage bolt through my ribs. I tried to grab it, but my bound hands slid across it and the water dragged me over the edge of the waterfall, plummeting to the pool below. I hit the water hard, and just kept going. The pain was everywhere now, inside and around me, like the water.

You have to fight it, I told myself. *You have to . . .*

Crack. Another boulder, this time against my back. I kicked and flailed helplessly as my head sank beneath the water again. The current was too strong; the stones in my pocket were too heavy; my leather shoes slipped on the riverbed whenever I tried to stand. The water kept pushing me on, on, on. *You can't fight a river.*

Another fall, another drop, another crack against stone. The river dragged me down, pulverizing me over and over. I could hear the roar of the turbine, getting closer with every second, screaming over the rush of water. There was no escaping it. I realized, with horror, what was about to happen: the water would drag me straight through the sluice gate and then under the wheel, crushing my bones and spitting me out the other side. Or it would break me and hold me under, and I would see out my final moments drowning and choking in agony in the dark.

And the truth suddenly became clear to me, even through the pain and the panic: I was going to die. I could fight against it as much I wanted, but, whatever happened, I was going to die. I had reached the point when I had to accept that life was going to crush me like a fly between two clapped hands, and that it could be done so much more easily to a man like me. Since the first moment that I had arrived at World's End – the moment I had opened that letter on my bunk – my fate had been sealed. I'd been flung into a river with no hope of escape, and the water went in only one direction. What made it worse, made it more painful, was to try to fight it.

So why bother?

The turbine loomed up through the darkness. The roar of machinery was everywhere. I closed my eyes and thought of Nan.

You can't fight a river.

My back hit the stone slipway.

But half the fun is in the fighting, Stephen.

I flung up my bound hands and grabbed the bar across the sluice gate at the final second. The metal scraped the skin from my palms, but the rope caught the bar and held me before I was dragged inside. The force of the current flipped me over, twisting my hands tighter. I was belly down, gasping for breath, inches from death. But I had stopped moving. I was alive.

I pulled up with all my strength, heaving my head above the water. I could feel the wheel pounding the river at my feet as I kicked and floundered to stay afloat. The river battered me over and over. I was stuck; all that stopped me from being dragged under the wheel was the rope that bound my hands.

I fought the current and dragged myself to my knees on to the stone slipway. The water pounded against my chest; the rope strained against the bar and cut deep into my wrists, but it held. I was inside the turbine shed: I could see the dusty wooden floorboards right beside me, at head height, but they might as well have been a million miles away. My hands and feet were bound; there was nothing to grab. If I pulled the rope from the bar, I would last perhaps a second before the river drove me under the wheel and crushed me to pieces.

But the rope was breaking: I could feel the strands splitting on the bar, one by one.

You have to jump.

'I'll die.'

We're all going to die.

'Not like this.'

Stop fucking complaining and get on with it, Stephen.

I cried out, and in one great leap lifted my knees and pushed both feet against the slipway, launching myself backwards and splitting the rope as I went.

My top half cleared the floorboards, but that was it. The river pushed me on. I slid across the dusty floor, my fingertips scrabbling desperately for something to grab ... and found a crack in the floorboards, just before my legs hit the wheel. I prised my fingernails into the wood, my whole body shaking with the effort, and heaved myself out of the water a hair at a time, throwing my legs on to the floorboards and over the edge.

And then, as easily as climbing out of bed, I rolled on to the floor and was saved.

I lay gasping in the darkness, as the wheel roared on and on beside me. I had made it. I was here. I was alive.

Miss Decima. They were going to kill her: Temperance, and whoever she was working with, were going to kill her.

I would not allow it. I would not, could not, let her die.

I sat up. Temperance had been banking on me drowning fast: she'd made the knots quickly, and badly. I could move just one of my arms properly – the other was broken, screaming with pain. I held it to my chest and untied the ropes with my good hand until I could pull my feet free, water gushing from my clothes as I stood up. I emptied my pockets, letting the stones thud on to the wooden boards. Then I limped out of the door and stepped into the forest.

The rain had stopped. I dragged myself up the slope, step by limping step, past the waterfall and over the bridge, faster and faster as I got used to the pain. I was bleeding a lot, from my arm and maybe a dozen other places, but I had to keep a clear head. There was Lowen's body, dumped in the ferns where I'd found him. My caulking iron was still beside him. I picked it up and made my way through the dripping trees, until Tithe Hall stood gleaming in the moonlight before me.

The storm had passed; the clouds had parted. There, hanging above the house, was the comet. The tails had come back, both of them. One blue, one white. Two tails disguised as one.

The house was fully dark. The power was still off. I could hear the shouts and chaos echoing all the way across the lawn. But there, at the Nursery window, was a single square of flickering candlelight.

Miss Decima's bedroom.

I heaved myself across the grass, limping past the maze and the stone fountains, up to the Nursery entrance. The door was still open; I could hear voices coming from inside. I crept down the hallway, staying as close to the wall as I could, knowing the floorboards would creak if I stepped in the centre. I was trying to make myself a ghost. Invisible. *Indiscernible.*

I came to the bedroom doorway, the iron held above me. The voices were even clearer now. I recognized all three of them, of course: I already knew who I would find in Miss Decima's room. Then I took a final breath, and in one swift movement I stepped inside.

The first person I saw was Miss Decima, sat in her chair, holding a metal tea caddy in one hand and a lit candle in the other. She tried to pretend that she hadn't seen me, but it was too late. The others had already turned to face me. I must have looked a state, soaking wet and bleeding from ten places with a broken arm clinging to my chest.

'How – how did you . . .' Temperance spluttered, gazing at me in horror.

I didn't reply. Instead, I let my gaze settle on the third person in the room. On the man cradling the crossbow aimed directly at Miss Decima's throat.

'Ah, Stephen,' said Mr Stokes, his voice sadder and wearier than anything I'd ever heard. 'You find us at something of an impasse.'

58

Monday, 23 May, 8.14 p.m.

We stood facing each other: me, Miss Decima, Temperance, Mr Stokes. Like four points in a constellation, with no one quite knowing what shape it made yet.

'What are you doing?' Temperance hissed at Mr Stokes. 'Shoot him!'

'I've already made my position perfectly clear,' said Miss Decima calmly, holding up the candle and rattling the tea caddy. 'Conrad confiscated the rest of my bomb-making equipment, but he never found this. *Picric acid* – highly explosive. Shoot Stephen, and I'll drop the candle, and this entire section of the house will be dust.'

'She's bluffing,' said Temperance. 'She'd never sacrifice herself for anyone. Shoot him, now!'

Mr Stoke's eyes flicked between us. The crossbow in his hands was scorched and burned, his hands smeared with soot and ash. He gazed at me with a face so heavy with guilt that he looked almost twice his age.

'I never thought it was you,' I said quietly. 'Not once. I always thought you were innocent.'

Mr Stokes shook his head. 'I never lied to you, Stephen.'

'I know you didn't,' I said. 'You looked me dead in the eye and swore to me that you didn't kill him.'

Holding the caulking iron, I reached out over Miss Decima's desk and batted a book off the shelf. It hit the floorboards at Mr Stokes's feet. A Bible.

'But you did let him die, didn't you?'

Mr Stokes said nothing. That silence told me everything I needed to know.

Miss Decima sighed. 'I *did* try to warn you, Stephen. Science is incapable of untruth: Mr Stokes was always the most likely suspect. But a *two-person murder*... I confess that I never considered that option. The fault lies with me: I spent far too long assuming that the motive was the inheritance. But the motive went back much, much further than that, to the moment of *another* death, twenty years ago – one in which Mr Stokes was also instrumental.' She turned in her chair. 'Care to explain how Lawrence Welt died, Stokes?'

'Don't do it,' snapped Temperance.

Mr Stokes shifted on his feet. His eyes darted between us, like he was trying to balance three plates at once.

'You've managed to keep the secret of what happened that day for twenty years,' Miss Decima continued. 'So why do it? Why protect a murderer?'

Mr Stokes smiled at that. It was the saddest smile I'd ever seen.

'That was the funny thing. It never *was* murder. Everyone was so convinced that Conrad had done away with his father that they never imagined it could be anything else. But the truth was far more complicated than that. It almost invariably is.'

'What are you doing?' Temperance hissed. 'Stop it!'

But Mr Stokes didn't stop. He kept going, his voice as calm and steady as the crossbow levelled at Miss Decima.

'Lawrence and Conrad went hunting on the grounds. I was there to assist, along with my father. It was our job to clear the way, reload their weapons while they talked.' He paused. 'They had a lot to talk about: Elsie, and the mess that Conrad had made of the whole thing. It became an argument, as it always did. It grew and grew, until finally Lawrence Welt told Conrad that he'd brought such shame to the family that he had already decided to write him out of the will completely. That Conrad would never have World's End, or Tithe Hall, or a single penny of the Welt fortune.'

He swallowed.

'I blamed myself for what happened next. I should have sent my father back to the house – put him on some errand, perhaps. By then, his drinking had long been out of hand. I had often glimpsed him sipping from a hip flask when he thought no one was looking. It had become my duty to hide it, to cover his errors and stop him from shaming himself. I was good at it. When we set out from the house that morning, I could tell that he was already drunk.' He took a moment to settle himself. 'At the very least, I should have insisted that *I* be the one to reload the crossbows. But my father was a proud man: he insisted on doing everything himself. I never did learn to stand up to him, until it was far too late.'

He paused.

'It happened quickly. My father was reloading Lawrence's crossbow and his hands slipped just as Lawrence turned to take it from him. The bolt fired directly into Lawrence's eye. He hit the ground and lay there, dying. My father was frozen to the spot; I somehow managed to find my strength and made to run for the house . . . but Conrad stopped me. He told neither of us to move. And then he sat down on a rock beside his father and watched him slowly die.'

He gazed at me.

'That is the truth of it. Conrad did not murder his father: my father was the one to pull the trigger. But Conrad let him die. After that, we were both bound to him, forced to carry out his every command. My father was responsible for Lawrence's death and, because I had stayed when I should have run, I became an accessory. From that point onwards, we were his prisoners.' He smiled. 'I suspect that Conrad rather liked that. He liked having power over people. That was why he had me take my father's place: so that he could continue to control me, to taunt me and humiliate me, for the rest of my life. To remind me that if the truth ever came out, he would see to it that *I* went to prison instead of him. And, as time went on, the hopelessness of my situation became so great that I simply became inured to it.'

Miss Decima nodded. 'Quite. But that's not the only reason you hated him, is it?'

Mr Stokes turned to her, his eyes almost pleading.

'Elsie,' said Miss Decima. 'My old ladies' maid. The one that Conrad used and threw away. You were rather fond of her, weren't you?'

Mr Stokes did not move. His eyes were the only things that changed, reddening at their edges.

'No, Miss Decima,' he said quietly. 'I *loved* her. When her employment was terminated, I wrote to her, confessing my feelings and telling her that I would leave Tithe Hall to join her in London. But then Lawrence Welt died, and I was trapped. Perhaps I could have run and left my father to deal with the consequences, but . . .'

He let the words drift into nothing. Miss Decima nodded.

'You stayed,' she said. 'You never came for Elsie, despite your promise. You never forgave yourself for that.' She turned to face Temperance. 'So when her daughter miraculously appeared from the past, asking for your help . . .'

Temperance stood in the corner, glaring at her like a trapped cat. Her face was twisted with hate.

'Yes, my dear,' said Miss Decima, her eyes gleaming like polished silver knives. 'Now we come to you. You knew all about your father, didn't you? How your mother must have ranted and railed against him: the heartless toff who'd abandoned her, cut her off from her people, left you both to rot. I dread to think what her life must have been like towards the end. *My word*, how you must have despised him.'

'She kept the letter she wrote to you, you know,' said Temperance. 'The one you had sent back. Did you know that? I found it when she died. The fine lady of standing, someone she'd loved like a mother, who could move heaven and earth if she wanted to, but who'd turned her back when she needed you most.' Her jaw clenched. 'She suffered for that. We both did. There's a cruelty to life, Miss Decima, which a lady like you will never understand. My mother died destitute in a workhouse, and Conrad – *that man* – carried on. I doubt he ever thought of her again. The only thing that kept me going was the knowledge that I would never, *ever* let him get away with it. That I would humiliate him, ruin his life, *kill* him, and, when I did it, I'd take his family down with him, too.'

I was shocked by the fury that lashed out of her, white hot and barbed. But Miss Decima just steadily returned her gaze, the candle flickering in her grasp.

'Naturally,' she said. 'But I think we can all agree that you were perfectly capable of doing such a thing by yourself. So, tell me, my dear – let's face it, there's no point being coy now – why *did* you ask Mr Stokes to help you?'

Temperance let her eyes flit between us. I could see her weighing it up: whether to lie, whether to stay silent, whether to tell the truth.

'My mother kept all her letters,' she said quietly. 'Even the ones from Stokes. Telling her of his feelings, saying he'd come to find her, begging for her forgiveness when he changed his mind. So I applied for a job at Tithe Hall. Made up all my references and got an interview with him. And then I told him who I was, and how my mother had never forgiven him for his abandonment of her. And when he explained why he couldn't leave, why he'd spent his life racked with guilt – that *he*, too, was Conrad's prisoner –'

Miss Decima smiled. 'Of course. He was the perfect accomplice. Stokes can hire whoever he wants. No one would ever question his decision, his integrity, when it came to staff. His character is unimpeachable.' She turned to him. 'I imagine it must have been a rather tempting offer for you, too. To make amends for your guilt; to find a way out of your own imprisonment. All you needed was an opportunity. And, before long, you had it. *The comet.* The lockdown. Plans that no one in the house knew about, except you.'

Mr Stokes nodded, slowly.

'Conrad had told me only a little of his plans,' he confessed. 'The rest I worked out for myself. There's an awful lot that you see, as a butler. I read correspondences between him and Herr Muller, and the notes on his desk explaining all his plans for World's End. I began to realize that there was a way to kill him that would create such a scandal that the house and the family would be tarnished forever. The similarities between Conrad's death and his father's death would be raised, and all the gossip about Conrad murdering his own father would be dredged up again, until it was simply taken as fact.'

Miss Decima smiled. 'Of course. All you had to do was plan a murder so outlandish, so impossible, that *no one* would ever be able to solve it.'

'I'll take it from here, Miss Decima.'

I stood on the spot, the caulking iron still held high in my hands. Miss Decima frowned. 'Don't interrupt me, Stephen. I'm just getting to –'

'No,' I said. '*I* want to explain how they did it.'

She snorted. 'Absolutely out of the –'

'*I* solved it, too, Miss Decima. It's only fair.'

She looked like she was about to explode, then thought against it and sulked in her chair instead, muttering furiously about ingratitude. I swallowed, fixing Temperance and Mr Stokes in my gaze. My arm screamed with pain and I felt weak as anything, but I had to keep going.

'You already knew two things,' I began. 'You knew that Conrad was planning to seal everyone in their rooms. But you *also* knew that he'd never seal up the study by himself, no matter what he told people. He was too lazy for that. When the time came, he'd get Mr Stokes to do everything for him. His faithful manservant – the one who kept all his secrets. And, sure enough, that's exactly what happened. Once everyone in the house was locked away, Conrad ordered you to seal his study door and chimney for him. He had too many other things to do: test out the rotenone on his fish, for example. You would even stay the night in the study with him; that had been the plan all along. Which was why he had *two* oxygen tanks in his room, not one.'

Miss Decima's eyes widened. I could tell, without her saying a word, that she hadn't thought of that.

'That's the thing about being a servant,' I said. 'You notice small things. Like that bonfire I spotted on the lawn yesterday. Odd, eh? A bonfire on the grounds, when all the grounds staff have been sacked. I knew something about it was wrong, and now it all makes sense. It was so you could get rid of *that*.' I nodded to the charred crossbow in Mr Stokes's hands. 'It didn't work, of course. The wood was still too wet, after you'd hidden it in the lake for a few days.'

Temperance and Mr Stokes stared at me in amazement. Miss Decima's eyes had started to sparkle with pride.

I turned to Temperance. 'On the night of the murder, *your*

job was simple. You knew you'd be sealed in the Nursery with Miss Decima. You'd spent months convincing everyone that you were wet, weak, hopeless. Crying all the time. That way, no one would ever think that you were capable of carrying out a brutal murder.'

Temperance glared at me, her eyes taunting.

'But then there was an unexpected surprise,' I said. '*Me*. It must have felt like an absolute godsend – an ex-convict, turning up to the house on the day you planned to commit a murder! You *knew* that I'd be the first person the police would blame.' I turned to Mr Stokes. 'Which was why you agreed to hire me in the first place, wasn't it? It didn't matter who'd brought me here: you had a perfect suspect in your sights. You both agreed to change your plan at the final second: *I'd* be placed with Miss Decima in the Nursery, sealing my guilt, and Temperance would go to her own bedroom. After all, it meant she'd still be right where she needed to be, wouldn't it?'

The room was stunned – it was like a curtain had been whipped back, the whole truth revealed.

'The roof,' I said. 'Where you already had a crossbow, set up and waiting. The original plan had been to sneak out of the Nursery side exit once Miss Decima was asleep and climb up the guttering, but now you didn't even have to do that. A crossbow's easy enough to come by, in a house like this. You'd taken the bolt from the suit of armour during the day and hidden it in your bedroom, carrying it upstairs in rolls of cotton wadding. All you had to do was make it look as if your bedroom window had been sealed properly, when in fact you spent all Wednesday afternoon loosening the boards. No one would have heard you, over the noise in the rest of the house. Once you were sealed inside, it was just a matter of prising off the loose boards and climbing on to the roof, until you found the study chimney.' I turned to Mr Stokes and smiled. 'Which is where you were waiting for her. Right?'

Mr Stokes had given up trying to hide anything now. He looked at that moment like a hand gripping an empty glass.

'It was simple, in the end,' he said quietly. 'I stood in the fireplace, under the pretence of fitting the final boards in place, and waited until I could see Temperance at the top of the chimney. Then I called for Conrad, saying that the comet was acting strangely, and that he should come and see it for himself...'

I nodded. 'Which was why...'

'Yes, very good, Stephen,' said Miss Decima quickly. 'You've impressed us all considerably. I'll take it from here, shall I?'

She puffed up with relief and turned to Temperance.

'By then, my dear, you'd been practising for weeks down by the turbine shed. You knew that you could hit Conrad dead in the eye if you had to – a nod to Harold Godwinson, lending the whole mystery enough drama and chaos to cloud the truth. One shot, and it was done. Stokes wasn't the murderer: it was *you* who pulled the trigger.' She turned to the Butler. 'But *you* let him die, didn't you? Just like Conrad and his father. Exactly how long did it take him to die, Stokes?'

Mr Stokes swallowed. The crossbow was trembling in his hands now.

'Longer than his father. I stood over him as he died, begging for my help, and watched until it was done. Then I sealed the fireplace and sat him on his chair. I cleaned the soot from his clothes and combed the ash from his hair, so that no one would ever know how he had been killed.'

Miss Decima nodded. 'And the wadding?'

Mr Stokes smiled sadly. 'I used it to mop up the blood

from the floor. I must have stuffed some of it under the door by accident. My head was ... not in the right place at the time. I had a lot to think about.'

'And all night to think about it,' said Miss Decima quietly. 'Because that's all you needed to do, for the final part of the plan to work. Stand beside the door with Conrad's evening tea tray and wait. That's a long time to spend in a room with the body of a man you have just allowed to die.'

Mr Stokes didn't look at her. He kept his gaze fixed on the crossbow, still shaking in his hands.

'In some respects, *your* job was easier,' said Miss Decima, turning back to Temperance. 'All you had to do was climb back through your bedroom window and replace the boards. The *real* challenge came in the morning: fooling everyone into believing that Mr Stokes was walking around the house, and not locked inside the study.' She adjusted on her chair. 'First, you quietly unsealed your bedroom door and sneaked downstairs to ring the staff bells – you figured that you'd have enough time to get back upstairs before everyone could get out of their rooms. There *was* no phone call from Conrad in the morning, no scratching at the door. That was all a lie – another clever distraction, to keep everyone confused.'

I took over. 'And it wasn't Mr Stokes who talked to me through the Nursery doors that morning, was it? It was *you*, pretending to be him. You always had a knack for voices. I knew that something didn't seem right; it took me ages to work out what it was. It was your footsteps down the corridor as you left. Mr Stokes is silent: you never hear him coming. Which is how he pulled off the final part of the whole plan. The most important one.'

Mr Stokes was staring ahead, faintly nodding, like a branch in the wind.

'What was the very first thing you told me?' I said. 'The most important part of being a servant is to be invisible. To draw no attention to yourself. No one could work out how a man was killed in an empty room, but that was the whole point. The room was never empty. *You* were there the whole time, standing in darkness, holding the tea tray, waiting for someone to break down the door. For me to run into the pitch-black room, and for Temperance to turn up pretending you were right behind her and shove Lowen towards the light switch. All you had to do was silently slip out of the darkness at the precise moment when no one would see or hear you, and stand behind Temperance in the corridor. As if you'd never been in there at all. No one else could have managed it. No one else could move that invisibly.'

The room was silent, unbroken.

'But it was still a huge risk. Which is why you removed the butler's mirror from behind the desk, wasn't it? So that no one would spot you in the reflection; so that when you later hung it on the second-floor corridor, everyone would assume it had always been there. That's why you made sure to drop the teapot in the corridor, to cement in everyone's mind that you were standing outside the study when the door opened. But that wasn't the *only* reason you had to get rid of the teapot, was it?'

I smiled.

'That teapot – I've been thinking about it for days. It's been bothering me like mad. And now I understand why. *It was the tea.* It was stone cold – it didn't steam. Because you hadn't just made it. You'd made it the night before, just as Conrad had asked. A single, tiny detail that could reveal everything. The whole truth. And that's why I noticed it. I tried to forget it, but it refused to budge. *Resilient*, it was.'

Everyone stared at me in confusion. I adjusted my grip on the caulking iron and set my jaw.

'*Resilient*,' I repeated. 'I looked it up. It means hardy. Which is what you'll have to be, when you're both arrested for murder.'

59

Monday, 23 May, 8.36 p.m.

No one spoke for some time.

'Brilliant, Stephen,' Mr Stokes said eventually, his voice soft. 'Really quite brilliant of you. I must say that I am . . . truly impressed.'

I was struck, as ever, by how serious he was. He'd always been serious, and I understood why now. There was something in him that had been broken a long time ago, and he'd spent his life building over the ruins, but he could never fully hide what had been lost.

'I am not ashamed to admit that our plan got out of hand,' he said. 'I take full responsibility for my actions. I knew, with Edwin in place, that there was every chance the staff in this house might lose their jobs. *That* became my focus: I thought that I could devote myself to ensuring that it would not happen. A recompense for the crime, perhaps. But it seems that it has all been in vain.' He smiled at me. 'Part of the problem was that I could not bring myself to let you take the blame. When the time came to accuse you, I simply could not do it. I could not let you suffer for what *I* had done. It was never meant to be so . . . ugly.'

'It's not your fault,' said Temperance quickly. 'It's theirs. They were never meant to get involved.'

'No, Temperance,' said Mr Stokes wearily. 'It's not their fault. It is not their fault that Lowen is dead either.'

Temperance's eyes were wide with panic. 'He attacked *you*! You had to defend yourself –'

'I wondered about that,' I said. 'It must have been right after I saw him by the river. Right after he'd stumbled on your target-practice site. He was going up to the house to tell Jarvis what he'd found . . . I'm guessing he found *you* instead, pulling the crossbow out of the bonfire.' I pointed to the ash on Mr Stokes's hands. 'He must have put two and two together. So you killed him.'

Mr Stokes swallowed. 'It was an accident. We fought – he fell back while I tried to reason with him, and his head hit a rock. It was never meant to happen.'

'And Jarvis?' I said bitterly. 'Do you expect me to believe *that* was an accident, too?'

'It was, sadly.'

We turned to Miss Decima. She nodded at Jarvis's notebook on the desk beside her.

'It's all there, in his final notes. He suspected that Edwin was the murderer – he'd decided to take his bust from the plinth, to get some phrenological measurements with his calipers. I think we can piece the rest together. He placed the bust on the mantelpiece, bent down beside the fireplace to tie his shoelaces, and the bust fell on his head and killed him. All rather humiliating.'

My mind went back. 'No – that wasn't why he was kneeling down. The soot in his hair and on his fingertips. He was peering up the chimney.' I smiled at Temperance. 'He must have worked out how you did it, just before he died.'

Miss Decima sighed. 'Poor old Jarvis. He was spot on about its being a woman, spot on about its being Stokes, spot on about checking the lake for a weapon, spot on about how the murder was done. He was just too useless to do anything about it.' She smiled at Temperance and Mr

Stokes. 'And his death *really* put a spanner in the works for you two. It was easy enough to hide that Lowen was missing in all the confusion but not for long. The police would be back at World's End in a matter of hours, and then his body would no doubt be discovered. Your plan went into high speed: framing Stephen for the murders. You'd cut the power to the house and lure Stephen out of my rooms by pretending that Lowen was dragging Temperance into the trees – that was you, of course, Stokes – then come back here to finish me off. No traces left, and a scapegoat for every step of the way –'

'And why not?' snarled Temperance. 'This is all your fault. You had to get involved, didn't you? Thanks to you, two more people are dead.'

Mr Stokes shook his head. 'No, Temperance. The fault lies with us.'

Temperance was panicking now. 'Stop saying that. It's not over. We can fix this.'

'We can't,' said Mr Stokes. 'Not in the way that you want to, at least. There is only one way to fix this now.'

There was a moment's pause and then he turned, aiming the crossbow at Temperance. She stumbled back, scrambling against the layers of paper pinned to the wall. 'N-no!'

Mr Stokes strode towards her . . . and thrust the crossbow into her hands. Temperance clasped it, stuck between aiming it at me or aiming it at Miss Decima. 'What are you doing?'

Mr Stokes didn't reply. He stood before me, trying to get past. 'Stephen, if you wouldn't mind.'

I stood in place, the iron trembling in my grip. The pain had been getting worse and worse. I was hurt, and bleeding badly. But I had to hide it. 'No, Mr Stokes. I can't let you go.'

'I insist that you do. There are a number of things that I must put right, and the sooner the better.'

'Don't!' said Temperance frantically. 'For God's sake –'

'Let me pass, Stephen,' said Mr Stokes. 'I am unarmed and entirely at your mercy.'

My arm throbbed. My head was spinning. 'What are you going to do?'

'I cannot tell you that.' He stayed gazing at me. 'I always believed in you. I always knew that you would redeem yourself. *That* is why I could never bring myself to condemn you. And I would very much appreciate it if you would do the same for me.'

I shifted. 'Sir –'

'Matthew, Stephen. My name is Matthew.'

He was begging me as much as a man can beg without kneeling. I held still for a moment longer, then glanced at Miss Decima. She nodded to me; I nodded back. Then I staggered to one side so that Mr Stokes could leave. Temperance backed against the wall in panic. '*Stokes!*'

But it was no use – he was gone. I listened as his footsteps made their way down the corridor from the Nursery, and I realized that for the first time that they were making a sound on the floorboards. He wasn't walking silently any more. The *click* of his heels faded into the distance, growing fainter and fainter, until it disappeared altogether.

'Well!' said Miss Decima. 'I believe this rather leaves you in a pickle, doesn't it, my dear?'

Temperance was trapped. She had one bolt in the crossbow and two targets. I was at the door, blocking her escape. Miss Decima kept her eyes fixed on Temperance, the wick of the candle dancing in her eyes.

'I am not without sympathy for you,' she said kindly. 'You were wronged – greatly wronged. I can admit to my fault in that. You were right to be angry, but you had no right to kill. No one does. It is time for you to accept that. The storm has passed and the causeway will soon be open. The police will be here any minute.'

'I'll deny everything,' said Temperance quickly. 'I'll tell them what I know about Stephen. No one will believe that I did it!'

'Perhaps not,' said Miss Decima. 'After all, you have proved yourself to be a fine actress. That performance you played on the telephone – Conrad arriving with a mystery man to change his will – all balderdash, wasn't it? A fake clue you made up on the spot, to keep us off the scent. But I suspect that no one could act their way out of this one. Your only hope is to leave before the police arrive, and, currently, time is not on your side. Which means you're going to have to kill one of us, so you can at least try to escape, and then hope for the best.'

'Miss Decima!' I protested.

'I can see what you're thinking,' said Miss Decima, cutting me off. 'The obvious answer is to shoot Stephen. After all, he's blocking your escape. But the moment that you do that, I'll blow us all halfway to Tregarrick.' She rattled the tea caddy once more. 'Or you could shoot *me* and take *me* out of the equation, but you'd have to make certain you got me in one, my dear, because it's hardly difficult for me to drop a lit candle into a jar of explosives, and quite frankly I don't plan on dying quickly.'

'You'd kill Stephen as well,' said Temperance.

'If you believe that's a concern of mine,' said Miss Decima coolly, 'you have underestimated me.'

The words cut deeper than I expected. I hoped she was lying to Temperance, playing for time, but she sounded like she meant every word. Temperance was stuck in the same conundrum, trying to work out what was true and what wasn't. 'You're bluffing. You've always been a lying hag.'

'Perhaps,' said Miss Decima, 'but you've already made plenty of mistakes; to suggest you've made another is hardly a stretch of the imagination. But, on this occasion, I'm afraid you cannot afford to make a single one.' She sighed. 'We find ourselves in a complete stalemate. Stephen won't leave, and you won't give yourself up. So . . . allow me to introduce a third option.'

I glanced at the two of them. I had no idea what Miss Decima was doing. The truth was, I was finding it hard to follow her. I'd lost a lot of blood; my head was still spinning. I was having to lean on the wall to stay upright.

'I will confess that I underestimated *you*, my girl,' she said fondly. 'You are no weak, teary-eyed maid; you are a woman of exceptional cruelty and startling inhumanity. It takes great strength of character to kill as you have killed, and not sacrifice yourself in the process. Your real name probably isn't even Temperance, is it?' She smiled, as if she had known this all along. 'I finally see you for who you are. You're no opportunistic killer. You're a product of your own bloodline. You're a Stockingham, through and through.'

'Miss Decima,' I said weakly, 'what are you doing?'

'Your father wasn't, believe me,' Miss Decima continued, all her attention fixed on Temperance. 'That man was Welt to the marrow. But I so often find that these things skip a generation. And you are in so many ways like your grandmother Isabella.'

Temperance shook her head. 'No. I'm nothing like her, or you.'

'We don't get to choose these things,' said Miss Decima. 'And if I were you, my girl, I would not so readily bite the hand that is attempting to feed you.' She shifted in her chair. 'We all know what Stokes is *really* doing – he will continue to be a decent man right until the end. So why don't you make the only smart decision that you've made so far and take the side exit, and we'll say no more about it. I couldn't help Conrad, but I can help you.'

I froze. 'Miss Decima, no!'

'Shut up, Stephen.'

I tried to step forward, but I suddenly found that I couldn't. The floor was swaying like I was on a ship at sea.

'Ignore him,' said Miss Decima, her eyes fixed on Temperance. 'Leave now, without hurting Stephen, and I won't breathe a word to the police.'

Temperance glanced at me. 'He's not going to let me leave.'

'He won't have a choice soon,' said Miss Decima. 'He's about to pass out.'

She was right. I'd lost too much blood. My eyes were spotting. I fought against it, but *you can't fight a river*. 'She might cover for you, but *I* won't. When the police get here, I'll tell them everything you just said! I'll . . . I'll . . .'

I dropped the iron and it fell to the floor with a hollow *clang*. Temperance stared at me, watching as I swayed on the wall. Then she slowly stepped towards me, the crossbow aimed at my heart. 'Stephen, it's like you've learnt nothing. Nobody is going to believe a single word you say.'

She stood, waiting for me to let her leave. We faced each other in silence. She looked so different. I suddenly remembered the first time I'd seen her, red-eyed in the corridor, her face in her hands. I wondered how much of the crying had been an act, how much of it was real.

'Did you ever like me?' I asked.

I had no words for the look that she gave me then. I would think about that look a lot over the next few days, and all the years following. There was pity in it, of course. Contempt, even. But there was something else, too, hidden under it. Something like surprise.

'I'm sorry,' she said quietly.

Then, as if I wasn't even there, she stepped past me and made her way out of the side exit and into the darkness.

Miss Decima waited until her footsteps had disappeared across the gravel. Then she let out a big sigh of relief and put down the jar and candle.

'Well! All things considered, that went better than expected. Good thing they never twigged that this jar's just full of old tea leaves.' She took out her dentures. 'Now pay attention, Stephen. You and I are going to have an *extremely* careful chat about what you're going to say when the police arrive . . .'

I didn't hear the rest, because I was already fainting, sliding down the wall and into a darkness that I knew there was no point in fighting.

Friday, 27 May 1910

LORD STOCKINGHAM-WELT MURDERED
SCANDAL AND MASSACRE AT WORLD'S END

The world has been shocked by a series of bizarre and tragic deaths on the tidal island of World's End in Cornwall this week.

Authorities were first summoned to Tithe Hall on the morning of Thursday, 19 May, where it transpired that Lord Conrad Stockingham-Welt had been discovered dead in his study in what police described as a 'brutal and inexplicable murder'.

Less than a week later, on the evening of Monday, 23 May, police were once again called to World's End after the alarming death of Inspector James Jarvis, who was found in the drawing room of the house following a tragic accident.

When the police arrived, the Head Butler, Mr Matthew Stokes, refused to answer calls and pleas at the door of his office. He was found dead in his chair, having taken his own life. A letter written by the deceased confessed to a series of shocking crimes, including the murders of Lord Stockingham-Welt and Lowen Hunt, 21, the first footman employed at Tithe Hall, whose body was found bludgeoned to death on the grounds.

Police are currently searching for Temperance Atkins, 20, who was employed as a ladies' maid at Tithe Hall but has not been seen since Monday evening. Police are appealing for any friends or family, or those with any information about her whereabouts, to come forward.

It has been a long time since England has seen a scandal of this magnitude, which has left society reeling. Indeed, the murders have cast further light on a number of other inexplicable incidents at World's End over the years, including the strange death of Lawrence Welt two decades ago. It is safe to say that this is not the last that we will hear of the Welt family over the coming months.

The funeral for Lord Stockingham-Welt will be held in Tregarrick this afternoon. The will reading will be held afterwards at Tithe Hall.

60

Friday, 27 May, 12.54 p.m.

I made my way, slowly, through the house.

It was the first time I'd been out of bed in days. My limp was better now; my left arm was strapped to my chest in a sling, which made wearing livery more or less impossible, but then my livery was torn to shreds anyway. Mrs Pearce had given me one of Mr Stokes's old jackets, but I couldn't bring myself to wear it.

At least I was sleeping better now. It was the first time in years that I hadn't dreamt about Nan.

I wasn't supposed to be up, really. But today all staff were expected to gather in the drawing room for the will reading, once the family were back from the funeral. The room was empty when I found it, except for the rows of chairs facing a desk at the front of the room. The last time I was here, Jarvis had been dead on the floor. The Viscount's speech, Edwin's lockdown . . . It all felt like a long time ago.

'Ah, Stephen.'

I wasn't alone. Miss Decima was sat in her bath chair in the corner.

'You're not at the funeral,' I said, surprised.

'Absolutely not,' she muttered. 'It's bad enough I have to come to this godforsaken will reading in the first place. To be frank, I was rather hoping that I might run into you.'

I didn't reply.

She shuffled. 'I trust you're resting well? You look slightly better than when I last saw you, but not by much.'

There was a stony silence. If she could be rude, so could I.

Miss Decima groaned. 'Good grief. Stephen, I *know* you're cross with me. Let's discuss it, rather than suffer these impertinent silences.' She rapped the chair beside her with her stick. 'Sit.'

I did as she said – it was hard not to, with Miss Decima. But I didn't meet her eye. I was worried what would come out of my mouth if I did.

'Now,' said Miss Decima, 'let us first begin by –'

'You shouldn't have let him do it,' I said.

There it was. I had to keep going now.

'You shouldn't have let Mr Stokes take his own life,' I said. 'You knew he was going to do it, but you let him leave anyway. If I'd thought there was *any* chance of that happening, I would *never* have –'

'That was his choice to make, Stephen,' said Miss Decima.

I shook my head. 'No, it wasn't. Mr Stokes was a man of God. To take his own life . . . it would have been a great sin for him.'

'He had plenty of other sins under his belt. It seems to me like it was his last chance to repent for them.'

I felt the flush burn up my neck. 'But he *didn't* repent. He lied to save a murderer. Temperance is still out there, unpunished. And that's because *you* let her go!'

Miss Decima bristled. 'I should think it's fairly clear that I did that to protect *you*. If Temperance was arrested, she'd have found a way to implicate you. Letting her go was the only safe way to proceed.'

'It was *wrong*, Miss Decima.'

'Interesting! And have you told the police otherwise?'

I fumed. 'You know I can't.'

'Well, there you have it,' she said firmly. 'There's an awful lot wrong with this world, Stephen, but, thanks to me, you get to experience it as a free man.'

The silence fell over us once again. There was no point trying to fight her: Miss Decima was too strong, too fixed, too intelligent, too unchangeable in her ways.

But half the fun is in the fighting. 'You were going to let me die.'

Her head whipped around. 'What?'

I knew that I'd never get another chance to say it. We both knew how the will reading was going to go. World's End would pass to Edwin, and, once that happened, the staff would be dismissed, Tithe Hall would be closed forever, and I would never see Miss Decima again. It was over. So why not say what had to be said?

'You were going to let Temperance kill me. You said that it made no difference to you either way.'

Miss Decima was shaking her head. 'I was buying us time –'

'I'm not sure I believe that.' I glared at her. 'And I don't believe what you said on the heath either. This *has* always been a game to you. I think, if it came to it, if you *had* to, you'd get rid of me, too.'

She looked horrified. 'Stephen, you could not be more wrong. I have been so grateful, *truly grateful*, for the time we have spent together.'

'You used me to get what you wanted.'

'I *needed* you.'

'As a servant.'

'As a friend.'

Silence again.

'You don't know what it means, to be my age and to find a friend,' she said. 'I haven't had anyone in my life that I cared even slightly about for *years*. It has made all the difference in the world to me, Stephen.'

She took my hand. And then I couldn't stop the feelings from coming out any more. My eyes swelled at the edges.

'We failed, Miss Decima. We spent all that time trying to find out the truth, and it came to nothing. The killer got away with it. Edwin's going to inherit everything. All the staff will lose their jobs. That awful family will go on just as they've always done. The only thing that's changed is that there are four people dead who didn't deserve to die.'

Miss Decima thought this over. 'I am afraid I'm going to have to disagree with you, Stephen. Take Comet Halley . . .'

I groaned. '*Miss Decima* –'

'Take. Comet. Halley,' she repeated, ignoring me. 'It continues on its course, century after century, never once erring or diverting, regular as clockwork. But every time it passes the sun, a little piece of it burns off. Did you know that? It's been getting smaller for thousands of years. And one day, long after you and I are both gone, it will make its final passage past the sun and disintegrate entirely. It will end, as all things must end. Traces, nothing more.' She held her arms around her. 'Everything is changing, all the time, even when it appears fixed. You simply cannot see change when you're close to it. This mansion, the money, the servants, the system that upholds it – none of it will stay. We've no need to punish the family, Stephen. I suspect time will do that for us.'

I wiped my eyes. 'When will that happen?'

'When will *what* happen?'

'The comet disintegrating.'

'Oh!' said Miss Decima. 'In about . . . 250,000 years, I believe. Give or take.'

Silence again. I glared at her. 'Is that supposed to make me feel better?'

'Stephen –'

'I have to wait 250,000 years for something to change!'

'Oh, stop being so bloody difficult.'

There was a sound outside of wheels on gravel. We gazed at each other in the empty room, surrounded by unused chairs. The family were back from the funeral: in moments, the staff would be called to the drawing room, the doors would be closed, and the will reading would begin.

'Well, Stephen,' said Miss Decima. 'I believe it's time for us to face the music.'

'Yes, Miss Decima.'

I stood up to leave, so that we could sit apart – she with the family, me with the servants – but at the last second she grabbed my hand and clung to me. Like I was that bar of the sluice gate, and she was trying hold back the river before it drove her under the wheel.

'Stephen,' she said gently. 'I would be most grateful if you would stay with me during the reading.'

I blinked. 'Servants are at the back.'

'Well, then in that case, I will go to the back with you.'

I smiled. 'Yes, Miss Decima.'

I wheeled her to the back of the room, and we waited like furniture as the family trooped inside.

61

Friday, 27 May, 1.00 p.m.

By the time everyone was settled in the drawing room, there was hardly any place to stand. It was just like the speech, all over again: the family sat at the front, all in black, with the Reverend Wellbeloved and Chief Constable Penrose. The servants packing the rest of it. A solicitor stood at the desk at the front of the room, and cleared his throat.

'First of all,' he began, 'I would like to offer my condolences on such a sad day. I knew Lord Stockingham-Welt for a great many years, and –'

'Get on with it!' snapped Edwin.

I glanced at the family with a wave of disgust. Edwin was tapping his foot on the floor like a ticker tape; Jolyon was already drunk; Lettice sat between them, holding both their hands so she could be first to congratulate whoever got the fortune. Gilbert sat at the end of the row, pale and drawn and much quieter since his illness. Being poisoned suited him.

The solicitor gathered his papers and coughed. 'Well, Lord Stockingham-Welt composed a number of wills throughout his lifetime. We believe this one to be his most recent and final. He included a letter to be read in the event of his death.'

He took a million years to find, polish and put on a pair of spectacles, then opened the letter. Edwin was grinding his teeth so loudly we could hear it from the back of the room.

'*My dearest family,*' the solicitor read. '*If you are reading this letter, I am sadly parted from this world. I have spent the last few months preparing for the future as best I can, but I know that my efforts may be in vain. No man can fully prepare for what lies ahead. I dearly hope that you find yourselves in better times, and the comet's electrical storms have not devastated the Wessex Downs.*'

There was an air of stagnant embarrassment.

'*I have made a number of small amendments to my last will,*' continued the solicitor, '*in sound mind, body and spirit, and it is my wish that these are followed to the letter. I shall begin with my servants, before moving on to members of my family.*'

There was a shifting of feet. You could have chewed the silence between sentences.

'*To the men and women of my staff: I would like to express gratitude for their work over the years. I leave each of them the sum of one pound, with an additional shilling for each year of service for senior members of staff.*'

The dark muttering around me said it all: it was a pitiful amount of money, far less than what a servant would usually expect. I was glad that Mr Stokes wasn't around to hear it.

The solicitor carried on.

'*To my cousin Edwin Welt.*'

I saw Edwin's shoulders lift as he leant forwards in his chair.

'*I leave my full collection of scientific materials on the smallpox vaccine,*' said the solicitor, '*which he is in desperate need of reading, given that he has voted against it several times.*'

Edwin stayed frozen in place like a photograph, blinking in disbelief.

'*To Lettice Welt,*' said the solicitor, moving swiftly on, '*I leave the sum of fifty pounds, and the large oil painting of myself hanging in the entrance hall, which she has always expressed great admiration for. To my cousin Rear Admiral Jolyon Welt, I leave six bottles of wine of his choosing, and the use of my least expensive automobile one weekend per month.*'

'I say, that's a bit of a result,' said Jolyon, perking up.

The room was shocked. World's End hadn't passed to the family – neither had the fortune. It was more of an insult than an inheritance. I tried to meet Miss Decima's eye, but she was staring straight ahead. She didn't seem surprised at all.

The solicitor cleared his throat nervously. '*It goes without saying that the estate of World's End, Tithe House and the remainder of my fortune should go towards the continuation of my vital work for the Cometary Cataclysm Society. Creating the Society has been the sum total of my life's work; humanity needs the clear-eyed guiding of science more than ever. As a result, the day-to-day workings of the Society will continue under the watchful eye of my co-founder, Professor Wolff Muller.*'

The penny dropped. The inheritance was going to go to the Society, just as Miss Decima had predicted. In the front row, I saw a triumphant smile spread across Lettice's lips. She could blackmail Herr Muller for anything she wanted – that money was as good as hers.

'This is an outrage!' cried Edwin, leaping to his feet. 'The fortune cannot pass outside of the family!'

'*But, unfortunately, I am unable to place sole control of the estate and fortune in Professor Muller's capable hands,*' the solicitor continued, with a slight tremor in his voice. '*Though I have no children to speak of, and no heir, it is imperative that control of the World's End estate and the fortune should be kept within the family itself.*'

Edwin sat back in his chair, mollified. Everyone held on expectantly while the solicitor kept reading.

'*I have spent the last few months in sad contemplation of the future. Now, more than ever, the world must be placed under the care of a number of men of science, dedicated to creating a brave new world. It has disappointed me greatly that none of my cousins on the Welt side of the family have taken the slightest interest in my scientific endeavours. As a result, I am left with no option but to bequeath the entire inheritance to the only member of the family who has ever expressed the slightest interest in science: the Honourable Miss Decima Stockingham.'*

There was a moment of stunned silence. Then, one by one, everyone turned to face us. Miss Decima sat still as a statue, calm as you like.

'*My only stipulation,*' the solicitor continued, '*is that Miss Decima uses the house and fortune for the growth and strengthening of the Cometary Cataclysm Society, under the proviso that Tithe Hall becomes the Society headquarters and that the fortune is spent on science-related projects. With her remaining time on this earth, she is to see that a member of the younger generation is found whom she adjudges to have the best scientific mind, and is educated suitably, in order to take over the running of the Society when she is gone.*'

The solicitor removed his glasses with an air of apology and placed the letter on the table. The room was in complete shock. Edwin, Lettice and Jolyon were all staring at Miss Decima with the same look that foxes have on their faces just before a bus flattens them on a country road.

'Well! I had a feeling that would happen,' she said. 'Stephen! Front of the room, if you please.'

Without even thinking I grabbed her bath chair and pushed her to the front of the room, squeaking all the way. Then I turned it around and kicked the brakes so Miss Decima could face the speechless crowd. She took a sheet of paper from her purse, cleared her throat and read aloud in the grand, steady tones I'd become so used to.

'The following people are to leave the grounds immediately . . .'

62

Friday, 27 May, 4.32 p.m.

Tithe Hall had only just managed to return to normal. The family had left in fury hours ago, vowing to fight every element of the will. Lettice had sobbed, Gilbert had wept, Edwin had a nosebleed from shouting so much, and Jolyon strolled cheerfully into the cellars. Miss Decima sat at the front of the room and watched, enjoying it all immensely.

When I found her again, she was sat in the conservatory, gazing up through the glass ceiling.

'Ah, Stephen. Come and look. Our comet is almost visible, even at this early hour.'

She was right – the comet was there, fainter than ever, but it was just possible to make it out.

'I think I might set up my telescope in here,' she said, glancing around the room. 'It's ideally positioned for me to make observations without having to troop out to the south-west prospect every time. I might ask you to set it up later, after you've brought me some sandwiches. And a slice of cake. And maybe a bit of pork pie.'

I was amazed. 'You're hungry, Miss Decima.'

'Ravenous. I don't know about you, but, after all this excitement, my appetite's come back with aplomb.'

I beamed. 'I'll get them for you now, Miss Decima.'

She shook her head. 'No! The food can wait. Sit with me for a while, Stephen.'

I pulled up a chair beside her. It was nice, being able to

do all this without having to worry about being sacked or arrested or murdered. 'Have you made any other plans for the house?'

She mulled it over. 'Hmm. We shall have to see what the next few months hold. I imagine Edwin is going to contest the will on the grounds that Conrad was temporarily insane, but I suspect he'll only last a few months before giving up. He'll decide that he's better off without World's End anyway: its reputation has been somewhat tarnished by all the murders. And I don't think the Rear Admiral's going to bother us either. Six bottles of wine and a car sounds like a fairly lethal combination. I give him two months.' She sighed. 'As for Lettice . . . well, I'm sure I can buy her loyalty with a one-off gift for little Gilbert. I'll send the snivelling little creep off to Eton, on the proviso that she does some blackmailing on the side for me. We'll start with Edwin and go from there.'

I frowned. 'Miss Decima –'

'I'm rich now, Stephen, don't preach to me.' She steepled her fingers. 'As for the rest of the fortune . . . well, I have a number of ideas about that. I think Conrad's suggestion of a scientific fund is, for once, entirely appropriate. A scholarship would be an excellent place to start: one for young women keen to enter the realm of science. An annual scholarship to attend Oxford, perhaps.' She shuffled in her chair. 'I thought Clemency might be a good first recipient. The Reverend's daughter. As a matter of fact, I cornered him earlier and offered to read that application essay of hers.'

I was surprised. 'I thought you said she was a dud.'

'Yes, I'm aware of what I said,' said Miss Decima quickly, her eyes on the floor. 'I think I may have been somewhat . . . unfair on the girl. I was . . . rather too quick to judge her.' She paused. 'I can do that sometimes.'

It was the closest thing to an apology that she was ever

going to give me, and it was more precious than any fortune in the world. 'I think that's a fine idea, Miss Decima.'

'The rest of the will is simple,' she said. 'I can leave Tithe Hall to that silly Society of his, though I imagine there won't be much of a rush to join between now and when the comet next appears in 1986. But it does mean I can ensure all the servants remain employed. It would be a fitting tribute to the memory of Mr Stokes, I think.'

I smiled. 'It would, Miss Decima.'

She took a careful pause before speaking again. 'You cannot blame yourself too much, Stephen, for what happened to him. The fact remains that —'

'It's all right,' I said, cutting her off. 'I did all I could to help him. I know that. Even if it didn't save him, I can still hold myself tall and say that I tried to do what was right, in spite of it all. That's how Nan raised me.'

Miss Decima nodded. 'I think she'd be very proud of you, Stephen.'

'I know she would be.' I paused. There was something that had occurred to me the other day, something that I'd been meaning to ask her ever since. 'Miss Decima, there was one part of the mystery we didn't solve. Something that didn't fit into any of this. That drawing you saw on the Viscount's desk — the symbol in his papers. What was that?'

She didn't reply for a long time. She gazed up through the conservatory roof, but I knew she wasn't looking at the comet. She just didn't want to look at me.

'Sadly, Stephen, that is something I cannot answer for you. Not now, anyway. Perhaps at some point in the future.' She shifted in her chair. 'On that subject, there is something I have been wondering about. Regarding your employment.'

I blinked. 'I was hoping I might stay here, Miss Decima.'

'I mean your *career*,' she said. 'There are a number of new vacancies to be filled in the house, after the events of this week. There's a position for first footman available, for a start. Not to mention Head Butler.'

I snorted. 'I'm not sure I'm cut out for either of those.'

'Perhaps not,' said Miss Decima quickly. She seemed incredibly uncomfortable – she couldn't stop fidgeting. 'So . . . you are determined to stay here, then?'

'Yes, please, Miss Decima. If that's all right.'

'Ah, I see.'

Her eyes were back to the ceiling, pretending to look at the comet.

'Stephen . . . I don't think there's going to be much need for me to stay at Tithe Hall. I've spent most of my life on World's End; there's an awful lot out there that I haven't seen. As a result, I intend to leave Cornwall at the soonest possible moment and place myself in Conrad's London apartments for the foreseeable future.'

I smarted. 'I'll be greatly sorry to see you leave, Miss Decima.'

'Well, yes, about that,' she said, flinging out the words like water from a leaking boat. 'I really don't want to have to go through the unnecessary inconvenience of finding and hiring some hapless maid who doesn't understand the first thing I need; that would be most draining. Under the circumstances, it seems it would make far more sense to take an existing member of staff with me. Someone who is trustworthy, already familiar with the city, has proved himself to be a very capable young man indeed, who can push my bath chair, and so on and so forth.'

My face had begun to turn red some time ago. The beacons did the talking for me.

'I've looked into it,' said Miss Decima, 'and I think the Monday afternoon train would suit us best. I have a number of things to attend to here before then, and you *really* do need to sort out that bath chair properly, Stephen; that squeaking is driving me to distraction. Then you can write to the Borstal Society and explain your change in circumstances, and say your goodbyes to everyone and come and stay with me at the Savoy, before we begin organizing Conrad's apartments.' She shifted. 'I've found I'm rather fond of all this detective work. I think I shall establish my own agency, and we can set to work immediately. I'm sure there is no shortage of mysteries in London for me – for *us* – to solve. That is, if this is agreeable to you.'

I smiled. 'It is very much agreeable, Miss Decima.'

'That's a relief. I already called the hotel and reserved your room. I have found, Stephen, that I am rather in great need of you.'

I held her hand. 'Thank you, Miss Decima.'

'And Stephen?

'Yes, Miss Decima?'

'I think, at this point you can start calling me Decima. If I hear the word *Miss* one more time, I'm afraid that I may commit murder.'

We sat together in contented silence, watching the comet pass above us, on towards infinity.

Epilogue

Comet Halley disappeared from sight by mid-June, just as Stephen and Miss Decima were getting settled into Conrad's apartments in Kensington. Miss Decima was applying for membership of the Royal Society and reading the first letter of enquiry sent to her detective agency. Stephen was unpacking his suitcase and placing a brand-new silver picture frame on his bedroom windowsill, bought with the first of his wages.

No one by the name of Temperance Atkins was ever seen again.

Edwin Welt, MP, spent several years contesting the will, before stepping away from his seat in the Commons in 1912 due to ongoing health reasons. He continued writing letters to national newspapers every single day until 1913, when he suffered an aneurism while shaking his fist at the squirrels on his bird feeder, and what was left of his heart shattered like a glass vase.

Professor Wolff Muller disappeared shortly after returning to Hamburg. He briefly resurfaced in 1914 following the outbreak of the Great War, marketing a weapon that released hydrogen cyanide gas from canisters worn by homing pigeons. He held a single public demonstration in Hamburg, which was hugely successful, in that every single person attending it died, including Professor Muller. His relatives burned his photograph collection.

Rear Admiral Jolyon Welt served his country for exactly twenty-three days following the outbreak of the Great War.

He was summarily discharged after he insisted on taking lunch on the ship's prow, and the enemy mistook the waiter flapping a tablecloth for a white flag. He was last seen selling a car for five dogs in a local pub in May 1917, and then three dogs for a glass of whisky in June 1917, before being found dead in his lodgings a week later, with one dog.

Lettice Welt found that high society was increasingly less welcoming to her following the scandalous incidents at World's End. She married the love of her life in 1915, and another in 1923, and another in 1927, and a final one in 1935. She died in 1938, of gastric flu.

Gilbert spent several years at Eton, before being expelled for imprisoning the matron. Following the many scandals that had befallen the Welt family following the murder at World's End, he decided to change his name by deed poll and follow his uncle into politics, where he eventually became Home Secretary.

The Halley's Comet panic of 1910 was quickly forgotten. It wasn't until 1981 that scientists calculated that the tail had missed Earth by almost 200,000 miles on the night of Wednesday, 18 May 1910. By then, of course, none of it mattered.

Comet Halley drifted past the planets for thirty-eight years, reaching the bounds of our solar system in 1948, before the forces that guide our universe turned it in a great elliptical arc back towards the Sun. It passed Earth again in 1986, before returning to the edge of our solar system in 2024, so that it can come back again, and again, and again, and again, and again.

The comet will return in 2061.

Acknowledgements

[Acknowledgements 2pp Text To Come]